HAMARTIA

SCARLETT DRAKE

Copyright © 2023 Scarlett Drake.

All rights reserved. This book or any portion thereof may not be reproduced or used in any manner whatsoever without the express written permission of the author except for the use of brief quotations in a book review.

Disclaimer: The material in this book is for mature audiences only and contains graphic content and themes of an adult nature. It is intended only for those aged 18 and older.

This is a work of fiction from the author's imagination.

Cover design by author
Cover design (Illustrated edition) by Caravaggia
Copyediting and proofreading by Lindsey Clarke
Interior formatting by Champagne Book Design

ISBN:978-1-7399127-5-8
FIRST EDITION

For Clo, without you this book wouldn't exist.

AFTER

Paris, 4th September 2023

Two and a half years after a leaked video changed the entire landscape of his life, Raphael Scott is ready to talk. His first solo album, Hamartia, released December 3rd, is the main focus of our chat, but it would be impossible to appreciate the destination without first looking at the route he took to get here.

Having been lucky enough to have an early listen, the album is certainly a departure from his previous persona as the swaggering, screaming, tattooed frontman of The Dead Poets. The album cover features a stripped back Raphael, tattoos covered, face bare, and heart even more exposed. Hamartia is a raw and shockingly honest exploration of love in all its forms. "It's just a few love songs," Raphael says during our interview. But from the outside looking in, it's also a study in those flaws we find within ourselves, the ones that threaten to destroy us, when faced with an all-consuming, life-altering kind of love.

My deep dive on his father, Finn Sullivan, a few years ago, should have made me the last person to whom Raphael would want to tell this story. (His refusal to acknowledge his father for the first five years of his career has been a subject of much journalistic discourse since The Dead Poets first arrived in 2017.)

But Raphael is not the man he was then. He'd listened to my podcast on his father. He'd enjoyed it. He'd even learned something, he said. (He doesn't elaborate on what that is.)

As we sit down in the large airy living room of his apartment in Les Halles in the 1st arrondissement, he looks entirely unlike the man I'd seen fronting The Dead Poets a few years ago. His band and his old persona are on hiatus indefinitely.

He offers me a variety of things I'm not expecting: Turkish coffee (he's addicted) or Bubble Tea (he drinks it like water) and nods happily when I ask him if it's okay to switch on the recorder after we're settled with our drinks. (We both opt for water in the end.)

He sits comfortably in a large armchair near the balcony, long white curtains billowing softly in Paris' late summer breeze. He's barefoot, wearing sweats, and a loose long-sleeved T-shirt, and his hair is long enough that he's scraped half of it up into a knot at the top of his head.

He looks young, I think. Too young to have experienced all that he has. To have his name and his life and his sexuality become a topic of mass discussion.

This isn't an exposé. That's been done already. But Raphael still looks a little nervous as I tell him I'm turning on the recorder. When I tell him not to worry, that I'll send him a copy of it after and remind him I've no intention of publishing anything without his approval, he offers me a bright smile. Warm and friendly. And it's in this, for the first time, I see echoes of his father in his face.

[*The distant sound of traffic below and the faint chirp of birds singing.*]
LQ: First of all, this apartment is incredible. It's entirely unprofessional for me to talk about that and I'll cut it out after. [*my laughter*] But I have an interior design obsession like you wouldn't believe. These are the only accounts I follow on Instagram. And you, now.

RS: [*Raphael laughs*] Ah, thanks. I love it here too. Paris in the summer is really special for me. Now, it's even more special.

LQ: And you didn't include it as a song on the album? New York and Seoul made it on there. Why not Paris?

RS: Ha, well. I moved here after I finished the album. It was too late by then. But you're right, it should definitely be on there.

LQ: And Camille is here too, right? You and her make it work now?

RS: [*Raphael nods, smiling wide*] We do. We make it work. It's working. She's incredible.

LQ: Was there a time where you thought it wouldn't?

RS: Of course, right after. I thought she'd hate me. It's what I deserved.

LQ: After the video you mean.

RS: I mean, yeah. But all of it really. She deserved better.

LQ: But you were the one exposed in the most awful of ways. Before you were ready. You didn't deserve *that*.

RS: [*shrugs*] No. But it was no different to any other paparazzi photo or video; there are a million of them out there. I expect it. I'm ready for it. I never cared much what people thought of me so I always thought that there wasn't anything that could hurt me. But not everyone is like me. Jae wasn't. And Camille wasn't. And they both got hurt, which was ultimately down to me.

LQ: But the video, you weren't to blame for that.

RS: You sound like my therapist. I mean, I know that. But it doesn't make any difference. Two of the people I cared most about in the world were hurt and I'd been a part of hurting them. But it's in the past now. She's happy, I'm happy, Jae's happy. We all got out of the other end, relatively unscathed.

LQ: You tweeted once about the inevitability of things. Of love and fame and death. It was a quote from your father. Do you believe that this was all…inevitable?

RS: [*A soft laugh*] Me falling in love with a guy? Ha, probably, you know. I'm sure the second he was born he was meant for me. People think that the video was the big moment, that something changed for me at that point. Something irrevocable happened. But it wasn't then, it wasn't that, it was the first time I set eyes on him. That was the moment. Nothing was ever going to be the same after that. I knew it. And it wasn't.

LQ: Are you talking about love at first sight or something else?

[*Raphael laughs again*]

RS: I mean, it sounds ridiculous, I know. But it was like I heard angels singing or something the first time I saw him. I'd never seen anything as beautiful or as…fuck…as perfect as him. It really was like a religious experience for me. He laughed when I told him that. It's funny you're asking about love at first sight because he said he hated me at first sight—so there's hope for us all, I suppose.

But yeah, it felt life-changing at the time, even more so later. Like some great event that would change me forever. I'd never had an inkling I liked men before that moment, and you know, I still don't know if I do. I haven't been able to definite it, honestly.

But him…well, he was my inevitability. *He* was when it started. When everything else ended. Everything I was before. He was the moon and the stars and everything in-between and all I wanted to do was worship at his feet. The band, my girlfriend, my dad, everything that I thought was important to me, just ceased to exist the moment I first saw him. I'm not proud of that. But it's what it was.

There was before him and after him, two sides, and I am two completely separate people on each.

SIDE ONE

HIM
LIPSTICK
SAYONARA SON
MANHATTAN MOON
GREEN TEA
SHIBAL

BEFORE
RAPHAEL

I've spent a lot of time thinking about the things that had to happen so that we'd both be standing in that bathroom at that moment. Staring at each other across, what seemed to me then, like a fucking ocean.

DP should have been performing the Global Union show in New York, but our flight got cancelled due to unplanned strike action by European aircrew that weekend. The organizers of GU shifted the billing so we could stay in Paris and perform our set there instead.

His band were supposed to perform their spot the following day in Seoul, but the same airstrike had them stuck in Europe after a show in Berlin, while the European Committee for Workers Rights hammered out some pay increase that was equal to about 0.36% of the artwork cost of our last album.

I'd been downing water since I woke up because I'd gotten wasted the night before and so needed the bathroom right around the time his band had just come off stage.

I was in the group of three who stood there, mouths open with shock, when one of the people we'd just been spouting shit about had strolled out of the cubicle looking like some kind of walking sculpture.

He'd given me a look. A look that shifted something inside me in a way that all those separate parts that made up the whole changed imperceptibly. So that they didn't fit back the way they were supposed to. Like I no longer fit inside *myself*. That's how I'd come to describe it. That was the power of that shift. The power of *him*. I was like a stranger to my own fucking soul.

I hadn't noticed any difference right away—couldn't see past the self-loathing and shame I'd felt in that moment. I wasn't fit to kneel at his fucking feet and lick his Louis Vuitton boots. In lots of ways, I'm still not. I still see him like I saw him then: like some ethereal being, untainted by the likes of us, me, far above us mortal men.

I wanted to tell him that. In fact, I felt compelled to tell him that.

But I didn't.

Couldn't.

I'd stared at him feeling like the small insignificant prick that I was. Watched him cross the tiled bathroom, silver boots melodic on the cold tiles, and come to stand between us to wash his hands. He was slow about it too. Unrushed. I'd glanced briefly at Mase who was watching him too. Had he felt as small? As big of an asshole as I had?

When he reached for a towel to dry his hands, I'd caught a whiff of his cologne. Sweet, but still masculine. It made my cock do a weird twitch thing. He smelled like money. He smelled fucking incredible. So good my head spun a little.

He met my eye briefly in the mirror, so the power of his stare wasn't as great as it could have been had it been head on, and smiled. A small flicker of a smile. Then he reached into his pocket and pulled out something small, something I thought was lipstick at first but was a ChapStick. When he swiped it over his lips, the way a girl might touch up her lipstick, I felt another vibration between my legs, then the base of my spine. He might as well have punched me in the fucking face for the impact that one act had had on me. I wish he had. I wanted him to.

I'd have let him do anything he fucking wanted to me right then.

Then, his lips red and glossy and so fucking kissable, he spun on his heel and left.

He hadn't said a fucking word to us but I felt reduced to ash. Small and unimportant. I hadn't felt like that in years. I hated it.

As the door swung closed behind him, Crawford looked at me, hesitating a beat before doubling over with laughter.

"Fucking hell. Thank fuck they don't speak English."

I could only blink, dumbfounded. Dumfounded and a lot of other things too. Things I'd think about later when I was alone.

As it turned out, Crawford was wrong. They could speak English. Because ten minutes later we'd listened to them thank the crowd of over 100 million people for their donations to the Global Climate Emergency. Every one of them spoke fucking English.

It's amazing what the mind does. How it seeks to protect you from yourself. Because by the time I'd collapsed into my hotel bed five hours later, I'd all but convinced myself we hadn't said anything *that* awful. Yeah, okay, we'd had a go at their music but who didn't? Their fashion sense. Again, who didn't? At their make-up. There was metro-sexual and there was…well, them. Like we'd never worn fucking make-up for a shoot. Like literally any person hadn't worn makeup for every TV appearance. Like I hadn't let Tom Ford put a set of fake eyelashes on me and streaks of green eyeliner for their Athleisure shoot last year. *Fucking hypocrite.*

But it was the suggestion of them all fucking each other, and the agreement that we'd take turns on the "pink haired one" because we were certain he "didn't have a dick anyway" that had kept me up that night.

It was also what made me log into my Instagram account to check whether he had a personal account. I told myself I was going to apologize. He'd see my verified tick and know it was really me and then I'd explain that I wasn't as much of a dick as he thought. As much of a homophobe as he thought. That I didn't think like Crawford. Or Zeke or Mase. That I wasn't like them.

He did have a personal Instagram. 20.1 million followers wasn't exactly personal, but from what I could tell he ran it himself. Unlike his group one—57.8 million followers—which was PR'd to within an inch of its life and curated like an art exhibition.

I'd planned to send him a message, to apologize, but then I'd gotten distracted.

Lots of his posts were professional magazine shoots; Asian Vogue, Elle Korea, GQ, but some—most—were just him. Some were completely innocent. Face mask on as he sat in a café, or outside in a park. Headphones in as he took the train somewhere (he had 20 million Instagram followers and still took the fucking train?). Him standing in front of a painting in a gallery. But there were some others in there that could only be described as thirst-pics.

I mean, I wasn't thirsty. I'm not into men. But they were definitely…unexpected. I certainly wasn't expecting to see him lying on his stomach in his boxers sprawled across an unmade bed, sunlight streaming in through the window. Skin smooth and back a flawless plane that made my mouth water. Who the fuck took that? Some of him at the gym, soaked with sweat and his eyes half-closed as though he'd just had an orgasm.

His messages were open too. Did he seriously read these? Surely not. There was little point in messaging him in that case, my apology would just sit in his DMs unread and then I'd feel like even more of a tool being left on read.

Finally, I decided I'd apologize next time I saw them in person. It was the decent thing to do.

So, I scrolled. And scrolled. Zoomed, then scrolled some more.

Had his skin been that flawless? Had his waist been that small? His lips that full? His hair had been pink in Paris, but his photos told me it had been every color under the sun. Silver, turquoise, orange, yellow, and black.

Before I knew it, I'd lost an hour scrolling @ljh's Instagram. I hadn't planned on following him but when I heard Mase shouting from the adjoined room, I panicked and let my finger hover over the follow button for a moment before impulsively hitting it. I figured if he noticed, maybe the act itself would look like an apology. If not, there'd be no harm done. Or maybe I could like a few of his posts. Comment. Maybe if he replied then I could work up to an apology by DM.

Yeah, that was the plan.

앞서
JAE

I can feel Kai's eyes on me from where he's sat across from me scrolling his phone. I'd felt them following me all the way from the hotel lobby to the car. I can always feel when that sharp focus of his is on me, exclusively.

He waits until we are seated on the plane—the private one YJK had chartered to get us home—before he speaks to me.

"What's wrong?" He doesn't look up from his phone.

Behind me Boohyin lets out one of his loud laughs. I shake my head and gaze out at the tarmac. It looks like an oil slick from where I'm sitting. Wet and black.

"Nothing."

"Well, that's a lie."

Irritation flares up. It's directed at Kai but he's not the source. I'm not entirely sure I know what the source is. Part of it is homesickness, part of it is exhaustion. Another part of it is back in the city, laughing with his band members about everything that's wrong with our band.

I didn't understand everything. My English is good but they were speaking too fast. I caught the general idea though.

Do they seriously think I don't have a dick?

When I sigh, Kai looks up from his phone, his eyes narrowed in study. His mouth is soft. Tinged with regret. He always looks at me like that when he thinks I'm sad. Like he alone is the cause of any and all sadness I suffer. It's due partly to the size of his ego and partly to do with his capacity for self-blame. Self-loathing. It's something we both have in common.

While Kai utilized that self-loathing into music, into production and writing for K: OS and anyone else who asked, I spent those hours in the rehearsal room. Pushing my body to its limit. Stretching it beyond its capabilities in the gym. Covering up my lack of talent with commitment and work ethic.

Because for me, anything less than perfect isn't good enough.

Kai says I can work as hard as I want, I can bleed and sweat and cry every day if it makes me feel like I have done enough, but it won't fix me inside. That needs something else entirely. A doctor most likely. I suppose he would know; he saw one for years. But I'm relatively certain that he still hates himself and so he isn't exactly a walking advertisement for therapy.

Anyway, a few choice words—words I've heard and read before—from a stupid American rock band aren't enough to break me. Not even close. It's rooted in some fruitless pursuit of masculinity. And that kind of masculinity is the destruction of everything else. Kindness, empathy, femininity, romance. Men like them will never really understand the hypocrisy behind it.

It's why I'm so bothered about it that is bothering me. It's not like I like this band. Maybe I'd had some vague passing kind of crush on the lead singer after that video of him, the one where he wore a leather jacket, bare-chest, and warpaint. Maybe it was the look he'd given me. Like a little boy. Big wide eyes I was sure I could see the moon in. The way he'd made me feel like I'd been the one who'd insulted him.

"You did well," Kai says then, yanking me back to the feel of the plane taxiing down the slick runway. "I know you were nervous, but you did great."

He's talking about the speech. The speech that had kept me awake with worry last night and the night before.

"Thanks, Hyung," I say, without looking at him.

For one stupid moment I want to cry. I feel so utterly alone. Then I feel guilty for feeling like that because I am surrounded by my best friends, people who would do anything for me, people who I love like brothers. And yet, I still feel like they really don't know me.

Loneliness haunts me most days, a looming grey specter that knows all of my thoughts. A chilly understanding that no matter what

I achieve—how much success we have—there will always be that part of me left wanting something else. Needing something more.

It's ironic because there are so many days where I have far too many things I don't need or want. When I find joy and peace through far simpler things; a bike ride through Yeouido Park, a solitary walk through a random book shop or art exhibition, the heat of the shower after a particularly hard dance practice.

"Drink before we take off?" A flight attendant asks as she stops at Kai and me, smiling a polished white smile.

"Whisky, please," I say and she nods, flicking her eyes at Kai, who's watching me still. Curious and concerned.

"Same," he says without looking at her.

She hurries off behind the curtain and I ignore the look while moving to fish my Air Pods and eye mask from my bag. Then I reach over my shoulder to wave Lua over.

"I've changed my mind about the pill," I tell her and she scurries back to retrieve the previously refused sleeping pill.

I'm already feeling tired, thinking about my bed, about cuddling with Shiro, about how long I'll sleep when we get home. Goodness knows when we will be back in Europe again. I should enjoy this moment, feel proud, feel something. The first Korean group to sell out a stadium tour in the west. But all I feel is bone deep exhaustion. Fear too, because I have a feeling that things are about to get crazier for us, like we are in the path of some massive tornado that we have no power of withstanding once it hits us.

With the pill and the whiskey in front of me, I down both just before we start our ascent. In the air I request another drink while trying to ignore the occasional glances from Kai.

He takes a deep sip of his drink before letting his head drop back against the seat, eyes closed, throat pale and long. He looks good, which is also messing with me. He's lost a little weight from his face but put on some muscle in his chest and arms. His hair is longer than I ever remember seeing it.

I'm staring at him as the pill and whiskey cocktail start to work their magic. How long has it been since the last time? Three months?

Four? We are not always drunk when we fuck, but most of the time we are. We just handle our alcohol better than the rest and so we're often still awake when the others have gone to bed. It's easy. Too easy sometimes. But mainly it's convenient. No strings, no feelings—aside from that residual love you carry around for your first love long after it's over. Long after you realize that it never really begun.

There's no risk of being outed or caught or anything else that goes with maintaining any kind of romantic entanglement while being an idol.

At ten thousand feet I'm contemplating going down on him in the airplane toilet. At twenty, I'm thinking I'll let him fuck me in there instead. That would help scratch some of the itch crawling over my skin. The whiskey and sleeping pill are doing a different job to what I need them to do. By thirty-five thousand feet, I'm nodding off and thinking instead about Raphael whatever his name is. Specifically, about how I'd disprove his assertion that I don't have a dick by bending him over that bathroom sink and making him take it. I'm not a natural top, but I would make an exception for him.

ONE
RAPHAEL

Two years later
August

"So, ma mere found a Chateau, just outside Lyon. She sent me some pictures of it. I'll forward them to you now."

"Right, sounds good," I tell Camille as I toss myself back onto the bed. Soft. How I prefer it.

The view from the ceiling height windows at the foot of the bed is of a lit-up Chicago, the night sky a wintery ink-blue.

Fuck, I'm hungry. When did I eat last? I skipped the in-flight meal, like I always do. Fuck, I want Sushi. I'll get Sam to go out and find some.

"I've sent them," she says a minute later. "Let me know what you think. It's not as nice as the house in Garda, but it's France. And papa will be much happier if it's in France."

"I doubt that. Doesn't matter where you marry me, he still won't be happy about it." I flick the call to speaker and go into my messages to have a look at the pictures. Yeah, it's a chateau all right.

Camille giggles. "He'll come around."

I doubt that too. It could be our twenty-year anniversary and Jérémie would continue to despise me. Continue to believe I'm not good enough for his daughter. Which I'm probably not, but it would be better if he didn't realize that.

Or maybe he's what'll force one of us to pull the breaks and bring this thing to a screeching halt. I don't know what the fuck we're doing. Well, that's not true. We're doing it because we love each other. But there's also a chance that what we love is the idea of us. I'm sure she said yes partly because of the aesthetic. Her mother: the Oscar-winning actress. Her father: the Palme D'or winning director. Her sister: the supermodel. Her husband: the rockstar.

Camille doesn't know anyone who has a normal job. Everything in her life has been carefully cultivated; a celebrity pedigree that's a Vogue editor's wet dream.

But yeah, she loves me too, and I love her. And if I'm gonna marry anyone, it's gonna be Camille Le Garde.

"So, what do you think?" She's eating something now. Something crunchy and loud in my ear.

"It's nice," I admit. It's a sand-colored building in the middle of acres of vineyard in the French countryside.

"Nice?" she snorts. "That the best you got? I thought you were a poet?"

"It looks expensive."

"My parents are paying," she reminds me.

"I told you we don't need them to pay."

She made two and a half million on her last film, and the last time I met with my financial advisor things were looking decent, thanks to the last tour and some sound investments he'd suggested that I'd been high when I agreed to.

"And I told you papa is adamant. Surely you don't want to piss him off even more?"

"Even more than I do by merely existing? No, I guess I don't."

"You are his favorite American if that makes you feel better."

"It would if it was true."

Fuck, I'm really fucking starving now. Feel a bit sick from it. I wonder what the room service is like. I haul my ass up from the bed and cross to the circular dining table by the window of the room to where the leather-bound book of Hotel Information is standing. Before opening it, I lift the remote and flick on the TV, scrolling until I find a music channel.

"Well?" She presses. "Do you think it's the place?"

"Hard to tell from a few pictures…"

I vaguely recognize the song playing on the screen but it's halfway through and I don't recognize the girl in the video.

"So, do you want to go visit it? You have a week off at the end of the month, right?"

Do I want to spend my week off looking at chateaus that I may or may not get married in? Ardently, no, I fucking don't.

"Babe, it's a nice place. If you like it and your mom likes it, then go for it." I try to sound both enthusiastic and submissive at the same time. "My feelings don't really count here."

"Of course, they count, Rapha!" A coating of French creeps into her accent whenever she whines. It happens in bed too, sometimes. "What are you talking about?"

Guess I didn't quite get the tone right. With a sigh, I try again.

"I just mean, everyone knows guys take a back seat in this arranging–a–wedding shit. The brides have thought about this day for years. They'll be the ones who'll look back at the photos for years. Who'll have all the regrets if things aren't how they dreamed they'd be. I want whatever you want."

Over the line Camille makes a mushy sound.

"You're really sweet when you want to be, you know?"

"I do know. I'm sweet as American pie, baby." Fuck, they have buffalo wings with a blue cheese sauce and a Chicago style pizza. My mouth waters. I can get sushi tomorrow.

"Mm, I miss you."

"I miss you too. How's London?"

"It's raining."

"Of course, it is."

"You know what I was thinking about earlier? That time we were here for Papa's premier…" and her voice trails off because the music video that was on TV has ended and another one fills the screen and then I'm staring at *him*.

He's dressed in some kind of white silk shirt and corset combo which makes his waist look small enough to get my hands all the way around. His white trousers lead down into feet that are bare as he dances across an empty theatre. He moves like the dancer he is. All elegant lines and ballet dancer motion. Fluid as water. The prickling starts at the top of my head and peels down my spine, settling around my stomach before clutching hold of my dick. Then he starts to sing. That fucking voice. High and sweet, soft and smooth. Men shouldn't have voices that high or that sweet. But he does. I don't know what the fuck he's singing about but it sounds melancholic, painful. It's not YouTube so I can't put the subtitles on to translate the lyrics. As he falls to the floor one of his bandmates fills the screen, voice deeper, more of a rap style, and I can breathe again.

Camille's voice floats down the line.

"Rapha, do you? Do you remember that? It was hot."

"Course I do…" I manage. "Yeah, it was."

"Fuck, now I'm horny."

Yeah. Me too.

"Listen, babe, I need to go get some food. I never ate on the plane and my stomach feels like it's about to eat itself. I'll call you later, okay?"

"I guess I'll just have to get one of my toys out…" She sighs, forlornly. "Think about you instead."

I groan. For all sorts of reasons. "Yeah, think about me. I'll do the same while I shower. Think about you, I mean. Not myself."

Think about him, more like.

Camille laughs. "Okay, call me tomorrow, not later. Because it's already later here. Love you, puppy."

I watch until the end of the music video—he appears again, in a black corset this time, looking like some kind of dark fae prince—then I place the call to room service and strip off to take a shower before it arrives. I need to come. I try to pretend it's because I know my beautiful girlfriend is in a hotel using her vibrator while thinking of me, and for the first minute at least, it is.

But then it's about him.

About how pale his skin looked under that black shirt, about how that corset would look against it with nothing underneath. Then I imagine him in just the corset and a pair of women's panties and stockings. It's not the first time I've imagined him in women's underwear. That all started because one time I googled him and found a photo shoot from about five years ago where they had him wearing fishnets. I thought about it all fucking day. The skin—smooth like a girl's—pressing against the criss-cross fabric. When the thought of his dick pressed against it burst through my head, I thought I was going to come in my fucking boxers.

It's crazy, all of it. How a single fucking picture of a guy can have this effect on me.

I'm not gay, I know I'm not.

Camille is my ideal woman. She's funny, talented, smart, and gorgeous. I love her and I constantly think about fucking her. But then...there's him.

In the two years since I became aware of this guy's existence, I've forced myself to think of other guys in the same sorts of ways that I can't seem to stop myself thinking of him—it just doesn't work. I mean, guys I know who are considered objectively hot. Fuck, I see Mason naked often enough and I can categorically say that it's never once crossed my mind that I want to fuck him. I'm not even sure that's what I want from Lee Jeyhun. I'm not sure I would know what to do if he bent over, spread his ass, and begged me for it.

Great. Fuck. Like I needed my mind to go *there*.

But then I'm coming into my hand with the image of him bent over in the shower, hairless ass dripping with water and my fucking come, those eyes dazed and spent as he looks over his shoulder at me.

I get out of the shower feeling dirtier than when I went in. But clearly I'm not done, because after I dress in a pair of sweatpants and t-shirt, I lie back on the bed and pull up YouTube on my phone to find the music video from earlier.

It's new, YouTube tells me. Released 3 hours ago. 12.5 million views and 800k comments beneath it already. Fucking hell. It would take close to six months for one of our videos to do those numbers, if it ever did.

But then, it's like everything these guys touch turns to gold. Feels like they're taking over the world and the rest of us can only sit back and watch as they do it. They'd been sort of big when we'd played the same bill back in Paris; now they're stratospheric. A monolith of popularity hanging over the music industry like one of those alien spaceships.

I watch the MV twice before the room service arrives. While I'm eating, Zeke messages to say they're going out to get trashed and to meet them in the lobby in thirty if I fancy it. I do, but we've got soundcheck at 1pm and now I've fallen down one of my Jaehyun wormholes I can't physically drag myself out of it, even if I wanted to.

I check his Insta after I've eaten, to see he's posted the new music video with the usual Korean caption that I have to ask the app to translate for me. It says, "Some Birds Don't Fly." The song is called "White Dove" and so it's apt, I guess.

There's a ring around his profile pic which tells me he's posted a story and so I click on it to find him cycling his bike around some city at night, Seoul I imagine. His eyes are creased with laughter behind his white face mask and ball cap. He's with someone, a guy, one of his bandmates maybe, but I can't tell which one because he's also wearing a mask. He's swerving his bike a little as he tries to film which only makes them laugh harder. He has a deep laugh. Not like his singing voice would hint at.

The next story is him in a restaurant, a bowl of steaming noodles in front of him as he slurps loudly and shows us out the window.

The final story is a screen cap of the new video showing it at

10 million views on YouTube with some crying and heart emojis. 10 million views in two hours. Mind blowing.

I throw my phone down with a curse. I need to fucking stop this. Like seriously, stop this. My obsession with this guy became weird a long time ago. Some dirty secret I have that no one knows about. Like watching furries porn or something. Worse maybe.

I try to imagine what Mase or Crawford would say if I mentioned it and a chill skitters from my scalp all the way down my spine. It needs to stop. I can stop. I still feel like I'm in control of it to some degree. Like I could stop if I want to—it's just that I haven't wanted to.

I go to bed hoping I have a sex dream about him because I still haven't gotten over the one I had a few months ago where he rode me wearing fishnets and a thick silver chain necklace I could pull on. His nipples were pierced and he played with them as I came inside him.

The cars pick us up at 1pm and then I'm being driven with Mase and Crawford to the venue.

They smell like a late night, the sweet stale murmur of tequila and beer fogging up the inside of the suburban. Crawford's dark hair hangs lank and unwashed, his face paler than usual. When Mason puts the window down, sticks his head out of it and groans, I can't help myself, laughing into my hand as I scroll through my phone. Mason glowers at me. He looks better than Crawf does, but then he always does. Golden skin that always looks like he's just stepped off the beach no matter how little sleep he's had, and dark, almost black, eyes that hide a multitude. His beard looks a bit scruffier than usual, but other than that he looks fresh. He drops his eyes to my phone and then away again before his head falls back and he closes his eyes.

I study the picture message from Cam, of her in bed wearing a white lace bra and nothing else.

Thought of you. Night babe x, it reads.

I text her back, telling her she looks gorgeous—which is true, she does—and that I passed out with the TV on, not a lie either. I try not to tell too many lies generally because I sort of feel like the big one I'm keeping is a fucking leviathan that leaves little room in my gut for much else.

The sound is shit in the venue and I tell the sound manager that. I can barely hear anything in the in-ear and that's before we pack the space with six thousand people screaming. The guys play shit too, but I don't tell them that. I just sing and play and hope that everything will be alright in seven hours. If not, it won't matter half as much, as I'll be shit faced by then.

There's coke in Crawf's hotel room after we get back from soundcheck. Gorgeous, perfect white lines that remind me of Jaehyun's body. The first line does nothing thanks to my tolerance. The second and third work wonders before I wander back to my room to shower.

I'm lying naked and damp on the bed when the notification comes in.

He's posted. It's a clip of him dancing to the Haven Williams song that's been everywhere for weeks. It's been at the top of the Billboard 100 for the last month at least.

The room he's in looks like a dance studio, white curtains and bright white sunlight. He's in loose black trousers that might be silk, a black shirt that's partly see-through, with only one button fastened low on his chest, glimpses of a hard flat stomach peeking out when he moves.

His hair is longer than it's been in other posts, but then he normally wears a hat. It's half tied up, but still falling perfectly around his face. His feet are bare as he dances across a polished wooden floor.

It's just him and the music, falling and rising, rising and falling. A spin and then a leap before his arms wrap around himself and he freezes, standing still to stare straight at the camera. The camera rushes toward him, stopping about a foot away to look at him dead on. His eyes are wide, he's breathing hard, then his lips part ever so slightly as the softest whisper of a smirk comes over his mouth. Then the screen fades to black. My cock hardens. Soft to rock hard in the blink of an eye. Or in the lift of a mouth. *His* mouth.

My journal is on the dining table. The lyrics are a mess, like they always are to start. My handwriting too. I just write words, some sentences that sound good, lines from books or other songs that I like. *Tongue, lips, skin of light. Nothing ever feels right. You're not right.* But I wipe that because Camille will think it's about her.

I call room service and have them send up a bottle of Jameson from the bar because I'd already had the whiskey from the minibar when I got back from Crawford's room. And because it's the only thing that helps dull the rising anxiety I get before a show.

I don't really remember getting dressed. The gig though, I remember. It's the only thing that settles me. Being that out of it, that loose, that free, that completely unhindered by anything that's going on my fucking head. I think about one thing, and one thing only: performing. It's all I'm here on this earth for. The only thing I can do that no one can argue with. I am born for this. Maybe I got it from Finn. Maybe I honed it myself after all these years of hard work. I want it to be the latter—I don't want to owe him anything.

For these two hours where I move and talk and smirk and dance, I am what they say I am. A person I recognize. The crowd are everything I need them to be. Present, faithful, focused. All things I'm not. I know I'm off-key throughout "Black River", the guys know it too, but the crowd don't. Or if they do, they don't give a shit.

We don't do encores. We never have. But tonight, I want to. Tonight, I don't want to go back to the hotel room and be left alone to think.

So, I go out with the guys to a club in West Loop where the company have booked us a section. It's styled like a dive joint, but it has high ceilings and a huge wraparound bar that has every whiskey imaginable lit up behind it. It's 4am when we're barreled out and into a few cars, and there are a few paps waiting. One of them I recognize because the guy literally follows us everywhere. Phil, I'm sure his name is. I'm not sure how much money I've made for Phil but it's substantial.

When I'm standing in front of my room, I realize I've lost my key card and because I can't be fucked going back downstairs, I bang on Mason's door. Crawford brought a girl back and Zeke and Cleo will be asleep already so my options are pretty limited. When I get in there, he's not ready to sleep and opens another bottle of champagne, sets up a few lines, and proceeds to talk about *How Atom Heart Mother* is Pink Floyd's most underrated album for the next hour before my eyes start closing over and I'm out cold on the sofa.

I don't dream about him.

TWO
RAPHAEL

September

We're sprawled across Crawf's sectional still half asleep. It's ungodly to ask rockstars—ha fucking ha—to be awake at this time in the morning. Normally we don't bother getting up for it, but this year it feels important. Feels like we might have a chance. Or we're deluded and have read way too much into that Rolling Stone article.

The last album was a shift, one we all felt. It was fight after fight with Cleo and me keen to push us in this direction, Crawf on the fence as usual, and Mase and Zeke stuck back in the fucking 90's. On the whole, Cleo and I won, coming out of the fights we'd had on top. It was Hell. Mainly. Every fucking day of it.

But the album was out. It hadn't done the numbers *Chopper* had, but it was early days and word of mouth was king—plus the reviews had been better than anything we'd put out previously. Could we seriously pull a Grammy nomination out of the bag for it? We'd scraped into the New Artist category three years ago but hadn't won, been disappointed the last two years, but this felt...different. It felt like we had it. Not just the nomination, but the fucking award.

I don't tend to examine these feelings too closely when I have them. This sure as fuck certainty that creeps up and curls a hand round my throat every now and again, and I never talk about it out loud—I've had it only a handful of times before. When I fronted DP for the first time, when we got signed by Halcyon four years back, two years ago in a Paris bathroom, and right this second.

It's like anxiety but more potent. Loud and rumbling. I can barely breathe.

Two categories before ours is the Pop Group/Duo award. I'm not expecting to see their name—I am *truly* not even thinking about him—but when they're announced as nominees this weird thing happens in my chest. All bubbles and warmth. Like pride or something. I'm sure they've been nominated before, I'm certain I read something about them being the only Korean act to have been nominated before.

Mason scoffs as their name pops up and mutters something to Crawford that I can't hear from here but that makes Cleo roll her eyes. They get one for best Pop Vocal Album too. Two Grammy nominations in a single year for an Asian act is incredible.

I think of his face smiling with delight and wonder what his posts are going to be—because he's going to post a celebration—I know he will.

Then it's our category. Best Rock Album.

That grip around my throat squeezes. I clutch at the fabric of Crawford's sofa because I can barely fucking handle it. If we don't get this, it's tantamount to me ruining our band. I know it is. I feel it not only in my blood but in the vibe of the guys scattered around me. Cleo wouldn't blame me. Her and I had been aligned the entire time we'd worked on this and we'd written almost everything. The rest, well, they'd blame us. Me.

I glance briefly at Crawford, who's rolling a joint on this stomach, looking non-plussed but it's an act. He pauses as the guy smiles and talks awkwardly about how great rock music is. About how it dictates the zeitgeist, about how it keeps the world turning, about how there has never been a time in the last 100 years where rock music has not ruled the world.

I don't breathe as he starts to read out the nominations.

Alphabetical order. It goes from Castreal to Klansman. And we're not there. We're not nominated.

My head is spinning, sweat licking up my spine. I think I'm going to throw up. We're done. We're fucking over, I think. There's not a sound in the entire room apart from the sound of the commercial that's just come on. I can feel Cleo look over at me, feel the air in the room stretched to breaking point. A phone starts ringing somewhere, then Mase is answering it and wandering out of the room and into the kitchen.

I move to sit, swinging my legs round and planting them on the floor. When I glance at Cleo, she has this look on her face and I don't understand it at first until suddenly I do. Pity. She looks like she feels…sorry for me. When I look over at Zeke and Crawford, they're still pretending to watch the TV. Stunned silence choking the air.

"Fuck. Sorry," I mutter and then I'm standing up and walking towards the bathroom.

I'm either going to shit myself, throw up, or burst into tears and I need to be alone for any of that. Inside, I slam the door closed and turn the lock, moving to turn on the cold faucet for some noise to fill the room. Then I open the toilet and empty the contents of my breakfast into it.

I need to get out of here. I need to go home, get wasted, and rethink my entire fucking career. The album was good. Great even. I believe that with every cell in my body—even now. It was the best thing we've ever done. So why does this bother me so fucking much? Why do I care about an award?

Because they care. Because they're the ones I had to convince to let me do this. I convinced them to trust me. The sales had been down on Silver River and Chopper and both those records were a fucking mess. Rolling Stone called "Sayonara" a fucking masterpiece.

I'm rinsing my mouth out with Crawford's mouthwash when I hear it. Screaming and swearing from the other room. At first, I think they're fighting, and I'm worried for Cleo so I rush out and back through towards the noise. They're all up on their feet now, laughing with their arms around each other and looking at the TV.

"What happened?" I ask.

Mase comes back in from the other room too, frowning with confusion.

Crawford turns and then he's barreling over the sofa towards me. I just manage to get a look at the TV before I'm crushed against him. It says, 'Album of The Year'. It says 'Dead Poets-*Sayonara Sun*' right fucking next to it.

"You're a beautiful fucking genius, Rapha! Have I ever told you that? Have I?" Crawford is saying as he lifts me up. "A BEAUTIFUL POETIC GENIUS!!" He puts me down, grabs my cheeks and kisses me on the lips.

Cleo is crying and Mase and Zeke are laughing their fucking asses off. I can still taste the vomit in my mouth and I think I might throw up again.

Album of the Year.

Album of the fucking year. Relief, happiness, pride, gratitude, and a whole host of other things are rushing through me. I want to call my mom. I want to call Camille. I want to spit on my dad's fucking grave and tell him that I'm better than he ever fucking was. That I did all of this myself. Without his name or his presence or his love. I wish he was alive so I could call him up and tell him that over the phone. Tell him that he was nothing to me.

Album of the Year. I did it. We did it.

Now we just have to fucking win it.

My phone doesn't stop ringing all day. Notifications from every app that I have, showering me with praise and congratulations. It feels good. We got a nomination for best Alternative Album and Record of The Year too, but that sort of gets lost in the buzz around the album nomination. I have this weird vision of me holding the award, accepting it, and giving a speech and my breath stops from how badly I want it to happen. I don't know if it's good to trust it as another choking certainty, but it feels like ours already.

Camille posts about it on her Instagram: '*So proud of you, mon amour x*' and the internet goes fucking wild over it. She calls me before she gets on the flight from London telling me the same. Her flight lands in eight hours and I can't wait to see her. I've missed her like crazy. I call my mom because she works Mondays and hasn't likely heard the news yet. She cries like she always does when we do anything, then asks me if I'm eating okay, like she always does. Fuck, I miss her too. I miss Colorado and I end the call with a promise to visit for Thanksgiving.

The label wants to throw us a party apparently, a nomination party. What they really mean is a 'your sales are about to sky-rocket and we're relieved we don't have to drop you' party. Sam calls us on Skype from Malibu with the news and a smile on his face brighter than the sun. I can see his relief too. And I'm glad I haven't let him down. He's been doing this a long time and we've given him a lot of stress. I'm convinced one day he's going to have a heart attack and it will be mainly my fault. I smile back, big and wide, as I tell him it was never in doubt.

It's close to ten pm when I get home. I'm exhausted, drained, the adrenaline subsiding bit by bit, leaving behind only a warm jittery afterglow.

Grabbing a bottle of beer from the fridge, I twist off the cap and carry it out to the pool, collapsing on top of the lounger to stare out at the night-time view of west Hollywood. There's nothing but contentment and warmth settled in my chest, so it's weird that my dad pops into my head then. Someone who never makes me feel warmth or contentment, someone who I wish made me feel nothing at all. And fuck him, but he does it again, takes that warm contentment I feel and turns it into something melancholic and empty. Something that makes me feel lost and adrift, like a little kid. Like the time I wandered off in Target while mom was at the cashier and thought I'd never see her again.

"Fuck you, Finn," I say to the night air. "You were nothing to me. You'll always be nothing to me." I down the beer and stand.

I'm standing in front of the body-length mirror in the bathroom, hair plastered to my head and body soaked with sweat. My fingers aching and bleeding from the show and the familiar feeling of euphoria a loud buzz in my head. I feel like a god. I'm hard as a rock, as often happens when I come off stage, and I smooth my hand over it but I need something more than my hand this time. I need…the thought fizzes through my mind and then I feel it. Hands creeping around my middle from behind, warm body pressing against my back. When I look back into the mirror, he's looking at me over my shoulder, as he mouths at my ear.

"Is this what you need?" Jaehyun says, his voice a whispered dream. His eyes are dark and hot and filled with lust. A surge of pressure pounds against my dick.

"Yes…fuck, yes," I groan, dropping my head back onto his shoulder.

"Say it, Raphael…tell me what you want."

"Your mouth, your hands, you…"

He laughs, this soft airy thing that tickles my balls, then he's sliding to his knees and I'm turning to look down at him.

He looks glorious on his knees, blonde hair hanging over darkly made-up eyes, pink mouth wet and fuckable. I glance at us in the mirror and have to choke back a groan at the way his back arches, his ass pushed out, thighs spread wide. His hands on my zipper are what drags my attention back, his perfectly long fingers peeling open my jeans and pushing them down my thighs.

"Have you been thinking about this?" he asks, stroking my dick against his cheek, his mouth, eyes closing in what looks like bliss. "About me being on my knees for you?"

"Fuck, Jaehyun…please." My hand reaches out to fist his hair and he lets out this delicious gasp, mouth falling open wide.

"Feed it to me. Feed me your cock, Raphael. I want it so much."

The instant I comply, pushing my cock into the warm, wet heat of his mouth, I'm coming. *Endless spurts of my orgasm onto his tongue, down his throat.*

It feels like divinity. And he's my god.

I awake to the feel of something cold and wet on my stomach. Fucking hell that was intense. The first sex dream I've had about him in months, and I came from it. I'd fallen asleep naked after finishing a half bottle of tequila and playing guitar for a bit.

The clock tells me it's 4am and Camille will be here shortly and I can't have her finding me in this state. After hauling the sheets from the bed, I drop them in the laundry basket and climb into the shower to wash off the evidence.

As I play the dream over in my head, I'm hard again. I jerk myself off against the tiles before climbing back into the unmade bed, but Camille won't notice anything out of the ordinary about that.

I hadn't checked his Instagram after the nominations, so caught up in our own that I hadn't had a minute alone to do it. I pull up his account now. There's a pic of him kneeling, head and hands pressed against the floor. The caption reads: *'Thank you to our fans, I'll work hard to make you proud. Be happy. You did this.'* I'm not sure why, but it reads so utterly heartfelt, so completely genuine, that I feel something thick burning in my throat. Then I feel guilty for jerking off to him and dreaming about him, for making him this dirty-talking minx in my head, for this whole weird fucking obsession I've cultivated from a single meeting. I know nothing about this dude. He seems sweet, genuine, hard-working, and probably isn't even fucking gay.

What am I talking about? *I'm not fucking gay.*

THREE
RAPHAEL

I wake up with Camille's mouth around my cock. It's half-hard and getting harder as she swipes her tongue over the head the way I like, as she flicks at the seam that connects my foreskin.

I hadn't heard her get home, had fallen back asleep while checking my phone.

"Fuck, baby." I look down to find her eyes closed and her cheeks pink, nipples poking through the cream silk vest she's wearing. "I missed you."

She smiles around my cock and pulls off. "Did you? How much?" She takes me to the back of her throat and sucks up and down a few times, then she's straddling me, pushing me inside her.

"Shit."

I arch my hips up into her, thrusting as she falls onto my chest, peppering kisses across my throat up to my mouth starting to move slow and sensually over my cock. Her thighs clench and release as she rides me with purpose, the familiar scent of her perfume flooding my nose. Having her in my arms is warm and familiar and feels really fucking good and with my brain still half asleep I've not the energy to fight off the orgasm. I'm spilling into her a few minutes later.

"Fuck, babe, sorry," I groan, wrapping an arm around her neck to pull her close to me.

She sighs. Disappointed. "It's fine." She presses another soft kiss to my lips and murmurs. "Missed you too."

"Was it this stamina you missed? Cause no one would blame you. A sex machine you have right here."

This makes her laugh and then she's sliding off me and rolling onto her back on the bed.

"It's the Grammy nomination. That's sexy, you know." Her smile is wide as she turns onto her side to face me. She looks fond and proud.

I grin. "You want me even more now, right?"

"A hundred percent more. I can't wait to marry you."

That weird feeling skitters down into my gut again. Like fear. Or dread. I avert my eyes to look at the ceiling instead.

"I honestly thought I'd fucked it up, Cam. That we weren't gonna get it. I've never felt fear like it. I was so sure and then when we weren't in rock, I was certain we were done."

It's always been easy to be this vulnerable with Cam. She understood me on a level most people didn't. She never judged and never expected and it was easy to just be myself with her. It's one of the reasons we've lasted this long. I *do* love her.

"You really think the band would have imploded if you hadn't gotten a Grammy nomination?" She sounds doubtful.

"I'm sure Crawford would have killed me, Zeke would have helped bury the body, so maybe they'd have found another singer. But Raphael Scott would have been dead. Buried."

"Mason wouldn't let them kill you, he loves you," she says.

When I look at her, she forces a smile.

"Cleo wouldn't either," she adds.

"Mase couldn't even look at me when he thought we weren't getting it. The thought of letting them all down." My chest echoes with the anxious memory.

She reaches out to squeeze my arm. "You're a band, Rapha. It is a team. The success or failure of Dead Poets isn't all on you, puppy."

She's right but fuck me it sure feels like it sometimes. It's my name all over the tabloids. It's my name on most of the tracks. It's me people see first. I *am* the Dead Poets for so many people. And I'd put everything into this album. It had taken hours of me convincing the others to trust me on it. I hadn't wanted that trust to have been for nothing.

"I know. I'm just glad you don't have to go to my funeral…" I turn to face her. "Though you'd definitely be the hottest widow anyone's ever seen."

"I don't think I count as a widow until we're married, but I'd still mourn like one." She kisses me again.

"How was the flight?"

"I slept for most of it." This prompts her to yawn. "This film is killing me. I seriously want to take a year off when it's over. Lie on a deserted beach somewhere doing nothing."

"Where would we go?" I ask.

"You'd come with me?"

"Can't think of a single other person I'd rather spend a year on a desert Island with."

Though as soon as the words are out of my mouth, I know it's a lie. There is another person I'd quite happily spend a year on a desert island with. The fuck is wrong with me. Guilty, I lean in, kiss her, and then climb from the bed.

"What do you wanna do today?" I stride naked towards the bathroom. "Hike? Beach? We could take the bikes and go on that trail down by Athony again? Cute couple shit."

She laughs at that as she curls deep into the covers. "Can cute couple shit involve staying in bed? I am jet lagged and you owe me an orgasm."

I stop and give her a hurt look. "Oh, we're keeping track now, are we?"

"I used to keep track, but I lost count," she says breaking into a laugh.

She yelps when I rush to the bed and pounce on her.

Camille flies back to London on Wednesday and I drop her at the airport just after lunch.

I'd offered since I have a meeting with one of the lawyers at the Halcyon offices to sign some paperwork. I'd put it off long enough. Made sense to do it today since I'd be driving to LAX anyway.

I sit in the car for ten minutes before going in because the traffic is nowhere near as bad as I expected it to be and I'm there almost forty minutes before I should be. I scroll my phone for a bit in the parking lot before getting thirsty, so decide to grab a drink in the restaurant inside. Can't do me any harm to turn up early for once, I guess.

I tell the receptionist who I'm here for and since I'm early she directs me to the visitors lounge anyway. I shouldn't, because I haven't been near the gym in a week, but I buy a can of coke and down it in four gulps, then buy another. I'm wandering out of the lounge, cracking open the can and not looking where the fuck I'm going, when I walk into someone. A guy.

"Fuck, man, sor–."

My voice literally dies in my throat as we make eye contact.

He's wearing a ballcap and tinted sunglasses but it's him. It's fucking him. I can't move. Can barely breathe. How is it possible? How the fuck is Lee Jaehyun standing in front of me in the offices of Halcyon Records in LA? He's in New York. I know this because I was just on his fucking Instagram page outside. He posted a picture from his hotel room last night.

"Sorry," I finally get out.

He stares at me a minute, blank, then lifts a hand politely.

"No problem," he says, his voice whisper soft. Exactly like it was in the dream I'd had the other night.

Then he's moving past me toward the counter. I can only stare after him. He's wearing all black. Black cap, black leather jacket, black jeans, and black boots with a buckle and a short heel.

He's there. Right fucking there. I want to talk to him. What the fuck would I say?

Hey, remember me from the Paris bathroom two years ago. I was laughing about your lack of a dick with my mates. Haven't stopped thinking about you since. Wanna grab a drink?

And then, like he can hear me, he turns his head and stares right back at me. He looks like he's smiling a little. Like he knows something I don't, or maybe like he's trying to place me.

"Mr. Scott," a voice says from behind me.

"Rapha," I reply, dragging my eyes to Amari's PA.

"Of course. Mr Amari is finished with his previous client if you'd like to come with me?"

I nod, looking back at Jaehyun. He's browsing the chilled drinks display, no longer looking in my direction. I have this weird pulling sensation in my chest when I start to walk away from him, like my body is fighting against me. Like my body wants me to go back over. Do something. Say something.

"Was that who I think it was?" I ask the PA as we walk towards the elevator. I know it was, I'm just hoping it might encourage her to tell me why he's here.

"It was," she affirms but says nothing more.

Before we disappear into the elevator, I glance back once more. He's on his phone with his back turned. Did I just miss the only chance I'd ever get to talk to him? My gut is churning tight with inaction, like it might be. If I was a person who believed in signs, this would be a huge one with neon lights flashing around it. I'd put this meeting with Amari off for weeks but I showed up today, finally, early, and Jaehyun is somehow here too. This fucking idol of my fantasies.

We're speeding up to the tenth floor now though and I can't very well ask her to take me back down.

Fuck. He was right there. I was right there. I just fucking spoke to him. Sort of.

Amari comes off like he was born to be a corporate lawyer. Sharply dressed, polished all over, and with a smile that looks somehow both deadly and genuine.

He congratulates me on the nomination then offers me a drink, before sitting me down with a more serious tone to talk through the redraft of the contract. It gives me a 28.84% share of the royalties off the next three albums. It's the most I've had and it's more than the guys are getting. There's also a separate conditional contract pertaining to a solo record, with an option to make and release it with Halcyon's full support within the next five years.

I'm not really listening, honestly. I'm thinking about Jaehyun. Wondering if he's still in the building. Wondering how long he's in LA for and where else I might bump into him.

"Perfect, Rapha," Amari says as I sign. He slides the contracts across the table to his PA to witness and sign, before she lifts them and takes them out of the room with her. "I'll have Emmy courier your copies over to you asap."

"No worries, man." I take a sip of the water he poured me. "Anything else?"

"I don't think so? Unless you've anything else for me?"

I shake my head and stand. "Nah, I'm good. Sorry about taking so long to get down here, you know how it is."

"I do, I do, No worries at all." He rises to his feet and shakes my hand. "Well, if there's ever anything I can do for you. I work for Halcyon, but I'm also here for the artists, you know?"

"Appreciate it, dude."

I'm out of there like a shot and Emmy the PA is ushering me to the elevator and keying me down to the ground floor again. I practically bolt out through the doors towards the restaurant. I've still not got a clue what I'm gonna say to him but that doesn't matter at this point. I'll deal with that when I'm standing in front of him.

He's not there though. There are a few guys in suits by the window and two women looking over a cell phone on the other side. But no Jaehyun. I feel like punching something. Kicking something. I glance at the young guy behind the counter who's looking at me expectantly and think about asking him when he left and in what direction, but what does it matter. He's not fucking here.

"Can I get you anything?" the guy asks. He's wearing a black apron and a big smile that tells me he's a fan.

"Nah, I was just…" I take a last look around the lounge. "Where's your bathroom, man?"

Should probably take a leak before the drive back as the two cans of coke and glass of water start catching up with me. He points me to the shiny black doors hidden behind a wooden screen and goes back to wiping the counter.

I've just finished pissing into the urinal when one of the cubicle doors open and he's striding out towards the sinks.

It feels like I've been kicked in the fucking face.

He falters very slightly when he sees me, but barely gives me a second look as he moves to wash his hands.

How is it possible that it's this again? An exact re-enactment of Paris. Except this time there's no Crawford, no Mason, there's just the two of us.

His phone is sitting face down on the marble counter as he rinses and I notice he has a pale pink Gucci cover on, his initials in gold: **LJH**. Silver bracelets hang from his wrists and rings decorate his hands as he makes a thorough job of cleaning them.

Heart pounding in my chest, I glance up to look at his face in the mirror. My breath catches when I find him watching me, the smallest semblance of a smile on his face, eyes dark and skin pale and smooth as marble under the crappy lighting.

"It's Jaehyun right?" I hear myself ask.

Fuck, is that my voice? It echoes clumsily around the bathroom sounding nervous and unstable. I'm not ready for what he says next.

"And you are Raphael."

He turns off the tap and shakes his hands gently into the sink before reaching for a hand towel.

He knows my name. Some weird noise goes off in my head. He knows my fucking name. I mean, a lot of people know my name but for some reason it hadn't occurred to me that he might.

"Yeah, hey man."

I do some stupid fucking wave thing at him before turning off the tap.

Jaehyun hands me a towel and then we're both standing there drying our hands while we look at each other.

"So, you're meeting with the label? I thought you guys were with YJK? That's under Sonar, right?"

When his eyes narrow, I get a weird flutter of panic behind my ribs. I just told him I know what label he's on. Is that weird? Is that something only an obsessed stalker would know? Is that why he's looking at me like that? I decide that no, it's completely normal. I'm a musician. Of course, I know who is and isn't signed to the same label I am.

"I was meeting with an artist on the label," he tells me somewhat tightly. Like it's none of my fucking business. Which it isn't. Vaguely, I notice his English is smoother than I remember it being, a little less awkward and stumbling than it was in the Paris speech. I'd noticed it in his more recent videos too.

"Ah, cool, gotchu." Though everything in me tells me he has no desire to share it with me, I ask anyway. "You not gonna say who? It a secret?" I offer some dumb grin that gets stuck partway on my face.

He looks confused, like he can't understand why I even care. He folds up his towel and drops it gently into the wicker waste basket before turning back to me.

"It is not yet agreed so I cannot really talk about it."

I nod. "That's cool, dude, I totally get that. Collab is cool though. A track with you and a western artist is gonna fly whoever it is. Hope it works out. Can't wait to hear it."

Is this what they call verbal diarrhea? Have I said anything of any substance yet? My ears feel hot.

Jaehyun nods, smiling politely, and then backs away from me towards the door the way you might back away from a crazy homeless person.

"Goodbye, Raphael."

"Yeah. Nice meeting you, man." I say.

He throws a last enigmatic look over his shoulder, nods again, and then he's gone, door swinging shut behind him. I can only blink after him, a little stunned, a little panicked as the sound of his footsteps echo away from me outside.

Then I practically fold into myself with embarrassment, hanging off the counter with a groan.

"You fucking moron. You actual fucking moron."

As I straighten, I spot it.

The Gucci covered phone with LJH lettering still sitting there on the counter. I grab it and turn it over, bolting towards the door. I glance down at it just as the screensaver lights up. It's him holding a cat up for a kiss. A furry white thing with bright blue eyes and a pink nose. It's cute as fuck.

I pull open the bathroom door at the same time it's pushed open and it fucks me, hard, in the face. Pain bursts across my nose and I hear what I'm sure is a sickening crunch as blood starts to pour from it.

Jaehyun makes a horrified gasping sound, his eyes going comically wide.

"You forgot your phone," I mumble, holding it out with one hand as I cover my bleeding nose with the other.

FOUR
RAPHAEL

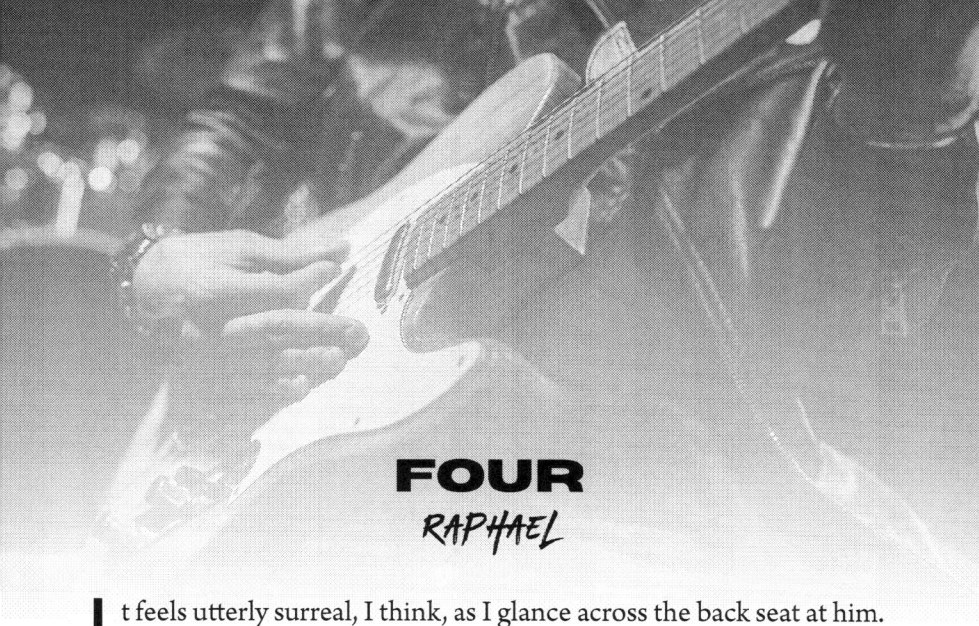

It feels utterly surreal, I think, as I glance across the back seat at him.

He's talking quietly on the phone in Korean, his head slightly turned so I can't see his expression. Though I've not a clue what he's saying, he doesn't sound angry. Like he's pissed off at having to ferry my clumsy ass to the ER.

The bandage the barista had pulled from a pristine first aid kit behind the counter is on my lap, the bleeding having stopped, but I'm still holding the ice pack to my nose. An ice pack that's melting quickly due to how hot my body feels.

He finishes his call and looks over at me, eyes still wide and worried behind his tinted glasses.

"Have I messed up your schedule?" I ask.

He smiles a little, but his eyes are still concerned. "No, do not worry. I was just calling my lawyer."

I laugh at that, and he smiles wider.

"I am so sorry," he says, eyes serious again.

"I told you. It wasn't your fault, man. I'm just clumsy as shit, honestly. And not in a cute, adorable way, in a really fucking chaotic way."

The smile he gives me makes my stomach flip like crazy and then he's frowning again.

"I really hope it is not broken."

He leans in a little and the scent of his cologne floods up my battered nose. Sweet and spicy. Like Christmas. Maybe mulled wine. Cinnamon and apples and fuck, my mouth waters. Up close his skin is dewy and smooth but not as flawless as his pictures make it appear, slight imperfections across the skin which only make him more attractive in fact. More real. His lips though, they *are* as perfect as they look in pictures: full and pink and wet. My cock stirs a little, so very interested in what my brain can't help thinking about in relation to them. He lets out a sigh and sits back.

"It wouldn't be the first time someone had broken my nose, so don't worry about it."

"You've had it broken many times?"

"Once or twice. People tend not to like me off the bat, you know, and they wanna make sure I know it."

It's an attempt at a joke but he doesn't smile. He frowns a little.

"So, you are used to making a bad first impression on people?" he says and my head snaps up, shame crawling up my spine, prickling over my scalp.

"Fuck, I was really hoping you didn't remember that..."

He blinks, slow and careful. "Remember what?"

I thought he meant I made a bad impression on him. He doesn't mean that? He doesn't remember?

Fucking hell, I feel like singing. Except now he's looking at me all wide-eyed and expectant and so I have to tell him something. I owe him a fucking apology. Cause even if he didn't hear it, we still fucking said it. *I* still laughed at it.

There's this calm, cool look on his face as he waits for me to explain.

"Well, it's just that, we've met before. Once," I glance down at the bloodied bandage, ass clenched tight.

"We have?"

I nod, fiddling with the thread on the cut knee of my jeans.

"Not properly, but we were in the same room once. I um, well it wasn't cool. I wasn't cool. I said some shit I shouldn't have said." I chance a look up at his face to find it utterly blank. Expressionless. "I was a dick, and well, I've thought a lot about it. Wanted to apologize to you about it." I give a pathetic half-shrug thing while I wait for him to respond.

Jaehyun says absolutely nothing. Just stares at me, eyes wide. Long legs stretched out, shoulders back, head high.

"I am sorry, I don't remember," he says finally.

"Honestly, I'm sort of relieved you don't."

"Because you weren't cool." It's not a question. Dark eyes bore into mine.

"Because I wasn't cool."

His gaze lingers on me a moment and then he glances down at his phone. I expect him to ask more about why I wasn't cool, but he doesn't. He shifts slightly, the sound of his leather jacket squeaking loudly against the leather of the car seat.

"Then you must be relieved at how cool you are being now?"

He flicks his eyes across to me and there's a fucking glimmer in them. Playful. Almost…flirtatious? Which is obviously wishful thinking on my part.

Either way, I have to swallow the grin that wants to break over my face. I feel suspended here with him, like the world outside the car doesn't exist. Or like I'm going to wake up in my bed drenched in sweat and come with just the memory of him burning behind my eyes. The throbbing of my nose tells me this isn't a dream though.

Suddenly the car's pulling into the drop off point of the UCLA Medical Centre.

"Ronald Reagan Centre," the driver tells us over his shoulder.

God, I don't want to get out.

"Listen, thanks for the lift, beats an Uber."

"It is no problem," Jaehyun says genuinely. "The company said they would drop your car at your home, yes?" I'd dropped my keys with Amari's PA, who promised to have someone drive it home.

I nod. "They did. I'll grab an Uber back once they fix me up."

He nods, hesitating slightly. Then he's lifting his phone out of his pocket again and typing something in. "Would you mind me sending to you a message? To check that you're okay?" He looks at my nose, then corrects himself. "To check that your nose is okay?"

He wants my number.

"Um, sure. Yeah, I mean I don't mind. Hit me up." My voice sounds all trembly and uncertain. *Get a fucking grip, Rapha.*

"You're on Instagram or Twitter?" Jae asks me, scooting closer and holding his phone up between us. "Show me?"

I deflate a little that he doesn't, in fact, want my phone number, but it's something, right?

With some work I manage to find myself on his Korean Language set-up Instagram.

"And you manage it yourself?" he checks.

"Yeah, just me," I nod.

"I've sent you a message now, so you can find me," he says, and I want to laugh at that.

So I can find him? I check his account more than I check my own.

"I won't follow you now because people notice these things. And sometimes it can cause problems," he says, smiling sadly before slipping his phone into his back pocket.

I suppose I sort of know what he means but I guess I also don't. Would people care if he followed me? I nod anyway.

He looks up at me and smiles. "It was nice meeting you, Raphael," he says, then adds. "Again."

"Yeah, if we could just pretend this was the first time, that would be fucking great, man."

He smiles wider, then gestures to my nose. "We can forget this time too, if you want?"

I laugh. "No way. This time, I want to remember." I realize too late how that might have sounded but find it hard right then to give a fuck. When I try to gauge Jaehyun's reaction to it, I can't. He's completely chill, nothing but a soft smile lifting the side of his mouth.

"Take care, Raphael," he says, as I push open the door.

"You, too. Thanks again for the lift." *And for breaking my nose.*

He gives me a little dip of his head and then I close the door. I stare after the black defender until it turns out of the hospital lot and disappears.

It's not broken—which honestly feels like a miracle because I was certain I heard something crack back there—just 'traumatized' according to the radiologist, Scott, with a body like The Rock and a smile like Jack Nicholson. After talking my ear off about our first album for almost forty minutes, he supplies me with some meds (the good shit) and some good vibes and sends me on my way.

I call an Uber from the front door and it arrives within five minutes. But at this time the traffic is like Dante's seventh circle of Hell and I'm trapped in the back of the car just staring at my DMs and waiting (pathetically) for his message to come in. Then I figure he might be on a plane—why didn't I think to ask him how long he was in town for? —and so, I hover over the little paper plane icon on his IG thinking it wouldn't look too pathetic for me to message *him*. I mean, he was clearly concerned about what damage he thinks he might have done to my face. He asked for my socials. Asked if he could message me. So why hasn't he then?

Jesus, I can't think properly in here. I need a beer and some weed to organize my thoughts a bit before I message him.

The driver doesn't seem to have recognized me and is talking to me about football instead. I always pretend to be into football because it's just easier, and I know enough about it to fool the casual conversationalist. But honestly, I could give less of a shit about the draft or the NFL or the fucking Superbowl. All things I'm sure are in Diego here's top ten reasons to get out of bed in the morning.

I'm just pulling up at the house when my cell rings. My heart flips out even though I know it's not gonna be him calling. I look at the ID as I hand the driver a $50 and thank him.

"What's up man?"

"You at home?" Crawf yawns. He sounds half asleep. Like he's just woken up. Or like he's wasted. Given how I know he can be on our downtime, it's either of those options.

I glance at my watch. Almost 7 p.m.

"Just getting home now, why? You good?" I punch the code into the gate and spot my truck straight away. Parked in front of the garage.

"Where you been all day? Camille's gone right?"

"She left this afternoon. I had to go to the ER, got a door opened in my face earlier."

He laughs first. Yeah, he's wasted. "Shit man, you're so fucking clumsy. You okay?"

"Tell me about it. Yeah, I'm fine. Nothing's broken. Hurts like a motherfucker though."

"I'll bet."

Rosita, our cleaning lady, has been because there's fresh flowers in the hall table—Camille insisted we get a subscription—and the place smells lemony fresh like it always does after. I literally cannot retain the information about which days she comes no matter how many times she tells me. Mainly as I'm never here, but also because my memory is disturbingly shit sometimes.

"So, what you up to now." Crawf says. "Fancy getting fucked up with me? I'm bored, dude."

It took me a surprisingly short amount of time to understand that Crawford hates his own company. He simply cannot fathom a period of time where he has to spend time with himself. When he doesn't have anyone near him or around him. Where he has to deal with whatever demons he's got hiding in his head. I've always found it curious too because he doesn't like other people very much either. His girlfriends never last more than a few weeks.

"You sound fucked up already, man." I go directly to the fridge and pull out a beer, holding it to my nose for a few moments. The throbbing eases slightly. I crack it open on the counter.

"Yeah, well. I plan on getting more fucked up. You in?"

On one hand, I don't particularly fancy the company. I was looking forward to having the house to myself tonight now that Camille was gone. Fancied gaming some, playing some guitar, drinking a bit, and jerking off over Jaehyun. But the drugs will help the pain in my fucking face and it's never a good idea for Crawford to be left alone when he's in one of these moods. I pull the good shit Scott at the ER gave me and pop open the cap with one hand.

"Yeah man, but head over here? I just spent an hour in an Uber from the Valley and I'll be fucked if I'm doing it again."

"I am on my way. Gonna grab some pizza on the way. Do you want anything?"

I toss back three of the pills and wash them down with a mouthful of beer. "Korean. See if you can find some Korean, will you?"

"Sure man, got it. I'll be there soon."

Crawford hangs up and I flick back to Instagram as I carry my beer through to the lounge.

I'm on his IG—because am I ever not—the moment he posts.

It's a video of a beach, the waves splashing melodically against the sand. The camera pans up to show the most beautiful sunset. Purples and oranges and pinks against the indigo water.

He's still in LA and he's online.

My heart is beating quickly at the possibility. If he controls his account himself then it means he's taken this and posted it immediately. It looks like Malibu but I guess it could be any beach in LA.

I'd wanted to word my message to him properly, after debating it for at least an hour, but if he's online now, then it's too good an opportunity to miss. I flick to my DMs to reply to the message he sent earlier and it appears before my fucking eyes.

@ljh: Raphael! I am hoping that nothing is broken and you are not in too much pain.

Then a second right away.

@ljh: (My lawyer did not want me to send you this message. Kekeke)

I hold my breath while I read it over a few times, blinking in disbelief. Then, for a reason I don't understand, I close the app, set my phone down and walk over to the window. I down my beer entirely, before coming to my senses and practically bolting back to the couch. Who knows how long he stays online for?

@theraphascott_: Never listen to lawyers. It's my life's motto

@theraphascott_: Not too much pain. And nothing's broken! (Except my pride.) Thanks for caring :)

My panic to get the message out quickly before he disappears offline means I don't overthink it whatsoever.

The little 'read' text appears below, telling me he's seen it, but no dots appear telling me he's typing. But something better happens. A picture comes through. It's the same beach from his post, except this one has his feet in it. Stretched out in the sand.

@ljh: I felt guilty enjoying this view while worrying about your nose! LA is very beautiful.

I laugh because my instinct is to reply, unironically, that it's not as beautiful as him. But I have to fight that instinct.

@theraphascott_ No guilt necessary. Great pic, man! Is it Malibu?

This time the little dots do appear and I feel fucking elated at the sight of them. Over a text exchange with a guy who almost broke my nose this afternoon. A guy I've been obsessing about for the last two years.

It's insane to me right then. But I don't feel any guilt about it, which is weird. Maybe because of the insanity of it. Because it is a guy. Because I know nothing is ever gonna happen with this person, because I'm not gay. If it was another woman then yeah, I would be a piece of shit. But he's not. So, I'm fine. This is fine.

@ljh: Yes, we are in Malibu.

My spine straightens. I'm not sure why the word 'we' has such a bizarre effect on me. But it does. I can't think of anything else to say to that, except to ask him who he's with but I honestly don't even want to know. Is it better if he's with a chick or a dude? Does it fucking matter?

Do I just leave it there then? I mean, it's hardly an open question.

But my body feels on edge, like I've snorted something by just talking to him and I'm not quite ready for that feeling to fade yet. I debate for half a minute over it, figuring it's absolutely something a guy could say to another guy he has no sexual interest in whatsoever. It's also got enough in it to suggest it could be something else, if the person reading it wanted it to be. My hands tremble slightly as I write it.

> **@theraphascott_: Let me know when you're next in town and I'll show you my favorite beach in LA! You'd love it!**

As soon as I hit send, I want to unsend. I feel the heat creep up my throat to my cheeks, my ears burning hot too.

The moment he sees it I think my heart stops. As the seconds tick by, I imagine him staring at it, feeling awkward and a little creeped out.

"Fuck," I mutter to myself, squeezing my eyes closed and digging my thumb and index finger into them. I want to gouge them out. I may as well have asked him to let me know when he was next in town so I could suck his dick.

But as I glance down at my phone, the relief, and something else, courses through my body.

> **@ljh: I will do that. And if you are ever in Seoul, let me know and I will show you my favourite sunset :) Take care, Raphael! J**

He's clearly ending the conversation, but for some reason I don't feel disappointed. I feel only elation. Giddy—is that even a word guys use?—nervousness giving way to a heady sort of joy.

FIVE
RAPHAEL

November

Camille walks into the room to the sound of whistles and cat-calls from the guys. She rolls her eyes at them and looks at me—I can only give her an apologetic smile. She looks incredible in white, in a dress that's really just a tuxedo jacket which stops just below her ass, and white heels that show off her dainty ankles and tiny feet. I love Camille's feet. Pretty sure I've a foot fetish of some kind because I genuinely get hard just thinking about them sometimes. Little cute toes that she's always got painted and these small little ankles that look sexy as fuck in open toe shoes like she's wearing now.

From nowhere the image of Jaehyun's small pale feet and a bejeweled ankle blasts itself into my mind. I'd spotted it in one of their videos, how I've no idea, but when I did, it had felt as intimate as seeing his cock.

"You look beautiful," I tell Camille as she comes toward me, sliding an arm around my waist.

"Thank you, puppy," she says, lowering her voice to hide the pet-name from the others. "And you look very sexy."

I'm wearing black: a black suit and shirt with an open collar and probably too much silver around my neck. But the way her eyes dip lustfully over them and the flashes of my tattoos, tells me it works. I lean in to kiss her, licking the taste of champagne from her lips.

We'd offered to host everyone at our place before we left for the ceremony. We were going in three cars; Camille and I were expected to arrive together of course, the rest of the band in a second car, and Sam and the rest from the label, in a third. I'd link up with the guys on the carpet for interviews when the cameras got what they wanted from Camille and me. I feel nervy, jittery, and it's about more than the award.

It's about the fact that he's going to be there.

I'm going to see him for the first time since the day he thought he'd broken my nose. We haven't spoken since those messages back in September, though with every picture and story he'd posted I'd wanted to reach out. Wanted to click that little heart or leave a comment, reply to some video of him in the dance studio, in a designer clothes store, eating some amazing looking meal, of his cat. But I hadn't. I hadn't unfollowed him—and he hadn't followed me back—but I hadn't liked any of his posts either and it was mainly because of his words in the car on the way to the hospital.

People notice these things. And sometimes it can cause problems.

Tonight would be the first time I've seen him in the flesh since that day and it's the reason I drink a little too much champagne and do three lines of white before we leave. Thank fuck I'm not performing. I doubt I'd be able to make my fingers and throat work at the same time if we were, not with the pressure of the night, coupled with him sat in the audience watching me. On some level I like the idea of him watching me perform, of him seeing me when I'm at my most confident, most assured, but mainly it just scares the shit out of me.

We're greeted by a few people with tablets and those headset things and then we're being led to the gauntlet. Unfortunately, I can't let Camille do the talking as I always do when it's just us, what with this being about our nominations so I keep my answers short and pretend I'm distracted by how beautiful my fiancé looks. I'm gonna have to circle back and do this with the guys in a bit anyway, where Crawf normally does most of the talking.

"You look so good, baby," she whispers at me while the cameras go off a few feet away from us. She brings her mouth to my ear. "I can't wait to fuck you later. Limo on the way home?" She pulls back to ask. Innocent as you like.

I grin and lean in to kiss her. "Sounds good."

The cameras go nuts.

We're being interviewed by a pretty English girl from The NME when I first spot him.

He's at the far end of the gauntlet, just arriving it looks like, surrounded by his band and about twenty other people. Of course, he stands out. His hair is a pale soft purple. His body looking tall and lean, all angles and grace under a dark blue suit. Moving through space like a fucking dream.

I'm talking about the album title but my words just break off, my whole attention caught in his snare. Only when he disappears behind a mass of bodies does my mind switch back online.

The night is long and fucking boring. We don't win in Alternative but we weren't tipped to. Record is up later but we don't have a shot in that one either. The album award is near the end and so I've been trying not to overdo it, but I'm aware I've had way too much to drink.

He's on the other side of the room, about eight tables away, but I can see him every time there's movement in between and he's often laughing with one of his bandmates—a small thing with bleached white hair. I'm staring too hard when I feel Cleo nudge me gently and I blink back in.

"Earth to Raphael," she says.

"Sorry, I thought I saw someone there who hated our album," I laugh.

She laughs too loud and then the others make me repeat it and they laugh too. It's hard. To stay focused and stop my eyes from searching him out, drawn to where I think he might be. I'm going to go speak to him at some point. I'd thought about it for weeks, since I heard he was going to be here. Now, I'm thinking that was a fucking terrible idea because I can't think. Can't speak without slurring. Not a single coherent thought in my head.

I need a drink. No, a line. Something to sharpen my thoughts.

"You okay?" It's Zeke, an arm slung around my shoulders. "You look like you've checked out."

"Bored as shit, dude."

He laughs and nods, reaching over to fill up our glasses.

The thing most people don't realize about awards shows is that they're fucking boring. They're long—real fucking long—and when you don't give a shit about who's performing or winning awards, you start wishing you'd stayed the fuck home. I'm not even listening when they announce the next performer. I'm listening to Zeke talk about the gig he went to in Calabasas again—some Latin jazz multi-instrumentalist that just lost out to someone in his category and Crawf thinks is the greatest musician he's ever seen—but then the lights are dimming and there's a blue spotlight pouring down on the stage lighting up a figure dressed all in white.

Behind him, another light drops from the ceiling, highlighting a black gloss piano with Haven Williams sat behind it dressed head to toe in black.

I know it's him before he even moves, before the first notes of the piano hit the air. But then he's dancing and I'm not breathing.

It's the song that's been everywhere for months. It's the song he dances to in the video I've watched countless times. It's move for move the same dance, though the arrangement of the song is stripped down for piano and a violin that appears in the background half a minute in, and then a guy playing a Spanish guitar.

But he's all I see.

He's wearing a more tailored version of the loose silk pajama bottoms and shirt he wears in the video, feet bare, hair covering his face slightly. Haven sings, incredibly raw and emotive. And he dances, matching every bit of that emotion. The song had been huge already, but his dance video had made it bigger. Last I checked there was 59 million views on it. Her original music video had a quarter of that. They're both in complete sync. I realize then that his moves don't just match the beat, like a dancer's should, but they match the lyrics too. It's like I get it then. Dance. The concept of it. A fucking epiphany.

When it's done I can only stare dumbfounded for a few beats, like everyone else in the place, then the applause starts snapping me out of it.

Haven gets up from her piano and crosses the stage to meet him, hugging him tightly. Like they're friends. A weird rush of envy comes at me as I understand how far away from being able to do that I am. Hold him in some way. Touch him.

"Lee Jaehyun," Haven says into the microphone, pointing at him with a clap and shake of her head, and the crowd cheers again. It's the audience behind us that make the most noise though, a roar louder than anything I've heard tonight. He puts his hand over his heart and does this little bow to the crowd, then waves at those making the noise behind us.

When they disappear from the stage, feeling rushes back into my body. My chest feels weird, my head too light, and my mouth is so fucking dry I have to peel my tongue from the roof of it. I reach out for the closest thing to me—a bottle of tequila—and down several gulps.

"Who the fuck did she say that was?" Crawford asks.

I can't figure out the tone of his voice but I know that I don't like it.

"Lee Jaehyun," Cleo says. "He's from K:OS."

When Crawf looks at her blankly, she says, "The K-pop band."

This seems to trigger something approaching recognition and I'm relieved when he says nothing else and just drinks his drink.

"Ah, that was magical!" Camille says. "I loved it. That song will win record of the year tonight. I'm sure it was number one in France."

"And everywhere else," Mase says, rolling his eyes, deeply unimpressed.

"Gotta take a leak," I say, standing. I need some air, some space from the noise in my head.

"Don't take too long, we're four away," Crawford shouts.

"It's a leak, not a shit. I'll be back in time."

I don't meet him in the bathroom as is normally our MO and I'm disappointed. I consider messaging him to congratulate him on the performance or something but it feels lame. If his band wins their award maybe I could do that, mention the performance then. Less lame, perhaps.

I'm walking back to my seat when I see him, lavender head thrown back with laughter. He's redressed in the black suit he was wearing when I saw him on the carpet, but he has the jacket draped over his arm. Floral silk shirt open at the neck to expose a pale line of skin. I've stopped in the middle of the floor of tables, my entire body vibrating with something fervent. Surge of blood going straight to my head and my dick simultaneously. I haven't seen him in person since September and he looks taller than I remember. All silk angles and exquisite tailoring. From this position his cheeks and jawbone look sharp enough to cut ice.

Before I can even think about it, I'm moving again, going over to his table. Straight through the herd of faceless bodies toward him. It must be a commercial break because there are a lot of people moving around, trays of drinks being carried aloft towards already rowdy tables. I bump the shoulder of one of the servers and he curses, managing somehow to stop the tray toppling over.

"Sorry, man, my bad." I hold my hands up and the guy's eyes go wide, recognition sparking in them.

"No, problem," he gets out, smiling nervously before he hurries off.

One of his bandmates spots me first. A guy with unnaturally green eyes and an undercut.

Jaehyun has his back to me now, as he talks animatedly to another guy with wide shoulders and a pair of sunglasses. The entire table stops talking one-by-one to look at me, the guy talking to Jae sliding his shades up off his dark eyes. He looks distinctly pissed off at the sight of me. The coke in my veins doesn't give a fuck though, and when Jae's head turns over his shoulder and his mouth and eyes widen with warmth, it makes it feel like a million little fireworks are going off in every blood cell.

"Raphael!" he says, turning all the way around to face me. His smile is big and warm and entirely genuine.

"Hey, how's it going, man? Had to come over and say hi. Good to see you." I stick my hand out to him. Without a thought, he takes it, shaking it gently. His fingers feel strangely cool, the tips cold even against the heat of my skin.

"I am good. How are you?" he asks.

"Good, great, yeah. That performance was incredible, dude. Honestly, mind blowing."

I do some weird wide-eyed thing that I'm scared makes me look unhinged. But he just smiles, shyly. His cheeks coloring visibly as he does the same short bow he did on the stage.

"Ah, thank you. I was so nervous. Haven was very generous to ask me to perform with her here."

I'm faintly aware of the entire table still watching us, of the stare of the guy Jae had been talking to before I got here, burning through me. But none of it really breaks through because he's still smiling at me.

"So, you're here for just this or you guys have a show or something? I'd love to check it out."

He looks surprised by this. "We are on the Late Night show tomorrow and then we go to New York on Monday," he tells me. "We have five nights there."

I blink at that because it means we are going to be in New York at the same time. We're in LA together now, and then we will be in New York together too. We'd been thrown together back in September too. Was that some fucking sign or what?

Except, I still don't believe in signs and we're not fucking together. I debate whether to tell him I'm in New York, but a glance at the dude growling at me behind Jae makes me decide against it.

"And your award is up soon, right? I have a good feeling about it."

He beams at this while shaking his head a little and the action is so adorable it makes my heart trip over. His table have resumed talking, even the guy behind him, and it's that which gives me the balls to say it. That and the coke and the tequila and the champagne. I use a lower voice than before, but not low enough that it could be considered flirting I don't think.

"Hey, let me know if you want me to recommend that beach I mentioned before. I mean if you have some free time here before you head out to NYC."

There's a flicker of confusion before it clears and his eyes widen again. "Ah, yes. Your favorite beach in LA! I would love to see it."

"Really?"

He nods, face warm and open. "Yes, we arrived three nights ago and I have not left the hotel and practice room. You must send me the details; I'll try to make it."

I'm not sure if he means he wants me to take him or go on his own but those are details I can work out later.

"I will, I will. Listen, I should get back to my table, I think our award is up in like five or something."

"You are nominated?" He beams. "That is wonderful! Good luck. You deserve it."

Even though I feel a bit deflated he didn't know, there's something so utterly genuine about it, so completely without the bullshit I'm used to hearing, that I can only stare at him a few long moments.

"Thanks, I appreciate it. You guys too. I'll be rooting for you."

He smiles before closing his eyes and lowering his head again. I think I say something like "Speak soon" before I'm moving away from him back towards our table. A glance over my shoulder has the guy talking in Jae's ear again, except this time they're both looking at me. One dark cold gaze, one warm and friendly, but fading a little.

My visit to the K:OS table seems to have gone entirely unnoticed by my own table because no one mentions a thing as I sit back down. They look relieved though, as if they half expected me to have passed out in the bathroom.

As they announce the presenter of our award, I realize that I've barely thought about it all night. It's been there, right at the back of my head. But it's been buried beneath this bigger, heavier, thing.

This thing that confuses and scares me shitless. But that thing lumbers out the way now, moving surprisingly fucking fast as they read out the nominees. Names I don't recognize right then. Names that sound like they're being spoken in another language, even our own.

A breath. The beat of my heart. A high-pitched noise.

I think maybe I've misheard, or that the entire place is so unimpressed with what's just happened they're not cheering. But then the sound rushes back in and Mase is standing and coming around the table towards me. He pulls me up out of the chair and throws his arms around me and then I'm being dragged toward the stage. Everything feels slow and dulled, like I'm underwater and then I'm on the stage and the lights are far too bright from this angle and I've had far too much to drink. I'm going to throw up. If I open my mouth, I'm certain that's what will come out, vomit. As the guys push Cleo towards the mic first, I try to stop the room tilting, attempting to focus on something to anchor me.

Then I see it.

The bright flash of lilac hair. Everything settles. Steadies. Calms. Not wanting to stare right in his direction, I keep that spot in my periphery as I suck a lungful of air in and let it out slowly. Then again. They're moving out of the way to let me talk now and because I wasn't listening, I'm not sure who they've thanked. It doesn't matter because there's only ever been one thing I wanted to say if I ever got to stand here. Only one person I ever wanted to thank.

"Thanks Mom, I love you."

Fuck you, Finn.

It's loud with the sound of people congratulating each other and themselves. I've already had people I know hate us come up and tell us how well deserved we are. A few even daring to mention Finn, but I'm too loose limbed and light-minded to care tonight.

We won. For an album I helped produce. For an album I wrote 90% of the songs for. For a direction I forced them down. I feel like a fucking king. We didn't get record of the year—Haven Williams did, Jae cheering for her on his feet and loudly even though his own band had just lost out in the category before—but it doesn't matter. Nothing matters except that I didn't fail DP. I feel weightless from relief. The stress and anxiety I'd worn for months now shirked off. I feel a hundred pounds lighter. I also feel wasted.

They'd arrived to the afterparty about an hour after everyone else had. Changed, but somehow still coordinated as a group. Another set of designer suits with bright colored shirts underneath. This one is the pale grey of a rain-soaked Colorado sky, his top a sheer white silk with a high collar, his shoes white too. I'd sensed him as he'd walked in, the hairs on the back of my neck tilting up, my blood heating when he'd gotten closer. They'd passed our table to get to their own which was on a raised section further from the bar, but he didn't make eye contact. Maybe didn't see me.

Now, he's standing with his back to me, talking behind his hand to a tall guy dressed in a white suit with black shirt. It's one of his band, but I still don't know their names. When he pats the guy gently on the shoulder and moves away down the stairs and in the direction of the bar, I'm standing. More than that, I'm following.

"Going to the bar," I say to Cam. "You want something?"

She shakes her head. It's table service, but the pace is slow and so she doesn't question it. I make my way through the huddles in the vague direction I saw him go. I've already decided I'm gonna try the bathroom if he's not at the bar. Maybe it could be our thing. A private joke about always meeting in bathrooms. Third time is a charm and all that.

But I see him before I get that far, attached to another small huddle, this time with Haven Williams, her tattooed English boyfriend, and another girl I recognize, but can't name. Haven has her arm looped through Jae's and is beaming up at him all sparkly-eyed and smiles. It's her boyfriend that stops me as I'm pretending to pass without noticing them. He played guitar in Dervish and I've met him once or twice at a show. He came to see us in Chicago back in August, because he tagged me on Instagram story and so I know he's being genuine when he puts his hand out and congratulates me.

"Raphael, mate!! Album of the fucking year—so well deserved. Truly."

"Jack, man, thank you." I shake my head as he pulls me into a one-armed hug and starts up about the album, sincere in his praise of it. From our chats before, he's always struck me as a guy who likes music, like *really* likes music. He knows stuff about obscure British bands that I've only vaguely heard of. He's talented too. I'm certain he's a fan of Finn also, but he's never mentioned him to me and that's always raised him in my estimations. He'd split from Dervish about a year ago and is working on his first solo album. So, I guess I shouldn't be entirely surprised when he asks me to work on something with him.

"Seriously? Wow, I'm flattered, dude, but the timing might be an issue right now," I tell him honestly.

I'm half distracted because Jae still hasn't noticed me, completely enraptured by whatever Haven is telling him. Something funny by the looks of it because he's laughing. Perfect, neat body shaking with laughter I can't hear because of the noise in this sound-muffling vacuum of a basement club area.

"I'm back in LA in a few weeks. How about I hit you up then?"

"Sounds perfect! Yes!" He beams at me and I nod.

As we swap numbers, I wonder how many contracts I've just breached. "Hey, you know Haven, right? She's on your label. Hey, babe." He taps Haven's shoulder and she whips round, still clinging to Jae. "Hey, you know Raphael, don't you? You're both on Halcyon."

"Of course! We haven't met properly. Nice to meet you, finally."

She's smiling prettily, slipping her arm out of Jae's to wrap it around me.

He turns then, eyebrows lifting in surprise, before his mouth pulls up in another of his shy smiles. I smile back.

"Congrats on the award," I tell her. "Amazing performance too."

She sighs, dreamily. "Wasn't it. Wasn't this boy INCREDIBLE?"

I look to see how Jae feels about being called a *boy*, but he just smiles, looking as shy as he did when I praised him earlier.

"I have been obsessed with that performance since he posted it," Haven says.

Same.

"And I just had to see if he'd wanna do it live here. Imagine the scream I let out when he said yes! It was loud. Like a banshee, loud."

"It was louder than that," supplies Jack. Haven hits him playfully.

"Jaehyun, do you know Raphael? He's from The *Grammy-Award winning* Dead Poets? That band with the incredibly hot lead singer? Well, that's him." She points at me.

I roll my eyes. Jae is laughing.

"We have met," he confirms. "Just once." His eyes flash me a private look that makes me want to grin stupidly wide. "I almost broke his nose."

Haven's eyes almost pop out of her head. Her friend—who I've just recognized is an actress called Nina something—gasps.

"That's an exaggeration, he didn't." I shake my head unable to stop fucking grinning.

"Tell us what happened!" Haven is glancing between us, expectantly.

It's me who tells the story, playing up my clumsiness and playing down Jae's role in the incident entirely. Jae just looks embarrassed. My mouth dries up when he brushes a hand through his hair, sweeping the pale lengths back from his forehead.

"Listen, good to see you all again, I need a drink. Jack, I'll hit you up when I'm back, man."

"Sounds good, can't wait, man."

I lift my hand in a wave, looking in Jaehyun's direction because I can't not. He's watching me with that small private smile on his face again.

"Hey, Raphael," Haven calls out. "We're having a party back at my place, pretty chill. Cool people, good vibes, great music. You should come?"

"Yeah? Sounds good."

"Yay! Bring your band, whoever you want! Be cool to see you there."

Jack is looking at me hopefully, Haven too. But it's Jae I look at.

If he's going to be there, then there's no question. To have the chance to talk to him out of this fucking goldfish bowl again. To hear him say my name in that quiet way he does. To have his focus and his energy and his attention. It had been heady that day in the car. I crave it again.

"It will be good to see another friendly face," he says so quietly I'm not sure I didn't imagine it.

"I am *not* a friendly face??!" Haven looks suitably outraged.

Jae only gives her this charming smile that makes my breath feel funny.

"You will be busy hosting," he replies. When he looks at me again, I am certain there's a plea in his eyes and I find myself nodding.

"Yeah, sounds good. I'll say to some of the guys. And Cleo." I lie. "DM me your address?"

"I'll do it right now," Jack is saying while tapping something into his phone.

Jae is still watching me, intense like, a little serious like. And then he's saying his goodbyes too.

"I will see you all later." He does his little bow thing again.

"No bailing on us!" Haven orders.

Jae bows again. "I will be there. Later." He flashes another look in my direction and then he's strutting back towards his table.

My phone buzzes in my pocket with Jack's notification. My head is a bubbling pot of thoughts. The loudest of which being how the fuck I'm gonna get someone to come to this party with me. There's only one person I could convince to come along to a party where he doesn't know a single person. One person who has no one to go home to and who hates his own company so much that he'd accept an invite to a lame party, as he'd probably call it.

SIX
RAPHAEL

Beside me, Crawford is twittering like a bird. High from the win and the drugs, he doesn't notice I'm not really paying attention.

In the end, it had been harder to convince Crawford to come with me to Haven's party than it had been to ditch Camille. She's flying out to Sydney tomorrow afternoon and didn't want to stop me from celebrating, so she'd kissed me goodbye and told me to have fun and took the car home with Cleo and Mason. Zeke had a date and had pissed off right after the show.

As Crawford launches into all the possible producers we could now pull for the next record, I try to figure out what the hell I'm doing here. Do I even know? Do I have a plan? Does that plan involve me cheating on Camille with a guy? Is that what the end game is here? Is it to talk to him about this? Whatever this is?

I think about him finding out that I've spent the last two years fantasizing about him. About us. And I think it's almost as bad as Camille finding out.

Almost.

The rest is a kind of breathless excitement, a sparking hot light feeling in my head and in my chest at the idea that he might actually…reciprocate this. I don't know his sexuality. I've guessed at it.

Hoped at it. And then thrown it away because clearly it doesn't matter—I'm the prime example of that.

"You okay, man? You look like you're gonna throw up," Crawford says before asking the driver to pull over. So, he had noticed.

"Nah, I'm good. It's cool. Just dropping…a little. Need another drink."

There's nowhere to stop anyway since we're stuck in a jam on what looks like Mulholland. I press the window down and suck in a lungful of congested gas-fumed LA air.

There's a tap on my arm a few seconds later and Crawf has a small amount of white held out to me on the top of his thumb. I only stare at it a few seconds before wetting my finger and swiping it up and into my mouth. He grins at me in the dim light of the car and the dread inside me evaporates like rain on a hot sidewalk.

Haven William's place is in West Hollywood. A modern, two-level with a gated entrance and big Spanish-looking front door. It's open when we pull up, the sound of EDM floating out from inside. There are a few cars parked in the driveway, one of which is a Bugatti. I'm not a car guy, but I know this one because Zeke has it as his screensaver.

We're in the door about two minutes before Crawford sees someone he knows or who he's fucked, I'm not even entirely sure who he's pointing at because my attention is scanning the room for Jaehyun.

As he wanders off, I move towards where I think the kitchen is to find something to drink. I don't think he's here yet, because he said it would be later, but I check out every corner and sofa in the most surreptitious way I can. It reminds me of a frat party, except with more money on show. More drugs too.

When I spot Haven herself, she's far away from where any of the illegal shit seems to be happening so maybe she's not partaking. She squeals when she sees me and pushes past the group she was with to come over. I met her about two hours ago, but she still flings her arms around me and hugs me like an old friend.

"You came!! Well, this party just got 80% cooler," she says giving me a wide smile.

"Haha, I don't know about that. Thanks for the invite. Nice place." I nod, looking around.

It has Spanish villa vibes inside, white walls and terracotta floors with lots of exposed wood.

"You think? I sort of hate it. But we're moving soon so…" She doesn't elaborate further. "Here, let me get you a drink. What's your thing?"

I let her pull me into the huge chef's kitchen where she pours me a tequila and lime soda and then tells me how happy she is I won record of the year. How much her and Jack love the album, how he's probably my biggest fan, all shit I'm certain he wouldn't want her to be telling me.

She talks at length about a show she did the week before in Colorado, after I tell her where I grew up, and I do my best at listening. She looks disappointed I didn't bring Camille but nods understandingly when I tell her why. Because I'm desperate to find out if Jae is in fact going to come, I steer the conversation back to her performance tonight.

She closes her eyes dreamily. "Honestly, wasn't it divine? I watched it back on the ride home and it's the best we ever did it. Jaehyun is an angel, like an absolute ethereal being not of this earth. I think he's the most beautiful human alive, I really do."

Same, Haven, same.

"And that's before he starts to dance. I had to beg his company for months to let me speak to him about this after I saw his video, and it was dead silence. They're so protective of them, and like, I get it. But in the end, I just reached out to him on his Insta. He replied within an hour. Said yes. I'm gonna stream the performance again later." She points behind me at a massive TV.

I'm not sure how to make it sound casual so I just say it. "Is he coming here tonight? You invited him, right?" I sip my drink as I affect an unbothered look.

Her eyes light up with something. "Ah, I really hope so. But we'll see if they let him." She sighs around her straw. "Listen, I have so many people I have to talk to, but let's catch up again later? Sooo glad you made it." And then she's gone in a cloud of pretty, fragrant energy.

I refill my glass which I've downed already and venture out into the party. I manage to avoid talking to anyone until the guitarist from Death Note stops me—they supported us on tour last year and I have absolutely no clue why Luca's here, until he tells me he's dating Haven's best friend. The actress I saw her with at the afterparty. He congratulates me on the win and has just started talking about having me on a song he's just finished, or even giving it to me because he thinks it would suit my vocal better, when I see him.

Impossibly, he's not wearing the suit he wore on the carpet or the dove grey one he wore at the afterparty. He's wearing a black wool sweater and slacks and pair of black-rimmed tinted glasses, his hair swept back from his forehead, his skin glowing and dewy.

There are two guys with him, one I'm certain is his manager or bodyguard, and another is one of his band members—the small one he'd spent a lot of the night talking to at the show.

Like when they'd arrived in the basement after the show, I feel his presence like a physical thing. A low thrum. A crackling of electricity that flows across the room from where he's looking around for Haven.

I hear her shriek before I see her. Louder than she did with me. But then she's hugging him too and he's smiling and doing his little bow and the crowd goes back to whatever they were doing before he arrived. No one anywhere near as interested in him as Haven and I are.

Luca from Death Note is back to telling me about the song, an 'alt-rock love poem about a bird' apparently, and I'm telling him to send it to me whenever and I'll have a listen.

When I finally manage to break away, I head in the opposite direction to where Jaehyun is, heading outside to the backyard where people are smoking in little huddles around the pool, and where the music is quieter and more sedate.

It's out here I find Crawford. Telling some wildly exaggerated story about when we were last in the Philippines and we all got arrested at the border by armed guards who wanted to have their dogs sniff our assholes. It's not quite the truth but I don't correct him. Just laugh along with the particular way he has of weaving stories to suit whoever the audience is. It's a skill. One I envy. He's the same on stage. The crowd hanging off every word he says in a different way they do with me. He's a great songwriter for this very reason too—except he never wants to put in the work. Playing guitar, he says, isn't the same. It's not work.

I've positioned myself with my back to house because I don't trust myself not to stare. When I've been out here a half hour or so, I make an excuse that I need a piss because I'm scared he might only have turned up to be polite and that he's gonna leave before I get a second alone with him.

I don't examine what the fuck I want to be alone with him for.

It's busier inside than it was when I arrived, and the kitchen looks too crowded, so I swipe a bottle of beer from the ice bucket on the dining table instead of going to refill my tequila, opening it with the keyring in my pocket. Panic skitters up my chest when I can't see him and I decide to check if he's still here by exploring the house a little. It really is a nice place. One that will need a deep clean tomorrow.

There's a mezzanine-type level at the top of the first landing overlooking the rest of the house, with a small library, some thoughtfully placed art, and a few comfortable looking armchairs currently occupied with an actor I recognize and two girls I don't, who are hanging on his every word. They don't even notice me. There's a bathroom at the end of the hall and I go towards it, glancing into each room as I pass. Not that I'm expecting I'll see him in any of them. The door to one is pulled open wide and then Haven is strutting out, wearing a pair of sweats and a hoodie as opposed to the dress and heels she had on earlier.

"You lost?" she asks, smiling brightly.

My brain momentarily struggles to come up with a reason why I'm wandering around her house so I hesitate, laughing as I try to come up with something.

"I was looking for Crawford, my bandmate—the guy I came with?" I say, finally. "I tend not to only let him off the leash outside."

Haven laughs but she still has a look on her face that makes me feel exposed. Like she's caught me in a lie.

"He's still here, by the way," she says, as we walk back down the hallway the way I came.

I almost trip over my feet because I know who she's talking about. I just don't know why. My face feels hot. I decide to play dumb.

"Crawford? I should fucking hope so, I told him not to run off."

"Jaehyun," she says.

We're at the open landing now, but the group of three who were there a minute ago are gone. It's just us.

"Jaehyun?" I turn to her, mouth twitching. "Oh, cool. I'll try and catch up with him."

"That's who you were looking for, right? Who you were looking for when you arrived too."

Her tone is still friendly but there's something new in it now.

I'm terrified at whatever look might be on my face. I know if I deny it then it'll come out too strong to be plausible. While I'm considering my options—what feels like hours is only moments—she goes on.

"I can get him up here if you wanna talk to him alone. I know how these parties can be, and he's rarely ever out in the wild without his security so the chance of you getting a second alone with him is non-existent, trust me. But if—."

"Haven, listen," I laugh, fizzing with nerves. "I think you've got the wrong idea about this. I'm not…I don't…"

"I saw you with Crawford outside when I came upstairs." She cuts over me, gently. "You were lying about looking for him. So, either you were looking for me, or you were just looking around my house…or…" She leaves it hanging there.

"What if I said I had a weird thing for interior design?" I make a show of looking around. "And I really like your house. I just wanted to check it out."

"I'd say I have a house in Malibu that I still have to style if you want a job?"

She smiles at that and I find myself smiling too. Despite the wild noise rushing through the space between my ears I feel something like...excitement? Not terror that this thing I'd managed to keep locked inside myself was in real danger of spilling out.

She seems to be waiting for me to go on, but I've no intention of saying another word. Let her say it.

"I noticed a while back that you'd liked a few of his Insta posts—which I thought was completely random—Raphael Scott following Lee Jaehyun of K:OS on Instagram."

I hear Jae's words then. *People notice these things. And it can cause problems.* I must have a look on my face as I'm thinking about how the fuck she would notice all of this, because she throws her hands up.

"I'm an Instagram freak, okay, and all-round Lee Jaehyun fangirl. Plus, I follow you both."

"Haven." I laugh, nervously. "I don't know what any of that means."

"Nothing, probably nothing."

"Right," I say.

"Right," she repeats and then she's stepping in a little closer. Like we're sharing a secret. "But you should probably tell your face that because when you were telling that little story earlier about when he almost broke your nose... and the way you were looking at each other. Sort of made me feel some kinda way."

"What?" I manage. "That wasn't...I don't..."

I have nothing. The terror that was absent before, the terror at the idea of someone finding out about this, comes rushing in. Did everyone else notice too...did he?

Haven reaches out and puts a hand on my arm. "Hey, listen, I don't think anyone else noticed. I mean, I know they didn't and I'm probably way off. I never know when to shut up, honestly. Ignore me. Forget I said anything. Let's get a drink..."

She pulls me gently towards the stairs. But then, it hits me. Smacks me right in the face.

"Wait. You said each other." I turn to her. "You said, *the way you were looking at each other.*"

She opens her mouth, then closes it, making a show of pressing her lips together.

"Are you saying we looked at each other the same way?"

I was looking at him the whole time though and I didn't see him look at me anyway but friendly. Right? She's wrong. She must be. Except…she's bang on the money where I'm concerned which makes it seem plausible that she might be right about him too.

"Yeah, yeah you did actually," she says after a minute. There's this look on her face. Almost sly but not malicious.

"Is that why you invited me here?"

She smiles. "Look, I just threw an invite out there to you both and here we are. Here you both are. You've spent the night waiting for him to arrive. And now you're up here looking for him, so why don't you wait here and I'll get him up here and you guys can…talk about whatever this thing is and see where it leaves you."

Something screeches to a halt. *Talk.* Talk about this thing? I can't do that. No. I'm shaking my head.

With a shrug, Haven says: "Well, then, I guess you'll just have to get over it."

"I'm engaged."

She rolls her eyes. "I'm not suggesting you fuck him in my bedroom, Raphael. I'm saying talk to him. If it's nothing, if I've gotten this completely wrong, then at least you know. No harm done, not really. What you do and don't decide to discuss with your fiancé is up to you." She's waiting.

For some stupid as fuck reason, I say. "I don't think…I mean, I'm not gay."

She smiles at this. "And maybe neither is Jaehyun…maybe this is all just a weird heteronormative case of a guy having a crush on another guy. Happens all the time."

My eyes widen, hopefully, but she's giving me this wry, smile.

"Look, I really have to get back to my party, but I don't imagine he'll hang around very long. Not unless he has a reason to. But I suspect he's only here for one of two reasons."

When she doesn't elaborate, I give her a look.

"Politeness or you," she clarifies. "Only one way to find out which it is." She gives me one last easy smile and heads down the hall in the opposite direction.

I have about four seconds to make the biggest decision of my life, it seems.

"Haven?" I call out after her. When she stops and turns back, I say, "Do me a favor and tell him to check his Instagram DM, in about ten minutes?"

She beams at me and gives me a salute. "Roger, that, soldier."

I don't bother telling Crawford I'm leaving. He's cozied up with some blonde influencer out by the pool. I'm in an Uber five minutes later with my finger hovering over the small paper plane. *A heteronormative case of a guy having a crush on another guy.*

I shake my head at that as I hit send.

SEVEN
RAPHAEL

If he doesn't show, then I can move on. That's what I tell myself in the thirty minutes it takes to get from Haven's place in West Hollywood to Manhattan Pier. It's what I tell myself as the word 'seen' pops up beneath the picture and maps link I sent him. A picture of the pier—one I'd taken myself about a year ago—and the words: **I'll wait until 1 a.m.**

If Haven was right; if we *had* been looking at each other the same way, then he'd come. And if he doesn't show then this has all been purely on me and I can move on, finally. I can marry Camille and live a life where his name is just something I hear occasionally and experience a rush of confused emotion about. Like Finn's is.

He doesn't reply to the DM. I stare at the screen of my inbox for ten whole minutes after he sees it, but he doesn't respond. I slide my cell back into my pocket and try not to think about what that means.

The beach isn't empty, it never is. It's the reason it's my favorite beach in LA. Even at this late hour there are people walking their dogs. A few joggers. A small bonfire surrounded by a group of laughing teenagers. The pier itself is well-lit and almost empty except for me, a couple kissing on a bench, and a guy sweeping the well-worn tread boards of The Pearl of LA's South Bay.

The sea is a melodic lull against the night air. It's not cold. It rarely ever is in LA, but there's the mildest of breezes skipping over my cheeks and ears and nose, cooling down my overheated skin.

There's a whole catalogue of feelings tumbling about inside me as I lean over the railing and stare down at the choppy black waters. Nerves and excitement, guilt and terror, but the worst, I realize, is the idea of him not coming. The idea of never seeing him or hearing from him again at all.

My thoughts slip to Camille, asleep and oblivious, and I decide right then that I need to tell her everything regardless of what happens tonight. She deserves to know where my thoughts have been the last few months, years. We're supposed to be getting married. We love each other.

And yet…here I am. Waiting at the end of a pier in the middle of the night for someone else. Waiting to find out if this mess of desire taking up prime real estate in my heart and soul means anything. If it's reciprocated. It's fucking insane.

What am I doing? I'm drunk. I'm high. And I feel part-way invincible because our band just won record of the year.

I should go home. Sleep it off. Next to my girlfriend. Fiancée. When I turn around to do just that, I freeze.

He's standing a few feet away watching me, black woolen cap pulled low over his ears, oversized duffel draped over his lean frame, and his hands shoved deep in his pockets. He's wearing a face mask along with his glasses which, coupled with the hat, make him almost unrecognizable. I wonder if it's a disguise of some sort.

There's something about his stance that makes it look like he might have been standing there a while. I'm not sure what time it is but I'm certain it's after 1 a.m.

He takes a small step closer, then another, then offers me a small nervous smile.

"Your favorite beach in LA," he says and all the second thoughts I'd been having the moment before I'd turned around tumble to the back of my head, discarded.

I nod. "I'd rather have shown it to you at sunset or sunrise but it was the best I could do at such short notice."

Too fucking late I realize how that sounds. How...*romantic* it sounds, but I can't find it in me to regret it. Jaehyun continues to stare at me. His expression is completely inscrutable. He says nothing. Barely moves. But his breathing looks calm and even, unlike mine.

"I didn't think you'd come," I say and realize it's true. I didn't prepare for it. Not sure what to do or say now that he has.

His expression turns searching. "But you hoped that I would." It's not a question.

"Yeah."

"Why?" He moves closer and then past me, to lean a hip against the railing of the pier. Pulls down his face mask. "Why am I here, Raphael?"

I shift slightly and mirror his position, staring down at him. His nose and cheeks are slightly flushed, his lips a strawberry pink pout against pale skin.

"You'll have to ask yourself that one." I dare a smile. "But I hoped you'd come because...I've been wanting to have this...to talk to you like this for a while. Since I saw you in September, but I guess since Paris, if I'm being honest and I guess tonight I'm being *real* honest. But we've been in a room full of people all night and tomorrow you go to New York, and I didn't want to do this over Instagram and fuck...I don't know what I'm even saying right now."

I let out a groan and turn my head toward the black waves instead. Except, I can feel his stare on me and it drags my eyes back to his.

"You wanted to talk to me since Paris?" Jaehyun says carefully, a perfect little crease appearing between dark eyebrows.

It's on the tip of my tongue then. The apology. The truth of that moment. What it meant to me, what it's done to me every day since. But I can't force it past my lips. Can't make the words form. Instead, I nod.

"Why? I do not understand any of this..." He looks around, a little lost.

"Me either," I admit.

Beside me, Jaehyun shivers.

"Are you hungry? I'm starving. Maybe we can sit down somewhere, eat something, talk?"

He gives me a look of surprise. Then nods. "Yes, I am hungry."

Two blocks from the pier is my favorite Chinese restaurant in LA. It doesn't look like much from the outside, or the inside actually, but it has the best Kung Pao Chicken on the west coast and it's almost always open.

Much like the beach, it's not busy this time of night: 1.45 a.m, but it's not empty either. We find a booth near the back and I slide in first, watching as Jaehyun takes a seat opposite, his back to the restaurant. He keeps his woolen hat on but slips out of his coat and hangs it on the little hook at the end of the booth. We order a pot of green tea and water and the tired-looking older waitress scurries off to get them.

We read the menus—which stand in as placemats—in silence for a few minutes until the tea arrives. Then we place our order. Jaehyun orders number '12' a pork noodle dish which I've had and is great, I tell him, and I get my usual chicken Kung Pao. Not that I've an appetite now. I think I lost it at some point between the walk from the pier and the sight of him blowing softly on his cup of green tea.

The proximity of him, the reality of the situation, the strange note of nervous anticipation singing over my insides filling my stomach with something else.

"This is somewhere you come a lot?" he asks me, finally breaking the silence.

I nod. "Yeah. When I'm home. Probably a few times a week. I really love the food." Obviously, I love the food. *You think he thinks you're here for the décor, you tool?*

He doesn't seem to notice, just nods softly as he watches me over the rim of his teacup.

"Do you like Korean food?" he asks. It's a simple question but it feels layered somehow. Important.

"Yeah, I do. Kimchi is amazing!"

This time I want to take the knife in front of me and cut my tongue out with it. My cheeks feel hot from embarrassment. I shake my head.

"Fuck, I'm sorry. That sounded racist or something. I know it's more than fucking Kimchi."

Though right now, I couldn't think of another Korean dish if someone did hold a knife to my tongue. My eyes dart around the restaurant desperate for something else to focus on that isn't his… perfection. The peeling Formica table, the paper menu, the steam curling out of the teapot. When I chance a look at him, he's smiling. Soft and small. He looks amused. Like I amuse him.

"I'm sorry," I say again.

He shrugs. "It is fine."

"Do you like American food?" I ask, chancing a smile.

He makes a show of thinking about it. "I think so. French fries are amazing."

I can't help but laugh and then Jae is grinning over at me. It's a sweet looking thing that accentuates his sharp cheekbones. It melts away when he takes another sip of his tea.

I tell him about some of my favorite American foods: philly cheesesteak, the po'boy sandwiches you can only get in New Orleans, my mom's thanksgiving turkey dinner, pizza pie in Chicago, and my favorite sushi restaurant in San Francisco. I tell him I know it's cheating cause it's technically a Japanese food. He corrects me, gently, by saying that Sushi was invented in China. As our dishes arrive, he tells me how good it is, and what Korean foods it reminds him of. He tells me some of his favorite foods too; samgyeopsal, sundubu jjigae, and fried chicken. Korean not American, he clarifies.

My appetite makes a reappearance as soon as my chicken is put down in front of me and we talk about food we loved in other parts of the world—his favorite is Japanese and Thai—before we move on to just talking about what countries we've visited that we loved.

It's surprisingly easy to talk to him. Or, rather, at him. He says he understands English better than he speaks it, but I don't notice that, apart from when he pauses to take his time finding the right word for 'monsoon' and 'alligator' and 'avalanche'.

The swirling, nervy anticipation in my blood ebbs away as we eat and drink and talk. He smiles and nods a lot. Laughs softly whenever I say something he finds funny. Smiles shyly when I say how he should have won tonight and how amazing his performance was again.

We accept the offer of more tea from the waitress before he gets up to go to the bathroom, and I pay the check while he's gone.

When he returns, I notice it immediately. The slight shift of his mood into something a little more serious. Into something similar to how it was when I first turned round and saw him standing on the pier. The echoes of laughter gone from his eyes and mouth. I twist my fingers around each other atop the table as I try and decide what to say now. Whether to suggest we head out, that it's getting late, that maybe we could—

"What have you wanted to say to me since Paris, Raphael?" he asks, making my stomach drop out of my ass.

Shit. I'd said that. I'd actually said that. What was I thinking? It'd felt different out there under the moon. In here it's too bright and the words too loud and I can't fucking do it.

"You have talked about every city in every country you have visited except that one."

I laugh, nervously. Fingers tumbling over.

"Sorry," I say. "I've wanted to say sorry."

He blinks at this, slow, then again. It's the same thing he did in the car when I brought up the first time we met. "You already apologized. In September."

I shake my head. "I mean, yeah. I did. I guess."

I can't think. Can barely look at him. When I do I find him frowning, that perfect little arch pushed in between his brows again. He looks confused. *I'm* fucking confused. I scrub a hand over my face.

"I don't know what I'm trying to say, or how to say it. But since then, since Paris, since I saw you..." I clench my hands into fists and then release them, splaying them across the table while beneath it my foot bounces maniacally. "I haven't been able to...I mean, I've just thought a lot about you…maybe it started off being about guilt, for not being cool that day, but then it wasn't just about that, and I guess I wondered if you ever, like, think of me. If you feel something like…about me. Fuck, I don't know, man."

I have literally no clue what I've just said, what disaster has come spilling out of my mouth onto the table. I want to get up and leave and never have to look at him again. Except when I lift my gaze, I find him watching me. So fucking closely, so completely, like nothing else exists but me and I fucking love how that feels.

He says nothing, just stares at me, hands curled loose but gracefully around his cup, breathing calm and even.

"You wonder if I *feel* something about you?" he asks, somehow with a straight face.

I don't know how he manages it because it sounds so fucking absurd I almost laugh.

I close my eyes and shake my head. "No. I mean, yeah. Fuck. Forget it, that sounds ridiculous. It is ridiculous. I just thought…"

Fuck, *Haven.*

"Are you trying to say that you want to fuck me, Raphael?" He says it in that same soft voice and this time my stomach does drop out of my ass.

The way he's looking at me feels like he's reaching inside me, pulling out something hot and desperate and raw, and showing it to me.

The silence stretches too long before I manage to get out, "I don't…know."

He smiles. But it's a different one, one I haven't seen yet. It's detached and a little cold and it makes a horrible sensation slither over my gut. He lifts his teacup, takes a final sip, and then slides out of the booth. He unhooks his coat from the hanger and pulls it on. As he types something out on his phone, he speaks.

"It seems you have a lot to figure out, Raphael. I do not know what you expected to happen here, but I am not the one to help you do it."

Inside my head there's a loud crashing noise, like a hundred teacups smashing on the floor. I blew it. I feel sick. Desperation coats my next words. "You didn't answer my question."

He gives me a long indecipherable look. "I am not certain I heard you ask one." It's a thinly veiled insult, but it's an invitation too. An invitation to ask it, properly.

"What if I ask you to help me figure it out."

Something moves over his eyes, something softer, something like understanding. Empathy. Pity maybe. Fuck, not that.

"I am not...the right person. I'm sorry."

He sounds sorry too. And then he's moving, away from me and towards the front of the restaurant where he'll get into a car and I'll never see him again. Panic propels me out of the booth and after him. He's on his phone on the sidewalk outside but turns at the sound of the bell ringing as I pull open the door. Into his phone he says a few quiet words in Korean before hanging up.

"I'm the one who should be sorry."

His sigh is loud. "Please stop apologizing to me, Raphael." He studies me a moment before coming a little closer. "You won a Grammy award tonight; you should not look so miserable."

I realize then that I'd forgotten. I'd fucking forgotten. I'd achieved one of my single greatest professional goals and a few hours later...I'd forgotten. I nod, sliding my hands into my pockets.

"So, you're going to New York on Monday, right?"

"Yes."

"Well, I'm gonna be in New York on Tuesday," I say, boldly. "If you wanna meet up and do this really awkward thing all over again there?"

He doesn't laugh at that. So, I try something else. "Look, I know this has been weird. Inviting you out here to see a beach in the fucking dark. To say whatever the fuck I just said in there." I pull my hand out of my pocket to gesture behind me, my cheeks hot. "But man, I'd *really* like to see you. Again. Maybe we could get a drink or something? In New York, I mean."

"A drink."

"Yeah, or like get something to eat or watch a movie or go to a museum." What the fuck am I saying now? "Hang out and talk, I don't know."

"I do not understand," he says, still frowning.

"Which part?"

"Are you trying to ask me out on a date, or do you want to hang out as friends?"

I open my mouth and then close it again. I don't have an answer. I don't want to say I don't know again because I think that's what made him want to leave before. Instead, I say, "Can't I want both?"

He stares at me through slightly narrowed eyes, trying to figure me out.

At last, he says, "I do not need any more friends, Raphael."

I can only stare dumbly at him. His decisiveness is impressive. Kind of hot too.

As we stare at each other in silence, a black SUV pulls up curbside and idles there.

"Do you need a ride somewhere?" he asks after a moment.

"Nah," I shake my head. "I'm gonna go back to the beach and wait for the sun to come up, maybe contemplate my entire life."

I say it light-heartedly but it doesn't matter, he still looks like someone's just delivered him a fatal diagnosis. He nods and turns, glancing briefly in the passenger window before pulling open the back door of the SUV.

"I don't suppose you wanna come watch the sunrise with me?" I call out, thinking fuck it. I'm still high or wasted or something and this might be the very last chance I ever get.

He turns back. And when I raise my eyebrows playfully, his face softens. A glimmer of a smile. It makes me feel powerful that I can have absolutely anything to do with making his face look like that. I really don't want him to leave. The last few hours have felt like a figment, as though I've been asleep inside some warm, comforting dream. One I'll wake up from like I usually do, panting and covered in come, loss and need echoing like aftershocks across my chest.

"I can't, I am sorry," he says.

It sounds like there's a lot more behind those five words. I want to press him against the car and kiss the unspoken words out of his mouth.

"Goodnight, Raphael." He gives me one last lingering look before he climbs into the car.

"Night, Jaehyun," I say just before he pulls the door closed.

The windows are tinted but I stare through them anyway as though I can still see him.

EIGHT
RAPHAEL

I blink awake on Crawford's couch to the scent of strong black coffee and him talking loud—too fucking loud—on the phone.

I hadn't sat on the beach; I'd walked the length of it from the pier to Dockweiler and then back towards Inglewood to Crawford's. He'd been passed out face down and fully dressed on his bed when I'd come in. No blonde influencer in sight.

We had keys to each other's places so after I'd checked he was breathing; I'd grabbed a bottle of tequila from the kitchen cupboard and sat on the balcony to watch the sunrise instead. Then I'd smoked a joint and scrolled social media, before finally passing out on his sofa around six a.m.

Camille had sent a text around five asking where I was. I'd stared blearily at it for a bit but made no attempt to respond. Not sure what to even say.

It should be clearer now, right? But he came, and he wasn't completely disgusted by the idea of me, only confused by what I wanted from him, and so it didn't feel over yet. It still felt...possible.

What did that mean for Cam and me? Do I call off my wedding? When I turn it over, I still love her. I'm still attracted to her, but all of it feels out of perspective now. Like I'm looking at it from a different angle and it's blurry.

Ironically, of everyone I know—aside from maybe my

mom—she'd give the best advice on whatever the fuck I should do about all of this. But she's not my therapist, she's my fucking girlfriend. And she deserves an explanation. Yet after what came out my mouth last night when Jae had asked, I don't imagine trying to explain it to Cam will go any better.

"Can't you just do this over the phone, Sam?" Crawford is saying. No, shouting. "Sensitive how? Well, I can't drive so you'll need to send a car. Yeah, okay, fine. Yeah, I'll wake him up."

He curses and then he's banging around in the kitchen loud enough to rival the jet that's just flown over the apartment. I haul myself upright with a groan and take a minute to assess my hangover. I think the joint helped, but there's a tight, sick feeling in my stomach. Not sure if that's entirely related to the alcohol and drug consumption though.

"Your coffee's there," Crawf says gruffly, pointing at it.

"Thanks, man." It's hot but not scalding, and sweetly bitter as I gulp it down.

Crawford can't cook for shit—the guy burns toast—but since he worked at Starbucks through college, he makes the best cup of coffee I've ever had.

"Sam's called us all in. Some 'sensitive matter' he wants to talk to us about in person."

My whole body goes stiff, my cup stopping just shy of my mouth. I cough to clear my throat which feels thick all of a sudden. "What sort of sensitive matter?"

Crawf shrugs. "Not a clue. Did you do anything embarrassing last night?" He comes to sit across from me, grinning wide.

A cold lick of fear flattens against my spine.

"Me? Did you?" I deflect. "You were at Haven William's teeny bopper party with a bag of Special K in your pocket."

He doesn't look in the slightest bit concerned. "Nah, we're good. I dipped after about an hour—had a look for you but think you'd gone?"

"I was starving, man. Went to Frida's and ate my bodyweight in

Kung Pao and then sat on the beach for a bit thinking about the win. Then walked back here. You were passed out."

He nods but eyes me, wary. I only sit on the beach when I'm in one of my moods. Which hasn't been for a while now.

"Figured when I saw you passed out there. Cam's gonna be pissed though? Wasn't she flying out this morning?"

I nod. "This afternoon. But she'll be cool. I think she figured I wouldn't make it back."

He gives me another of his looks. "Everything okay with you two?"

"Yeah, fine. Just…yeah."

"Pre-wedding jitters?" he asks slurping a mouthful of his coffee. If fucking only.

"Yeah, maybe man. Who knows." I scrub a hand over my face to dislodge the sleep still lingering there. "So, Sam called you first?"

My mind flits back to last night and whether anyone might have spotted me and Jae together, whether anything we did could be considered 'a sensitive matter'. I'm certain not. I'm also certain that this is not how Sam would do this if there were pictures of me on a fucking date with a male K-pop singer. In fact, there are no calls or texts from Sam this morning at all.

"Cleo, then me. When I told him you were here, he said to wake you up. You wanna grab a shower? Car's gonna be here in ten."

"Yeah, thanks man. You got anything of mine here?"

He nods and stands, gulping down the rest of his coffee as he does. "I'll leave it by the door."

While the shower steams up, I open Twitter. My heart in my chest as I check my name, then his, letting out a breath when I find nothing except pictures and videos from last night.

His performance is still trending. Our win and me thanking my mom made the rounds too. Some pictures of Cam and I on the carpet. There's nothing else. It's not about me.

I close the app and move to Instagram to do the same, but my eye is drawn to the numbers on the little paper plane. There are thousands of DM's in there, thousands that I'll never read, but his name is near the top and there's a new message there. Sent 2 hours ago.

I stare at it a few minutes, the nervy tightness in my stomach growing more intense.

I hit on it. It's a picture of the sunrise from what must be the balcony of his hotel room. A cityscape. The amber glow of the sun peeking between the silver and grey of downtown, bursts of early sunlight reflecting off the windows. There's another message, sent ten minutes after the picture.

It says: *Perhaps another friend would not be so bad.*

I'm smiling so fucking wide when I step into Crawford's scalding hot shower.

"I don't see what the fuck it has to do with our band?" Mason is saying, turning on Sam, eyes black and angry. "Why the fuck are *we* here?"

Sam looks at Mason like he's just said something particularly ridiculous.

"Because it's Dazed fucking Magazine. You're going to be asked about it."

He looks at me, hoping I'll back him up that this is absolutely the kind of thing he should have called us into Halcyon offices at noon on a Sunday for. The day after we just won a Grammy for Album of the Year.

I give him a blank stare.

Obviously, I'd been relieved it hadn't had anything to do with me and Jae, but this isn't our fucking business. It's Cleo's. It's her I'm worried about. Cleo who had flown out to New York first thing this morning and wasn't here for this.

"You dragged us all in here for this?" Crawford says. He looks deadly pissed off, like a cornered alligator with a hangover.

"You're on Dillon on Tuesday, you've got a string of interviews coming up, your Grammy win is gonna seem like old news next to your bandmate's brother being *America's Next Top Gay Porn Star*."

I have to stop myself rolling my eyes. Sam is a great manager, but he's a fucking drama queen. I'm not sure if one is related to the other.

"It's really not a big deal, Sam," I say, calmly. "It's not our business. It's his. Cleo's maybe, but even then..."

I'd met her brother a few times; and he was sweet. Gorgeous. Like androgynous Greek god kind of gorgeous, and that was before Jaehyun. Before I looked at men that way.

Not men, him.

"Makes no difference to us if her brother wants to take dick on camera..." Mase grumbles, shifting in his seat. "Little fucking faggot..." he mutters.

I only hear it because I happen to be looking at him, because I'm watching his mouth. My blood turns cold as ice, spine going ramrod straight.

"*What* did you just say?" I ask him.

Mason straightens up, eyes narrowing.

"What?"

"That's what I asked you. What did you just fucking say, cause it sounded like you called Cleo's brother a faggot." I stand up and glare down at him, snarl barely kept in check.

I feel Zeke standing up too, coming towards me.

"You said what?" Zeke is growling at my back.

"Guys, let's just calm down here, yeah?" Sam is urging from across the table.

"And what if I did?" Mase stands up too, facing me, head up.

"Since when are you *this* fucking guy? Seriously?"

"Since when do you care what kind of fucking guy I am, Rapha?"

"What does that even mean, man? You're a fucking homophobe now? Since when?" I'm holding Zeke back with one hand as I glare at Mason.

"Oh, fuck you," he spits and then he's squaring up to me. Shoulders pulled back, fists clenching by his sides.

My blood feels hot as lava in my veins, anger loud in my ears as I take another step towards him.

"You wanna hit me? Fucking hit me, go." Mason says, a cruel

smirk on his face now. "I'd love to sit there and tell everyone how amazing you are with a black fucking eye—go. Hit me."

"Don't fucking tempt me, you piece of shit!" I growl.

Mase flinches, looking fucking *hurt*, before he reaches out and pushes hard at my chest with both hands and storms out of the room. Everyone stares after him for a beat before looking each other.

"Who pissed in his fucking cereal?" Crawford says, unbothered.

After the meeting, which continues without Mason, Crawford and I head back to his place and pick up his truck, then drive out to Malibu to a restaurant with good reviews and an all-day sushi buffet. It's busy, but after filling our plates we manage to find a seat by the windows, which look out at a choppy pacific. I order a beer and Crawf gets a lemon Kombucha and we eat in an easy silence for a bit, until he feels the need to talk.

"Did Cleo know he was doing porn?" he asks, before swallowing a piece of nigiri whole.

I shrug. Cleo was one of the most private people I knew—we knew she'd run from a super religious family, that Asher had followed her out when he turned eighteen—but she was closer to Zeke than she was the rest of us, so was unlikely to offer this kind of information had she known it. I'd known her five years but I still knew nothing about this part of her.

"How old is he again? Seemed like a kid the last time we met him?"

"He's like four years younger than Cleo, I think, so, twenty-one? Two?"

"Hardly a kid." Crawford points out. "The fuck does it matter what he wants to do?"

"It's a non-issue, yeah." I wash my seaweed salad down with a gulp of my beer.

"So, what about Mase? You gonna call him?"

"No. Fuck him," I spit, angrily. "What even was that?"

Crawford shrugs. "The same shit he's always doing. Question is, why are you surprised by it?"

I frown at that. "What are you talking about?"

Crawford laughs a little, shaking his head. "Mason. He's always coming out with shit like that. Fuck, remember when they tried to put eyeliner on him for that shoot we did for Dark Sound? He nearly hit that makeup artist."

"Are you serious?"

I cast my mind back to that shoot. It was over a year ago, just after Cam and I came back from Costa Rica when we got engaged. I remember Mase was in a shitter of a mood most of the day, but I just assumed he didn't want to be there. He hates photoshoots and anything like it. Always says it has nothing to do with music.

"It was a dude, don't worry. But I think he thought the guy was coming onto him or something. Fuck, and remember that club in Berlin, no, Frankfurt, with the dancers in cages and this guy grabbed his ass and he head butted him?"

Now that, I *did* remember. We'd all got thrown out after that.

"Yeah, but that was *because* the guy grabbed his ass, Crawf. That's something else."

Crawford shrugs. "I'm just saying. Not the first time he's overreacted about this shit. You and me? We'd laugh off a guy grabbing our ass. Zeke too. Mason just…he can't fucking handle it."

It feels shameful somehow that I hadn't noticed any of this before. The latent homophobia living and breathing inside one of my best friends. Then I do remember something, the night in Paris when Jae walked into the bathroom. All three of us were there that night though, and we were all fucking disgraceful, but Mason had been the loudest. I think about him saying the word faggot about Jae and my fists curl, violence humming through me.

"Well, he'd better work on it because the next time I so much as sniff that shit from him, I'll give him more than a black eye."

Crawford eyes me for a minute, then nods, and focusses back on his plate.

We spend the rest of lunch talking about last night, about the blonde influencer he's planning on meeting up with in New York, about a few of the songs he's been working on that I agree to come back to his place to listen to.

He's in the bathroom when I pull out my phone and send the message I've been debating over all day. I pull up our conversation which ended with his picture and his words about another friend not being so bad and hit reply. Settling on:

Maybe it's me who doesn't need any more friends. Let me see you in New York.

There's no immediate response, no 'seen' notification below it. So, I put my phone back in my pocket and resolve not to check it again for a few hours.

Hours later, I'm stoned and sitting on the floor of Crawf's living room replaying the bridge from what I'm convinced is the best song we've ever written together, when my phone rings. It's not the first time it's rung tonight, it's not the first time I've ignored it either—Cam had tried calling me, sent a few texts too, all of which I'd ignored—but this time some unknown force makes me reach across for it. It's a number I don't recognize. I'd never answer those. No exceptions. But that same force urges me to make one this time. Crawford is downstairs picking up the pizza we ordered, so I'm alone.

"Yeah," I answer.

There's a small pause. "Raphael," he says.

I must be asleep or hallucinating or something because it sounds like him. How much did I smoke?

"Jaehyun?"

"Yes, it is me."

"*Fuck.* I mean, hey. Hi. How are you?"

My mouth is dry as a desert, my tongue scraping the roof of my mouth as I speak. I reach for my beer and gulp a large mouthful.

"I am in New York," he tells me.

"Already?" I cough as I swallow too quickly. "That's great. Cool. I mean…great. Glad you got there safe."

I seal my mouth closed tight after that because I don't know what the fuck I'm saying.

"I got your number from a friend; I hope you do not mind me doing that."

I'm shaking my head for a while before I realize he can't see that. "Not at all, I'm glad. Glad you did that. Glad you called."

Glad. Glad. Glad. I don't think I've ever said glad before in my life now it's the only word I seem to know.

I need air. I stand up and head for the balcony. Sliding it closed again behind me. I immediately regret it because it's noisy out, life going on a few floors below while I feel suspended here in whatever dream this is.

He called me. He called a friend and asked for my number. Then he *called* me.

"I want to be very clear with you, Raphael," he says sounding very fucking serious. Sobriety rushes at me like a wave. "Our language difference already makes things a little difficult. Difficult to understand the…intention behind some of what is said and how it is said, and so I do not want to make assumptions about things which are not the case, do you understand?"

I swallow, desperately trying to wet the inside of my mouth. It makes no difference, my voice still sounds rough and cracked open when I say, "Yeah, I think so. Clarity. Got it."

"So, what I am going to say now is because of this: because I do not want there to be any misunderstandings between us." He takes a deep breath, building up to something. "I do not *want* to be your friend, Raphael. I do not want to watch sunrises and think of you. I do not want to close my eyes to go to sleep and see the image of your mouth when you smile. I do not want to spend a five-hour flight daydreaming about your eyes or the sound of your voice or the way you say my name. I do not want it. And yet… all of these things I have done just today."

"Jaeh…" I start but he's not finished.

"If you come to see me in New York, then I will assume—based on what you have said—that you wish for there to be something between us which is not friendship. I will also assume, even though you did not confirm it when I asked you, that you wish to fuck me."

"Ask me again," I reply before he can say anything else. "Ask me again if I want to fuck you, Jaehyun."

I can hear his breathing change, soft and almost imperceptible, to something quicker, a little heavier.

"Do you want to fuck me?"

"Yes." I breathe the word out, the lightness of its release making my head spin. I close my eyes to re-center myself because I feel fit to splinter apart from the confession. "I want that. I want…"

I open my eyes and stare out at the flickering lights of downtown LA, sparks of amber that bleed together the longer I look at them.

"I want *you*. I don't know what this is but I haven't been able to think in a straight line since I saw you and it's driving me insane. I want…to touch you, breathe you in, kiss you, taste you, and I don't know what any of it means. It's…it's like I'm fucking obsessed. I feel obsessed. Have you ever been obsessed with anything? Ever wanted something so much it makes every breath you have to take without it, pointless?"

I have a moment of panic as the words leave my mouth. Panic that I've said *too* much. I *have*, I know it. I've turned this thing that's been curled up deep down inside out in front of him and he's going to run from it. From me.

He should run. I should too.

"Yes," he says quietly. "I have."

My heart is still thundering, louder than Zeke's drum line on Bombay Blues, but my head feels clear, suddenly. Clearer than it has in weeks. Like that moment when a fever breaks and finally you can think past the heat in your brain.

"That was a lot, fuck. I'm sorry."

I sort of want to take it back but I really like how it feels having said it out loud. To know he's heard it. And he hasn't hung up.

"You are apologizing to me again."

"Yeah, I guess I am. Should I apologize for that?"

"I will hang up if you say sorry one more time."

I laugh softly. "Please don't hang up on me."

On the other end of the phone, I hear him shifting, like he's getting comfortable. I take a seat at Crawford's old rusting patio table and fold my legs into the most comfortable position I can, given how fucking uncomfortable it is. With a glance over my shoulder, I see Crawf peppering and tabasco-ing the pepperoni pizza on the counter. He looks up and I give him a wave to tell him to start without me.

"You are confusing," Jaehyun informs me.

"I am?"

"Yes. You look at me in a way that makes me confused."

I go to say it but he's expecting it and cuts me off again.

"***Do not*** say it."

A smile pulls at both sides of my mouth. "Well, I find you confusing too."

He makes a noise of disagreement. "Well, I have done nothing to encourage any of this. All of it has been you."

"That's definitely true. Does that mean you're not interested?"

"Do not put words in my mouth, Raphael."

It's out before I can even think. "Would you prefer I put something else in your mouth, Jaehyun?"

I hear him take a small, surprised breath. "We are really going to do *this*?"

"At this point, I honestly fear for my sanity if we don't *do this*."

I'm not expecting the whiplash that comes from his next words. "And what about your girlfriend?"

I think about lying but I don't have it in me. The less I have to lie about any of this, the less I have to apologize for it feels like.

"This *honestly*…has nothing to do with her."

Maybe it makes me a piece of shit to say it, maybe all of this makes me a piece of shit. But this, here? It feels so far from Camille that it almost wipes out the guilt swirling in my gut. Almost.

He's silent for a long moment. "I see."

"Does it bother you?"

He thinks about this, then says, "You want *me* to be the one to feel guilty about it? Though I am not the one who has made promises to her."

His words are like a slap across the face. Again. The lack of any subtlety in how he expresses things is refreshing, but like diving into an ice-cold river refreshing.

"Whatever is between you and her is your business. But I do wish to know one thing, again so there are no misunderstandings."

"Yeah?"

"You do not come to New York, to my bed, *unattached*. Correct? You are with her, still."

The words are hard to push out for some reason. "Yes. We're still together. Technically."

"Technically." He repeats.

I pinch the bridge of my nose as guilt flares from my gut to my chest. "I mean, we're gonna have to talk, obviously. About what this is, you, and what I've done. But as of right now, we're still together, yes."

"Then I am clear about what this is."

There's no trace of disappointment in his voice, or anything like it, it's just cool and matter of fact. I'm not sure why that makes me feel the way it does. Turned on. Hot. Desperate.

"Right. Okay."

"You arrive in New York when exactly?" he asks.

"Tuesday morning. We have a TV show recording in the afternoon, then a couple interviews after—but I should be done around six."

"We have a schedule all day on Tuesday, but I will be back by eight."

"Can I...come and see you then?"

There's a pause. And then: "Yes, you can. I will send you the address of where I am staying." He takes another pause. "If you change your mind, I will not be offended."

"I won't."

"There is some time between now and then."

"I think you underestimate how much I want you. How *long* I've wanted this."

There's a slight quake of nervousness maybe in his voice when he says, "You were able to control yourself last night."

"I barely breathed the entire time," I say. "It's kinda hard to think about first base when you're just trying to keep yourself alive."

"What is *first base*?"

"It's nothing." I drop my head back to look at the sky; a sheet of indigo velvet scattered with diamonds. "I'll take whatever you're willing to give me, Jae."

The nickname just slips out and when he's quiet for a moment I worry it's too much, too soon.

"Sshibal," I think he says. I make a mental note to google what it means. Then with a sort of whispered finality he says, "I will see you in a few days, Raphael."

"Yeah, okay. See you in New York."

He ends the call without saying goodbye and I sit on Crawford's balcony playing over the entire conversation in my head. It feels surreal. All of it. He watched the sunrise and thought about me. He thought about me as he tried to fall asleep. He called me. He wants to see me in New York. He wants —

Crawf knocks the glass behind me and slides open the door.

"That Camille? You fight? Need a drink?"

"Drink sounds good," I say, standing. "I think we're almost there with this track, you know. I played the bridge through again with that last part you added and it flew, man. It's really fucking good."

"Yeah?" he says as he heads for the fridge. "I was thinking about that line from earlier that we tossed, the one about *lost my head and found myself*? It might not sound as lame if we bury it in the back somewhere. I sort of like the line the more I hear it."

I nod, agreeing with him, but I'm only half listening as I google the words `Sshibal Korean meaning` on my phone. I smile when I see the translation.

Fuck.

So, he swears. That perfect mouth swears.

There's a notification from Twitter saying that he's posted something. I open the app to see a video of his performance with Haven from last night. The angle is from a camera somewhere in the audience, maybe even from his table, and it's close enough and clear enough to show every expression on his face as he dances. It's better than the view I had last night and I'm mesmerized, again. I'm not sure what I'm thinking—I'm not thinking, not clearly anyway—when I hit 'retweet' and repost the tweet with the quote: *Best performance of the night!! This guy can dance. Can you teach me, man?*

I'm smiling at the innuendo as I grab a slice of pizza and switch my phone off.

NINE
RAPHAEL

We finish the recording for Dillon around three, an hour later than planned due to some issue with the lighting on the stage they'd rigged for us. It's unusual. From experience, pre-recorded shows tend to run smoother than any other sort of booking; live shows are always hit and miss and rarely ever go according to plan. Tours always throw up all sorts of unexpected shit (overbooked hotels and delayed flights, injuries, equipment failures) that someone—usually Sam or our tour manager Marianne—has to fix. So, this having run over means one of our interviews has to be rescheduled. It's not a massive deal since we have some time off after this. Only Mason seems to have an issue with it.

We'd not spoken a word to each other. On the flight—private, paid for by Halcyon, now that we'd won a Grammy I guess we were important—he'd already been seated when I arrived and hadn't looked up from his phone when the others had said hello.

After landing he'd pulled his hat low and his hoodie up and slept on the drive from the airport to the studio where we'd been sent straight to makeup. As we'd waited for the lighting issue to get sorted, he'd slept some more and during the Times interview he'd said all of four words.

This isn't unusual for him though so nothing would have seemed off to how he normally is, but the band felt it. We had been asked about Asher, but Zeke had shut it down pretty quickly and that had been that.

Cleo and I had talked during the delay and she was okay about it, seemingly happy that Asher was happy, and satisfied that her brother wasn't doing porn out of financial desperation. Turns out he is some kind of superstar in the industry. He's doing well. Really well. He's been offered brand campaigns for underwear and sex toys and basically can't move from offers from adult film studios. From sheltered religious choir boy to New York's porn darling in less than three years. It's impressive. It's a blockbuster movie waiting to happen.

Camille has called every day since she landed in Sydney but I've managed to successfully avoid every single one. The morning after Jae's call, I'd texted her, saying Crawford and I had gotten wasted the night of the Grammy's and I'd crashed at his place and hadn't woken up until Monday morning. I'm sure she bought it; she trusts me. And it's something I've done a lot of times before, so there's no real reason for her not to.

I've drafted more than one 'we need to talk when you get back' text in my notes app. It's on its eighth redraft at this point. But it's still unsent, because I can't quite bring myself to do that while she's thousands of miles away and working. It's a bullshit excuse, I know it. I'm just being a coward; I know that too. It makes me think that maybe I am my dad's son after all.

I'm back at the hotel and just out of the shower when the text I'd been checking my phone for all day arrives with a ding and rumble on the bathroom counter. The floor beneath my feet tilts slightly as I read it. The address is there. Along with:

I will be free from eleven.

I read the address over and over until the characters blur together and the words mean nothing. I conjure the apartment in my mind, along with his bedroom, him, me, us. Arousal, nerves, anticipation, and guilt all swirling together in my gut until it becomes overwhelming. I only just make it to the toilet before the Five Guys and Iced coffee I had for lunch empties itself into the bowl.

After, I sit with my back against the shower door and breathe. Deep and slow. Just like how I do before going on stage, when that same overwhelming panic that I'm gonna fuck up massively in front of thousands, threatens to drown me. With my eyes closed I focus on the way my diaphragm contracts and expands, drawing a square in my head each second. I pull the air in, hold it there at the base of my lungs, and then slowly push it out. I'm on my third one of these when his next text comes in, vibrating against my palm.

If you have changed your mind, please let me know.

I stare at it a minute before going back to breathing. When I've done another couple, I feel a lot better, my stomach more settled, my head clearer. The panic and reality of it might have set in, but I haven't changed my mind, I know that much. I still want him. I still want all the things I told him I wanted on that phone call, and more than that—I need those things now.

I text him back:

I haven't changed my mind. I'll be there at 11:30.

I rinse out my mouth, brush my teeth, and then place a room service order for a bottle of Tequila. I'm doing this. I may just have to be a little drunk while I do it.

The apartment is one of those buildings that has been gouged out from the inside and remodeled, the outside still the face of the 18th century, the inside modern and sleek.

I look down at his message again: Apartment 106. I press each number with a trembling finger, counting each one as an inhale as I do.

As I'm waiting, another message from Camille comes through. Another one I read and ignore, but which sits heavy in my back pocket as a reminder that my life is waiting for me on the other side of whatever this is. Whatever *he* is.

"Yes," he answers, voice deeper but still recognizable.

Takes me a second to find my voice.

"Hey, it's me. Raphael." My voice sounds weird, rattling with something I can't name.

There's a pause before he unlocks the door, then there's a buzz and the sound of the door lock unlatching, and I'm pushing it open into a dark stairwell lit by the huge skylight several floors above. I don't remember the journey in the elevator to the 10th floor but suddenly I'm at his door, which he's left open for me.

The sound of music drifts out from within; Korean, grungy, and lo-fi with a deep male voice groaning out lyrics.

Inside, it's all wood floors and sleek modern furniture. Muted greys and burnt orange accents which don't seem entirely him somehow. He's standing in the middle of the large sitting area with a small nervous smile on his face and it gives me some strength to see it. To know he's nervous too.

He's barefoot and wearing jeans that are tight around his thighs and ripped across the knees. A black t-shirt hangs looser over his frame, a few silver necklaces draped around his neck. He looks good. Really fucking good.

"Hey," I manage to smile a little.

"Hello," he says, holding my eye a few moments. "I did not know if you would come."

"I told you I would."

"Then you always keep your promises?"

"Like maybe..." I make a show of thinking about it. "86% of the time."

He smiles, intensely, and then turns towards a small ornate bar trolley in the corner of the lounge where he begins pouring something amber into a glass. He drinks whiskey then. I file it away. Along with all the other tiny bits of information I'd picked up, polished, and stored away in a Jae-shaped jewelry box to admire whenever I was alone.

"Drink?" he asks, without turning.

I busy myself by looking around the apartment. "Yeah, whiskey is good."

He comes toward me holding out a glass and I take it from him, knocking back a large mouthful which burns its way down. He drinks his in the same way he drank his green tea, dainty neat sips, letting the whiskey sit on his tongue a moment before swallowing it. His pale smooth throat moving gracefully as it goes down makes my cock twitch, a filthy image searing itself to the inside of my brain. The whiskey settles comfortably next to the quarter bottle of tequila already sitting in there.

"So," he says.

"So," I echo. My voice sounds calmer, but I don't feel it. My heartbeat loud in my ears and skin tight and stretched thin over my bones.

"Do you want to sit?" he asks me, glancing toward the large sectional.

He doesn't wait for my answer, just floats toward it where he folds himself neatly into one corner. I follow, sitting somewhere in the middle, about an arm's length from him. It feels further.

When I turn my body slightly to look at him, he looks smaller, younger. I'd noticed that he can make himself look like an entirely different person by turning his head or lifting an eyebrow or showing his teeth. Or in this case, widening his eyes just a little. It's mystifying. Like he's a million different people all at once.

"Where is your girlfriend tonight?" he asks, sipping on his whiskey.

It takes me as much by surprise as the last time he asked about her.

I hide it with a frown. "I thought you didn't care about her?"

"I thought I told you not to put words in my mouth."

This, said the way he just said it makes my cheeks heat, like I've been scolded. I find I don't hate the feeling. Not from him anyway.

"I ask only because she seems like a nice person."

"She is. She's fucking fantastic. Beautiful, kind, talented, funny." *She's just not you.* "But can we stop talking about her? *Please.*"

His eyes widen with interest before it melts away and he lifts one shoulder. "If you like. Is there something else you would rather we talk about?"

"Fucking hell, Jae, I didn't come here to talk. I thought that much was clear in LA? Wasn't that the whole point of that call? Clarity?"

Did I miss something? No, I didn't because he'd been clear. We both had. And I'd replayed it over and over in my head since. Is he…? Is it *him* who's having second thoughts? It's not the reprieve I might have wanted once.

"It was, yes. But I want to hear you say it now, here." His voice is gentle, but there's heat in the command. "I want to see your face when you say to me why you have come here."

The words do something to my head. My dick. My entire fucking body. He's going to make me say it. Here. In person. Under that powerful black stare of his. Fuck, the way him just looking at me makes me feel like nothing else on earth. Enthralled, raw, vulnerable. As though he can do and say whatever he wants to me, and I'd take it. As though he'd command me to do anything for him and I'd do it.

I despise too the way he seems almost completely unaffected by me. Almost. Those glimmers I see now and then though…he's a master at hiding it, but there's something under there. Something that's slowly unfurling, getting ready to bare its stomach for me.

"I told you, I'm here because I want you. Because if I don't get to have you at least once I'm gonna lose my fucking mind."

Maybe I could have gone with something more poetic, something like *I'm here because I haven't been able to stop thinking about you for two and a half years. Because I've never wanted to touch and be touched by another person as much as I want to touch and be touched by you. Because just looking at you feels like I'm drowning, and I like that feeling more than I should.*

But it seems to have worked because he's looking at me differently now. He's looking at me like he wants me a small fraction of the way I want him and I really fucking like how it looks.

I let out a sigh and sit forward on my thighs.

"Since you're big on clarity I guess I should also say this: I have no fucking clue what I'm doing. I don't *understand* any of this."

It's maybe the wrong move given how he reacted to my uncertainties back in LA, but I don't have the strength to hold it in right now, every ounce of strength going to my heart and brain just to keep me alive.

Graceful as a swan he unfolds himself from the sofa and comes to stand in front of me, his drink dangling in his long-boned hand as he gazes down into my eyes. He knocks back the rest of his drink and then takes my empty glass and sets them both down on the coffee table. He looks unruffled. Utterly calm.

When he reaches down to take my hand, I feel his touch like a match striking, hiss and spark and then heat spreading all over.

"It's okay," he says, softly. "I do."

TEN
RAPHAEL

I follow him through the apartment like he's the pied fucking piper and I'm under some spell and then we're in his bedroom. Some huge space that looks and feels like an expensive hotel room and it occurs to me that perhaps he doesn't live here. Perhaps this is just some place he rents when he's in town, where he can fuck men. Men like me.

This thought makes me freeze just inside the door, and I watch as he wanders barefoot over to switch on a glass table lamp. The bed is low and huge and raised slightly on a wooden platform. Above the headboard hangs a piece of abstract art the size of a room. Grey and black with a splash of red in the center.

"Do you live here?" I ask, looking around.

"Sometimes."

I nod. Unsure of what to say as he comes toward me and runs both hands through his hair. When it's pushed back from his face and I can see the smooth skin of his forehead, I have the weirdest urge to kiss him there. On the head. Press my nose against his hair to see what it smells like. Camille's always smells like a summer garden. I draw my eyes over his face, eyes, cheek, nose, lips, chin. Every part of him is flawless. Like a painting or a sculpture.

I saw Michelangelo's David once and I think Lee Jaehyun is more beautiful than that slab of perfectly-shaped marble.

He stares at me a few moments, waiting for something, before he asks in a soft voice, "Do you want me to kiss you?"

It's not asked seductively, more like he's asking for consent, I think.

"Is that what you want?" I reply because I want it to be what he wants; I want to know that he wants me a fraction of the way I want him.

"I want a lot more than that, Raphael." This time it is seductive. Stars in his eyes and a promise in his voice and my cock throbs with want. "But I thought it might be a good place for us to start," he says softly.

"Then yeah." I breathe. "I want you to kiss me."

His mouth twitches with a smile as he leans in, lips edging towards mine. Fuck, his mouth looks wet and tempting and I can't help licking my tongue across mine in anticipation.

He slots his hot mouth over mine gently, whiskey-kissed lips and spiced tongue making me yield immediately. I have to stop myself letting out a groan because finally, *fucking finally*. His hand comes up and slips around my neck as he presses his body against mine, dominating the kiss from his slightly shorter position. When I wrap an arm around his waist, he deepens the kiss again, licking his tongue into my mouth filthy and slow, and God help me, because this time I can't stop the moan that slips past my lips into his mouth.

He matches it with one of his own, before sliding his hand up and into my hair, pulling on it to drag my head back further. I'm glad I didn't cut it then. Glad I'd left something for him to hold onto. Open and wanting, I pant into his mouth as he pulls back slightly to look down at me.

"I have thought about doing that since I saw you shoving Kung Pao chicken into your mouth," he says, breathing hard.

His pupils are huge and his voice a little breathless and I want to kiss him again immediately.

"I've thought about it a lot longer that than," I admit, leaning in to kiss him hard. My next words aren't ones I ever thought I'd say to another man. "Please, let me suck your cock."

Suddenly, I can't remember wanting anything as badly as I want to taste his dick. Feel the weight of it on my tongue, watch him grow more and more aroused around it. His eyes are studying me carefully, a dark penetrating gaze that bores deep into mine. I feel crushed under it.

"Are you sure that is what you want?" He looks...worried for me?

I smile, nodding, bringing my hand up to brush my thumb over his slight frown. "Yeah, I'm exceptionally fucking sure."

His mouth lifts into a small careful smile, frown melting away.

"Okay." He slips his hand through mine so he can walk us toward the bed. Then he lets go and sits down, leaning back on his elbows to look up at me and I can only stare. Long, elegant body arranged like a wet fucking dream, head dipped back and legs parted slightly.

"You're so fucking beautiful," I say out loud.

I've thought it a million times since I first laid eyes on him, but never thought I'd ever be able to say it out loud. Certainly not to him. But all I want to do now is compliment him, praise him, worship him. Maybe I should kneel?

Jae's eyes round, softening, and *fuck me,* his cheeks flush a little. Like he's not used to being complimented like this, which can't be true. When he scrapes his top teeth over his bottom lip, my cock twitches. Then he lifts a hand and beckons me forward with a flick of his fingers. I'm on him in a second, pushing him back on the bed as I drag my mouth over his lips and down his throat, pulling on the neck of his t-shirt to kiss to suck my way across his collarbone to his shoulder. He moans, soft and loose, and tilts his hips up to press our cocks together and I can't stop the groan that tears out of my throat.

"Fuck, Jae..." I moan, finding his mouth again. "I want..." I'm biting at his lips now, nibbling the plump wet skin too roughly but I can't stop myself. I feel like something's unravelling inside me and I've not a fucking chance of wrapping it back up.

"Tell me what you want, Raphael," he says, as I move my mouth to his throat again, scraping my teeth across the smooth skin encasing his Adam's apple. He smells incredible; sweet and delicate, but with an undertone of masculinity. Where my voice sounds ragged and torn, his voice is completely controlled, cool almost. He pushes at my chest slightly and forces my head up to look at him. "Tell me."

"I told you. I want to suck your cock. Let me, please."

I can't even process that in the space of two minutes I've begged a guy twice to let me suck his cock. I'm not even drunk anymore. I'm very fucking aware. Present, sober, and so turned on my whole body feels like a single exposed nerve. He keeps his eyes on mine and sits up ever so slightly, reaching between us to unbuckle his belt—black leather with the Gucci buckle—and push down his torn designer jeans and black briefs. I fall back at the vision that's slowly revealed.

He's mainly shaved, neat dark hair shorn close to pale smooth skin. He's cut. Not huge but not small either, though smaller than I am. His pretty, hard dick sits darker against the pale skin of his thigh.

He has mirror piercings just below his hip bones, small silver studs which look like freckles, and then lower down, just above his pubes, he actually does have a freckle. Along with the piercings, it makes his torso look like a constellation. There's a bead of precome on the head of his cock and fuck me, my mouth waters with a thirst unlike any I've ever known. He doesn't need to say anything else, I'm moving down in some kind of lust-led daze, towards that pretty fucking cock and swallowing him down in a single go.

His body arches off the bed, my name whispered like a prayer on his lips, as his hands dive into the lengths of my hair. His dick is warm and smooth and hard all at once, but more than that, life-changingly more, is that there's nothing weird about it. Nothing that feels even remotely odd about having a cock in my mouth. It feels like it belongs there. Like my mouth was shaped in just this way so that it could hold him like this. So that it could feel the hot perfect weight of him grow inside it.

I try and think about any time a girl has ever gone down on me, what I liked, what I didn't, to figure out what I should do now that I have him in there. I take him deeper, push him further towards the back and try not to preen when he swears in his own language, pushing himself up off the bed to watch me. His cheeks are bright pink now, his throat too, and his mouth is bright red where he's been biting on his lips. It's the hottest thing I've ever seen. *He's* the hottest thing I've ever seen.

"Use your hand too," he says and I immediately obey.

I wrap my fist around the base, before pulling off with a wet sound to lick and suck softly at his head. He hisses, his head dropping back to expose that pale sharp Adam's apple, and then he's thrusting up into my mouth. The studs in his hips glitter in the low light and I tighten my grip and hold my head still to give him something to fuck up into. It's good I don't have to do anything right now because he looks that fucking good doing it I can't think straight. Soon though, he stops thrusting, and I take him back in, swirling my tongue around the sweet hot head before pushing my tongue into the slit. This makes his whole body flinch, and so I do it again, using just my lips to brush back and forward over the head as I jerk him off with my hand.

He sits up, alarm burning bright in his in his eyes as he releases his lip from his teeth.

"Raphael…I'm going to…"

I can only nod, unable—unwilling—to let him out of my mouth. He grabs hold of my hair again and pulls me down onto his cock, thrusting once, twice, then a final time before he's coming down my throat.

The moans that come from him are raw and high and delicious and I have to use my other hand to clamp hold of my balls hard so I don't come in my pants. I don't even think about it, I just swallow. Every fucking drop of it until all that's left between us is the soft tremble in his legs and the softening weight of his spent cock.

He falls back on the bed when I slide my mouth off, and not having him watch me do it makes me bolder. I lick my lips like I've just eaten some delicious fucking meal, before leaning forward to kiss each of the small pelvic piercings softly, then the freckle a little lower down. This makes him laugh and he tilts his body away from my mouth.

Ah, so he's ticklish here. Good to know.

I move up to lie next to him on the bed so that we're side by side and I turn my head to look at his profile. He looks incredible from this angle. Sharp jawline, straight nose, full lips. Cheeks flushed from his orgasm.

"Was that...okay...?" I ask.

He turns his head to me and I feel something tighten in my chest. His smile is slow and sexy and my cock throbs loudly in my jeans.

"You have really never done that before?" he says. His voice sounds wrecked.

"No. But I've thought about it a lot."

Some look flits across his face and he looks at the ceiling. I can see his mouth harden a little.

Fuck, I'm an idiot. I shift closer, reaching my hand across to his cheek to nudge his head to face me again.

"With you, I mean. I've thought a lot about doing it to you."

He stares at me hard as his top teeth bite down on his lower lip.

I want to kiss him so fucking badly.

And so I do.

I surge toward him and crash my lips to his, licking into his mouth which opens straight away. All warm and wet and perfect. I stretch over so I'm half on top of him, he's leaner than me, and smaller overall and I hold myself up on my elbow so I don't crush him as I devour his mouth. I want to climb inside him and never come out. My cock rubs against his muscled dancer's thigh and I groan, desperate. Then I feel his hand between us and he's touching my cock, palming it through my jeans.

"I suppose I do not need to ask if it was all you thought it would be," he asks, squeezing the head gently. "I am going to assume you enjoyed it."

"Yeah, yeah I enjoyed it a lot." I groan as he tightens his grip and drop my head into the crook of his neck to inhale deeply. "Fuck, Jae, you smell insane here."

He turns his head to offer me more of his neck and I lick it first before biting, sucking the warm flesh into my mouth. It's his turn to groan and the sound of it goes right to my dick again. He grips me harder, tracing the shape of it with his ringed fingers, fingers I'd fantasized about having in my mouth, around my cock.

"Take it out," I whisper. "Please." I can't remember ever saying please this much during sex, begging this much, but fuck me, I feel desperate enough to beg him. "I want to see your hand around it."

He makes a thoughtful sound. "You take it out," he says. "Take it out and show me how hard you are."

I'm about to say that he can feel exactly how hard I am, but I don't want an argument about it, I just want his hand on my cock. I lean off him to lie where I was before, on my back next to him. Then I begin unbuttoning my jeans. I'm not wearing a belt, so it's quick work. I push them open and my boxers down, sliding my hand under the waistband to pull my dick out.

When I look up at him, he's not looking at my dick, he's looking at my face, propped up with his hand under his head. He drags his eyes over my mouth and then down my body slowly, so fucking slowly. When his gaze lands on it I see his mouth open a little, his tongue darting out to lick his lip so that it shines.

"So, the rockstar has a big cock," he says, sounding distinctly unimpressed. "Isn't it too obvious? What is the word…" He thinks about it. "Cliché?" He pronounces it *cleech-ay* but I get the meaning and it makes me laugh.

"Yeah, that's me. A walking fucking cliché." I wrap my hand around it and give it a few slow strokes while he watches.

"I do not know, but maybe a walking *fucking* cliché would not be here, doing this, with me."

He flicks his eyes back to me, looking for something, before shifting his body closer. Then he angles his hips towards mine and leans over to kiss me. Somehow it feels like the first time again. It's slow and sexy and I feel it in my balls. I have to grip my cock harder to stop myself coming over my hand. From a fucking kiss. He kisses around my mouth, licks up under my top lip, across my teeth, then sucks on the bottom lip. When I feel his hand wrap around mine at the base of my cock, I tilt my hips up off the bed and into his hand, desperate.

His hand, covered in those delicate silver rings he always wears, feels like heaven as it starts to move. The cool friction of the metal mixed with the soft heat of his skin.

"Let me," he says, as he presses a kiss to my throat.

My hand falls away and I reach out to touch him, my fingers sliding into his hair. It's silky and smooth and part of me wants to grip it hard and force his head down to take me in his mouth but this is also fucking great. He jerks me slow and teasingly to start, flicking his wrist so he almost circles over the head, before smoothing it back down. When he brings his hand up to lick it wet, before gripping hold of me again I swear out loud.

"Fuck, Jae, I need…" I manage, as he kisses me again.

"Mm? What do you need?" He nips at my throat, scrapes his teeth over my Adams apple, licks across my collarbone.

"Everything. All of it. I need…everything."

I groan, leaning up to watch as he moves down my body to kneel on the floor between my legs. It makes no sense spoken out loud, but in my head it does. His lips are red and wet from kissing me and I love it. He pushes my dick toward my stomach and kisses beneath it, licks over my balls, then on the place where my thigh meets them, soft breathy kisses with small kitten licks of his tongue. When he sucks one of my balls into his hot wet mouth, I almost pass out. *Holy fucking shit.*

"Hang, on, stop, wait…"

He pulls off and lifts his head to look at me. When he realizes why he gives this low breathy laugh and it's the sexiest thing I've ever heard. I let my head fall back on the bed, trying to steady my breathing as I feel him scrape his nails softly up and down my thighs, gently impatient. He places a kiss in the inside of one, then the other, then in the crease. A full body shiver rolls through me.

"I know you've never fucked a man, but have you ever let one do this to you?" he asks in that low voice.

"Suck my cock, you mean?"

"Suck your cock, I mean."

I lift my head up to look at him. Then shake it.

He nods and then raises an eyebrow. When he lowers his mouth over my cock again, it's so he can take me all the way to the back of his throat. He swallows around the head and I see fucking stars, before he's pulling off to dip his tongue into the slit, then lifts off it entirely. He flicks his tongue softly over it, playing with it a moment, before he curls it around the crown and repeats the whole sequence all over again.

It's no more than a minute before I'm coming into his perfect mouth, one hand fisted in his hair, the other splayed across his cheek and throat so I can feel my cock moving inside him. I don't even see him swallow, too blacked out from pleasure to really see anything, but I do see him use his hand to wipe the corner of his mouth.

As I enjoy the afterburn of bliss, Jae stands, discards his jeans and wanders out of sight and out of the bedroom.

I lie there staring at the ceiling, that sense of peace settling over me like I normally have after sex. I expected to feel guilty, ashamed, weirded out that a guy has just given me the kind of pleasure I've been programmed to get from women, but I don't. I feel at ease with everything that's just happened. In fact, I want more.

Suddenly, the music that was playing earlier in the lounge, floats out of the speakers above the bed and he's back. He's still wearing the shirt he had on before which stops just below his ass and he's holding the bottle of whiskey. I'm still lying where he left me, but I sit up when he comes to sit on the bed, shuffling back against the headboard. He gives me a crooked smile and moves around the bed to climb on and sit next to me. After a healthy mouthful he offers it out to me. It's good, and it's curiosity as well as the weight of his eyes, that force me to look at the label. Japanese single malt.

"You like whiskey?" he asks.

"I like anything. But this is good."

"My favorite is a Scottish one, but they do not have it here. I have some of it at home."

I take another gulp and hand it back to him. I let it sit on my tongue a moment before swallowing. "Home in Seoul?"

"Home in Seoul."

A moment later, I feel Jae's eyes on me.

"Where is home for you?"

"California. But I grew up in Denver. Colorado." I add just in case, "I went to LA for college and never left."

"What did you study at college?"

"I was a math major," I say and he nods. Most people laugh when they find that out. He doesn't. I smile. "I'm good with numbers."

"But you wanted to be in a rock band instead?"

"I mean, I guess. Music was something I loved but did for fun." I didn't want to take it too seriously because of *him*. "It all sort of happened by accident. I used to do open mic's, you know, like turn up at bars and sing for something to do and the free beer. One night after I played, Crawford and Zeke asked me to jam with them. They needed a lead singer and they liked my voice. It took them months to find out who my dad was."

Ironic maybe that I'd used his money—the money he left me in his will after he died—to pay for my slot at Chapman, but didn't use his name to pay for my slot in the Poets.

"Turned out they hated his music as much as I did." I laugh a little at the memory.

"Your father makes music too?" Jae questions.

"He did. He's dead now. I guess he was sort of a big deal."

Not to me because I never met him, but to other people.

"He was in a band called Rapture of Malice. There was a tour bus accident in Switzerland in '99…I was a kid. He'd left my mom just after I was born—so I didn't know him."

It's the most I've ever spoken about him to anyone but my mom. A few sentences. More than he deserved. Jae's expression doesn't change—he doesn't know the band and so doesn't know Finn's name and it makes me happy then that we come from such completely different worlds. That what is common pop culture knowledge here, just isn't, over there.

"He left you too," Jae says.

I blink. "Huh?"

"You said he left your mom. But he left you too."

He's not being cruel about it; it sounds like the opposite. Like he's angry with Finn on my behalf. He takes another gulp of the Yamazaki. He drinks whiskey like water. The way rockstars are supposed to, the way I can only dream of. Tequila, I've trained myself to handle. Whiskey still burns like a mother fucker on almost every sip.

"Do you get along with your parents?" I ask him. "Are you close?"

Did your father leave you as a kid too, is what I suppose I mean.

I see him swallow, the glow in his eyes fading slightly.

"My relationship with my parents is…complicated." But then his expression changes. Lightening. "But I'm very close with my brother and sister. They both live in Daejeon, but I visit them when I can. They are so proud of me." It embarrasses him this, I can see.

"But your parents aren't? They don't approve of what you do?"

I know Korea is a conservative country in lots of ways, that their kids are very well educated and that parents there are strict. Maybe they wanted him to be a lawyer or something.

"No, it is not that. Being an idol is a matter pride for them too. They are proud of all that I've achieved since I debuted. It is only that my father is very…traditional. The fact I am attracted to men is still…" He searches for the word again, something he does carefully and unhurriedly. "A challenge for him."

Fuck. "I'm sorry," I say for some dumb as shit reason.

"It's okay, Raphael," he smiles, but there's sadness in it. "What about you? You are close with your mother?"

"Yeah," I nod. "We're close. It was just the two of us for so long, you know. So, she's my best friend." I feel my cheeks redden, but Jae only smiles, warmly.

"Then no brothers or sisters?"

I shake my head. "Nah just me. Mom was a single mom for so long—she's an art teacher in high school—so she just focused on working and raising me, I guess. Two days after I left for college, she met a guy and they've been together since." I laugh. "It's like she was waiting for me to fly the nest. Ironic since the guy is a pilot…"

I'm rambling now. I have to force myself to stop talking. There's loads I want to know about him, loads I want to ask, but I don't want this to feel like an interview. Plus, sitting with him here, both of us half-naked and with the taste of each other in our mouths, feels like something I should savor, because fuck knows if I'll ever get to have it again.

Fueled by want and a sudden notion that this might all be over when the sun comes up, I lean over and kiss him. Soft at first, before bringing my hand up to hold his head and pull him closer, kiss him deeper. The whiskey tastes sweeter from his tongue and I lap at it as he moans into my mouth.

He places a hand on my chest before fisting my t-shirt and pulling me closer. Then it's heavier, hotter, us panting into each other's mouths as he moves closer. When he throws a leg over and straddles me, our cocks harden against each other in an instant.

Pulling back from my mouth, he takes a final sip from the bottle before offering it out to me. I swallow a large mouthful and he takes it back and sets it down on the nightstand. When he kisses me again his mouth is full of the whiskey, warm from his tongue which I suck at before nibbling on his lip. The liquid drips from our parted mouths down his chin and I chase it, sucking it from him. Under his jaw and back to his ear, down the column of his neck to his shoulder. His hands sink into the lengths of my hair and he pulls my head back, gently, as he begins to move. Soft sensual movements of his hips so that our dicks rub together.

When I bite down on his shoulder, he moans, and I wonder what he'd do if I sucked hard enough to mark him here. It turns me on thinking of his perfect pale skin bruised from my mouth. It's sobering, because when the fuck did I become *that* person? The person who wants to mark their lovers up. Is the thought more palatable to me now because he's a guy? A muscular, fit guy who could probably fight me off if he wanted to? Have I ever or would I ever be turned on at the thought of leaving a mark on a woman's skin? The answer is instantaneous: hell fucking, no.

His movements begin to speed up, filthy rolls of his hips that turn my head to noise and my cock to stone. I move my mouth away from the spot on his neck and back to his collarbone, but his t-shirt is in the way. I urge it up and he pulls it off and the second it's gone I lean forward to mouth at his nipple, sucking it into my mouth.

His reaction is fucking instant. His whole body coming alive—I feel his cock harden all the way against mine. So, he likes that. I do it harder, looking up at him to find his eyes dark with want and his wet mouth open and panting. With my free hand I reach between us to grab both our dicks, curling my fist tight around our erections. The slide is pretty dry, and he notices, because then he's leaning across me to his nightstand and pulling open the drawer.

I almost laugh when I see what it is. Or, what it's not. It's not cheap ass lube anyway; it's expensive-looking fragrant oil that goes straight for my synapses the second he pumps it into his hand. It's sweet and musky and sexy all at once. It smells like him. It's arousing as fuck.

He slides his hand over mine, nudging mine out of the way and then he's slathering this almost hot shit over our cocks. I groan out loud, my head dropping back against the headboard so that I'm just watching him jerk us both off. He's still rolling his hips, but it's slower now, in time with the slide of his hand.

I drag my eyes up over his abs and pecs, strong and defined, and up to his shoulders. He's ridiculously toned. He's got a small-ish looking frame but it's elegant with it, and under his clothes it's all sculpted muscle that hardens and pulls as he moves. He's mesmerizing.

"You think I'm beautiful?" he asks.

I can only blink up at him, stunned that he's seemingly read my mind. But most likely it was evident on my face as I drank him in. He has this almost cocky look on his face, but there's something hiding behind it, beneath it. Something…vulnerable.

I nod, gasping as he twists the head of my cock against his.

"I think you might be the most beautiful thing I've ever seen." The scent of whatever oil he's using has gone straight to my head clearly. Both heads. But I'm not done. "Sometimes I wonder how you can be real. How the hell…ah, fuck, Jae." I gasp as I feel him slide a hand under my balls, stroking them, kneading the skin beneath them. It feels incredible.

"Go on," he says.

"Huh?"

"You think I cannot be real. What else?"

He wants me to speak while he's doing *that*? Fucking hell. "I don't know…I can't think while you're touching me there."

"Then maybe I should stop."

"No! Fuck, please don't!"

He laughs and then he's riding me harder, fuck I wish he *was* riding me, wish my cock was deep in that perfect fucking ass, his hole grabbing onto me as I pound up and into him, into that—

There's literally no warning before I'm blowing all over his hands and his cock. An orgasm so intense I can barely believe it's my second of the hour. Lights sparkle behind my closed eyes, my heart hammering out of my chest and my breathing heavy, like I've just run a fucking marathon.

When I open my eyes, it's to find him watching me behind that dark heavy-lidded stare. He's still jerking me slowly as he watches me come back down to earth, and as I glance down to where I just emptied, I see he's still hard. There's also come on his chest.

"Did you?" I ask.

He shakes his head. Fuck, then that's my come on his chest. I groan out loud from how hot that is. He's moving slowly now, like it's almost mindless.

"I want to watch you," I say. "I want to see you come."

His eyes drop closed for a brief moment and he whispers something in Korean. Then his hand speeds up around his own erection. He arches his back away from me and starts to lift his hips so that he's fucking up into his own hand, strong thighs pushing him upwards. It's beautiful to watch. Like watching him dance. His movements graceful, even in this.

When he brings one hand up and starts to play with his nipples I honestly think I might pass out. The oil from his hands quickly makes his skin slick and shiny and I suddenly need to touch him somewhere, anywhere.

I do what I've dreamt about doing more than once and reach

out to wrap my hands around his waist. It's small, not small enough that my hands go all the way round, but small enough to make my hands look huge and tanned as they hold him. I kiss the middle of his chest, but he comes out of his daze and uses a hand to push me back toward the headboard again.

He looks me in the eye when he says. "You wanted to watch. So, watch."

And so, I do. I watch.

When he comes, it's on a low growl and another Korean curse and then he's falling onto me. I can feel his come, wet and hot, as he presses it into my skin, and I feel nothing but satisfaction. More than that, even. Bone deep contentment. He settles his head on my chest, breathing fast and hard, as my arms come up to settle around him.

I wonder how weird it would be to kiss his hair, but the two orgasms and expensive whiskey decide for me that I don't care, and so I press my lips gently to the soft hair on the top of his head. Not like a garden in summer, like the ocean at midnight.

SIDE TWO
(FEAT. JAEHYUN)

NEW YORK
WHISKEYKISSED
SEOUL
DAL
DEATH OF A POET
HER

ELEVEN
RAPHAEL

I'd passed out cold with Jae in my arms. But I'd woken later, the room dark and the music off, when he'd climbed off me and wandered into the bathroom. He'd come back with a warm wet cloth and gently run it over my chest and around my sleeping cock. I'd been still mainly asleep, but I remembered him whispering something in Korean—words I told myself I'd remember but which had disintegrated as sleep pulled me back under.

Now, he's asleep on the other side of the bed. On his back with one hand over his chest and the other by his side, legs sprawled almost diagonally so that his head is furthest away from me and the tips of his toes are pushed against my calf. The covers are kicked off and the grey New York sunlight streams in through the window. He looks peaceful. Deeply asleep and utterly calm. His mouth is a full pink pout, lips pushed out and kissable.

I expected that when I woke up today, I'd feel something like shame. Like guilt. But I don't. There is something in there though, in the deepest part of my gut, or higher—in my chest. Something that when I look at him only tightens and squeezes, the breath in my body turning hot and quick.

It's terrifying. It's not a new feeling. I'd felt it before, or a precursor to it at least. The moment in the men's bathroom in Paris. The first time I saw him. That time he doesn't even remember.

What did it mean that the first moment I saw him everything inside me changed color and flavor, while he didn't even remember it? It meant I was insane for thinking that this was anything more than us messing around. It meant I couldn't ever be to him what that deep place in my gut wanted to be to him. We're from completely different worlds. Our cultures intrinsically opposite. It would never work.

I know this and yet I still want it more and more each moment I spend with him? Why am I fully prepared to move to another continent and learn a language that may as well be spoken with a different body part. It's ridiculous. We hadn't even fucked. A blow-job and a hand job and I'm ready to change citizenship.

With a soft huff of a laugh, I slip out of bed. I need to piss and brush my teeth. Then I need some water and a coffee. Then I need to check my phone and find out how many times my fiancée rang me last night and hope that maybe she's had enough and I won't have to be the one to end it. *Fucking coward.*

I piss, splash my face with water and check his bathroom cabinet for a spare toothbrush. I hit the jackpot when I find a small basket under the sink stuffed with necessities like floss, brushes, and toothpaste. After brushing, I wander back into the bedroom to find he's not moved an inch. He told me the night at Frida's that he doesn't sleep great, and so seeing him like this is comforting. I've no desire to wake him. I lift my jeans and t-shirt from the foot of the bed and pad quietly out of the room and close the door.

In the daylight, the apartment looks bigger. Tall ceilings and large windows that flood the place with light. The kitchen is spotless, all dark cabinets and light marble with gold accents. After three glasses of water my head and mouth start to feel normal again and I gravitate towards the coffee machine next to the stove. It's not difficult to work, and after a second I've got it brewing away while I switch my phone on and check the damage.

There's nothing. Not a single message from Camille, or the guys, or my mom. Nothing. It's eerie. Like I imagined turning my phone on and finding accusations and insults, but it's like no one even cares. I just spent the night with Lee Jaehyun from K:OS's cock in my mouth and literally no one cares. I flick open the Instagram app and open his page. It's automatic now and though I know he can't have posted anything because he was with me all night—fuck me, that's wild—I still look.

His last post was 19 hours ago and it was the one from the concert. It's just him and his bandmates smiling at a packed-out MetLife Stadium and the words 'Thank you. I was happy' and a white heart.

I register a dull beeping somewhere in the apartment but I don't think about it. I hit like on his post. Again, nothing happens. Raphael Scott liked another Instagram post of Lee Jaehyun and no one fucking cares. Haven Williams would, but then she's the only one. Feeling wild, I like a few others too. One of him on a bike. Another of him at the gym. Then the last, a still of him from a video mid dance move. He's drenched in the spotlight, the room behind him totally dark.

"Who the fuck are you?" I hear a voice from behind me.

I startle so much my phone slips from my hand and clatters loudly to the floor.

The guy is big, wearing an oversized hoodie, a ballcap and a white facemask. He's holding a takeout bag and two coffee cups as he glares at me.

"Who the fuck are *you*?" I reply.

"Where's Jaehyun?" he asks, ignoring me.

He's Korean, but his English is better than Jae's. The edges smoothed out to something approaching American. It's how I recognize him. Kai. Kim Ji-hoon. Their band leader. He's the one they speculate about with regards to Jae. I've read some of the analysis articles, fallen down the Reddit holes, the Twitter threads, the YouTube videos. All of it I'd passed off as the product of bored teenage minds. Minds who think about celebrities far too much, it's not normal. But now, here, with him looking at me like he is...well, I'm not too fucking sure. He looks furious. Dark eyes gleaming with violence. He's about my height and wider. Could probably take me to be honest, but I'm not about to let him know that. I square my shoulders off and give him a small smile. I'm glad that I decided not to put my t-shirt on. I like that I'm standing in Jae's kitchen topless and barefoot. I want this fucker to know.

"He's still in bed," I say, bending down to pick up my phone. The screen is cracked. Fucking great. I make a show of locking it before sliding it into the back pocket of my jeans. "You're Kai, right?"

He says nothing. Just continues to glare at me. I give him a nod and turn towards the coffee machine, taking my time to pour. I can feel his eyes on me as I do, and he hasn't moved an inch when I turn back around. We stare at each other as I sip my coffee and I realize then that he's studying me, trying to place me, figure out where it is he recognizes me from. Well, I'm not about to help him out.

It's Jae's voice that cuts through the malevolent silence growing between us. He says something in Korean as he wanders up behind Kai that has him turning, wide eyed.

"*Neo jejeongsin-iya?*" Kai says harshly.

This makes Jae roll his eyes as he comes toward me. His eyes dip appreciatively over my body and then he's nudging me gently out of the way to get to the coffee. He doesn't pour it into a cup though, he gets a glass, fills it halfway with ice, and then tops that up with the black coffee.

Kai's face has taken on a sort of sneer now. He has mean eyes, I decide. Cold and sharp with a thin mouth. Still objectively good looking, but in an anime villain kind of way.

Jae rattles the ice around his glass to cool the coffee and asks Kai what sounds like a question. Kai snaps his answer back in a low growl, making Jae let out a sigh. Jae's next words in Korean make Kai glare at me fully.

"*Dangsin-eun?*" he says.

It sounds like an insult so I glare back, lowering my cup to lift my head up.

"Ji-hoon Hyung, this is Raphael," Jae says, tiredly. "Raphael, Ji-hoon is our band leader." He points at the guy just in case I'm not sure who he means. "He says he's really happy to meet you."

Kai snorts. "I suppose I will leave this, then. You both must be hungry." He dumps the food bag down on the counter and looks at Jae. "I'll be back in one hour."

It sounds almost like a threat. Then he's leaving. Striding toward the door and out of the apartment. The door banging shut behind him.

Beside me Jae lets out a soft breath. When I turn to look at him, he lifts his head, eyes a little uncertain as he takes a large gulp of his iced coffee. He's wearing loose grey pajama bottoms and a striped long-sleeved t-shirt with a wide neck. He looks soft. Sleepy. Young.

"He just came in," I say. "He has a key?"

Jae shrugs and moves to slide up onto one of the barstools, dragging a hand through his sleep-ruffled hair. I'm not sure what the shrug means, and I don't feel like it's my place to press him on who does or doesn't have a key to his apartment. I hate the way my gut clenches at the thought of it though. That they're this close, that Kai walks in here first thing in the morning, that he's angry about other men staying the night.

I stay where I am, watching him as I drink my hot coffee.

"You have another show tonight, right?" I ask when the silence gets a bit too much for me.

He nods, not looking at me. He has his phone in his hand now and is typing away furiously. I wonder if it's Kai. I push up off the counter and go toward the bag his band leader ceremoniously dumped there. It's Korean food. My stomach rumbles.

"You hungry?" I ask, as I start pulling out the still warm containers from the paper bag. There's soup, noodles, rice, and some long-rolled things that look like uncut sushi. When I look up at him, he's not typing anymore, he's just looking at me.

"What are you doing?" he asks, frowning a little.

"You're not hungry?"

"No, Raphael. I mean what are you doing? Here."

When I can only blink in confusion—where the fuck has this

come from?—he sighs again. "I mean what were you doing last night? With me. What is this?"

I place the container on the counter and swallow. Then lick my lips, which feel dry suddenly. Run a hand over the top of my head.

"Is that what he was asking?" I gesture my head in the direction Ji-hoon stormed off in.

"No. But he worries about me. He was surprised, that's all."

"I think if there had been a knife nearby, he'd have cut my balls off and had them for breakfast. That would have been a surprise."

Jae smiles a little but doesn't deny it. He gives me another look. Expectant.

What am I doing here? I decide to be as honest as possible.

"I told you last night," I say. "I don't know. I don't know what the fuck I'm doing."

Jae looks sad about this. "And now? Even now you still don't know?"

"Was it supposed to be clearer this morning?"

I mean, some things are, I guess. Other things aren't.

"I had hoped it would be, yes." He fixes me with a look that's both thoughtful and soft, then decides on something. "Men experiment all the time. You do not have to feel weird about this…it's normal, you know."

"I don't feel weird about it."

It comes out sounding defensive, but it's the truth, I don't. I come around the counter towards him and stand beside him, reaching out. I think about touching his cheek but I end up running my hand through his hair past his ear to the back of his neck.

"I promise, I don't. Last night was incredible."

I smile, and then I'm pulling him into a kiss. He tastes of toothpaste and coffee as he lets out a soft little moan against my lips. We kiss soft and sweet for a minute before some strangled noise bubbles up from between us. Then he's pulling back to look up at me, eyes all big and round and filled with sunlight. He looks horrified.

"Was that…*your stomach?*" I look down at it, like it might have grown its own mouth.

He covers it, curling into himself as he groans in mortification.

"Yes! I'm hungry, okay." When I burst out laughing, he swipes a hand out to hit me, pouting like a child. It's cute as fuck. "I'm always so hungry the morning after a show. Because I cannot eat during the day; the nerves, and adrenaline…I do not eat properly."

And Kai knew that. He turned up here at breakfast with a bag of Jae's favorite food because he knew he'd be starving. Another knot of jealousy flares up in my gut. I move away from him back towards the food and slide it towards him.

"So, eat," I say as I go to find forks.

When I come back, he's already shoveling cold black noodles into his mouth with those single-use chopsticks, biting into the large sushi roll he's holding in the other hand. I hide the other fork under the paper bag and watch him eat for a minute. And boy, is he eating. Huge mouthfuls of food that make his cheeks round like a squirrel as he chews, utterly lost in the taste of it. Umm-ing and ahhhing at each bite. He seems to remember I'm there after a few minutes and gives me a grin around his food, then pushes one of the containers towards me that has another of the long sushi rolls in it.

"*Kimbap*," he tells me around a mouthful as I stare at it.

He demonstrates just biting the thing he's holding. So, I do that. It's delicious. It tastes a little like sushi, only better. When I look up a moment later, he's holding out his chopsticks towards me, laden with black noodles.

"Open," he says.

I do and then he's feeding me, a big, adorable smile on his pretty face. It makes my stomach do a weird flipping thing.

I'm so fucking fucked.

When we're done eating, I gather the containers and toss them in the trash while Jae wanders through to the living room. When I get there, he's lying spread out on the large sectional, legs wide, one arm thrown over his head and the other rubbing small circles over his flat stomach. I sort of stand there feeling awkward for a minute, thinking I should probably split, but then he turns his head and looks at me, this little easy smile on his face, and splitting is the last thing on my mind. But I've been here twelve hours now and neither do I want to overstay my welcome.

"I should probably get going," I say, scrubbing a hand through my hair.

I need a shower. Some fresh air. A long talk with myself.

He stares at me a long minute before he moves to sit up. The neck of his T-shirt has slipped so low it gives me a view of a perfect collarbone and the very top of a dusky pink nipple. My body *wants*.

He blinks super fucking slow a few times before giving me a nod. "Okay," he says.

I nod. "I'll go…dress."

Jae nods once more and then I'm wandering around trying to find my jacket and boots. He'd placed my boots neatly by the door next to his own, and hung my jacket on the hook above. When I get back, dressed, he's staring hard at the TV but looks miles away. Something grabs his attention though and then he's standing, coming towards me.

"I will walk you out."

He walks past me, not looking at me, and so I trail after him, my eyes fixed on the back of his pale neck. He has another freckle there, just below his hairline, and it hypnotizes me as we walk to the front door. At the door he turns, peering up at me with those big soft eyes and I can't help but compare it with the Jae who rode me as he fucked his hand to orgasm. The confident, glittering postshow Jaehyun who was high on adoration and exhaustion. He still looks exhausted, but he also looks smaller, more delicate, more vulnerable. They're almost polar opposites, but I want both versions of him equally and in entirely different ways.

A thousand and one things run through my head that I want to say, things I don't want to say, things I should and shouldn't say. All of them fighting with each other so it's just useless chaos and noise inside my head.

"Good luck tonight," is what comes out. "You'll kill it, I've no doubt about it." I want to kiss him. Should I? Everything feels different now, he seems different now, but inside *I* feel exactly the fucking same. I still want him. Not less. Not at all. More; the want is bigger now, altered irrevocably.

"Thank you," he says softly, turning to open the door.

My hand shoots out completely independent of my brain and I'm covering his, holding the door closed. Jae looks up at me.

"Jae, I..." Okay, I need to say something, clear and concise just like he likes it. "Look, I don't want last night to be *it*."

"You don't want it to be it?" He looks lost.

I rethink the words. *Clearer, Raphael. More concise.*

"I mean, I might not know what this is, but I do know that I want to see you again. Let me see you again." Then, not feeling pathetic at all, I add, "Please."

My cheeks are hot, my heart thumping hard, and I'm not quite prepared for what I'll do if he says no. Except, I have that feeling again. That echo of certainty that he won't. That this isn't over yet.

His smile is small and slow, but it lights up the entire fucking hallway. "Yes, okay."

I'm kissing him the next instant. Pushing him back into the door as my lips and tongue devour him. He grabs hold of me, clutching at my arms and holding on. I slip my hands under his shirt to find the warm soft skin of his stomach and hips before wrapping my arms around him to pull him against me. I want to climb inside him. He's not small, but he feels small in my arms. Like something I need to keep safe, need to protect. I've never felt that before. He *mewls* into my mouth, breathy and high, and then he's rutting gently, thighs open and a hardening cock pulsing against my own.

When he pulls away from my mouth he drops his head back against the door, panting, his full lips kissed red as he looks up at me.

"This is crazy, no?" he asks, his voice a hoarse whisper.

"Is it?"

When he answers by licking the taste of me from his mouth,

I lean in and kiss him again. When I palm his cock through his pajamas he groans, using what feels like all of his strength to shift me back.

"We cannot…not now." His eyes tell a different story; and it's about how much he wishes we could.

He stands up off the door and brushes a hand through his hair, cheeks flushed. "I can text you the code to the apartment. I will be home around eleven again. If that's too late—."

"I'll be here," I tell him.

TWELVE
RAPHAEL

I manage to sneak back to the hotel and shower before collapsing on the bed and drifting off for a few hours. It's four p.m. when I wake up and check my phone—I missed another call from Cam at two p.m. Another voicemail that I delete without listening to.

I need to talk to her, I know I do, but I've no idea what to say, what lies I should tell. I don't want to break up over the phone or have a conversation that sounds like I'm breaking up with her over the phone, so I reason it's best to say nothing.

It's over. I feel that in my heart and in my gut. And lying to her about it isn't who I am. We've always been honest with each other, and she deserves better than that now, but this just isn't a talk I want to have when she's not in front of me. The right thing to do would be to stop seeing Jae until I do, but that makes me feel ill. Feels like panic and loss and no, definitely not the right thing to do. My head is fucked up and backwards but not seeing him feels, resolutely, wrong in ways I can't begin to fathom.

After showering and writing in my journal a bit, the room starts to feel like a prison. Like I can almost see bars on the windows. Seven hours. What the fuck am I supposed to do for seven fucking hours? I miss him and I've no idea why. An ache crawling under my skin, making it buzz and tighten. I need to get out of here.

I pull on some clothes: a hoodie, my leather jacket and sling on a pair of sunglasses and a ball cap. I'm at the door when my cell phone rings. I contemplate ignoring it, certain it's Camille. Maybe I'll leave it behind. But I'm a fucking Gen-Z'er; I'm not wired to leave home without it. When I pull it out of the back pocket of my jeans to look at the call ID, I sigh with relief.

"Hi mom," I answer, moving back to sit on the bed.

"Hey baby, you okay?" Her panicked voice bleeds down the line.

"Yeah? Are you?"

"Camille called me."

"She did?"

Fuck. I can count on one hand the number of conversations my mom and Camille have had. They don't dislike each other; they just have absolutely nothing in common.

"She was worried. Said she's been trying to get you but you're not answering your phone."

"I'm okay." I think.

"You don't sound okay. What's going on, baby?"

I let out a breath, a tangible release at the notion that my mom knows me that well.

"Honestly? I'm not sure I know…"

"What does that mean?" She sounds edgy, her voice pitching higher. "You're scaring me."

"You don't need to worry about me, mom. I'm okay, really, I just…fuck I don't know."

"Is this about Camille? Have you had a fight?"

"No, not really. I've just…been dealing with some stuff." *Cheating on her.* "It's my fault. All of it. She hasn't done anything wrong. Fuck, she shouldn't have called you."

"She was worried about you, and now I understand why. You're not making a lot of sense right now, Raphael."

"I know."

"But, if you tell me you're okay, that you're not thinking of hurting yourself or—."

"Mom, fuck, of course, I'm not!" I almost yell. "I'm okay. I promise you don't need to worry about that. It's nothing like that."

"Okay…then that's okay." She sounds relieved. "Do you want to talk? I'm here for you, always baby, you know that."

"I know, mom. I know you are. And yeah, I do. But not right now, yeah? I'm still trying to figure shit out in my head first. Make sense of it all."

I hear her let out a soft sound. "You and Camille are gonna sort this though, right?"

I can't tell entirely how she feels about that, but there's a definite sadness there.

"Honestly, I'm not sure, mom."

She makes a soft sound. "Oh, baby I'm sorry."

"Yeah. Me too…"

I try to imagine what her reaction might be if I were to tell her how I feel about Jae and a rush of anxiety floods my chest and prickles over my scalp. I'm not there yet. Not even close. How can I talk to my mom about something I don't even understand myself? I ignore the part of me that says maybe talking to my mom will *help* me understand it. I ignore it because that part of me thinks that once I say it out loud to my mom, she'll know exactly what it is and I'm not fucking ready to hear it. Not yet.

"I can't wait to see you. I'll pick you up at the airport, okay? Just let me know what time and I'll be there."

Colorado. Thanksgiving.

Suddenly, I can't fucking wait to go home and see my mom.

I'm sitting in the Shake Shack when I get his message. I see his name first and I'm fully expecting it to be him cancelling our plan for later, but it's not. It's a six-digit code: 140312.

That's all it is. A text message with six numbers on it.

I drop my burger onto the paper wrapper and scrape a hand over my mouth as I think about a response. I want to encourage him to respond, but at the same time I've done nothing but beg and plead this guy for shit and I want to play it somewhat cool here.

Me: I'll be there. Good luck tonight, dude.

I watch it deliver, then turn to read, and then nothing. No three blinking dots to tell me he's replying. Fucking nothing. Cold. The guy is fucking cold. It turns me on even more somehow.

I laugh to myself as I pick up my burger, gazing out the window and thinking about how much I like New York. I haven't been recognized once. Not in the clothes store or the record store, not on the subway, and not as I ordered a burger, cheese-smothered fries, and a beer. I love LA. Denver too. But NY has always had a buzz I've never found anywhere else. Berlin had something similar. A vibe that said the people here were cool but indifferent to fame and celebrity. I want to live here at some point. Then Paris. London too maybe—but then I remember the rain and push that idea away again.

I take a picture of my half-eaten burger and fries and upload it to IG, then I think better of it because if Camille sees it, she'll know I'm out eating junk food and not contemplating our entire relationship.

I've finished eating and am sipping my beer when the message comes in. I almost ignore it because I'm honestly not expecting a response from him now. But I flick to my notifications to see his name.

JH: You are very American sometimes :) Thank you, I will do my best!

I reply with something which feels clever in the moment but I'm sure isn't.

Me: I'm very American all the time. I'm American. Is there something else you'd rather I was?

This time he reads it and replies immediately.

JH: Korean?

He puts a Korean flag after the word. Then a prayer emoji in the next message. I'm not ready to cut the convo yet, so I pull up google translate quickly and type in the response I want.

Me: 당신을 위해 최선을 다하겠습니다

For you, I'll do my best.

I wait on him correcting me or something, but he just sends a load of smiling emoji's that have *me* smiling like a fucking clown. Fuck, I want to see him. It's 6:15 meaning I've got five and a half hours to kill until I can do any of that.

It hits me like a brick.

I can see him before that. In fact, I want to. I pull up Sam's number on my phone and dial. He answers on the third ring.

"Rapha, my dude! What's up? How's Colorado?" He's driving, I think.

"I'm still in New York, man. Fancied hanging out a few more days."

"Sounds good, you and Camille or?"

I debate telling him about Camille, since he'll have to field the calls from Deborah and the label, but it feels shitty to do that without talking with her first.

"Nah, just me. She's still in Sydney. Her shoot has a few weeks left."

"Gotcha, what's up? You just checking in?"

"I was actually looking for a favor."

"Wow, okay, but I'm not gonna fuck you, man. You're hot and all, but it's just not my game, you know?"

"You're breaking my heart here, Sammy."

"You wouldn't be the first." He laughs. "What can I do for you, my man?"

"I'm looking for an in to a sold out show tonight. It's at the MetLife."

"Yeah? Who's playing?"

"K:OS. I fancy checking them out."

He practically explodes in laughter. "Seriously?"

"Yeah, why not? I'm here for a few days, there's fuck all else on, and they're our competition. Plus, I wanna see what all the fuss is about."

"It's all bullshit, bud. Their label is fixing it, manipulating the lot. It's a farce."

"You don't seriously believe that? They have fans on every

continent—you can't manipulate that. Their fans buy and stream their records, that's it."

"Teenage girls don't have that much disposable income, Rapha, it doesn't add up."

I say nothing for a minute, hoping it looks like I'm thinking about it. Of course, chart manipulation goes on, but this isn't what's happening here. The reason I know that is because I've followed this band closer than I should have, read more articles about their popularity than I should have, and fallen into a lot of Reddit holes the last two years. I know more about this band than Sam does.

"Yeah, maybe. Anyway, can you sort out a ticket for tonight?"

"Yeah, it shouldn't be an issue. You want VIP?"

Did I? Did I want him to see me there? To know I'd come and watched him? It was one thing to tell him later, but another to have him see me there, uninvited while he was with his band.

"For the bar, yeah, I don't need backstage."

Sam makes an affirmative noise. "Okay, leave it with me. You want two? I thought you guys had scattered to the four corners of the earth?"

"Fuck you, I have friends that aren't in DP." I lie. "Just one."

He laughs again. "Cool. Talk later. Enjoy your gig," he scoffs and I roll my eyes.

His attitude has no right to piss me off, but it does. Success on their level confuses people, and people are distrustful of things they don't understand. It's fucking textbook. At the end of the day, they'd sold out five nights at the MetLife Stadium which has a capacity of eighty thousand. No one could argue with that.

Now I can't wait to see him perform. To see him command a crowd of that many people. I wonder if he does it as easily as he does it to me.

I dump my trash in the can and head out into the crisp New York air. I get to see him perform in a couple of hours, and the thought of it causes something like butterflies to start an air dance in my stomach.

THIRTEEN
RAPHAEL

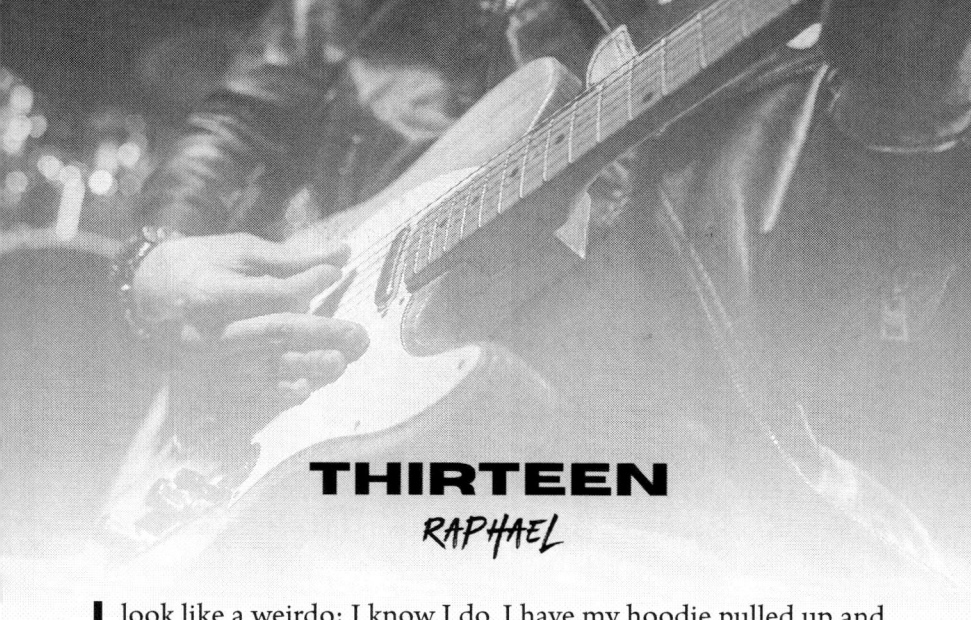

I look like a weirdo; I know I do. I have my hoodie pulled up and my ray-bans on, but the risk of being seen here was damn hard to explain on its own. Checking out the competition was fine to say to Sam, but there's no way to explain that to a journo or paparazzi. So, I'm hoping the crowd are just way too into the band to give me a second look.

Which isn't too far-fetched given what I'm seeing so far. It's insane. The merch stands are the biggest I've ever seen, full-blown pop-up stores inside and outside the venue selling every kind of merchandise imaginable. Stuffed toys, hoodies, t-shirts, scarves, phone cases and these light-up stick things that almost everyone is carrying. They're wearing bespoke-looking costumes and artistic face-paint and every second person has these hairbands shaped like cat ears. Every third person is carrying a homemade banner.

The crowd is mainly women, but not teenage girls as Sam had implied. They're all ages. I pass a group of women the age of my mom, giggling and laughing and carrying a banner with Kai's face on it and some words in Korean. There are lots of little groups hanging around inside the food court section, laughing loudly and recreating the dance moves. The vibe is pure fucking joy.

Yeah, people are happy at our gigs too, but men just bring a whole different fucking atmosphere. The guy's bathroom room is empty compared with the mile-long queue for the ladies, and so I nip in quickly before trying to find the VIP bar area.

A beer in my hand, I make my way to the entrance to my section. It's on the first level, not too far from the VIP bar. The security guy gives me a weird look as he scans my ticket but I'm not sure if it's because he recognizes me or because I'm one of about 100 guys in the entire place.

As I climb the stairs into the main arena, I stop dead. The place is packed to the rafters with colored light sticks, banners, and that same sheer joy. The whole place radiates positivity and excitement. I should hate it. I should. But when I see Jae's face on posters and banners and hear them singing and chanting his name, I can't find it in me to hate any of it. I struggle to think of any concert I've ever been to where the energy is as bright as it is in here.

Thankfully, I've got a seat at the end of the row. When I glance along it, I notice there are a few guys on it—albeit they're sitting next to their wives or girlfriends, and in one case: two young daughters. The two girls who can't be more than ten are dancing and laughing together to the music playing over the sound system, all big smiles, face paint, and glowing headbands. The guy catches my eye and gives me a friendly smile which I return.

It's only a few minutes later before the lights go down and the place explodes in a cacophony of screams unlike anything I've ever heard. I feel the hair on the back of my neck stand up as they shoot up from beneath the stage in a cloud of fire and smoke. Each of them doing nothing but standing there looking cool for almost a full minute as the crowd goes insane. The big screens pan along the six of them in turn, the screams changing imperceptibly for each member. No one gets a louder scream than any other, but Jae's feels more intense to me. He looks insane; his hair slicked back from his forehead and his expression bad ass as he soaks up the applause. I can barely breathe as the camera lingers on him. In fact, I barely breathe for the entire three hours of the show.

Wanting to avoid the rush, I leave before the encore and take the subway back to his apartment. My ears ringing and my heart beating wildly over what I've just seen these guys do. Most of their music isn't to my taste, but the production on each one is immaculate, along with their choreography and the sheer energy they put into it. There were also a couple rap tracks in there that I'd listen to again.

In all my hours spent deep-diving Jaehyun, I hadn't really listened to them as a band. I'd watched a lot of their music videos, but I'd never listened to an album from beginning to end. I decide it's the first thing I'm gonna do when I'm next alone. Watching them do what they do, the way they do it, it's fucking clear that the hype is more than justified.

There was a duet in the middle between Jae and Kai that made the crowd go particularly insane and I'm certain it's an album track without a video because I've never heard it before. The contrast of Kai's powerful rap and Jae's sweet voice was hypnotizing. I try not to think too much about the sexual tension I saw between them because I know there's fanservice at play. We do it too. Not on their level but watching them laugh and flirt with each other for close to three hours cemented the notion that they play up to this idea that they're all fucking. The fans love it. Fuck, I'd read the odd article about Cleo and me because of the chemistry we have on stage. We just don't lean into it the way these guys do.

The doorman gives me a look like he doesn't quite recognize me but moves to open the door for me anyway and I make my way to the bank of elevators. There's another guy inside and I give him the floor and he nods, not saying a word as we shoot up.

I'm outside his door when I start to get the weird fluttery sensation in my stomach and my chest. Nerves. I'm nervous. Last night I was halfway wasted and high on adrenaline, tonight I've had a single beer and a whole day to overthink it. Except I haven't overthought it. I'd barely thought about it at all, really. I'd known it was happening, that I was going to see him tonight, and that something was—is—going to happen that will change how I look at myself and my life forever. But my head has been surprisingly chill about it. My head is very rarely ever chill about anything, so this is nothing short of remarkable.

But this second my body seems to have figured out something before my head has and its scared fucking shitless. The thought goes through my head to turn and bolt, run as far away from this apartment and this guy as I can get. Take a flight to fucking Tibet or something, hide out in a monastery for a month until I find myself again, but my feet don't move. They don't want to move. Not really. And not away from the door.

Taking a deep breath, I punch the code I'd memorized into the small black keypad beneath the handle and push open the door. I call out, just in case he got back early.

"Jae? You home? It's me." Then, wondering that same thing I had last night when I wondered if this was a place he brought guys to fuck them, I add, "Raphael."

But there's no answer and so I move into the apartment. Having the place to myself means I have some time to calm the fuck down, pour a drink, maybe check the place out.

He said he only lives here some of the time, but the living area feels more than lived in. Maybe because he's been here the last few days. There's an iPad on the low wood coffee table and a book with a bookmark sticking out of it. Picking the same spot on the sofa he did this morning to sit, I reach across to pick up the book. '*Almost Transparent Blue*' by Ryu Murakami. It's in Korean. Making me marvel, not for the first time, how fucking incredible he is. He sings and dances, looks like a supermodel, and speaks two languages fluently. Wait, three, because he told me that night at Frida's that he speaks some Japanese too.

I fancy a drink, so I go to his table/trolley thing and browse the options. He has a bottle of Canadian Club which I haven't had in ages, so I pour three fingers into one of the crystal glasses and amble over to his sound system. It's high spec and looks more like a piece of sculpture than a sound system, but this shit I can do. These things always look complicated but everything you find in a home sound system has a more complicated counterpart in a studio, so it's not hard to work back from that and figure it out.

After a minute I have my current playlist playing from my phone's Bluetooth. I move to look out at the view while sipping my drink, mind flitting to Camille briefly. Soon. I'll deal with all of it soon. I'm not quite sure what I'll tell her but I'm sort of hoping it's one of those things that as soon as I start doing it, it'll come.

I want to look around the rest of his place but I'm not sure if he'd like it. Doesn't sit right to go snooping either and so I just down the last of my drink and pour myself another.

I'm sitting on the couch, head resting against the back, a nice low buzz in my blood when I hear the front door unlocking. The quiet beep of the mechanism before the soft whoosh of the door being pushed open.

My heart kicks up a level, that fluttery sensation coming back full force. I hear him kick off his shoes by the door then curse myself for not doing the same, glancing down at my sneakers like they've committed a felony. Then, he's standing in the large open doorway looking at me. He's wearing an oversized hoodie with the hood up and a long dark blue winter coat over it with big gold buttons. Dark sweatpants and white-socked feet.

I'd seen him this morning without his usual designer gear, heeled boots and make-up on, but this is different again.

"Hey." I smile. It feels dorkish on my face.

Jae looks like he's in a trance as he stares, wordless, then he blinks and comes into the room toward the couch.

"I did not know if you would be here."

I can't tell if he's annoyed that I am, but he certainly doesn't look happy. He sits down next to me with a sigh and looks straight ahead, reaching up to pull the hood of his hoodie down.

"Do you…want a drink?" I ask, tense.

He lets out a soft laugh and turns to me. "Did you just offer me a drink, in my own house?" He's smiling now, full pink lips quirked up.

I smile back. "I did. Was that a yes?"

He looks at my glass. "What is that?"

"Rye," I say and move to stand.

"I will have that too, then."

I can feel him watching me as I pour, but he doesn't speak. I've come to realize this about Jae, that he's perfectly comfortable with silences, even when they're slightly uncomfortable. He just owns them. Lingers in them. Happy in the quiet.

When I'm moving back towards him, he stands and unbuttons his coat, shrugging it off and dumping it beside him on the sofa. He takes the drink from me and sits back down, knee pulled up and his body turned slightly so that he's facing me when I sit down. I take a deep sip of my drink, watching his mouth as he does the same.

Fucking hell, he's so beautiful. I wonder if I'll stop being stunned by it.

I think about how hard he worked tonight, how he moved and how his voice sounded in that huge stadium, and I get it. I get why he's adored the way he is, almost fervently so by his fans. It's a turn on.

I mean, it shouldn't impress me as much as it does since I do a similar thing, but seeing it from this perspective hits different. I still haven't decided whether I'll tell him that I came along tonight or not. I'm not sure how he'd feel, if he'd see it as weird or something. I decide to play it by ear.

"How was it? It went good?" I ask, keeping my expression neutral.

He nods. "I think so. I always feel like I could have done better. Could have given more. Kai says it is a sickness I have. That I strive for perfection in an unhealthy way, and that since I do not recognize any level of perfection in myself, I will never find it."

He shrugs, nonchalant despite the depth of the words. I don't know if this is his usual comedown after a particularly grueling show—mine is the opposite in that I feel high as the clouds invincible, but he looks almost morose and I don't know if he'd rather be alone or not. A greater kind of man would probably offer to leave, but clearly I'm a lesser kind of man.

He's picking a fleck of lint from his dark sweatpants and avoiding my eyes.

"Did something happen?" I ask, inching a little closer. He lifts his head. "You seem...down."

"You think you know me so well already?" His eyes turn a little hard.

"No. I just..." Okay, maybe I should be a greater kind of man. "Look, do you want me to go? If you've had a shitty night and you want to be alone, I get it, man. It's cool."

"I do not want you to go, Raphael."

"Okay, good, good." I nod. "What do you want then?"

He catches his bottom lip between his teeth as he stares at me. "I want you to fuck me."

Some loud bang goes off in my head, my breath whipping out of my chest.

"Do you think you can do that?"

With a confidence I'm not sure I feel, I nod once. "Yeah, I can definitely do that."

FOURTEEN
RAPHAEL

"Okay, then I am going to take a quick shower." Jae says, standing. "If you want to wait in the bedroom."

It sounds somewhere between a suggestion and a request.

"Um, sure," I mutter, dumbly.

He downs his rye and then he's gone. I lift my glass and do the same. Then grab the bottle and take it with me to the bedroom, sipping as I go.

The bed is freshly made, different sheets to what I saw last night. I move to turn the lamps on, and wander towards the window to stare out at the city below.

He wants me to fuck him. I agreed.

Now it feels like I'm just waiting here, like some kind of gigolo, to service him. The thought shouldn't turn me on as much as it does. I should probably be googling 'how to fuck a guy' while he showers because I'm still certain I've no clue how to go about this, where to start. I've thought about it a lot, but that isn't the same. One night when I was particularly wasted, I'd even ventured so far as to watch some gay porn. I'd gotten four minutes in before I'd had to turn it off. Not disgusted, just not particularly turned on either. There's a part of me that thinks maybe once we get down to it, the actual bread and butter act of it, my body will refuse to do it. Like it's gonna know it's not programmed that way and that will be that.

But I mean, I've done anal, and that's what it is at its core, right? I've already had his cock in my mouth and that's the same kind of hurdle as this. A hurdle I made, cleanly. I made him come. If all else fails maybe I can just do that again? Otherwise I'm gonna need to learn real fucking fast.

I'd learned guitar in about eight months. This couldn't be much harder than guitar, surely? Except, I don't have eight months to learn how to do this. I don't have hours alone in my bedroom making mistake after mistake in order to master this. I likely have about eight seconds of Lee Jaehyun on all fours in front of me before I blow my load all over his fucking ass.

And what if there's something entirely innate to sex with a guy that I don't know? What if I do it, or don't do it and I fucking hurt him or something? Or what if it's just the worst sex he's ever had and he spends the rest of his life cringing over it? The thought of either of those realities makes me want to bolt. Or throw up. Or both.

This is the most important performance of my life, and my body knows it.

I turn to bolt for the bathroom and find him standing at the bedroom door watching me. Towel wrapped around his slender hips and his hair dripping wet onto his chest. All thoughts leave my head, and the need to throw up my Shake Shack from earlier disintegrates as I focus on staying upright. Because my knees almost buckle from how good he looks.

It's crazy that he's real, I think again. That he's made of the same matter that I am. That beneath all that flawless skin he's just blood and muscle and bone like I am. And I get to have him. He wants me to have him.

"You're so fucking beautiful, dude," I say. "Like, it's seriously fucking distracting."

His cool expression cracks, and he smiles. It's fucking breath-taking. "You're so fucking American. *Dude.*"

"You don't like *dude*? I can find something else to call you." I move toward him slowly. "What else would you call me?"

I study him as I get closer. His lean body and sharp elegant features, his high cheekbones and pretty mouth. Then I think about how he moves. Graceful and fluid. Precise and smooth. I almost don't say it because it's too fucking cheesy. But then I think about how he might smile at me if I do and so I can't not say it.

"Kitten?"

He laughs loud. This fucking beautiful musical thing that bubbles out of his throat and makes his eyes almost close. "Kitten," he repeats. "It is ridiculous."

"Yeah, well, I'm ridiculous."

His eyes turn serious. "No, you're not ridiculous. You are…" He thinks about it, hard, as I hold my breath and wait. "*Teug-ihan, nollaun.* Unusual. Surprising."

"I really hope that's a good thing in Korea," I smile.

His face is soft as he reaches out to take the bottle from my hand, warm fingers grazing mine gently. He doesn't look away from me as he drinks. I watch his throat move as he swallows, feeling every single nerve of my body come alive. I'm aware of everything. My eyelashes, the soles of my feet, my fingernails, every inch of skin buzzing with awareness.

Jae lowers the bottle and leans in. Our height different seems more noticeable then, as he stretches up on his toes to press our mouths together. The sweet burn of the rye stings my lips and tongue, but his are there to soothe it away. He does that thing where he licks into my mouth, then kisses around my lips, tender presses of his mouth above and below, before sucking on my lip. I reach a hand up and hold the back of his damp head, pressing our lips harder together. He smells of whatever expensive shower gel he used, sweet and spicy, and tastes like nothing I've ever tasted before. Like heaven probably. The wet kiss turns heavy quickly, tongues and teeth and lips, and though I can feel the wetness of his body start to soak through my t-shirt and jeans I couldn't care less, because my body is hot. So fucking hot.

He pulls back so that we're just panting into each other's mouths. I want to lick the water still dripping down his cheeks from his hair, and so I do. Reaching in to catch it on my tongue, licking up towards his temple. Then towards his ear. And he purrs. Actually fucking purrs. My dick, half way there, goes rock hard in the same instant.

I pull back to look down at him. His eyes are closed but he blinks them open and looks up at me, lust-drunk.

"I want you so fucking much," I tell him.

He licks his lips. "I want you too, Raphael."

"Will you show me? Show me how to make you feel good?"

Something so fucking fond moves into his eyes, a small smile tugging the side of his perfect fucking mouth. "Yes. I will show you."

My thumb stroking close to his mouth, I lean in to kiss him again. Slow this time. Soft. The inside of his mouth is so warm. Wet and soft and hot and it's driving me insane thinking about how his body is gonna feel around my cock. The groan leaves my mouth and melts into his.

He pulls back and gives me a look of intent before moving towards the bed. He sets the bottle down and unwraps himself from the dark towel. I can only gape at the full sight of him, uncovered, bare as the day he was born. Wide-ish shoulders, sculpted back, small waist, round ass leading down into lean muscular thighs. Miles of pale smooth skin. I think of that marble sculpture of David again.

He takes his time removing the rings from his fingers and setting them on a ceramic bowl thing on the bedside before he pulls open the drawer. He retrieves the bottle of fragrant oil and climbs onto the bed to settle his body upright against the headboard, legs spread. His cock is pink and hard and lying flat against his toned stomach.

When I come back to myself, I realize I'm just standing there staring, so I move toward the bed too, looking to him for direction.

He eyes the space between his legs, and I go to sit there but he says, "Perhaps you should undress, first?"

Well, this is going well. Can't even remember the fucking basics.

I give him an awkward nod, which just makes him smile, and pull off my t-shirt before moving to unbutton my Levi's. I leave my briefs on because just sitting there buck naked while he does whatever he's about to do feels weird. When I'm sitting there, cross legged and watching him, he gives me another of those fond smiles. I have this startling realization that he could be here with anyone right now. Literally anyone. Someone who at least knows what the fuck they're doing, someone he doesn't have to teach for shit's sake, but for some reason he wants me. Convenience? Curiosity? Fuck knows, but I'm filled with gratitude.

He pulls his left leg up so his foot is flat on the bed and squirts some of that expensive oil into his fingers. Then he reaches between his legs. It's the first time I get a proper look at him there. This small pink hole that's been scrubbed and shaved. It's…pretty? I'm not sure what I expected.

At first, he just circles it. Slow and deliberate with the index finger of his left hand. I flick my eyes up to his face to find him watching me intently. Why is it I'd never thought to do that to a girl first before anal? My cheeks heat. Was I supposed to? Fuck.

"Do you know why I am doing this?" he asks me. Like he can read my thoughts.

"Yeah, I know."

"Tell me," he says, as he tilts his finger down so the tip slides into that little hole.

My breath quickens when he lets out a soft gasp as he pushes it deeper.

"To open it up," I manage.

"Yes," he gasps as he begins to move his finger in and out of himself. "What else?"

I frown. Is this a test? If I fail, do I not get to fuck him? My brain legitimately scrambles. I've not a clue.

Jae lets out a soft laugh as he slides a second finger in. "Because it feels good, Raphael."

Oh. Yeah. Okay. Well, yeah.

"Does it look good?" he asks me and I'm sure my brain short circuits.

I don't have to think about it, not for a second, but I take a minute to just drink him in. Legs splayed, long fingers fucking into that tight little hole, pink blush spreading across his chest, mouth kissed and bitten red, cheeks flushed.

"It does. You're so fucking hot. The sexiest thing I've ever seen, Jaehyun."

He smiles at me, shy from the compliment, and I feel a burst of pre-come seep from my dick. I have to squeeze it hard to stop it from doing anything more than that.

"But I really want to fuck you, so if that's not gonna be anytime soon..." I eye his fingers, still doing their thing to his ass, "...you're gonna have to tell me so I can prepare."

He laughs and it's that soft breathy one he has.

"Not too much longer now," he says, with a sigh as he pulls his two fingers out, slots a third next to them, and slides all three back in.

I get bold then and I shift a little closer to marvel at how that hole has *widened* before my eyes. Still not big enough for my dick, but almost twice the size it was when he started. I slide a hand up his calf, squeezing and massaging the hairless skin. He likes this, because he lets out a soft moan and his head falls back against the headboard. I move my hand up over his knee, and then further, smoothing it over the firm muscle of his thigh until it meets the forearm of the arm he's using. His eyes have a dare in them as I walk my fingers down to his wrist. When I wrap my fingers around the hand he's using, he bites down hard on his lower lip and minutely shifts his hips upward, urging me. Then I'm fucking him with his own hand.

I don't even think about it, I slide my hand into my briefs to wrap it around myself, groaning as the pressure eases. He watches me as I start to stroke myself and I honestly have no clue how to tell him I have about thirty seconds max before exploding over my hand.

It's him who loses patience first though, he shoves my hand away from him and extracts his fingers and then he's shifting across the bed. As he pulls open the bedside again to grab a condom this time, I yank off my underwear and toss them behind me, sitting back on my knees to wait for further instruction.

He hands me the condom and I roll it on without taking a single breath. When I'm done, I look at him, swallowing.

"It's your first time, how do you want me?" he asks. I give him a look and he laughs, kind of sweetly. "I mean, with a man. Did you have something in mind?"

It shouldn't take me by surprise, not since Jae is always clear and concise about things. But because I'm not expecting it and because my brain is overloaded; I'm surprised any response comes out at all.

"Will you ride me?" I hear myself say. It doesn't sound like my own voice. It's so rough and desperate. But it's what I've wanted since the dream I had about him doing it wearing fishnets.

Jae looks surprised, but in no way reluctant. He gives me a smile and a nod and then urges me down to lie down where he'd just fingered himself. I smooth my hand over my cock, which hasn't softened even a fraction, and watch in awe as he straddles me in one fluid motion. He places his hands flat on my chest and caresses it softly, before stroking both thumbs over my nipples at once. They're surprisingly tender I find. He leans in to ghost his lips over mine, not really kissing me just breathing me in. I kiss him, pushing my tongue between his lips as I settle my hands on his hips. He bumps his perfect ass over my cock a few times which only makes it throb harder, moving so that it slips and slides between his oiled cheeks.

"Fuck, you're perfect." I groan against his mouth.

This makes him hum softly, and then his hands are in my hair as his mouth moves to bite and suck softly at my neck.

"Please." I beg. It feels like torture. I keep seeing that pink puckered hole, and those little balls and that smooth taint and…

"Are you sure this is what you want?" he asks against my ear. It sounds weighty. It's not seductive at all. I know he's asking for consent again.

I open my eyes as he lifts his head from my neck, his movements over my body halting.

"This is not sucking cock, Raphael." He clarifies, eyes dazed but serious.

My cock wants it, I know that much. My head and heart do

too I think, but I take a second to check in with myself. There's a marker here that says 'no turning back'. How do I feel if I stop now, get dressed, and leave? Regret or relief?

That does it.

"Sounds cliché as fuck, but I've never been surer of anything," I tell him. "Yes, Jae, I want this."

He studies me a moment then nods again. He reaches for that little bottle again and pours some more on to his hand, reaching around to spread it between his ass and then over my cock. Rising up on his knees he grips hold of my cock to position it at his hole. I can't stop the embarrassing noise that leaves my throat as he pushes me inside him. It's halfway between a groan and a gasp.

"*Seong-gyo hada*," Jae whispers as he stops, moves, stops again. It takes hours it feels like, but then he's seated all the way. His eyes are closed and his hands flat on my thighs as he takes a few deep breaths. "Sshibal, you feel so good, inside."

"Fuck, Jae, you do too."

He's tighter than anything or anyone I've ever had around me. Scorching hot too. As close to the most perfect sensation I can imagine. Tight and warm with ridges that heighten the pleasure each time either of us shifts or breathes. It takes every bit of control I have not to fuck up into him, but I've still no real clue how I do this and be sure I'm not hurting him so I need to wait for him to lead. I clutch at his thighs instead, gripping them tight as he smooths his hand over his cock. His movements are slow and deliberate and I slip into a sort of trance watching it.

He starts with a slow trial roll of his hips, groaning low with undeniable pleasure. As he speeds up, he lets out this soft mewl like a fucking cat and then there are fireworks going off all over my body, under my skin, and in my balls and I know I'm not going to last very long. If my brain was capable of it, I'm sure I'd be embarrassed about that, but it's not. It's capable of very little right now. Breath and thought and not the proper amounts of either. I tighten my grip on his waist and do little more than aid his movements.

"You can move," he says, smiling through labored breaths. "You won't hurt me."

It's all the encouragement I need.

I lift my hips off the bed every time he slides down, his movements altered now from shallow circles of his hips to lift and drop. Soon we have a rhythm and it's both the most pleasurable thing and the most torturous thing I've experienced. Why on earth did I ask him to ride me? I want to hold him down and fuck him into the mattress. It's not enough.

Jae lets go of his cock and drags his hands over his body, caressing his nipples before sliding his hands up into his hair as he really starts to lose himself. It's a sight I'll never forget. He looks fucking incredible. Another fucking performance that he's practiced his entire life for. I can only watch in awe as he uses my dick to put on the best show I've ever seen.

I can feel it then. The edge. And I'm rushing towards it without a hope this time of pulling it back. I reach for his cock, hard and dripping, and start to jerk it as I bend my knees and put my feet flat on the bed so I can fuck him harder.

His eyes spring open and they go wide as he gasps. "There, yes, there. Don't stop."

I feel it too. Some little nub scraping against the head of my cock, and so I focus on it. I lose it a few times, slipping past it when I miss the tempo, but I hit it more often than not and after a few more thrusts he's coming. He's moaning my name and a few words in Korean and spilling hot white come over my chest and hand. As he tightens round my cock, clenching and spurting at the same time, I'm done for.

I empty inside the condom as my vision sparks and I'm pulling him down on top of me to squeeze him against my chest and fuck the last of my orgasm inside him.

It feels like it lasts fucking hours. Hours of me lying there holding him too tight and too close, breathing hard against his hair. The smell of him is sex and lavender and that sweet spicy shower gel and

I wonder how the fuck I'd managed to live without it. Without this. Without *him*.

Once our breaths have slowed, he places a little kiss to my chest just above my nipple. Then another, before lifting his head to look at me, eyes sparkling. He looks blissed out. My cock slips out of him, soft and spent, and it's Jae who reaches between our bodies to pull off the condom and discard it in the wastebasket by the bed, barely lifting from my chest while he does it.

"That was...fucking incredible." I sigh when he's settled again. "I mean, you were incredible. I mainly just lay here while you got fucked. But I feel like if I'd participated any more, I'd have ruined it, you know?"

He laughs at that, but its soft and so fucking sexy and then his mouth is moving across my chest and he's kissing and licking his way across my pecs. Those same soft little kitten licks that he does to my mouth. When he burrows his nose in my armpit and licks there, I gasp out loud. It's ticklish as fuck but it also makes this hot spark of arousal shoot down my body right to my cock. What the fuck was that? When I look down at him wide-eyed, he's smirking like he knows exactly what he's doing.

"You did just fine, Raphael," he says gently, kissing my chest again.

Fine. Well. Only one way to go from there I suppose. Up.

I move quickly, holding him tight as I flip us both over so he's under me, legs spread around my hips. His eyes are wide and his breathing's a little fast again. He's waiting to see what I'm gonna do. What am I gonna do? Having him pinned under me like this feels nice, despite the come drying stickily between us. First, I lean in to kiss him softly, before pressing deeper into his mouth. He moans and curls his hands into my hair, lifting his hips in search of friction.

"I don't want to do just *fine*." I growl against his mouth. "I want to be the best you've ever had." *I want to be the only one you ever have from now on.* I'm so fucked.

He makes a soft tutting noise. "Arrogant rockstar."

"That's what they call me."

I move my mouth to his neck, sucking hard on the skin there. He tilts his head to let me change my angle. Almost like he wants me to leave a mark.

"Who calls you that?"

"Aside from you? Wikipedia."

"Your girlfriend?"

I freeze. Then slowly sit up and back on my calves to look down at him. He folds an arm behind his head and stares up at me, face calm and utterly expressionless. No accusation, no malice, nothing. It feels wrong to talk about her with him. Certainly, before I've spoken to her about him, but given what we've just done together, I realize that Jae also deserves an explanation. I take a few deep breaths as I try to think through the mess my head.

"It's over." I sigh. "With Camille. I mean, we need to talk, but when we do I'm gonna tell her it's over, Jae."

I watch his face closely for some sort of reaction, any sort of reaction, and I think I see a brief flicker of something in his eyes. It's gone in less than an instant. Maybe I imagined it.

"I see," is what he says, flat, almost unemotional. Then, "You are sad about it."

I blink down at him. "I mean, yeah, of course. We've been together a while, we were gonna get married. We were good together too. I mean I thought we were, you know, but maybe we weren't. I don't know." I drag a hand through my hair and shrug. "I don't really know anything anymore, I guess."

Or more accurately, everything I thought I knew has turned out to be complete and utter bullshit. I'm not sure what I'm expecting from him by admitting this. Empathy maybe. Some soft words of comfort. Sage advice. Anything other than what he does, which is to extract himself from under me and climb out of bed.

"Where are you going?" I stare after him.

He gives me a look like it should be completely fucking obvious, and says, "To run a bath."

FIFTEEN
RAPHAEL

He strides into the ensuite without a look back.

In my bewilderment I still register that his ass looks incredible; firm and round and pale. I want to fuck it again. Again, because I just did it. I just fucked him.

It seems incredible to me. I was inside him. I made him come. He made me come. I've just had one of the best orgasms of my fucking life, with a guy. This guy. And now he's what? *Done with me?* I'm dismissed?

Maybe poetic justice for all the times I'd done the same to women. Fucked them and moved on like they were nothing. I'd never been cruel or unkind, just superficial and dismissive. Even when they'd made it clear they wanted more.

Yeah, I deserve this.

And I'm realizing now just how much pride and dignity each one of them had, because they got up and left, no questions asked. Whereas all I want to do is follow him in there, kneel at his feet and ask him to let me have him again.

While I could watch him do no more than breathe for hours on end, his fascination with me seems almost non-existent, fleeting at best. It's one way traffic. It's never been more obvious than it is right now. Me sitting here on his bed covered in his come while he goes to run himself a fucking bath. The most pathetic part? I'm half-hard again. I still want him. Just thinking about sinking into that perfect body again has some kind of Pavlovian response happening to my cock.

Had I seriously been thinking that I could get him out of my system by fucking him once? I'm a bigger clown than I thought possible. I need air. I need to walk and think and then maybe speak to a priest or an exorcist or something because this guy is simmering in my veins like demonic possession.

I find my T-shirt and jeans on the floor and pull them on, trying to ignore the way the come has hardened and is starting to crust and flake on my chest. I'm sitting on the edge of the bed lacing my boots when he reappears naked and perfect as sin.

"You are dressed," he says, stopping to look down at me.

I look back down at my boots before I say or do something pathetic. "Yeah, I'm gonna split."

"*Split*?" He repeats, sounding confused. "Oh, you mean you are leaving."

When I stand up, he's closer and well, he looks almost…pissed. "Why?"

I frown. "Isn't that what you want? You got out of bed and said you were taking a bath and so I figured we were done with whatever that was."

Now he looks pissed *and* hurt. "With *whatever that was*? We fucked, Raphael. Surely you cannot be confused about that." There's a note of mockery in his voice that gets my back up.

"Dunno, Jae, felt a lot like I was the one who just got fucked." An image of him fucking himself on my dick projects itself onto my brain and my cock hardens all the way.

"And then I suppose you are disappointed?" he says. "Disgusted perhaps? Your *experiment* did not turn out how you thought it would."

I feel like he's slapped me across the fucking face. "*Experiment*? What are you talking about?"

He narrows his eyes and turns towards the bathroom. "If you want to leave, then go."

I'm after him in an instant, curling my fingers around his wrist to stop him, tugging him back to face me.

"You think I'm *disgusted*? *Disappointed*?" I'm not sure which is more insulting. "I told you it was incredible?" He doesn't pull his wrist from my grip, but I see the insecurity on his face. It's so completely unexpected. This perfect fucking force of a human being… vulnerable about anything. I take a step closer to him.

"Jaehyun, *nothing* about you is disappointing. Not a fucking thing. And I'm certainly not disgusted. Fuck. It was…" I scrub a hand over my face. *Life-changing. Soul-shifting.* I settle on: "Perfect. It was perfect."

He studies me a second, checking my sincerity, then his expression transforms. The shadows lift from his eyes and his mouth reshapes into this adorable pout that makes my stomach flip over.

"Then why do you want to leave?"

The vulnerability in his voice almost brings me to my knees.

"I don't. I thought that's what you wanted. I thought you were done with me." I shrug and gesture toward the bathroom. "You said you wanted to take a bath and I assumed you wanted me to leave so you could do that."

"Then I am sorry," he says. "For not being clear with you. I enjoy taking a bath after sex and I thought you would enjoy taking one with me." He has this soft little smile on his face now and it has the same effect that his hand wrapped around my cock would have.

"I…" My throat feels dry and my head fried. "You want to take a bath with me?"

He lifts one shoulder, nonchalantly, and then reaches out to slide his hand under my shirt, scraping his blunt nails over my abdomen. "Or you can watch…I don't mind."

I almost groan from the mental picture that provides. Jaehyun in the bath. Wet, pink, glistening, his hair soaked to his skin.

"So then…you don't want me to go?" I smile, reaching out to him with my other hand, sliding it over his waist and then around to his ass, squeezing gently.

He sighs, airily. "No, Raphael. I don't." He drops his eyes and his hands to my belt buckle and pulls at it playfully. "I am annoyed that you put these on again. I like looking at you naked."

I grin stupidly. "Yeah? I really like looking at you naked, too."

When I lean in to kiss him, he makes that soft mewling noise that goes straight to my dick. Then I feel him, his hardness, bare and tempting. I want nothing more than to sink to my knees and take it into my mouth. But I also really wanna take a bath with him so figure I can wait until we're in there and kill two birds with one stone. He steps back from me and watches while I undress again, eyes roving appreciatively over my tattoos, watching my hands as they undo my belt and unbutton my jeans.

"Nothing about you is disappointing either, you know," Jae says very quietly and I'm certain my heart stops beating for a second. "You are also very beautiful. Like a bright American sunrise."

I can only stare at him, stupefied. Maybe I do affect him then? In some way at least. I want to sing from how happy that makes me.

"Does that make you a dark Korean sunset?" It sounds cheesy as fuck and I regret saying it until he gives me the most incredible smile I've ever seen. Open mouthed and bright, perfect white smile glittering as his cheeks pull up, eyes seeming to disappear.

He rolls his eyes. "You have never seen a Korean sunset; you have never been to Korea"

"Baby, I'm pretty sure I was in Korea about ten minutes ago."

I raise my eyebrow and he bursts into laughter.

"You are ridiculous," he says and saunters into the bathroom.

"But not disappointing! And as beautiful as an American sunrise!" I call after him as I finish undressing.

His laughter is musical as it bounces around the bathroom. "Hurry up, the bath is ready, you big American idiot!"

Camille and I never shared a bath.

That thought occurs to me as I stare at Jae across the lightly fragrant steaming water. Now I'm sharing a bath with a guy I've been intimate with twice—like it's the most normal thing in the world—and yet not once with the woman I was going to marry. I don't take a lot of baths generally, but there's intimacy here. The echo of the water every time one of us shifts, the brief touches of wet skin beneath the surface. Is he hard under there? I am. My skin too warm and my head too light from the steam. I'm both tired and yet very, very alert at the same time.

Jaehyun's cheeks and chest are bright pink, his hair swept back off his forehead which is dappled with water.

It's a big bath. Huge. And on one side of it is a view of downtown Manhattan at night, which has absolutely nothing on the view across from me.

"This is nice," I say, grinning stupidly. "Not what I thought I'd be doing tonight, but nice all the same."

"You thought we'd be fucking all night?" Jae says, his voice low and scratchy.

My cock certainly likes the sound of that idea.

"You overestimate my stamina. I worked very hard tonight."

"You sure did," I smirk and he smiles, a little shy.

He turns his head to look out at the view. I don't think too much about it before I say it, never normally a great idea, but I'm too relaxed to really care.

"I came to see you tonight. At the MetLife."

His head twists back to me, utter surprise on his face. "You did?"

When I nod, he says nothing for a few moments. Then: "Why?"

"Why not?"

"Because you are not a fan of our music. Or our band. I don't know why you'd want to."

I frown at that. "How do you know I'm not a fan? I could have a whole room of K:OS merch for all you know. Every version of every record. A pair of those little cat ears all your fans wear. They'd look great on me."

He doesn't smile like I hoped he would. He looks a little suspicious, like maybe he thinks I'm mocking him. I sit up, sliding through the water towards him, so that I'm sitting in the middle of the tub.

"I wanted to see you perform. I was curious."

"Curious about?"

I shrug. "The hype, your K:Otics, the phenomena that is K:OS. I wanted to see it for myself."

His eyes are sharp, trained on me like a cat. "And?"

"And I've never seen anything quite like it. You killed it."

There are a few moments silence as he digests this, looking for any mockery again. The tension in his face melts away and a slow smile spreads over his perfect raspberry-pink mouth. Then he looks down at some point on my chest, almost shy.

"We've performed better. I wish I could have done better. My voice felt weak, though it always does when we do so many nights. I'd have liked—."

Beneath the water I grip his hand and pull him against me.

"Hey, I said, you killed it. I've no clue how you remember all those steps. To move like that and sing like that for three hours. Are you even human?" I pretend to study him. "If you were an alien then it would not surprise me. Would actually make a whole lot of sense."

It would explain why he makes me feel like no other person on earth does. Like there's a buzzing under my skin whenever he's close to me. Like he's on some frequency not of this universe.

He giggles and drops his head forward onto my chest, shy as he tries to hide under my armpit. "You are an idiot." He laughs.

"Yeah. And you are incredible," I whisper against his neck.

Sliding my arms around him I move my hands over the skin of his back, dancing my fingers up the nodes of his spine. When he lifts his head, our faces are close, mouths almost touching. I let out a soft breath and with his eyes open he kisses me. Soft and tender before he kisses me deeper and climbs into my lap. My cock jabs awkwardly against his thigh and he reaches between us to adjust it, so that it sits flush against his.

Our mouths move lazy and slow, not really kissing but licking and sucking our way across wet skin. I move my mouth across his jaw to the spot below his ear, to the crook of his neck, to his clavicle—I think I'm obsessed with it—lapping up every drop of wetness puddled here.

When he starts to grind, my control slips, and I sink my fingers up into his hair and pull his head back to expose his throat. He gasps a little, eyes going wide as he grinds harder, wrapping his legs tight around me.

He's panting now, his mouth a wet kissable thing, and it sends my mind somewhere else. As soon as the thought enters my head, I think I might come from the idea of it. From the idea that *he* might come from it. From the sounds he might make and the way his body might move against my tongue. I lean up to kiss him once more, then nudge him gently off my lap.

"Turn around," I say, my voice hoarse.

He blinks once, slowly, then he's moving up onto his knees facing the view and I'm looking at the elegant arch of his spine that leads down to his perfect ass. An ass that's pink and hot and dripping from the heat of the bath. I turn my body and smooth my hand across both cheeks before sliding my index finger between them.

Jae shudders, a small noise escaping him.

"Spread your legs a little for me," I ask, and he does. It sends a jolt of lust roaring through me. Him obeying me like this.

Because I like the feeling too much to let go of it, I try another. My finger between his cheeks I press it gently before saying: "Show me it."

My voice doesn't even sound like my own, and I'm not sure he even hears me because he does nothing right away. But then he's reaching back and spreading himself with both hands to show me his perfect pink hole.

I wasn't aware I could get any harder, but the sight of it, and the thought of all the things I want to do to it, things that had never entered my mind in all the years I've been aware of sex, makes me harder than I've ever been in my life. I glide my finger over it first and he shudders again, a deep body tremble that causes the water to ripple and his legs to shift. Then I circle it with my finger, like I saw him do earlier, pressing the pad of it flat against it the puckered skin and moving it in gentle circular motions.

Jae edges forward over the tub which makes his grip a little awkward. He lets go of his ass and settles himself on his stomach across the ledge before moving again to hold himself open for me. My finger looks big and tanned against the smooth pink-white of his ass. It's dangerously hot.

"Fuck, Jaehyun, you're really fucking pretty here," I say in wonder, moving my finger again. Round and round, *tap tap tap.*

He lets out a soft whimper and pleads, "Raphael, please…."

He hangs his head between his shoulders. I know what I want to do. Well, rather, I have a list of things I want to do, but there's a want that's louder than all the rest. It's the reason I wanted him in this position to begin with and suddenly I don't know why I'm not already doing it. I lean in and kiss his fingers first, then cover them with my own as I nose between his cheeks and replace my finger with my tongue to lick over his hole. It's clumsy and without finesse, but his reaction is still instant, visceral. He gasps in Korean and arches his back, pushing his ass into my face.

"English, Jae, I want to hear it in English," I say.

He laughs a little but then he's back to whimpering and panting, thrusting back as I curl my tongue and try to push it inside him. He's warm and wet and so fucking tight that I can barely get past the rim, but he's not complaining. I start to fuck him a little with it and his legs wobble again, his body slipping so that he has to hold himself up. I wrap an arm around his waist, between his body and the bath, and it helps me pull him closer and it also helps him, cause now his hand is free to hold his dick.

"That feels so good, please, Raphael, yes, please," he's saying now—in English—and my dick almost explodes from the need in his voice.

I go back to kissing it, sucking on it, listening to the noises he makes, how his body reacts. Focusing on what makes him let out those particular little whines and groans that sound so fucking good to my ears, and doing it again. He's fisting his cock, but the angle is awkward for him and so with my free hand I take over, lowering my mouth to lick the length of his cock from behind, all the way back up to his hole.

When I feel him go boneless in my arms I take it as a good sign, so I repeat that, sucking his cock into my mouth this time and swirling my tongue around the tip. His precome is sweet and savory at the same time and when I dip my tongue into the slit to taste it, more bursts across my tongue.

I really want to fist my own cock now, because it's starting to throb, dangerously, my balls tight and verging on painful, but I want to make him come first. He's close, I just need the right combination of chords. I let his cock slip from my mouth and take it in my hand as I circle his hole with my tongue again, gathering the saliva on my tongue to make the slide in easier. He's thrashing a little in my arms now, body pulled taught and on the edge.

"I am...I am going to come, Raphael, please do not stop."

He's pleading now, thrusting into my mouth and then my hand, back arched like a cat.

I time a particularly deep thrust of my tongue along with a gentle twist of my wrist and then he's coming. Hard. His hole clenches, actually clenches around my tongue, and I feel him spurt into my hand, thick and burning hot.

When he's done, I gently slide my hand out from under him and sit back against the side of the tub, watching as he tries to catch his breath. He's still folded over the edge trembling a little, his cock hanging between his legs, spent and softening. I wonder what it would feel like in my mouth like that but I'm sitting too far away, out of the water on the edge of the tub now as I fuck my fist with everything I have. I drag my eyes over his arched back and narrow hips, that perfect ass and pretty cock, and let out a low moan.

Soon enough he's turning round to watch me with fucked-out eyes and a mouth that he's bitten raw. He rests back on his arms, the New York sky glittering behind him as he licks his lips and eyes my cock. He makes no move to come forward, to help me out, content to just watch.

It's hot, having his eyes on me while I do this. My orgasm when it hits tears through my body like a hurricane, turning me inside out.

My chest tightens, my vision turns white, and my heart seems to stop. I feel wrecked.

While I try to catch my breath, Jae stands, reaching out to run his hand gently through my hair. Something soft pulls at me and I sit up, wrapping my arms around his middle and resting my head against his stomach. When he starts to smooth his hand over my head, I get the weirdest urge to cry. It's not melancholia. It's more like euphoria. I'm not sure I've ever felt this way before and certainly not after just having an orgasm. I feel it in my throat and in my chest, the weight of tears pushing behind my eyes.

"*Dangsin-eun na-ege neomu keun sangcheoleul jul geos-ibnida. an geulae?*" Jae whispers.

I want to ask him what it means, but I'm scared of how weak my voice will sound, so I say nothing and just hold him while he strokes his hand through my hair.

SIXTEEN
RAPHAEL

I can't stop staring at him. Watching the slow up and down of his body as he sleeps.

I'd fucked and eaten him out last night and I want to do both again now.

After we'd dried off and brushed our teeth, he'd put on a pair of shorts to sleep in. Black cut–off sweatpants that dwarf him. Is that how he'd look in my clothes? He's a good few inches shorter than me, and leaner. Narrow waist and compact frame where I'm broad shouldered and a bit more muscular. Not that I worked out, not really, and certainly not often. Jae's muscles were less obvious; tight abs and slightly raised pectorals, hard thighs, and shapely calves. He was fit but he was delicate too. A physical duality that was hard to wrap your head around. The way he dressed made it more confusing. He wore perfectly tailored designer suits or oversized hoodies and sweats with t-shirts that were two sizes too big, or tight jeans and elegant cashmere sweaters that looked like they had been knitted onto his body they fit so well.

He shifts slightly in his sleep, pulling his knee up towards his chest which only opens the leg of the shorts more. Which only exposes that perfect fucking hole more.

He's fast asleep as far as I can tell. On his stomach, face–planting the pillow in that same diagonal shape he was in yesterday when

I woke up. It's not how he'd gone to sleep. We'd both been on our backs staring up at the ceiling, as we'd talked about everything and anything: films to TV shows to sports and music and back to food and countries we wanted to visit again. I told him I still hadn't been to Japan, though it had been top of my list of places I wanted to visit since I was twelve and read my first manga. It had become obvious to me then that I wanted to travel with him, wanted to see things with him.

He'd been pretty much everywhere except Africa, it sounded like, and wanted to do a safari so he could see lions and tigers and elephants up close. He preferred Korea to anywhere on earth and though they were huge there, he said he was still able to live a pretty normal life. Their private lives were carefully protected by their label apparently, romantic entanglements, sexuality, families.

He'd looked round at me at one point during this, as if to say that *no one can ever find out about this*, or, *do you know how much I'm risking for this?* I'm not sure which. While his label, his band and his family knew about his sexuality, he still had to hide it from the world. From his fans. I'm pretty sure most of his fans would still love him regardless of who he was attracted to, but I didn't say this. Instead, I'd said that maybe the people who knew were the only ones who needed to know. That the world wasn't entitled to know about it. He'd gone quiet for a bit before saying, softly, "yes, maybe."

I edge toward him now, desperate to be closer to him, and press myself against his back. My morning arousal pushed against his ass as I bury my face into his neck and inhale, sleep and Jae flooding my nose like a balm. I settle my hand on his hip before walking my fingers towards the hem of those ridiculous shorts, tugging it up slightly to reveal the smooth skin of his taint and the hint of the tiny pink opening I want to bury myself inside again. My cock jerks at the sight of it, stomach flipping with want.

I remember how he fell apart on my tongue last night, the breathy whimpers and soft cries, and I almost groan out loud from how much I want to make him repeat them. I graze the pad of my index finger over it watching as a tremble moves through his entire body.

Not as asleep as I'd thought, then.

When I begin to circle it, I hear a quiet gasp and then he's pulling his leg up a little higher and pushing his ass out toward me. I lower my mouth to the nape of his neck and breathe him in again. He lifts his head and arches back, turning to grant me better access. When I push my finger against his rim, he lets out a small whimper that wraps around my dick and squeezes.

I'd slept naked so it doesn't take much to have the head of my cock sliding between his legs.

My brain is hot and loud and buzzing between my ears. Arousal pumping through my body, a need so fucking strong I can't think past it. I slide my hand under his head and tilt it towards me so I can kiss him, hard and dry. My fingertips trace the high cheekbones and sharp jaw, threading through his hair as he opens his mouth and feeds me his tongue. I can feel him pulling open the leg of the shorts to offer me more of his ass, then he's reaching behind him for my dick and jerking it sleepily, lazy strokes which match the movement of his tongue in my mouth. My finger slips in dry and he pulls away from my mouth to gasp.

"Fuck, sorry," I say, pulling it back out. "I'll get something…"

"I don't mind it…" he says, eyes dreamy as they blink open at me. But then he reaches for my hand and pulls it to his mouth, sucking on my index finger. He keeps his eyes on me as he sucks on the middle one, then the index again, then both together. "But this cannot do any harm."

He smiles and pushes my hand back down. He's still half on his side with his head twisted back to look at me. When my finger finds his hole again, it slides in with a soft wet noise and he arches his back. Dropping his head back down onto the pillow, he starts jerking my cock again, making a little purring sound when he swipes the tip to find it wet.

"You're so warm inside…" I groan, as my mouth finds his nape, kissing and scraping my way to his shoulder. I get that same desire to mark him, wanting to see him bruised and red from my mouth and it takes a degree of strength to pull back and not give into it. "So tight too...fuck, baby..." I groan.

His hand falters on my dick and so I just start rutting against it as I finger him. As I kiss and suck across the skin at the top of his spine. I want to consume him. His breathing is a little frantic now, his movements sensual as he fucks himself on my finger. I pull it out all the way and slide two back in and he mewls a breathy noise that is like music to my ears. I wanna record it and listen to it repeatedly.

"Fuck me," he says, turning his head to fix me with a half-lidded look. "I want you to fuck me again."

"Yeah, okay."

I slide my fingers out and turn away towards the nightstand drawer where I suit up quicker than I ever have in my life. When I come back, he's still in the same position, but his shorts are gone and he's running his hand up over his chest as he jerks himself off slowly. His cock is hard and the tip is a delicious creamy pink that has me reaching for it with my mouth. I lean over to suck the head into my mouth, swirling my tongue around it a few times before sliding off and moving back behind him.

He coats his fingers in saliva and spreads them over his hole before giving me a look that almost sends me over the fucking edge. He's going to be the fucking death of me. As I thread my fingers through his hair again, I line myself up at that perfect tight ring and push inside. It's a struggle, even with Jae spreading himself open for me, long shapely fingers digging into one perfect ass cheek as he holds it apart. It feels resistant. Tight. Too fucking tight. I don't want to hurt him.

"Let me in, baby," I whisper against his ear.

Jaehyun lets out a low sound and then something gives and I'm in. Pushing past hot tight muscle to that fucking paradise of sensation.

"Holy fuck, how can you feel this good?" I hear myself wonder aloud and then he's pushing back on me so his ass is pressed snugly at my balls. Then I feel it. A tightening from the inside, like there's a fist wrapped around my cock that's clenching and releasing. It makes my eyes roll back in my head. "What the fuck was *that*?"

And the fucker giggles. Actually fucking giggles. He props his head up on his hand and looks over his shoulder at me. Big eyes all innocent and glittering.

"You mean this?"

He does it again and something spurts out the end of my cock. I'm certain it's all over but some high power takes mercy on me and keeps the rest of my load in.

"You need to quit that or I won't be able to do that fucking thing you asked for."

He frowns. "But you are not doing the fucking thing anyway?"

He gives me a sort of pissy look that only makes me smile.

Without another word, I slide almost all the way out and then ram myself back in. Jae cries out, mouth falling open and eyes falling closed. I do it again, watching his face for pain or discomfort. He turns his upper body so that it's flat on the bed, his lower half still turned sideways. Sort of reverse cowgirl—boy—but not quite, and I go again.

On the third thrust I change my angle and the noise that leaves him is a high-pitched thing that tells me I've hit my jackpot. His eyes go very serious all of a sudden and he gives me a fervent nod. He pulls his legs up and this changes the angle again and this time I don't need to thrust to hit it, it just grazes it on each pass and then Jae is gasping and jerking and thrashing in my arms. My head drops to find a nipple which I suck into my mouth. This makes his noises change again, growing more unabashed, less contained, like he's lost all control now.

I fucking love it.

It's a little awkward, the angle, but we make it work and I manage to wrap a hand around his dick while I fuck him. It's only a few more thrusts until I feel it in my balls. The perfect close heat of his body around my cock, the little clenches he does when I hit it just right, the sounds he makes between breaths. All of it undoes me quickly.

Miraculously, I feel his cock start to spurt at almost the same time as my own, and he curses in Korean as his body arches up from the force of it. The clenching around my cock as he comes, turns my mind to white noise and my body into one giant dick. I feel the orgasm everywhere; the top of my head, the tips of my ears, behind my eyes, my fucking asshole. Incredible. It's like each time with him some new part of me that I didn't even know was there, is uncovered. Like sex with him is some archaeological dig. Who knows what else is lying under all this fucking dirt?

After, I gently ease out of him and tug off the condom.

When his breathing returns to normal he cracks open an eye and gives me this massive, pleased, smile that turns me inside out.

"Mmm. You are getting better at that," he says, dragging a finger down my softening cock. It tickles but I don't pull away. He looks fascinated with it, and I like the look of fascination on his face. Especially when it pertains to me. He circles the end, then pushes into the foreskin to the slit with one long pale finger which feels really fucking nice actually. Soothing. Like a foot massage after a run.

"I've had a pretty good teacher," I grin, and he huffs out a laugh.

"Ah, yes. You wanted me to teach you how to *dance*."

He's talking about the Twitter post I'd made after he called me in LA.

"You got that, huh." I grin. "That's what's called an *Innuendo*."

"Inn-u-en-doh," he repeats. "I like this word."

His finger leaves my cock and goes to his mouth where he sucks it inside. It looks almost thoughtless, just some absent action, but the gleam in his eyes tells me he knows exactly what he's doing. Like when he licked my armpit and almost made me come from it. Like when he giggled after clenching his ass around my fucking cock. He knows what he's doing.

Because unlike me, he's done this before.

The thought makes me feel irrationally pissed off, but I'm not sure why. Jealousy seems the obvious answer but I've never been particularly jealous about this kind of shit before, so I don't know. I've also never fucked another guy before so I guess anything is possible. For me, at least. Him? I don't really know. Because I still don't really know what he's doing here with me. What this is for him. We were sort of enemies to sort of friends to sort of fuckbuddies. I'm straight. I mean, I was. What happens when he goes back to Korea? Do I go back to being straight? The idea seems laughable to me now.

"You leave New York when?" he asks, eyes roving over my tattoos.

"Technically, today."

He blinks up at me. "Today?"

"I'm only booked into my hotel until today…" I hesitate, not sure how much to reveal here. What makes me look less pathetic? "I wasn't due to stick around this long."

He nods, slowly. Understanding that I *am* pathetic.

"I'm due to head to Colorado for Thanksgiving. See my mom. But I never made any firm plans outside of that because I wasn't sure. I was gonna hire a car, do the whole road trip thing. Been so long since I've driven anywhere really except around downtown LA which is more like a human safari through Hell…" He looks lost. "So yeah, I was looking forward to it. Just me and the road, you know. But then…well."

You, I infer.

"I'm sorry I ruined your plans," he says, in a small voice.

"I didn't mean that. You didn't. Not at all." I scoot a little closer. "I mean technically I can still do that. It's three or four days tops from here to there and my mom's not expecting me until Friday. So, I still have time. Or it's a four-hour flight, so really it's not a big deal. You didn't ruin my plans."

"But technically you leave New York today?" He seems a little guarded still.

"No. Technically I leave my room at the Mandarin Oriental today. But New York has other hotels, I think."

I chance a half smile but his expression is frozen. Totally unreadable.

Clarity, Rapha. Jae likes clarity.

"I could stick around for a few more days," I tell him. "If that's something you would want."

When he lowers his eyes, I think I've fucked it. Come on too strong, again. Been too clear, again. What am I trying to do? Date him? A guy who lives on the other side of the fucking world. *A guy. Who lives on the other side of the fucking world.*

"But either way, it's no problem. I know you're super fucking busy, we both are really. And this has been fun so, no pressure, dude."

He glances up at me.

"Next time we're in the same city or whatever, maybe we can catch up?"

Catch up? Stop. Fucking. Talking. Raphael.

"*No pressure, dude,*" he says, in this weird tone that I realize is supposed to be mine.

I frown at him and he glowers up at me.

"What? What did I say?"

He rolls his eyes and turns onto his side, reaching across to the nightstand for his phone. "Forget it, Raphael."

Why do I always say the wrong thing with this guy? We're communicating in English, but he may as well be talking to me in Korean for all the shit I don't understand.

"I don't want to forget it, Jae. I want you to tell me what I said that's wrong so I don't do it again."

I hate how whiny my voice sounds and it looks like he does too, because the look he gives me does nothing to settle the curdled milk sensation in my stomach. He fixes his eyes back on his phone and starts scrolling. I'm pretty sure he isn't going to answer, but then he does, and in a quiet voice says:

"I cannot teach you everything."

It feels like I've been slapped again. I sit up, staring down at him but feeling small.

"I'm...I'm not asking you to, but you need to give me something here. I don't—"

"If you tell me again that you do not know what you are doing, or what this is I will scream, Raphael."

It's enough to silence me, my face and tongue burning hot. I deal with it how I deal with most things. Bravado.

"Yeah, well, I kinda like hearing you scream to be honest."

His fingers pause their scrolling and he slides his gaze up to mine, something warmer in them again. I reach out to run my hand up his thigh, skimming over the divots beneath his hips, and up to the little piercings he has there.

"Look, I'm not asking you to teach me everything, Jaehyun. But you have to help me out a little. I feel like I'm pissing in the wind with you sometimes. This is new for me—really fucking new. And honestly, I've never been all that great with knowing what women want either, so it's not necessarily a guy thing. But with you, especially, I'm scared to say or do the wrong thing, okay? I'm scared that you're gonna realize that there are a million other guys out there more experienced and better equipped to deal with…" I stop myself saying *whatever this is* just in time. "…better for you and you'll be done with me."

He gives me a long look. "Raphael, when I am done with you, you will know it."

"Yeah, and maybe that's part of the problem. Like I'm sitting around here waiting for you to get bored of me and it's stressing me the fuck out."

His eyes round, all big and guilty. "I am stressing you out?"

"No, not you. Just…this…a little. I mean, fuck…I don't know." I sigh and drag a hand through my hair.

Jae vaults up to sitting, shuffling closer so he's in my space. He places a hand on my cheek and forces me to meet his eyes.

"Hey, it's okay. Things are fine. You are doing really well." He soothes, like he's used to assuming this role. Of reassuring. Comforting. "I am sorry I am so difficult." He leans in to kiss me, chaste and soft. "There is no stress here, okay. Only fun. Only that."

Only that.

"*Fun?*"

He nods and kisses me again, deeper this time. "Fun." He reaches up to run his fingers through my hair. He looks to be thinking hard. "You could stay here for a few days. Until you must go to Colorado. We have one more concert the day after tomorrow and then some schedule before we leave for Korea."

Chest expanding with happiness, I smile at him. "You're inviting me to stay here? With you?"

There's a hesitant smile on his face. "Yes. If you like. But there is…no pressure, *dude*."

When he pulls this cute as fuck pouting face, I feel this strange fluttering in my stomach. Not butterflies, but close enough. I pull him onto me so he's settled on my lap, straddling my thighs, and kiss him roundly on the mouth.

"I'd really like that, *dude*."

He pulls back to grin happily at me before dropping his head into the crook of my shoulder. Drawing my fingers across his back, I do the same, inhaling deeply—he smells so fucking good here.

"And you're not difficult, by the way," I say softly. I didn't like how he said that, how his eyes looked when he said that. "You're just a bit of an enigma. At least to me."

"What is *enig-i-ma*?"

"Kinda mysterious, hard to figure out."

"Ah, I understand." He sighs. "I am sorry."

"Don't be. I like it. I like you…sort of a lot."

"I like you too, Raphael." He says very quietly.

It's only half true, that he's an enigma, because the Jae in my arms right now feels a lot less mysterious than he did a minute ago. This one is soft and sweet and likes to cuddle. It isn't a Jae I'd seen in any interview or music video, any photoshoot or Instagram story.

This was the real him and I'm pretty fucking sure I'm falling harder for him than all the others.

SEVENTEEN
RAPHAEL

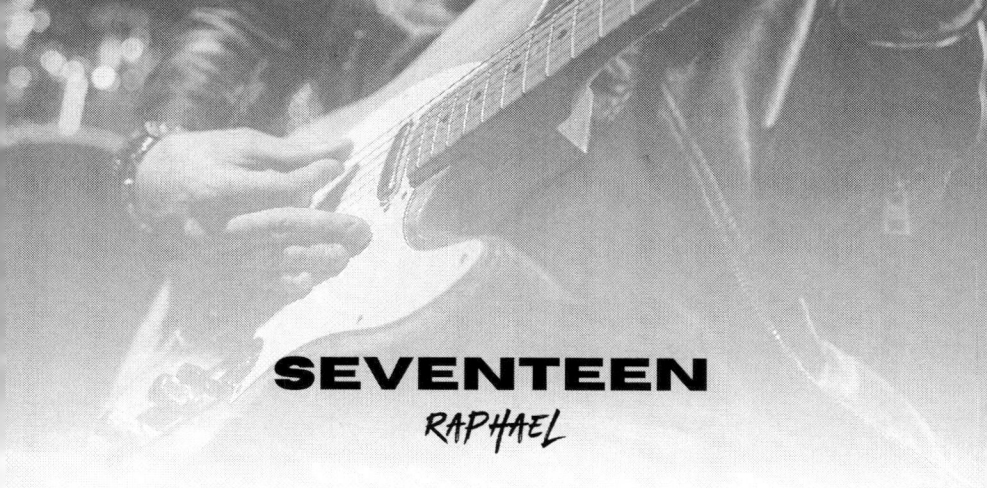

We make it to the Mandarin just after noon checkout. Not that I think they'd have thrown my shit out in the corridor or anything had I not gotten back in time, but I don't like being late for things. That *does* stress me out.

Jae had offered to come with me. Well, technically, he'd asked if I wanted to come with him to his 1 p.m. personal shopping appointment which I'd agreed to. I'd thought little about what might happen if we were spotted together—if he wasn't worried then I wasn't worried—and lots about what it would feel like to hang out with him for the day doing something *normal*. Not that having an appointment at a 5th Avenue designer store was exactly normal. It's the kind of shit Camille would do whenever we were in Paris, while I stayed home and gamed and it strikes me that Jae and Camille would probably get on well, in another universe, if I wasn't in the way.

In any case, I feel idiotically upbeat and stupidly excited by the prospect of spending the day with him, of staying at his apartment for the next few days, that not even the consequences of a rogue pap photo of us together can dampen. It's not like anyone is gonna assume we're fucking. I had heard him on a call with someone who I gathered was his manager, or certainly one of his people, and I also gathered that they weren't too happy about my going with him. But he seemed to have won out in the end and so we were going together.

I push all thoughts of Cam, and the conversation we're going to have to have real fucking soon, to the furthest recesses of my mind. I'm already thinking that I might be able to put it off until after Thanksgiving. After I spend some time at home. After I talk to my mom. After Jae and I see this thing through for the next few days and he flies home. *Then* I can look at everything with the benefit of distance and hindsight. I know I've no right to feel so fucking buoyant about all this, but I still do.

"I don't have too much stuff," I tell him, glancing at the driver. "I'll be ten minutes tops."

"I can come up and help you to pack?" He says 'pack' like he doesn't mean pack, he means fuck. It shoots straight to my dick.

I lean close and ghost my lips over his. "If you come up there we'll definitely miss check-out. They charge for that you know."

"I always miss check-out." He shrugs.

I give him a quick peck on the lips. Well, I mean for it to be quick, but his mouth is as hot and wet and addictive as it always is and it turns heavy. Then I remember we're not alone and so I pull back and glance sideways at the driver.

"Shit, sorry." I lick the taste of him from my lips.

He reaches up and puts his hand on my cheek, tenderly as he looks at me.

"Don't ever apologize for that." He smiles. "We are safe in here." To punctuate the point he kisses me, licking into my mouth a touch before pushing me away. "Go, hurry. I have many designer clothes to buy."

I debate settling my bill before I go upstairs, but the reception desk is busy given the time and so I swerve it and head straight for the elevators instead, slipping in just as they're closing. I've got my sunglasses on, but I keep my head low anyway. An older guy in his 60's asks for my floor number just as the doors sigh closed. I have a moment of panic when I reach my room, in that I've not a clue the last time I saw the key card, whether I even grabbed it as I left yesterday. But I find it in the inside pocket of my leather jacket, cursing with relief as I push open the door.

The room is spotless—the housekeeping service here alone is worth the five-star rating—and it takes me next to no time to throw what little I have into my weekender. A second pair of jeans, a couple t-shirts, a pair of gym shorts and vest, sneakers, a toilet bag, and my journal. I spend a few minutes looking for my laptop before I remember I didn't bring it. I'm wrapping my cell phone charger when there's a knock at the door I assume is housekeeping.

"Yeah, I'm almost done here," I shout as I glance around. I like to pack, wedge the door open with my bags, then do a last 'idiot check' before letting it close behind me. "You can come in."

I check the drawers by the bedside and am on my knees looking under the bed when a second knock comes. Room looks clear as I sling my bag over my shoulder and head for the door.

I'm *expecting* to see a housekeeper and a trolley there, but I'm *staring* at Camille gripping the handle of a small overnight suitcase.

I feel like I've been kicked in the face. She's wearing big sunglasses, an oversized coat, and one of those floppy hats she loves. She takes off her sunglasses and I see her make-up free face is blotchy and swollen. She looks miserable and tired and sad.

Wordlessly, I step back to let her into the room, closing it again as I drop my bag to the floor. She throws her shoulder bag and case on the bed and takes off her hat and tosses it on top, then turns to me.

"What are you doing here?" I manage. My body feels like I've just come off a rollercoaster, my legs weak and my breathing all out of sync with my heart.

She frowns at that. "What do you think I am doing here, Rapha? Trying to save our relationship. Checking you are alive. Making sure I am not paranoid and insane."

"But you were in Sydney." I point out. Like she was unaware. "When did you get here?"

Some look comes into her eyes that makes me feel cold and a little sick.

"I landed at seven. Got to the hotel just after nine."

I know what's coming before it does, and a cold sweat rises to the skin at the back of my neck.

"Of course, they wouldn't let me into your room even though they knew who I was. Who you were. Not hotel policy," she quotes. "They called up though."

I know I've got two options right then: lie and say that she knows how deeply I sleep when I'm drunk or high. Or tell the truth and admit that I didn't sleep in my hotel room last night.

I decide on a third. Silence. *Coward.*

"There was no answer, and your phone was turned off, so I waited in the lobby." She doesn't say that she saw me come in because she knows I know she did. "Where were you?"

I hold her eye as long as I can. While I run through all the scenarios in my head of what she might say or do if I tell her the truth. If I explain to the one person aside from my mother who knows me the best and gets me the most what the fuck is going on right now.

But I can't find the words. I know the longer it goes without me answering her question only makes it worse, but I'm confident there's no best way out of this. Not for her. Definitely not for me.

I swallow. Lick over my dry lips. It's enough of an answer for her because she lets out a horribly fragile breath and shakes her head, turning away from me. As I take a step towards her, my phone vibrates in my pocket. I had turned my phone off last night. I'd been trying to conserve energy after having it on me all day. I'd forgot to ask Jae for a charger. I'd only switched it back on as I'd packed. It doesn't have much juice left in it; I know that much. I can also guess who's just messaged me. Have I been up here longer than ten minutes?

"Cam, I'm sorry," I start, and she whips round to face me.

Angry silent tears streaming down her face. I feel like the biggest piece of shit that's ever existed. Maybe I am.

"Babe…look…I'm sorry I've ghosted. I just needed some space to think. I've been feeling….fuck, I don't even know. But I'm gonna head home, see my mom. Try and forget everything that I'm supposed to be and do and just try and figure it out. I didn't want to say all this over the phone, when you were out there working, alone…"

It sounds all over the place, but not untrue, not disingenuous. But Camille looks lost in it. Sad and angry and lost. "I don't know what's going on with me right now, okay…none of this is your fault." I drag a hand through my hair.

"Are you in love with her?" she asks, surprisingly calm.

I blink. "What? Who? No, it's not like that. There is no…her. It's more than that…it's…me. It's…"

Him.

Fuck, this is the worst I've ever felt. This right here. Like someone's peeling my skin open with a paring knife, slow and torturous.

"Then you were not with another woman last night?" Her tone is taught, hopeful.

I shake my head feeling like a liar and a charlatan and a coward all at the same time.

She lets out a soft breath, shoulders dropping with relief she has no right to feel. She nods and fixes me with a new kind of look.

"I don't understand where this has come from? We were good. We were happy, no?"

I nod. "I was happy…I was. But we're young, Cam. Like, stupidly young. The same age he was when he decided he wanted a wife and a family, and the same age when he decided he didn't."

Six months between that first decision and that second decision and my whole life had been tainted because of it.

"Twenty-four is too young to be standing in front of our friends and family and saying we wanna be together forever. I mean you're older, I know, but I still feel like a kid most days. And kids should not be anyone's husband. It's crazy. We'd be crazy to do that, don't you think? When we're still trying to figure out who we are? Who we want to be?"

I'm rambling now but she's listening, and she doesn't look quite as hopeless as she did and so I think—hope—maybe she agrees with me.

"So, this is about the wedding? You don't want to get married?" She makes a very French noise. "Rapha, puppy, I don't care about the wedding. You proposed to me? I said yes because I love you and because I thought it was what you wanted, what you needed. But we don't need to get married." She laughs, sounding relieved as she comes toward me. "We can take our time, focus on us or our careers or whatever, if that is what you want."

She reaches out to touch me, her hand threading through my hair. Jae had done something similar this morning. It had felt just as comforting as this does. I close my eyes and lean into her touch. I feel selfish for taking it.

The vibration of my cell phone ringing again disturbs the heavy moment. My eyes flash open and she's peering up at me. When I reach into my pocket and see his name on the screen my chest feels tight again. When I glance at Cam the soft understanding look on her face from a second ago starts to bleed into suspicion.

How long will he wait for me? What the fuck is he going to think when I don't answer and when I don't appear back at the car like I promised I would? My heart feels like it's being ripped in two.

But then all at once, I see everything really clearly. I see what I want and what I need and my body and mind move toward those goals without thought.

"Sorry, I need to take this," I tell her as I move toward the balcony. Outside, I close the door behind me and answer the call.

"If you make me late for my shopping appointment I will not do as I planned to do later. Which is too rude to say in front of others." He purrs this last part down the phone.

I swallow to clear my throat. "Jae, um, I got here and…well, Camille's here. I didn't know. I mean she was in Australia, and I never expected—."

"So, you are not coming?"

"I can't. I'm sorry. I have to talk to her. Explain…"

"Very well," he says bluntly. "Good luck with your talk."

And then the line goes dead. I hold the phone to my ear for a good thirty seconds after he hangs up, wondering how on earth it can feel like I have everything and nothing at the same time.

When I turn, I see Camille sitting on the bed inside, watching me cautiously. I let out a breath and turn my back to her to look out over Central Park.

If I give up on this thing with Jae, whatever it is, whatever it might come to be, I know I'm going to spend my life wondering about it. Wondering who I could have been. Is this really where it has all been heading? Towards him? Am I a guy who is sexually, artistically, and emotionally open to whatever comes his way, or am I a guy who keeps promises and doesn't hurt people? Am I a guy who takes after his father? Is this the great awakening I'd always assumed would hit me at some point? I'd always thought it would be about Finn. That I would finally believe that I was absolutely the best version of myself without him. I thought too that it would be some kind of creative awakening, something spiritual in some way. Not this kind of...awakening. Except, being with Jaehyun does feel spiritual on some level, holy and right; like enlightenment.

What sort of person would Jaehyun make me? What sort of person would Camille make me? Because we take on parts of those people we love and are loved by, bad and good, and though I'm not sure I can use the word love when it comes to Jae, not yet. I know I've never felt this kind of all-consuming passion for someone before. For music, yeah, but never for another person.

That alone should be all the encouragement I need. To turn around right this second and tell Camille it's over. To go for this. To see where it takes me.

Except, going for it, for him, is about a lot more than amazing sex in New York apartments where no one could see us. It's hurting people I care about and having the way people see me change forever. The latter doesn't bother me, not really. Sure, I don't want my mom or my friends to see me any differently, but I could give two shits about how the world at large sees me. I think about the band: Cleo and Zeke would be fine with me being with a guy. Mason and Crawf less so. While where I stuck my cock had never been an issue for them before, I'm not so sure they'd be quite as understanding about its new direction.

And this is before I consider what Jae wants. He'd spoken

about the fact that he keeps his private life private. About the issues with his parents. For all I know, a proper relationship with him is out of the question. Because being with me means that it's gonna be loud and public. The paparazzi will have a field day with this.

I've almost forgotten about Camille and what I owe her, when the sound of the glass door sliding open tugs me from my thoughts. Soft footsteps of her walking across it. She leans on the balcony next to me, mirroring my view out onto the park. I'm not sure how long it is before she speaks, her voice stronger than it had been since she'd arrived.

"This is about more than the wedding, isn't it?" she says.

When I look at her, she's looking up at me, searching my face for clues about what it *is* about. I nod and she lets out a deep breath, nodding too as she straightens her spine.

"Is there someone else?"

It's a slightly different question to the one she asked earlier. The one that allowed me to use a contortionist's trick to get around.

"Yeah," I admit and my voice is so fucking small. "I'm so sorry, Cam, I don't know how it happened. I really don't. It was nothing, and then it was..." *everything*. "But it happened and I don't know what I'm gonna do. I never wanted to hurt you. It wasn't like that. It's never been like that with us...I've always been...it's always been you."

Maybe it's how small and weak and pathetic I sound, but she doesn't look pissed at me. She looks like she feels sorry for me.

"Not always," she says. "Not now."

I bite and chew at my mouth. "I just need some time, okay? Can you give me that? Until after Thanksgiving? I need to figure some shit out. Talk to my mom. A priest. A Rabbi. There's a famous goat outside our town that can see the future. I'll talk to that too."

She gives me a small smile I don't deserve. "Will you also ask it if I will win an Oscar this year?"

I laugh miserably and she smiles a little wider, some life flooding back into her eyes again.

"I do love you, you know," I tell her.

"I love you too."

She drops her head onto my shoulder, and I rest mine against hers. I want to keep her in my life. In whatever form that is. I hate losing things and I'm not ready to lose her, which is what I'm sure will happen as soon as I say this out loud. A deep breath in and her hair smells of summer and flowers. Light and familiar. While my heart feels almost like a stranger.

막간
(JAE'S INTERLUDE #1)

I barely hear Sung-Ho speak over the noise in my ears. Panic. Fear. Anger. *Idiot. Idiot. Idiot.* They all make the same noise in my head. It's over. So soon? Except it's not too soon. It's too late. It's already too late. *Idiot.*

"Straight to the store now, yes?" He checks.

"Yes, Sungho-ssi."

He nods and pulls away from the drop-off area of the hotel and into the heavy New York traffic. I don't know New York very well, but I think we are still on time for the store, though the last thing I want to do now is try on pretty clothes and stare at myself in the mirror. At all the parts of myself I don't like. At all the parts of myself that are not enough for Raphael.

Sudden and loud, my cell phone rings and my heart trips in my chest. I hold a breath as I look down at the ID. Hope deflates. Kai-Hyung.

Ji-hoon hasn't spoken to me for two days. Not a word since he told me, in front of Raphael that he didn't know who I was anymore. That he hasn't known me for a while. Which is ironic because he'd once told me the problem with us was that he knew me *too well*. As a friend. A bandmate. A brother. It was why he couldn't truly see us as anything else. He believed that to be true, and so I always let him think that I did too.

But of course, I knew the truth, I was not enough; I never have been. Not for him. Not for my parents. Not for Raphael.

"I am busy, Hyung," I answer, entirely not in the mood to have this conversation now.

We would have to deal with our argument soon, the others

would force the issue sooner. But I do not want to have it right this moment. Not when my head is this loud.

His tone is short when he asks, "With your American?"

I hate the sense of loss I get at the idea that he will never be my American.

"With Gucci."

"You are shopping?"

Why does he sound so surprised? It's the only thing I do when we're in New York. I hadn't had a chance to do it yet, with schedule and work, and Raphael, but he shouldn't sound so shocked by the notion certainly.

"I am on my way there now."

"Alone?" The implication is clear.

"Alone."

"Then I'll come. Where are you?"

I sigh. "Perhaps I wish to shop alone, Hyung. Just because you wish to speak to me now doesn't mean I feel the same."

He lets out a tired sounding sigh not unlike my own, but his voice is soft when he says: "Jaehyun-ah. We need to talk. Ji-u spoke to me last night. You know how he feels when we fight."

"We are not fighting." I decide to correct that statement. "I am not fighting."

He sighs again and I relent.

"Fine. I will send you the location."

I hang up without a goodbye. An uneasy weight sits on top of the already heavy feeling in my chest, because despite my protest, we *are* fighting. And I hate fighting with Ji-hoon. I hate fighting with anyone, but especially him. When we fight it always feels like a physical thing, like an ache or a pain somewhere deep inside my body that I can't reach with stretching or mindfulness. It's only that I've had a distraction these past two days. A surprisingly sweet, surprisingly nuanced distraction. A distraction that tastes of whiskey and want and who looks at me like I might be the only one he has truly desired.

I glance down at my cell as I worry my lip with my teeth and imagine all the things that might be happening between Raphael and his girlfriend. The woman he told me was to be his ex-girlfriend. I imagine tearful words and weighted apologies. I imagine being painted as a horrible mistake and moment of madness. I imagine tight hugs and fervent kisses.

The taste of him floods my tongue, hot whiskey-spiced kisses, and I reach for the bottle of water in the cupholder so I can wash it away. I should laugh at myself. I have been such an idiot. I was being careful, so careful. It was nothing. It had been only fun. Right up until last night, at least. When he'd looked at me over the softly popping bubbles in the bath, cheeks and mouth bright red, eyes a glittering Californian ocean I would have been happy to drown in and I'd felt something I cannot ever remember feeling before except on stage. I had felt enough. More than enough.

You're incredible.

You're so fucking beautiful.

I contemplate deleting our text conversations and blocking his number, but the pathetic part of me is not ready to give him up just yet.

They have several private rooms on the first floor of the building to which they lead me, Sung-Ho acting as driver and security today following me inside. He speaks very little English, so I act as interpreter for him when the personal shopper offers us both a drink. He refuses and takes a seat by the door, pulling out his phone to busy himself while he waits. I accept water and follow the petite woman to the three racks of clothes she has pre-selected for me.

"I have someone joining me soon, I hope that is no problem?" I tell her as I flick through the items.

"Ah, of course not. No problem. I'll just make a quick call down to advise the front. Please feel free to try on whatever you like. The dressing room is just there." She points to a carpeted area behind the racks. "I'll be right back."

I pull out a long grey coat with vintage style buttons on the front and cuffs, checking the size before I drape it over my arm. Then I move along the rack. There's a light shirt of blue silk with handcrafted yellow embroidery that would look perfect on Raphael. A pair of jeans and a pair of the high-tops he wears. His leather jacket. I think about buying it for him and then I laugh because the chances are I won't even see him again. I shove it back on the rack.

"Ah, I love this," the assistant says as she reappears behind me. "Such a great color. The poplin cotton means it's an all-season item too. Coats aren't just for winter."

She smiles, sticking her hand out to take it from me. She moves to hang it carefully on an empty rack she's set aside from the others.

"I watched the show online," I tell her. "You have the monogram military jacket?" I'm scanning the row of outerwear but can't see it. "And the padded blouson? In green?"

She looks a little off kilter.

"Of course! I didn't select it because your team said you were keen on greys and neutrals."

"It is not for me."

She nods, gesturing toward a sharply dressed guy in a suit who looks to be around twenty standing off to the side.

I hadn't even noticed him before. A silent sentinel. She asks him to bring both items from the stock room and he marches off to obey, not before blinking a kind of startled, dumbstruck look in my direction. He's cute. Asian descent with nice hands and a full mouth. His ass looks good in the pants he's wearing too. She points out a few more items before getting the message that if I need her help, I'll ask for it. So, she steps away with her tablet and busies herself.

I'm wearing a navy trunk striped kimono jacket and admiring my reflection when Ji-hoon appears behind me in the dressing room. He's dressed in what I'd call military casual. A style that I'm certain went out of fashion a decade ago but somehow still looks good on him. Oversized green bomber with a black Balenciaga hoodie beneath, Supreme cargo pants, and ridiculous colored (bright yellow) trainer boots. He's wearing sunglasses and a ballcap which he takes off as he sits down. He runs a hand over his head and sits forward, legs spread, as he leans on his knees. Appraising me, there's a familiar heat in his eye that I drink up greedily. It fills some of the cold inside my chest.

"I like it," he says.

"Then I won't buy it."

He laughs quietly and sits back in the seat as I go inside to change out of it.

Of course, I'm buying it. It looks great. Everything I've tried on has looked great, has given me the familiar warm bubbly feeling from trying on nice things and looking good in them.

The feeling that disappears as soon as I take them off. Some jewelry will help too. Dressed in my own clothes, I wander outside to where the jewelry has been laid out in a wide but shallow display box, lights affixed to each corner.

Kai wanders over to stand beside me, scent of rich wood and citrus flooding my nose, warm body a comfort pressed next to my own. It calms my racing head. Slows my pulse. Eases the tightness in my chest. He's always had that ability. Calm. Strong. Dependable. Like the Sobaek Mountains. It's why he's our leader. It's why everyone turns to him when they're lonely or sad, especially me.

"I'm sorry," he says quietly.

It doesn't matter since the assistant and her…assistant do not speak Korean, but I appreciate the gentleness with which he says it. There's no bitterness or resentment. No weight or expectation that I will return it. Just an apology. Genuine and warm. Like Ji-hoon.

"I am sorry too."

He's quiet for a moment, staring at the pretty silver jewelry in front of us. "I don't want to lecture you, Jaehyun-ah, but sometimes I feel it is my job to."

"It is not your job to lecture me about who I fuck." I look at him. "Even when it was you I was fucking."

He blanches at that as he lifts his head up. Whatever he sees in my eyes has him looking away again. Guilty. "I know that."

"Do you?" I ask. "Because it has not always felt like you do. I never saw you as my leader when you were in my bed."

He raises an eyebrow. "No. You didn't."

My cheeks heat. "I don't always need a leader, Hyung. Sometimes I need a friend."

And outside of Ji-u, Ji-hoon is my best friend. It was what made our sleeping together so incredibly stupid. It was why we had had to be careful. In the end, Ji-hoon had been far more careful than me. I could not have survived without him. He was more than my band leader and friend—he was my confidante. The first person I told when I knew what I was. The person I called when I held those pills in my hand and thought about how easy it would be. The person who I clung to when my father told me no matter what I achieved I'd always be a disappointment to him. Because of what I was. What I wasn't.

"And then as your friend, I am asking why would you do this? *Him*?" He's wide-eyed now, cool demeanor cracked.

"You are sure you are asking this as my friend?" I give him a skeptical look.

"Yes. I am, Jaehyun-ah. I don't get it, him. After what you told me…how he made you feel."

His eyes harden, glassy with anger. I should never have told him what Raphael and his bandmates had said that day. I look down.

"He…he's not good enough for you. He's not fit to touch you…"

"He is sorry," I say.

"What?"

"About what he said that day. He has apologized." I look back at the cabinet. "I pretended. I told him that I didn't remember. I'm not sure if he believed me. But I believe him. That he is sorry. He sounded sorry."

I see Ji-hoon swallow, still angry, cheeks tight and hard. He's furious actually, but it's not with me. It's with Raphael.

"Why did you pretend you didn't remember?" he asks, still frowning. "Why didn't you tell him how he made you feel?"

"I don't know."

It's the honest answer. I don't know why. Except that we were in the car after I'd almost broken his nose and he looked embarrassed about it and I hated seeing him like that. I don't think Ji-hoon would understand that reasoning, however. I'm not sure *I* understand it.

"He insulted you. He insulted your friends," Ji-hoon says.

I feel exceptionally small then. Foolish and small. "I know."

I hate this. Ji-hoon, disappointed in me.

"I'm sorry I upset you."

He sighs. "Fuck. I'm not upset, Jaehyun-ah. I could never be upset with you; I've never been upset with you." He looks utterly sincere and it makes me want to cry. "I just don't want to see you upset. Hurt. By someone like him."

"I don't…think he meant to say those things. You know what these kinds of men are like. They don't like what they do not understand. But the man I know now, he's different, softer. Sweeter. He says what he wants and what he feels. Except when he's unsure. And sometimes he's so unsure. Like a child."

"You need a man, not a child, Jaehyun."

"Now you are so well versed on what I need?"

Especially as Ji-hoon has always been silent about the things I seem to want and need from men. About the things I needed and wanted from him once.

He stares at me a long time. "I have always known, Jaehyun. It was that I could never give them to you."

I feel guilty about that, about the sadness in his tone. It has always felt like there is a secret part of Kai, some sad tortured part that he hides from the world, something that would finally explain why he could never give me the things I'd once asked him for, begged him for.

"You like him," Kai says after a moment. It's not a question.

"Yes. I do. He makes me feel…" I don't know what he makes me feel. Not sad. Not a disappointment. Almost, *almost*, enough. "Special. The way you do."

He looks very serious when he says: "If he hurts you, I will ruin him."

Oh, he is going to hurt me, Hyung. It is only a matter of time before he hurts me. He may already have. It's what I almost tell him. But I don't see what good it can do.

Instead, I reach out to cup his cheek which is soft and warm. I love him. His protective nature. His solidity and dependability. His existence so integral to my own in a way. He's always been there. Comforting me in whatever way I need whenever I need it. When I needed discipline, he was there. When I needed a large pair of arms, he was there. When I needed a warm, tender, body to make me feel something other than bone-deep exhaustion and self-doubt, he was there for that too. I climbed into his bed time and time again and he gave me what I needed. Except that final part of himself. He is love and stoic loyalty; there is no man on earth as loyal as Kim Ji-hoon.

"Thank you, Hyung," I whisper.

Just then the assistant nudges into our private moment to ask if there is anything in the lightbox of trinkets that I want. I choose a few rings and a couple of sets of earrings and tell her to bag up my purchases.

Kai spots the grey overcoat I pulled off the rack when I first came in and his eyes light up.

"This absolutely isn't your color," he tells me, clutching the fabric to his chest covetously.

"I know. It is for you," I say as I hand my card to the assistant.

Kai flashes me a wide grin of thanks, which makes him look ten years younger.

As she's ringing it all up, I wander back to first rack and pull out the blue silk shirt with yellow embroidery, in what I'm certain is Raphael's size, and add it to the pile. I suppose if this is all over then I can wear it while crying over bokkeumbap.

Ji-hoon comes back to the apartment with me, and we order in while catching up with Kingdom on Netflix. He'd already seen the episode but seems content enough to sit through it again. I didn't feel like being alone. I'd switched off my cell phone and left it charging by the bedside while we ate and talked and got comfortable on the couch.

It's around 9 p.m. when the doorbell sounds. I glance at Ji-hoon for some reason, as though he can see through walls and doors, though I'm certain I don't need him to, because I know it's Raphael. I *feel* it. No one else would turn up here, not without calling. And since my cell is next door and the members know we are together, they would call him if they couldn't get me. It's Raphael. I know it is.

Ji-hoon makes no move to sit up but reaches for the remote to pause the show. He gives me a look.

"Do you want me to answer it?" he asks.

I'm not sure if he also knows who it is, but he looks a little tense.

I shake my head and stand, running a hand through my hair as I go. Had he tried to call before coming over? If this is finished, would I rather have heard it from his disembodied voice over the phone? Probably. Except Raphael is exactly the kind of person who would feel the need to do this in person. I'm sure of it. Stupid, ridiculous, American.

I pull open the door to find him standing there like a dog who has been lost for weeks and has somehow found his way back home. Eyes big and round with uncertainty. Then I notice his bag. A hopeful warmth rushes at me so fast I can't breathe.

"Hey," he says. "So, I was hoping that offer to stay here for a few days was still valid?"

I'm not sure what look I have on my face but it doesn't deter him at all, because he leans in and ghosts his mouth over mine. Gentle and unsure but so warm.

Stunned, I let him kiss me.

"I'm sorry about earlier," he says. "I never expected she'd show up. I mean, I should have, Cam is…well…she's forward, kinda like you are, but yeah, I'm sorry I ditched. I just had to speak to her you know." He looks down, guiltily. "I owed her that."

"Everything okay, Jaehyun-ah?" Kai's stern voice comes from behind us, and Raphael's head snaps up.

He straightens, eyes darkening as they go over my shoulder. From innocent and sweet to…suspicious, angry. The thought that it might be jealousy has that awful part of me singing. They watch each other, these two men who are terribly important to me, like cats might. Stiff and tall. Eyes hard as glass. I wonder who will hiss first. When the atmosphere is dense enough to see, I speak.

"You are still welcome to stay," I tell Raphael as I open the door wider.

Raphael still looks suspicious. Glancing from me to Ji-hoon, biting the inside of his lip. Something he does a lot.

"For God's, sake come in. I am not going to hit you," Ji-hoon hisses before leaving us alone in the hallway.

Raphael watches Kai go before flicking his eyes back to me, indecisiveness playing in his ocean eyes. They're so blue when he's unsure. Greyer when he is.

"He won't hit you," I confirm.

"I'm not afraid of him hitting me," he scowls, throwing a death glare back in the direction of the living room.

I step closer to him, placing my hand flat on his chest. His heart is beating hard and fast. Like thunder under his skin. Body warm to the touch.

"Then what are you afraid of?" I ask him.

He gives me an open look. Childlike.

"Honestly? Everything. I'm scared of everything right now, Jae."

And he sounds afraid. Voice trembling with vulnerability. I want to protect him. From anyone and everything that might want to hurt him. From Ji-hoon. From myself. I reach up and stroke my fingers across his cheek.

"Everything will be okay," I say as I brush a section of his dark blonde hair off his forehead. "I promise it will all be okay."

He leans into my touch and closes his eyes. A soft noise escaping his throat. When I reach up and press a kiss to his neck, over his pulse, a shiver moves through his whole body. He grips my hips and pulls me into him, pressing his nose to the top of my head where he inhales deeply.

"Fuck, I can't think past you," he whispers like a confession.

He squeezes me tight and then he's moving inside the apartment and closing the door behind him. Holding me to him, he noses at my hair and scents my skin and then he's kissing me. Forceful and a little desperate.

"I missed you," he breathes. "How can I have missed you this much?"

He kisses down my jaw to my throat and then he's sucking over my pulse, beneath my ear, along my collarbone. I must stop before I let him fuck me in the hallway with Ji-hoon next door.

"I missed you too," I say, pulling back to smile up at him. "But let's wait until we are alone for this. Okay?"

He blinks, seeming to remember we are not alone. "Fuck. Yeah, sorry, I just… sorry." He looks a little embarrassed.

I give him a warm smile and grab his hand, before reaching down to lift the leather bag he practically kicked into the apartment. When we reach the living room, Ji-hoon is sitting back on the sofa looking at home. He glances at us as we come in, noting our joined hands with a flicker of surprise. I see him consider something, then he stands and comes toward us.

"Kim Ji-hoon." He sticks his hand out to Raphael. "Or Kai. I don't mind."

Raphael looks at Ji-hoon's hand like it might be about to bite, before reaching out to clasp it in a firm grip.

"Raphael. Or Rapha. I don't mind either."

I observe them both as they stand face to face. Raphael standing a little taller but not by much, leanly muscled—American boy pretty—against Kai's darker, more threatening persona.

There's nothing similar in them. Nothing at all. But I think they're possibly the most beautiful men I've ever seen in real life. Exceptionally attractive but in completely different ways. I try not to think about what it might feel like to be fucked by both of them at the same time, but of course it's impossible.

"For some reason, Jaehyun has decided that you are important to him. Which means that if you so much as think about hurting him, in any way whatsoever, that face of yours will not look so pretty when I am finished." From anyone else the threat would sound overly dramatic, ridiculous, but said in Ji-hoon's low careful way, it carries weight.

Raphael blinks but recovers well.

"You think I'm pretty? Wow, dude, I'm flattered." He flashes some sexy smile at Ji-hoon that I can only gape at. "You're not exactly my type, but I can appreciate the aesthetic you're going for all the same." He draws a leisurely gaze down Kai's body before pulling me closer to him. "But you don't have to worry about him. I've no intention of letting anything hurt him."

Kai stares at Raphael for a few long moments, nostrils flaring angrily, before he lets out a breath. His eyes soften when he looks at me.

"I'll see you tomorrow," he says. He moves to grab his bomber jacket from the barstool, throws one last death glare in Raphael's direction, and leaves.

When the apartment door closes, the silence swells into the space, between us tense and brittle.

"So, you and him were together then," he turns to face me. "As a couple. That's true?"

I try to process *that*. "What?"

"You know. All that fucking crazy shit online about you two, it's true, isn't it?"

He read *crazy shit* online about us?

"Is that a question?"

He shifts on his feet. "Yeah. I mean… if you and him are a thing then I figure I should know."

"You wish to know if Ji-hoon and I are a thing?"

"Yeah."

"Do you think I would be here with you, fucking you and having baths with you and inviting you to stay in my apartment if Ji-hoon and I were together?"

He looks around as though he has lost something. "I don't know… maybe… yeah. I don't know what sort of situation-ship you guys have going and whether I'm just, like, a spare for you." He looks painfully uncomfortable as he rubs the back of his neck and avoids my eyes.

A spare for me. I am not even sure if I understand what that is, but I do not think it's good.

"I mean, you don't owe me anything. Like this isn't a relationship, I get that, I'd just like to know where I stand before this goes some place. I mean, if it is going to go someplace, if it even can go someplace…" He struggles. "I just…"

"Ask me what you want to know, Raphael," I say, snappier than I mean to. "You want to know about my situation boat with Ji-hoon, then ask me. Do not assume anything about what we are. If you want to know something, then ask me. I have tried to be clear with you, no? Always. So, then I will be clear with you now, ask me what you want to know."

He stiffens, eyes going from ocean blue to twilight. "Are you fucking him? Like, do you fuck him?"

"Right now? No."

His nostrils flare. "But you have? In the past."

"Yes."

He wants to ask more, and I realize that feeding him it in this way is not helping either of us. And it makes things decidedly unclear. I sigh.

"But not for at least six months, perhaps more. It is something we did when we felt…alone, I suppose. It was easy for us. What else do you want to know?"

He swallows, straightens up, something soft and vulnerable creeping into his eyes. "Do you wish he were here right now? Instead of me? Like, do you wish I hadn't shown up tonight? So, you could have…been with him instead?"

"No, Raphael, I don't." I shake my head. "I haven't stopped thinking about you all day. Wondering whether I would ever see you again. Wondering whether you and your girlfriend were fucking in your room while I looked at pretty, overpriced clothes." My mouth is completely out of control at this point but I can't seem to stop it from moving, admitting things. "Wondering if you told her about us. Whether you lied about me. Wondering if you told her I was a mistake."

I didn't want to be that to him. God, please not to him. Because I don't understand how I could ever be anything else to anyone else now.

"But when I opened that door and saw you standing there..." I take a deep breath. "I felt relieved. Happy. *Warm* and happy. When I am with you, I feel... happy." And enough. "Happier than I can remember feeling for a long time."

He stares at me a few beats, the softest hint of smile inching over his mouth, before walking towards me slowly. My chest starts to feel very strange and tight. And as he licks his lips, I feel the want stir between my legs. Those soft red lips he's always biting or licking around me, those small white teeth that I love to feel pressing into my skin. He brushes a hand through the thick locks that sit messily on top of his head and my gaze clings to the shape of his fingernails, the golden tan of his arms, the jumbled ink over them, surprisingly dainty wrists.

He is perfect, I think with a cold sort of clarity. Like the hero in an American high-school movie that always gets the girl. *The girl. The girl.* A walking Abercrombie and Fitch poster boy. Calvin Klein model in a rockstar skin.

"Is that all or is there something else you want to know?" My voice is scratchy and low.

His mouth curls up, a sexy smirk that would look arrogant on someone else but looks playful on him.

"Yeah, there's one more thing," he wraps his arms around me, warm and strong and just a little too tight. I enjoy the sensation. When he pushes his hips into mine, I feel the hardness at the front of his jeans and it causes my stomach to somersault, arousal to kindle.

"What?" I whisper as he leans in to kiss me. His eyes wide open.

"Do you only ever take a bath after sex?" He rubs his slightly stubbled jaw against my own before nosing behind my ear. "Cause I really wanna take another bath with you."

EIGHTEEN
RAPHAEL

Happier than I can remember feeling in a long time. Warm and Happy.

They aren't complicated words. They're simple. Really simple. I know what they mean. And yet as he lies sleeping next to me, snoring softly and cutely I still can't comprehend them. That he said them, about me.

Jae has always been like a complex puzzle with a hundred moving parts and where the instructions are in another language. I'd blundered my way through this thing with him by instinct and raging lust alone. This beautiful enigma lying next to me is still a virtual stranger, and yet by telling me that I feel like he's just given me the instructions. Or some of them anyway.

I made him happy. I have *that* kind of power. Knowing I have any effect on him at all is a heady fucking feeling. It makes me feel important. Terrified too, because if I have the power to make him happy, then the opposite had to be true, right? Despite what I told Kai. I could hurt Jae. It was possible. It's the last thing I want but it's still *possible*.

It hurts my head and my heart to think about that. I sit up and look down at him. He's clutching a pillow to his chest, another between his knees. Soft almost-smile on his face.

We'd fooled around in the tub, making out for what felt like hours, his hands tracing over my tattoos as he rubbed himself against me. Slow and languorous. I'd pulled his tongue and fingers and nipples into my mouth, marveling at how he tasted. A forbidden thing that made me feel more alive than I ever had. I'd sucked the water from the dips of his throat and bitten down on the soft warm skin of his shoulders as I'd gotten him off with my hand. Then he'd urged me up onto the side of the tub and swallowed me whole until I saw heaven in his eyes.

After, silent in words but loud in looks, he'd shown me a few drawers and places inside his closet where I could put my stuff. Domestic shit that I hadn't done with Camille until we'd moved in together. There had been a blue silk shirt hanging by itself in this section of closet, Gucci tags still hanging from the cuff, yellow bees or something on it. He'd gestured vaguely at it.

"I picked that up for you today," he said, suddenly not looking at me. "It is the same color as your eyes. It will look good on you."

It would. I reached up and slid it from the hanger. The size was mine, the richness of the fabric making it feel formal but with a casual look. When I pulled it on, he'd turned, a small, satisfied smile settling over his mouth.

He'd picked it up for me today. When he thought I was fucking Camille. When he thought I was telling her he was a mistake. I could only stare at him in complete worship a few minutes, as he went back to refolding pajamas.

It was easy to imagine it then. Us. Together. Easier still to forget everything else that would need to be fixed and explained first and just imagine us existing here as…a couple. I want it too. Fiercely. I'm sure I just need him to say it's what he wants too and I'm all the way in. Fuck, I already am most likely. I don't have all the instructions yet, but maybe I don't really need them. Maybe all I need is a nod and look from him so I know I'm doing something right.

As he sleeps on, I lean down and kiss his cheek, nosing over his pulse before climbing out of bed. I grab my journal from the front pocket of my bag and slide closed the bedroom door behind me.

The page in front of me has a few lines about New York. About its scale, its mass, about the way you can lose yourself in it. Words and sentences that I like but that don't necessarily mean much until I start to pull them together. I haven't written anything in weeks. Not because I'm dry, but because I'm afraid of what will come out. Now, I don't feel that same fear. Now I scribble down words of self-realization and fate, of regret and guilt, of lust and need. The raw taste of twilight. It sounds like a love song. But not about New York. About something New York possesses tonight. One single perfect thing that no other city on earth has.

And he's asleep in the next room.

I realize it's the first love song I've ever written.

Mase calls me the night before I'm due to leave for Colorado. Voice weird and weighty like he would rather be doing literally anything else but this. I pay little attention to it, too wrapped up in Jae. He was due back soon and I'd had this awful antsy feeling all day.

He'd been a little weird this morning. Distant. It had taken most of the day, but I think I'd figured out what it was: he was starting to pull back. To make arrangements for when he went home to Korea. Maybe I should start doing the same. But the words *happier than I can remember feeling in a long time. Warm and happy,* feel like a reason to cling on. Like they're a life raft in the middle of a dark ocean. I don't even know if after four days together, or rather four nights because his days were packed full beyond belief, if it was still even true. Did I still make him feel like that? I'd never ask.

"So, I guess we should talk," Mason starts with.

"Yeah, I guess we should." I wait him out because yeah, he might have made the first move and called, but he was still an asshole.

"Are you seriously this pissed about what I said about Cleo's brother?"

"You think that's what this is about?"

"Isn't it?" His voice sounds a little uncertain now.

"I mean yeah. And no. You were out of order, man. I'm not having that shit in our band, Mase."

He scoffs a little at that. "*Our band?* Feels like your fucking band a lot of the time, Rapha. Now you're gonna tell me what to say? What to think?"

I ignore most of that. "Yeah. If you're gonna think like a fucking red neck, I'm gonna call you out on it."

"Well, I am a red neck, my dude. What do you want me to do about it?" He smooths out his Arkansas drawl most of the time, but he lays it on thick now.

"This what you called for? Cause I've got shit to do, man." I pinch the bridge of my nose. "But you best fix your fucking attitude before we're back in the studio, cause this isn't gonna fly."

He sighs, loudly. "What's going on with you and Cam?"

The change of direction brings me up hard like whiplash, tilting the hairs on the back of my neck.

"What are you talking about?"

"She called me," he says, like it's the most normal thing in the world. It isn't. "Told me to talk to you as you 'might need a friend right now'. I guess you didn't tell her about our little fight."

No, I hadn't told her, because I'd been avoiding her.

"So, you're what, my girlfriend's *bestie* now, dude?"

"No but, she's under the illusion we're friends, I guess."

"Yeah? You tell her about *our little fight* then? What you said about Asher?"

He does another of his sighs. "We've been friends for nearly six years Rapha, you know I'm not a fucking homophobe."

"Do I?"

"Yeah, you do!" he growls. "It's just words, man. I don't give a shit about any of that, okay, Jesus. Let it go."

"Okay, how about this. You tell Cleo what you called her brother—Cleo who fucks women by the way—and if she's cool with it, then I guess I am too. Tell your bestie Cam too while you're at it and let me know if she still thinks you're a stand-up guy."

"You're acting like an idiot, man. This shit never bothered you this much before."

"Yeah, well, it does now."

"Fine. Well, now I know."

"Fine," I snap.

We're both angrily silent for a few seconds before he says, again. "What's going on with you, Rapha? What does Cam mean?" He waits me out but I don't say a word. "Look, I know you hate me right now but I am still here if you wanna, like, talk."

Right now, he's the last person on earth I'd talk to about any of this.

"I'm...taking some time," I offer. "To think about some stuff. Relationship stuff. Personal stuff."

He makes a weird scoffing noise, like it's the most ridiculous thing he's ever heard. It makes me want to reach through the phone and punch him.

"*Relationship stuff?* You're getting married in three months. The fuck do you need time for, dude?"

"Honestly, Mason, it's none of your fucking business."

He seems to ponder this and agree, because next he says: "Have you been writing?"

"A little."

"So, you're back in LA when?"

"I'll see you at the studio on the 30th. As planned." It comes out sharp as a knife.

"Listen, I didn't call to give you shit."

"No, you called because my girlfriend asked you to."

"No, I called because I acted like a prick and I don't know how else to say sorry, okay?"

This shocks me into silence.

"Look, Rapha, you're my best friend. I just...ach, I don't know. But I'm here, okay. Like if you want to talk. About whatever."

He sounds miserable and it makes me feel guilty. Great, so I'm two from two on how shit I've made two of my best friends feel the last two days. Maybe when I go home, I can shit all over my mom too.

"Yeah, okay. Thanks." It comes out sounding less than sincere. "We'll talk when I'm back in LA."

I sense movement behind me, and I turn.

Jae is standing at the edge of the kitchen counter, watching me closely. His eyes skip to the oven, then back to me, then at the table by the window which I'd set and prepared with I guess what looks like a romantic dinner for two. There's a candle and some flowers and a bottle of wine chilling in the cooler. He smiles and it's this beautiful shy thing that warms up my insides immediately. *Warm and happy.* That distance and coldness from this morning nowhere in sight.

"Gotta go, Mase," I mutter before hanging up.

"Sorry I'm late. I didn't know you had plans." Jae gestures at the table.

"You're not late," I lie. He is. Almost an hour, in fact. But he'd texted and so I was prepared. Had been for the last hour. "Wine?"

He nods. "Please."

He looks tired. Beautiful but tired. He's dressed in a formal white shirt which is open at the neck. A flash of silver at his throat, silver hanging from both ears, and scattered across his fingers as he drags them through his hair. A rush of lust so strong moves through me that I have to plant my feet into the floor so I don't march over to him and do something feral. I swallow hard as he moves toward me, the scent of him muted at this point of the day, but still powerful. That sweetly spiced cologne only enhanced by the smell of his skin. The expensive shower gel. The creams and lotions he pushes into his skin each night and morning. Layers of enticement that I want to peel away. Kiss away. Lick away.

I hand him a glass of the white wine. One he had in his wine fridge with a Spanish label. He takes a large sip, staring at me over the rim.

"I thought you might be hungry," I say.

"You cooked for me." There's a pleased look on his face.

I shrug. "It's only mac and cheese. My mom's recipe." I'd messaged her earlier for it. Said I was feeling homesick. She said she'd make it for me when I got home but had sent it anyway. "You can eat like…dairy, right?"

He grins and nods. "I can. I love it. Mac and Cheese." He sniffs in deeply and rubs his stomach adorably. "I'm very hungry. Let me go and change, it's almost ready?"

"Yeah, it's done. Just waiting for you."

He nods again and leans in to kiss me, soft and quick. "Thank you," he whispers. He sets his wine down and goes to change.

I'm sitting at the dining table in the corner of the kitchen, two steaming plates of mac and cheese sitting before us, when he returns. He has half of his hair pulled back in a small ponytail, a white t-shirt with sleeves that fall past his wrists and the Chanel logo emblazoned across the chest. Black sweatpants and a pair of those white hotel slippers on. He throws me a small smile as he slides into the seat and pulls his knee up in front of him. He leans in to sniff the plate of food, miming a fainting scene as he does. First, he takes large sip of his wine and then lifts his fork to dig in.

I hold my breath. Nervous.

Jae moans obscenely. Pretends to fall back into the chair, dead. Then bursts awake with a giggle and continues to eat. I can only watch him a few minutes utterly enamoured. Big scary feelings swirling in my stomach and my chest. Feelings I know the name of, but which shouldn't be there. Not yet. Not this soon. The fact that they're about a guy is the least troubling aspect.

A few mouthfuls in, Jae stops, glances up at me a moment, before sitting back. "What is wrong?" he asks, settling his fork down. "It really is good."

"I know. It's not that."

He nods. Like he knows what it is. Like he understands what it is. Probably because he does. This likely isn't the first time some purportedly straight guy has fallen head over heels for him. Maybe he collects them. Like necklaces or earrings.

I curl my fingers around my fork to focus on something solid. Jae wipes his mouth with the napkin, sets it down, then lifts his wine again.

"What happens tomorrow?" I ask, watching him drink.

He frowns. "As I understand, you get on a flight to Colorado from JFK. Two pm you said?"

"After that, Jae. Shouldn't we talk about it?"

He sets his glass down and takes another forkful, chewing slowly and thoughtfully while staring at the plate of food.

"I don't think we can," he says. "Not until you know."

"Know what?"

"What this is." He continues eating.

Until I know. I do know. I think I do. But knowing it and saying it feel worlds apart. My entire life changes the moment I say it.

I eat a few bites, suddenly not hungry, but desperately thirsty. I gulp a few mouthfuls of water, then a large one of wine. Then repeat. When his plate is clear, he reaches for another helping, then tops up our wine. Beneath the table his leg brushes mine, warm and solid.

"Have you plans for New Year?" he asks, conversational.

"This year…no. We're going back into the studio to record on the 30th right up until Christmas and then some time off over the holidays."

Last year we were in London for a show, so we hung out at the hotel. The year before that we played a gig in Rome.

He nods, watching me. I want to kiss him so fucking badly. My skin feels tight and warm, my blood loud. I don't remember the last time we'd spent this much time together and not fucked, or touched, or licked, or kissed. I don't think we ever have, and maybe that's important so I hold myself back.

"I am going to Tokyo with some friends. They have a boat—a big one—and there is a party on the water. Fireworks. Dancing. I do not know if you will know by then, but if you did. Or maybe even if you don't." He looks at me and drags a hand through his hair. "Maybe you'd like to spend it with me. You said you wanted to visit Japan, so maybe you could, with me."

It's said not like a question really, but like a suggestion. I'm not sure what look I have on my face, but it prompts him to say: "It is private. Only friends. No cameras, nothing like that. I would not be going otherwise. There is Disneyland too. Not on the boat, but in Tokyo city." He adds this at the end with a small smile I can't help but mirror.

Spend New Year's with him. In Japan. Away from LA. Away from everyone who knows me. Whether I know what this is or not? He's offering me that? To have something to go towards to work towards, to wait for. I still don't know if he's offering me anything more than that. More than a party on a boat in Tokyo, and maybe I should check, but how can I when I don't know whether I'm even going to take it. *You're going to take it.*

"That sounds...great." I nod.

Beneath the table he curls his leg around mine. Smiles.

"I'd love to come."

It doesn't feel like a choice. Or if it is, I think I made it four nights ago when I came here. Or in that Paris bathroom. Any choice in which he's an option, I'll always choose him.

Jae nods, eyes looking full and warm and happy. Then he flounces back in his seat with a huge sigh, rubbing his stomach the way he does after eating. (Another habit is that to fall asleep he strokes one foot back and forth across the other.)

"So, after tonight, I won't see you again until New Year's, in Tokyo?"

"I suppose not," he says. "But we have tonight. And after tonight we have video call. And if you really miss me then you can always jump on a plane. It is only thirteen hours." He's grinning.

"Would you ever live anywhere else?" The question is out before I can second guess how it might sound to him. "Move away from Korea, I mean."

He thinks about this a long time. "Two years ago, I would have said no. But my English is getting better every day, so maybe. One day." He meets my eye. "Home can be anywhere, I think."

I think about that as we sit on the couch together watching some Korean anime series that he thought I might enjoy (in English with Korean subtitles turned on). About home being anywhere. I think about the weight of his head on my thigh and the silkiness of his hair under my fingers. I think about that big feeling that keeps building and building inside me and about how I'm going to say goodbye to him tomorrow. Is this what our life would be like together? This right here? Dinner and anime and soft touches on the sofa. It seems too easy. Way too easy.

Jae's hand rubs circles around my knee as the voices on the screen hold his attention. I can only see his profile when I look down, but he's fixated on the show, long legs stretched out, t-shirt riding up a little to show the strip of skin across his stomach. The sight of one of his pelvic piercings is visible.

It's what does it. That slice of skin. That delicate jewel glittering against the hard muscle.

He doesn't miss the way my cock jerks inside the sweatpants I'm wearing. My free hand rounds his body as he settles onto his back, fingers skimming across his abdomen, circling the piercing, to his navel and around his belly button, dancing over the waistband. There's a bulge between his legs that wasn't there a minute ago, or maybe it was and I just didn't have a front row seat.

The fingers that I had in his hair I move down to hold his jaw instead, and I stare down into his eyes. Eyes that look black in the TV's flickering light. He's writhing a little now, hips tilting off the couch up into my hand. Without taking my eyes off him, I slip my hand beneath his waistband and wrap it around him. He gasps, then moans, then turns his head to suck my fingers into his mouth. The want grows hot and bright, singing up my spine and across my scalp.

"Raphael..." he mutters, as my fingers slip out of his hot mouth.

I release his cock and bring these fingers to his mouth too, pushing them inside for him to suck. His eyes go half-lidded as he slides his tongue between each finger, curling it around knuckles and pads. I'm fully hard now and the thought of my cock in his mouth instead of my fingers causes a needy groan to spill out.

When I wrap my hand around him again, he whines, a soft breathy sound that goes straight to my balls. The tip of his cock is wet and he lifts his hips and pushes down his sweats and kicks them off. Then he turns himself sideways and pulls my own down to take out my dick. It's in his mouth an instant later and I can't think, let alone keep jerking him off.

"Fucking shit, Jaehyun, your mouth…" I groan.

He pushes me to the back of his throat and then pulls off, nosing and sucking the shaft before pulling my balls into his perfect fucking mouth. He's fucking my hand as he does this, totally in control, multitasking. It's impressive really.

"Jae, I can't…fuck."

I let him go so I can hold his head with both hands and move up into the heat of his mouth. Jae shifts, turning so that he's on his knees and taking my cock deeper into his throat. He turns his head to look at me and smiles around it, eyes drunk with lust like he just fucking loves this. His hand slips between my legs as he sucks me off, massaging my balls and the sensitive skin behind them, then I feel it.

His finger there. Circling.

Without a thought my legs widen to give him better access to it. He pushes against it, soft and suggestive, his eyes watching me intently. He pulls off my cock and licks his lips.

"Have you ever had anything in here?" he asks, still fingering the rim.

I can't find words, my tongue lost somewhere in the roof of my mouth, so I just shake my head. He presses against it a little more firmly and I tense. His finger disappears instantly.

"I'd never do anything you don't want me to."

"Yeah, yeah I know." I choke out, raw. My voice strangled with arousal.

He climbs onto my lap then, straddling me, his ass fitting snuggly over my throbbing dick. He grabs my face and tilts my head up to him, eyes dark and serious.

"I am sorry, I shouldn't have done that," he says. "I got carried away."

But it wasn't that. It *isn't* that. Not at all. It's the opposite of that. The thought of it doesn't terrify me nearly as much as I assumed it would. It excites me. It feels like some final, loud realization. A door closing behind me. Another opening in front.

"I...it's okay."

He tilts his head, studying me in the dark. "Is it? What are you thinking now?"

I almost laugh at the thought that pops into my head.

Jae notices. Frowns. So, I try and flatten my thoughts, folding them into something ordered, that I can verbalize.

"I just thought about how...well, like how I'd basically be a virgin, right? Is that how it works?"

I hadn't been a virgin for a long time. And when I had been I'd hated it. Had wanted rid of it at the first opportunity. Now it was back. Now I do laugh. Because it is funny. When I focus on Jae, he's smiling, but more at my amusement I think than the fact he finds it funny.

"I suppose so...yes." He looks distracted, still worried, I think.

I lean up and kiss him hard.

"I'm okay," I tell him. "You touched my asshole and I liked it. Please stop looking so worried."

When I kiss him again, he smiles, dropping his arms to loop around my neck and pull me closer. Then he's grinding. Sliding that perfect fucking ass over my cock. Then I wonder how he'd feel inside, raw, and I groan around his tongue.

"You liked it?" he whispers, pulling back to look at me.

"Mmm, I did. I'm not saying I'm ready for anything to be pushed inside it, but the door is unlocked."

He laughs as I catch his lips between mine.

After we make out for a bit I flip him round, settle lower into the sofa, and eat him out again. Angling him to sit on my face while he babbles half in English and half in Korean about my tongue and my mouth like it's a fucking god he worships. He plays with his nipples as I jerk him off, and when he's about to come I throw him on his back and motion for him to do it on my face. His eyes go a kind of black I haven't seen before, as he lets it tear through him. Hot white come shooting up into my open mouth. I'm two seconds from blowing when he surges up and kisses me hard, licking his tongue over his orgasm as he cleans my face. Urging me onto my back, he proceeds to give me the best blowjob I've ever had, almost passing out from the pleasure, then again from the over-sensitivity that pulses through my cock as he suckles the softening head.

After, we lie together on the couch, him drawing circles on my chest in shapes that feel foreign and my fingers twisting through in his hair.

"I think I have a fetish for your hair."

He chuckles sleepily. "It will be silver when you see me again."

"Mmm. I like it silver." I think I'm halfway asleep. "I also like it pink and blue and purple."

"You liked it pink?" he says.

"It was the first color I ever saw it. I wanted you so fucking much. Even then."

He doesn't answer, but his fingers still on my chest. That's when I know. He remembered. I guess I always suspected he did, I was just happier pretending he didn't.

"I know."

I open my eyes for this and move my arms so I'm holding him tighter against me.

"Baby, I'm so fucking sorry. I think maybe...I was a different person back then." I think about Mason, about *this shit never bothered you this much before*, and I feel sick. "I'm sorry for what I said. For what we said. I'm just...sorry."

"I know," he says again.

NINETEEN
RAPHAEL

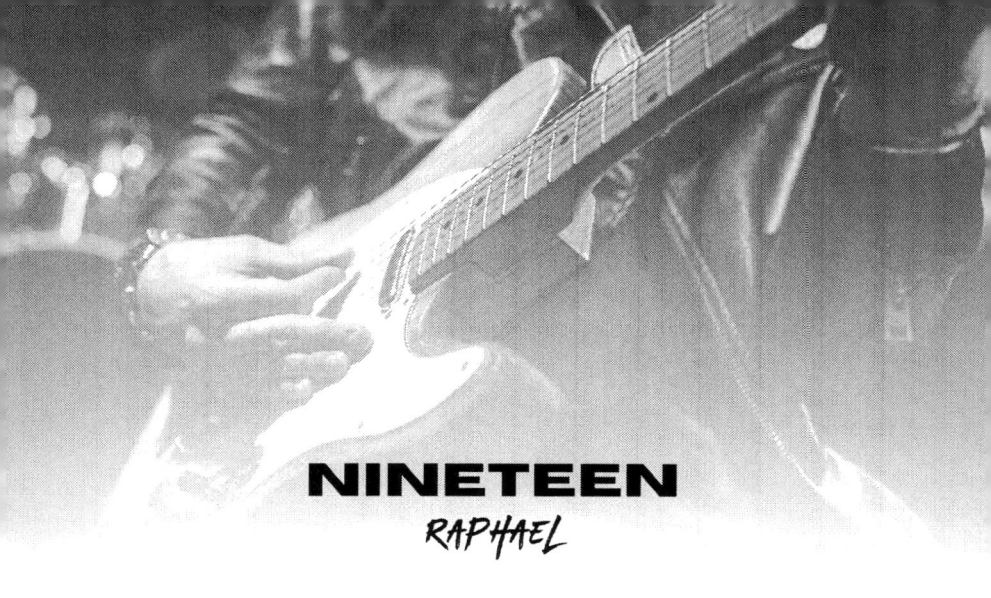

Mom is wearing mittens, an oversized lumberjack shirt with jeans, and a pair of lined fur boots when I spot her at the airport. She's waving both arms at me like she's drowning, red curls bright and shining, and I'm hit with a rush of love and warmth and home so strong it almost knocks me off my feet.

"Baby!" she shouts, in case I haven't seen her. Which would be impossible. "Here!"

I pull my ballcap lower as I move toward her. She pulls me into a tight hug. "Hey mom."

That smell. Of cooking and paint cleaner and cut grass. It settles some flux inside me. She clings to me as she presses wet kisses to the bits of my face she can get to.

"Look at you! Look at my baby. Have you lost weight, I think you have? Are you on one of those silly LA diets again? Let me see you properly."

She goes to pull my cap off but I stop her. She forgets. She always forgets. When she's in LA—which is rarely—it's better, she already feels out of place there and thinks basically everyone is a celebrity, but here she just forgets entirely. Here we're both who we've always been. Airports make me nervous though. A glance around tells me there's no paparazzi here, but there are still people with cameras. There always are.

When I pull back to let her look at me, I notice she has some purple paint on her cheek and a little in her hair.

"You definitely look skinny, Raphael." She pinches my cheek with her mittened fingers and gives me a sad smile. "I can't wait to fatten you up. This all you got?" She glances at my bags.

"Yeah, just these."

She fights over the backpack which I eventually let her have and then we're strolling out of Denver International towards my mom's car. She's parked her white SUV on the drop-off point and it takes us far quicker than I expect to get out of the Thanksgiving traffic at the airport and onto US-40. She'd been listening to some podcast with a British host which she switches off, and then Sayonara Sun is blasting through the car speakers. I half chuckle half groan.

"We really don't have to listen to this."

"What?!" She sounds insulted. "But it's so great, Rapha, I love it. Gavin loves it too. Listens to the entire thing on his runs. I never have it off in the Studio." There's a few beats. "I'm so so proud of you."

"You weren't too embarrassed when I mentioned you, were you?"

She'd said on the phone she screamed and then burst into tears.

"Embarrassed?" she squeaks. "About what? My beautiful boy won a Grammy award and thanked me on national TV. What is there to be embarrassed about?"

I just shrug and smile and she goes back to singing along to our now Grammy award winning album.

It's just under two hours from the airport to the house just outside Granby. Not the house I grew up in—that's in Arvada—but the one I bought for her two years ago when we got our first Grammy nomination. The label had advanced the band a seven figure check for the next four albums. She sounded nervous when I called while she'd opened the parcel with the key inside. I'd told her to drive to the address on the card and call me back. She'd done so crying and yelling. *I don't need a new house, Raphael! Why did you do this? I can't move! I don't want to move!*

I'd asked her to go inside and look at it first, and if she still felt the same then I'd sell it right back. Then she'd seen the studio, the views of the snow-capped mountains over Sunset Ridge and she'd cried some more.

Her, Gavin, and the dogs had moved in a month later. She didn't need to work anymore, though she still did. A few days a week at a high-school in town. But mainly she painted in her studio and sold stuff via her online shop. She did what she loved. She was happy. I'd helped make her happy. I was proud of that.

Mom doesn't mention Camille on the drive at all. Not our call in New York either. She just tells me about school and the dogs and Gavin, about Aunt Rebecca and Uncle Lyle, Jessie and Ana, and what she's cooking for everyone this weekend. I'm listening, but my mind is also wondering about Jae. What he's been doing since I left him at the apartment, whether he's sad that I'm gone. While mom gossips, I pull my phone out and see that a few messages have come in since I switched it off of flight mode.

Crawfish: Mase called. Said you and Camille had a fight? Everything good?

JH: I just checked and saw it is going to be snowing there. Please wrap up warm and don't catch a cold! Happy Thanksgiving, Raphael.

Some warm feeling tugs at my chest as I read it. Longing, I think. I want to call him, hear his voice, smell him. I *miss* him. It's sort of pathetic.

I see mom glance over at me as I stare down at the phone but she says nothing. I slip it back into my pocket and turn to face out the window.

Later. I'll call him later.

The dogs come bounding up the driveway at the sound of the car crunching over the gravel. The coppery red hair of Samson and the dark short coat of Delilah. They yip and bark around the car while mum shouts at them through the window whenever they get too close.

Gavin is standing on the steps in front of the house, hands in his pockets and a big smile on his face. He's a nice guy, mom's boyfriend. Really nice. Tall and grey-haired with a permanent tan and a genuine smile. He calls me 'son' though I have never once called him dad. He makes mum happy. But all I can think about when I see him is how different he is from *him*. From Finn Sullivan. Tall where he was shorter, wider where he was leaner, tanned where he was pale. I've often wondered if that's why mom loves him.

He comes down the stairs to help with my bags and pulls me into one of his bear hugs.

"Rapha, son, so good to see you. It's been too long."

Gavin is originally from Georgia and his accent and his deep voice gives off these comforting vibes that immediately put people at ease. Useful, given his job. He's a commercial pilot for Delta and still flies large planes over the Atlantic four times a week. Mom worries a lot about plane crashes.

"How was the drive, sweetheart?" he asks mom as he wraps a wing around her and pulls her close.

"Fine, fine, not too bad once we got onto I-70." They kiss and I avert my eyes. "Did you lower the heat on the turkey?"

"To one fifty at 4 p.m. yes, ma'am."

"You're a good listener, I've always said that about you."

Inside, I tell mom I'm gonna take a shower and Gavin tells me my room is ready and leads me to it, still carrying my bags. It's not technically my room; it's just a room that I sleep in when I stay here. Which admittedly is not very often. So by this definition only, this is my room. Gavin drops my bags on the ottoman by the foot of the bed and turns to me. Warm smile on his face.

"It's real good to have you, Raphael. She was worried you weren't gonna make it."

Like I didn't make it for her birthday, or last Christmas, or the last family wedding. It's not an accusation he's levelling, that's not Gavin's style, he's just making sure I know it's real good to have me.

"Yeah, I know. It's good to be home." I nod. "I need to get back more."

I glance around the room. At the glass doors leading out to the small balcony that has a staircase down to the one leading off the main floor below. There's some snow on the ridge outside, but its melting. Or it's not fallen too much yet. It's cold though, that biting sharpness in the air for sure.

Please wrap up warm and don't catch a cold!

"We forecast for snow?" I ask Gavin.

"Tonight, sure are! Should get out and cut some logs before the temperature drops."

"You need a hand with that?" I offer though I want nothing more than a hot shower, fresh clothes, and to talk to Jae.

Gavin shakes his head, mildly insulted. "Not at all, son. You get cleaned up and head down when you're ready." He pats me on the shoulder, fatherly, and then he's gone. Whistling as he goes.

I do exactly that, in that order. The scalding hot shower, then the fresh clothes—from the chest in the room where mom keeps spare stuff for me—then I pad across to close the bedroom door, grab my air pods, and then sit on the bed with my back against the headboard.

His flight from JFK isn't until just after midnight but he's two hours ahead—so it's only 9 p.m. there. I'm not sure I'll even get him, but I decide to call him anyway. I need to. Video too, because fucking hell, he feels like a figment from all the way out here.

It rings for almost a full minute until I'm sure he's not gonna answer, but then it connects and he's there, smiling. He looks surprised and a little shy, fixing his hair furiously. He's wearing glasses, round gold-rimmed ones that look great on him. He looks to be still in his apartment.

"Hello," he says. Then he smiles, wide, his cheeks rounding.

Tension I didn't even know was there seeps out of me at the sight of him. My shoulders release and I let out a soft breath as I drop my head back against the headboard.

"Hey." I smile back. "Sorry, for calling, I just wanted to hear your voice. See your face too, I guess?"

It comes out like a question. He licks his lips, glances briefly away from the phone, shy but flirty.

"You cannot call me without warning me first," he says pushing his hair back. "I look terrible. My face is so puffy"

"*Puffy*?" I frown.

I'm not even sure what that means. He looks immaculate. He's wearing a butter yellow sweater and long silver earrings which hang past his hair. His rings he took off before sleeping, but his earrings he always left in.

"From sleeping. I went to bed after you left. I woke up about ten minutes ago."

"Did you dream about me?"

He laughs, then squeezes his eyes closed. Embarrassed.

"You did! You dreamt about me." I punch the air in celebration and he covers his face and shakes his head.

"You are ridiculous."

"I'm the man of your dreams though."

He laughs again and the sound of it is like a fucking song.

He takes the piss out of me, deservedly, and I flirt with him, unashamedly, for the next ten minutes before he tells me another call is coming in. It's okay though because he'll call them back, he says. But I know he needs to go. He needs to get on a plane to fly thousands of miles away to another continent and I have to let him. Because he's not mine. *Not yet.*

"I'll call you in a few days," I tell him.

Jae nods before reminding me of the time difference again. Saying if he doesn't answer then he'll call me back. That sometimes he's not alone. I hate the hot jealous feeling that I get from the idea of that.

After we say goodbye, but before we hang up, I say it. The thing I'd thought about in the car to the airport, on the flight, in my mom's car on the way here.

"I know what it is, Jaehyun," I say, quiet.

He stops moving around—packing—and stares through the screen at me. His eyes are wide and expectant.

"I think I've always known. Since the first time I kissed you. Fuck, maybe even before that." Could it have been since Paris?

He nods. "Okay."

"I miss you so fucking much, that's stupid right?" I sigh, dragging a hand over my face, tears welling up for some stupid reason. "I just feel like I've wasted so much time."

He frowns. "We only had a few days."

"I don't mean this week. I mean before that...I mean, everything else."

I think he gets what I mean because the frown smooths away and he smiles again.

"Let us talk in Tokyo, yes? About what this is. What we want, what is possible."

I don't like the sound of that, about how he makes it sound like there are some things that aren't, but he's still looking at me in that soft warm way and it's enough to calm me.

"For now, enjoy this time with your mom. Do not think of me or anything else. Or if you must think of me, then make it good thoughts."

"I'm always thinking good thoughts of you, baby." I smirk and he blushes, actually fucking blushes. My dick perks up. "You'll dream of me?"

He laughs. "I'll try. Stay warm, okay? Happy Thanksgiving tomorrow."

"Safe flight."

It takes me a few moments of lying there on the bed, stupid grin on my face, dick half hard in my pants to realize my mom is watching me from the bedroom door. Her mouth is open, but her eyes are narrow. And she looks pissed.

But there's something far worse in her eyes. Disappointment.

"Now, I know that wasn't Camille you were talking to, Raphael. So I'm hoping you have a real good explanation for calling another woman '*baby*' and telling her to dream about you." She closes the door behind her and comes toward the bed, perching on the end. "Start talking."

TWENTY
RAPHAEL

"How long were you standing there?" I ask, pulling out my Air Pods as I sit up.

"If you think you're going to figure out how much I heard so you can lie to me, think again, Raphael Alwyn Scott."

I roll my eyes at the use of my full ridiculous name. "Mom, I'm not fifteen. You've not caught me smoking pot."

"No, this is worse! This is cheating. Which is far *far* worse." She scowls. "We talked about this, Raphael. When you *were* fifteen! About how you treat women that you're sleeping with? I thought you understood what was acceptable to me and what wasn't?"

I sigh. "This isn't about what's acceptable to you, mom." At this, she shoots me a murderous glare.

"I meant acceptable. Period," she corrects.

"It's complicated."

"Oh, don't give me that shit! I'm twice your age. I've been married. To your father, *your father.*" My mom is the only person on earth who calls him that. "You think I don't understand *complicated*? Or rather, what men *believe* to be complicated."

She has her hands on her hips, body stiff as a pole as she marches across the room. Then back. Still glaring at me.

"Sex isn't complicated, Raphael. It's one of the simplest things there is. Men have been breaking promises to women since the dawn of time. You might have been told a million times out there that you're special, sweetheart." She points out at the ridge. "But there are a billion men just like you out there, doing exactly what you're doing now."

Her eyes soften as she says the next words: "But you are special in here, to me." She puts her hand over her heart and curls her fingers into a fist. "Don't make me think of you like this. Like him. You're not him. You never have been, baby. You're better."

I sit up, swinging my legs over the edge of the bed as I set my Air Pods on the nightstand. I hate this. I fucking hate this. Just like I hated looking at Camille as I let her down too. I cover my eyes with my palm and squeeze, hard.

"It's not another woman," I say, carefully.

"Raphael, I heard you, I heard you say—."

"No, mom," I cut in. "I mean it's not another *woman*."

I lift my head to look at her and I can't read a single expression on her face now. It's blank. Until suddenly, it's not.

Her face is a picture of pure and utter confusion as she tries to figure out if I mean what I just implied. Why can't I say it? If I know what it is, then why can't I say it? I'd have to say it at some point. Then I'd have to say it over and over again. *This is my boyfriend. I have a boyfriend. I'm gay. Bi. I'm not straight. I like men. And women. I'm not exclusively into women. This is Jae.*

When Mom's mouth falls open, I wonder if maybe I've just said all that out loud.

"Not another woman. So you mean…that wasn't a woman on the phone? You were…that was a man?" She points at the phone I'm white-knuckling on my thigh. "You were talking to a man?"

I give her a slow nod and all the small fragments of the conversation start to sink in for her, with meaning. Whatever look she sees on my face makes her move and sit next to me on the bed. She's staring at me hard, searching my eyes for something. Not like I'm a stranger, that would be terrifying, but like I'm an old friend she hasn't seen in a long time and she's looking to see what's different.

"You're gay?" she asks very gently.

I shrug. "I don't know. I mean I guess I like both?" I like him.

She's nodding now. "So…you're experimenting? That's okay."

"Is it?"

"Well, cheating on Camille still isn't. Regardless of what you're going through, baby. That's never okay. She loves you and she trusts you. You need to talk to her. She deserves that."

I nod furiously. "I know, and I have. I guess, I went dark on her and she knew something was off. Now she knows there's someone else. We spoke in New York. After Jae and I…" I trail off realizing I just said his name out loud to my mom. It's real. I know what it is. "She came to see me and, fuck, she was great. She doesn't know about this…about him but she was…Camille, you know?"

Mom nods, though I'm not sure she knows Camille that much to say either way.

"She's a great person, mom. Really. And I don't want to hurt her. I know I have already but, I didn't know…I wasn't even sure what this was because it's big, you know? It's really fucking big, mom. Maybe even blow-my-entire-life-up big and I'm not quite ready to do that yet. I'm scared, I guess. But he makes me feel like maybe the aftermath wouldn't be bad at all. That what we'd be left with after the dust settled would be all I'd need. Perfect, actually. I don't think I'd need that much if I had him. He's kind of everything…he's enough. And I'd be enough too, you know?"

I look at her to see if anything I've just said makes any sense at all—honestly, it's the most succinct I've ever been inside or outside of my head when it comes to Jae—but she has these big fat tears in her eyes and then my vision blurs too and she's pulling me into her, arms tight around me.

"Oh, baby," she says against my hair. "My beautiful baby boy. I love you so much."

I hadn't meant to cry. Hadn't expected to. I don't really cry. I cried a lot as a kid, too much, and then one day, mom said, I just stopped. I can't remember the last time I cried. It feels kind of nice. Soothing in a weird way, like those deep breaths I do before going onstage.

"Am I making a huge mistake?" I whisper so quietly I'm not sure I even said it. "I really don't know what I'm doing here, mom."

She pushes me away from her. "Listen to me, baby, listen. Mistakes are part of life okay, they just are. And if you try and avoid them your whole life then, well, you're not really living."

"Not getting the full experience, huh?" I laugh, sniffling.

"Exactly." She ruffles my hair. "You're so smart. You're beautiful and smart and brave and talented, and you have more heart in this little finger here than anyone I know." She tugs on my little finger once before giving me a very serious look. "Follow it."

"My little finger?"

She laughs, wetly, before wiping her eyes. "That too!"

"And what about this whole dating a guy thing? You'd be okay with that?"

She frowns at me, looking genuinely perplexed. "Why wouldn't I be?"

I shrug. "All the usual reasons I guess."

"Which are?" She puts a hand on my cheek.

"Grandkids?" I offer weakly.

She slaps me on the shoulder, insulted, and stands. "You think I want to even contemplate being a grandmother at forty eight? Do you know your mother at all? AT ALL, RAPHAEL!" She walks toward the bedroom door shaking her head, stopping to gesture for me to follow. "Dinner's ready, come on. Pride & Prejudice is on PBS at nine and I want us all to watch it together."

I groan, but get up to follow her, wiping the dampness from my eyes. "Again? Surely there's some other movie about stuck-up British people we can watch?"

"Mmm, if you'd prefer we could drink beer on the porch and talk about *Jae*?" She throws a wide-eyed look over her shoulder. "It was Jae, right? Yeah, it was. I'm going to need to know all there is to know about him eventually so..."

"Actually, it's been a while since we've seen it? Like two years maybe?" I hook my arm through hers. "I told you Camille worked with her once, Kiera Knightley? On a film about Freud. When I met her I told her that you made me watch this film every Thanksgiving."

I can see mom's eyes go wide before she hits me again, gently.

"You never told me that! Why didn't you tell me that? What did she say?" She stops, eyes narrowing. "Wait, I see what you're doing. You're not going to get out of it that easily, we are going to talk about him."

I smile. "I know. We will."

As if on cue, my phone vibrates in my back pocket. Lifting it out I see his name.

> **JH: I am leaving for the airport now. I will dream of you. See you in Tokyo xx**

My mom doesn't miss the stupid ass grin that spreads over my face as I read it over and over and over again.

Thanksgiving at my mom's is tradition. She's always cooked for the family and despite how stressful it always appears to me from where I sit drinking beer, she loves doing it. Even when we were in the smaller house, Mom, Gavin, Aunt Rebecca, Uncle Lyle, Gramps and Grandma Jane, and I would crowd around the dining table crammed with enough food for a road crew on tour. I'd only missed two Thanksgivings with the family which I thought was pretty damn great. I was in a rock band. I toured most of the planet. But I still made it home for mom's mac and cheese, green bean casserole, and pumpkin pie once a year. It was birthdays and Christmas I wasn't great at.

For the most part, it's normal. My aunt and uncle ask me about the band like it's a normal job (how are the people you work with, is there health insurance?) which I always find amusing. My niece and nephew—seven year-old twins—are getting close to the age where they're going to realize what I do for a living and think I'm cool. I'm looking forward to it. There was no gramps and Grandma Jane anymore, even though there's plenty of room at the dining table in the

Granby house now, but it still feels like they're around because we always talk about them.

I snap a few pictures of mom's table, the food, the snow outside—which did come down as he predicted—and send them off to him. I work it out quickly and see it's about 5 a.m. and I know his flight was getting into Seoul late and so I don't particularly want a reply right away. I want him to be sleeping.

As the table talk amongst themselves I imagine him here, sitting between Aunt Rebecca and my mom as they admire his earrings and rings and style. I imagine going for a long twilight walk with him as the dogs run around our feet, the tip of his nose pinking in the cold. Fuck, I want it. Could I have it? Does *he* even want that? He talked about things that were possible like there were things that weren't. What did that mean?

Tokyo is everything to me then. It's almost five weeks away and I've been away from him about thirty two hours and I don't know how I'm gonna do—my brain also works this out quickly—another eight hundred and forty.

After dinner is the usual food coma and NFL game that Lyle and Gavin invite me to watch with them after doing the washing up. Mom and Aunt Rebecca drink wine on the porch, the log burner blazing, laughing like teenagers while I wrap up the leftovers that I'm already eyeing with want.

Mom hadn't asked me anymore about him. Not last night or this morning while we set the table and laughed about the time gramps had thought the creamed corn had been ice cream and ate it with his pecan pie without complaint. But after everyone is gone and I'm sitting on the porch with a beer, she finds me.

She hands me another bottle and sits down, reaching forward to throw another log into the grate. It crackles and pops, hissing its warmth up into the dark chilly sky.

"I love this house," she says with a deep sigh. "I think that every single day I wake up here." She reaches over and squeezes my knee. "I'm so grateful for it. For everything you do, you know that, right?"

I smile over at her. "I'm glad you're happy here, mom. That's all I wanted. For you to be happy."

She was sad for a long time, my mom. Around the time when I cried a lot, I think. I thought maybe me crying so much was what made her sad. But I know now that it wasn't that, and that maybe deep down it was knowing my mom was so sad that I cried so damn much. It's one of the reasons I hate Finn. It's the main reason.

"You've always made me happy, Raphael," she says, like she can read my mind.

Fuck, I always forget she does that. The way I can sometimes feel something before it happens, she can read my mind. I used to think it was because I lived inside her once. But I think it's because it was just the two of us for so long.

"I've always been so proud of you, sweetheart. Every single day. I am sooo stinking proud of the man that you are."

I'm going to cry again, I think, so I close my eyes and turn my head, groaning.

"Please stop. Too much emotion. No one's dying."

"Heterosexual Raphael died, and I'll miss him. Even if you won't." She pouts.

"Jesus! Seriously?" I choke on my mouthful of beer. When I look at her she's giving me this sad face. "I don't know how I feel about you talking about my sexuality like it's a dead relative."

"Wait until you see my new painting of it. It's gonna be so incredibly sad. So much death, it's going to leap from the canvas! Alive but dead, you know? At the same time. It'll sell for thousands once you come out."

Then we're laughing and everything feels fine. *I* feel fine. Everything will be fine. Because no matter what the fuck happens out there, how much Camille is going to hate me, I still have this, with her.

"It's serious," she says, as she takes a drink of her wine. "You're serious about him."

"I think so. I mean, it hasn't been long at all. Not really. Not us being…together. But yeah, it feels really serious, mom. I just…" I trail, gulping half the bottle as I stare out at the view. She waits for me to finish.

"You just what?" She prods, gently.

I'm scared if I say this, then it will color him in her eyes, and I don't want to do that. But I want her advice. Because I think this must be how women often feel in relationships. A little lost. Like men are a different species where the behaviors and patterns are sometimes predictable but sometimes not. Jae and I are the same species, but we're fucking worlds apart.

"I just…don't think he feels the same way."

Mom frowns, like I worried she might. "What makes you think that?"

I'd have to tell her. Everything. About how I'd fantasized and pined over this guy for two years. About how I met him the very same night I met Camille, and yet his was the number I wish I'd gotten at the after show. How I'd studied him and followed his career and socials, maybe even about my disgusting fuck up in that venue bathroom.

"It's like…" I start, turning to face her a little. "I've never looked at another guy before him, mom, not one. It's never even crossed my mind. But the second I saw him, I felt it. Something big had happened. I didn't know it at the time, or I was in denial about it—but I know it now." I shake my head. "I guess what I'm saying is, that's what he is for me. This life-changing, soul-shifting event. But for him I'm just another guy, right? Like he's done this before. Before me. Plenty of times before me."

She says nothing right away, staring at me in what looks like… awe? Wonderment?

"But he hasn't done this with *you, baby?*" She sees a look on my face and her eyes go wide. "*What? Already?* Okay, no, that's not what I meant. That is not my business. But you are pretty special, sweetheart, and I'm gonna assume he's not blind or stupid. You're beautiful, and kind, and smart—does he know about the math thing?"

I laugh and shake my head.

When she reaches across and takes my hand, her eyes go serious again. "You are something very very special Raphael Alwyn Scott, and he's gonna see that."

"There's only one problem with that, mom, and it's that you're exceptionally biased where I'm concerned."

She makes a show of thinking about it, then holds up her thumb and pointer finger an inch or so apart. "But I'm also always right."

When I nod at this, she grins.

"So, tell me about him. Where'd you meet this life-changing, soul-shifting event?"

I smile, cheeks and ears burning. "Paris. Two years ago."

She almost spits out her wine.

"But nothing happened, he didn't even look twice at me. I was a total dick. But I guess I just never stopped thinking about him. Then we met again a few months ago in LA. At Halcyon. He's in a band, too."

Her eyes widen with surprise. "A band I'd know?"

"A band you'd probably know, yeah." They'd had billboard hits, a few number ones too, and they'd done the Late Night Show just last week—a show my mom watches almost religiously. She's definitely gonna know them.

Since she looks like she's going to hit me if I don't tell her this fucking second, I say, "You like K-pop, right?"

She looks confused for a second before her mouth drops open and she *literally* squeals out loud.

"No? No way! You are kidding me?" She's sitting all the way up in the chair, eyes peeled wide.

"Everything okay out here, hon?" Gavin says, popping his head out of the sliding door to look between us both. Mom looks at me and I give her a smile and a half shrug thing and she stands up, turning to Gavin.

"Sweetheart, we have some news. And it's that Raphael and Camille are separating—and my baby's rediscovering his sexuality.

With a K-pop idol. That's what they call them. Idols. It's Jaehyun isn't it? *Jae,*" she asks, looking back at me.

I can only nod, too impressed by her deductive skills to speak.

She turns back to Gavin. "That pretty band we watched on Late Night last week, hon, remember?"

Gavin's eyes are wider than saucers as mom pulls up Jae's picture on her phone and shows him. I down the rest of my beer and stare up at the moon trying to work out what time it is in Seoul. It takes me a little longer than normal with the food and beer weighing down my brain, but I still get there quicker than most. 9 p.m. in Colorado is 1 p.m. in Seoul.

It's not until I'm going to bed at just after midnight (4 p.m. in Seoul), my head a little blurry from the beer and all the honesty, that my phone goes off with a notification from him. It's a picture. He's lying in bed with his eyes half closed and the duvet pulled right up past his chin. Kissable pout on his bare, sleepy face.

JH: I woke up alone.

JH: I dreamt of you.

Me: I hope it was a sex dream.

JH: It is a secret ,)

JH: Did you have a nice Thanksgiving?

I debate whether to say it, not knowing how he'll react, but I need him to know that I'm not messing about here. That I know what this is. That *he's* important. A life-changing, soul-shifting event.

Me: I told my mom about you.

There's no response right away. Then I see the dots flickering. Disappearing. Flickering again. My heart is beating so loud and quick in my chest I can feel it rocking my whole body. Fuck. Fuck why did I tell him that? It's too much. I try to imagine a girl saying that to me after a few nights together and then I'm *certain* I'm going to throw up.

I might know what it is but I still don't know what I'm fucking doing here. I'm thinking of a way to walk it back a little, make it seem more casual than it is, but then the dots are back and I'm holding my breath.

JH: Okay ☺

I'm not entirely sure how to take it. The word or the addition of the smiling face. But it's his thing, he uses this particular emoji a lot. So I decide not to take anything from it. He texts back a moment later.

JH: Do you want to talk?

With a smile, I hit on the little call icon next to his name and wait for it to ring through.

TWENTY-ONE
RAPHAEL

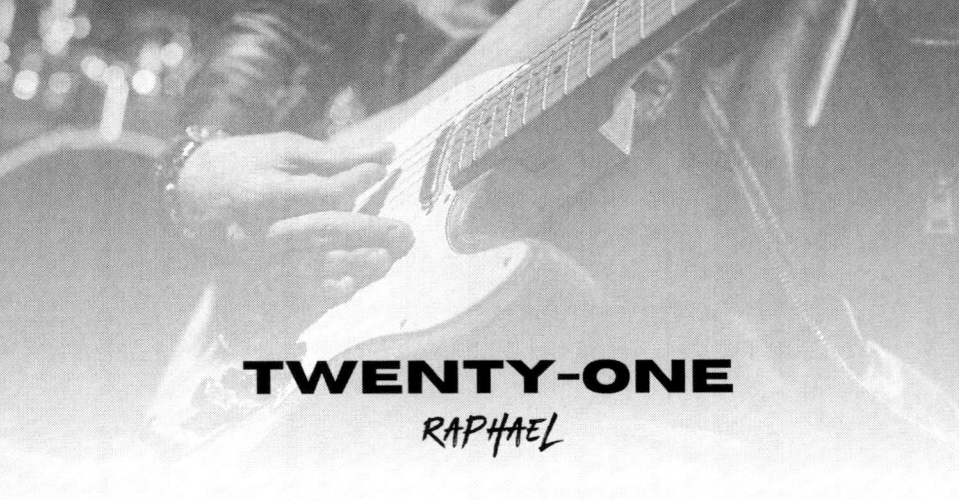

L A is the coldest I can remember it ever being. Not as cold as Colorado, or Seoul (Jaehyun had sent me a pic that morning of the snowfall from his window) but it's not t-shirt weather either. Global warming is fucking real.

I wait until I'm in the cab from the airport before I text mom to tell her I landed safely. I've got messages from Cleo and Zeke which I tap out responses to. Nothing from Mase since our talk in New York meaning Monday should be fun. Our first day in the studio after a break is always like that, like the first day back at school after summer. Friendships redefined, grudges either amplified or forgotten.

There's been nothing from Camille either, which should make me feel something more than relief, but it doesn't.

The cab driver recognizes me and talks to me about music for the entire journey from LAX to Sunset. Then he mentions my dad and I give him my standard response. *Never knew him so I know less than you, man.* His taste had been good and I'd planned to tip him a hundred, but I cut it in half for that. He seems grateful all the same when he drops me at the bottom of the drive and speeds off with Faith No More pouring out of the open window.

I take a long hot shower, change into a pair of sweats and nothing else, before doing a twenty minute run on the treadmill. After, I grab a bottle of water and collapse on the sofa to check his social media. I still look at it several times a day—out of habit more than anything else now. I've decided that I like looking at his pictures and videos more now I have this new insight. His captions, I hear in his voice. His pictures, I can see as moving images in my head. He's the same person, but now I know the Jae behind the phone camera. I've tasted him and felt him come under my fingers and around my cock. It's all more vivid and intense.

It's just after 1 a.m. there but I know he's a night person so he will still be awake. He told me he only sleeps normally when he's on tour, otherwise he can be awake to see the sun come up before sleeping the day away. I hate that he doesn't seem to sleep well, but it will certainly help this long distance thing.

Me: I'm back home in LA. Are you awake? Free? I miss you.

There's no response straight away so I lose myself through his Instagram again. Though I know his grid off by heart at this point. He's not a prolific poster of pictures to his grid but he does use his stories—once every other day or so. His last story was a video of a TV show he was watching. Looked to be some kind of talent show. He was congratulating the finalists, according to the translation.

I stop on the picture of his from a magazine photoshoot from a year or so ago, like I always do. Zooming in on it, back out. He's wearing a tartan skirt with white thigh highs underneath, the lace band of them around his thigh just visible beneath the hem of the tartan. A white t-shirt with the Chanel logo, a thick silver necklace that looks like a collar, and a pair of black biker boots. His hair is silver and his lips look cherry red.

My dick is hard in a matter of moments. I'm not sure when or why I started imagining him wearing white lace panties under that skirt—but it happened and it's impossible not to think of now whenever I look at it. Which used to be almost daily. Less now definitely. But now I know how his pretty pink cock would look through the material as it hardens and how his perfect firm ass would look spilling out of the back of them, it's almost worse.

I'm about ready to slide my hand into my sweats and jerk myself off when my phone rings with a video call, Jaehyun's name emblazoned on the screen. My heart leaps in my chest as I settle back on the sofa and lift the phone up. Then he's there. Smiling wide on the screen, hair wet and…fucking hell he's topless. The sight of his tiny pink nipples makes my dick *want*.

"Hey," I say first, reaching down to squeeze the head of my dick to calm it down. "You're wet."

He grins. "I have just had a shower. I was in the dance studio."

"At 1 a.m.?"

He shrugs. "I had so much energy today so I worked late. Practicing."

"You don't need to practice."

I can see his blush from here.

"We all need to practice. What about you? What are you doing?"

"Ah, nothing much. I got home about an hour ago. Took a shower, did a run. Looked at some pictures of you."

"Pictures of me?" He lets out a full-bodied laugh. "Why?"

"Because I missed you. And I was…" I close my eyes and groan. "You know." I hope the look I give him says what I haven't.

"I don't know." A mischievous smile tugs at the side of his mouth. "Tell me."

Tell him. Tell him that if he hadn't called I was gonna jack off to a picture of him in stockings and the mental image of him wearing lingerie. I try to decide how best to say that. How would he take it? Would it be an insult? If I said it to a girl, it would be sleazy as fuck, so surely it's the same here? But he's not a fucking girl. He's a guy. It's completely different. Fuck, I really have no idea what I'm doing.

I cannot teach you everything, Raphael.

Fuck it.

"That picture of you on your Instagram." I cover my eyes with my free hand. "The one where you've got a skirt on. And stockings." I peek through my fingers to see his reaction and I know right away I made the right call. He gives me this fucking smirk. One that makes the low thrum of heat at the base of my spine pulsate. I decide to keep going. "What were you wearing underneath?"

"I don't know what picture you are talking about." The lie makes his mouth look downright sinful. His lips pouty and pink. Fuckable. I think about how good it was to see my dick moving in and out of that mouth and I almost groan out loud.

"You know what picture I'm talking about. Your hair is silver. You're staring at the camera like you want to fuck it, and you're wearing a fucking skirt."

"It was a kilt," he says airily. "A traditional garment from Scotland."

"What were you wearing underneath this traditional garment from Scotland?" I ask, letting my fingers drift back down to my sweats-covered cock.

"What do you think I was wearing?" He lowers his body down the bed, settling his head on the pillow and lifting the phone up. "Surely you don't think I was naked? At a photoshoot? At work?"

"I was hoping you might have been…" I swallow. *Fuck, Raphael. You fucked this guy a few days ago. You had your cock in his fucking ass. You can certainly tell him that the idea of him wearing lingerie turns you on.* "Then I thought about you in, I don't know…something lacy maybe. Something feminine."

His eyebrows shoot to his hairline before he blinks, his expression smoothing, and then he's smiling like a sexy as fuck version of the Cheshire cat. "Raphael Scott. I had no idea you were so…kinky. That is the word, yes?"

"I'm not kinky. *You're* kinky. You're wearing lace fucking stockings, Jae."

"And you find them sexy."

"I find you wearing them incredibly sexy."

"And you'd find me in lingerie sexy too." It's not even a fucking question. He states it like it's fact. It *is* fact. "Or maybe it is the skirt?"

He's still smiling and damn I really love his smile when it's like that, all loose and open. Everything with Jae is so careful and precise, executed with thought, but not this smile. I really want to be the only person he smiles at like that.

"It's all of it. It's you and all of it."

His smile falls a little, then changes into something else. Something warmer, less flirtatious.

"I wish you were here," he says, in a low soft tone that pulls that same longing from my chest.

"I do too."

"It is not so long until Tokyo," Jae says.

It's not, but it also is.

When I don't answer Jae adds, "You still want to meet me there?" The uncertainty in his eyes makes him look younger. Vulnerable.

"Yeah, of course. I'm coming. I'll look at flights tomorrow."

The relief is clear on his face and he's soon smiling again.

After a moment, he says, "I was wearing, how do you call them, undershorts. White undershorts."

"Well that's disappointing." I sigh and he pretends to be insulted. I'm still hard though. "What about now? You wearing undershorts now?"

He shakes his head, licking his tongue slowly over his lips. "I'm wearing..." He looks down at himself. "Nothing but a towel now. What about you?"

"Um, grey sweats. Nothing else."

"It is warm there? In LA?"

"It's colder than any December I can remember since I moved here, but still warm."

He nods. "Don't catch a cold."

I smile. "That's not about to happen anytime soon, don't worry. I'm still hot from my workout and you're basically naked. I feel like I'm burning up, and I'm really fucking hard."

His eyes widen and I see his hand come up to his chest as he brushes it across his left nipple. "Show me," he whispers.

My eyes almost bug out of my head even as my breath trips, before speeding up.

"You wanna see? My...cock?"

"Mmm. Please. If you are comfortable."

It takes me less than a second to decide that I'm comfortable. I flip my camera around first and point it at my crotch, which is hard and tenting the fabric. Then I slide my hand into the waistband and push it down, exposing my cock and balls to the cool air. I hear Jae let out a low appreciative sound, then another, louder, as I wrap my hand around it and jerk it a few times.

"So hard," he remarks.

"I was hard before you called me."

"Because of my photo? Or because you thought of me in lingerie?"

"Both. It's just…you, I think. You always make me hard, Jaehyun…" I manage through half gritted teeth. "So fucking hard."

"Spit on your hand," he says calmly. "Then touch yourself again."

I obey without hesitation. Smoothing the saliva over my dick, as he makes soft appreciative noises. I miss his face so I flip the camera back and find him sitting up again. The hand that was rubbing his nipples isn't anymore.

"What about you? You hard?" I ask.

"Yes." He nods, flipping his camera to show me. The towel is open and his cock is hard against his open thigh, but he's not touching it. His knees are pulled up as he touches himself lower, past his cock, between his legs. "I cannot wait to feel your cock here again… my fingers are good, but not as good as you."

I let out a groan. "Fuck, I miss your hole, baby. So tight and warm…it's perfect."

"Mmm, yes. Did you like stretching me open, Raphael? Making me fit you?" He's breathing hard now, through his nose as he bites his lip. "Did you?"

"Yes…I fucking loved it." My hand speeds up, thumb scraping over my cockhead, spreading the precome over the crown. I want to touch my balls with my other hand but that would mean putting the phone down and that would mean not seeing his face.

"I liked it too. So much. I felt you for days after… I still feel you a little now." He's moaning now and his cheeks are pink and it's the hottest fucking thing I've ever seen. "I want to feel your come inside, Raphael. Feel you spilling out of me. Would you like that? To see your come dripping out of my hole?"

"Jesus…fuck, Jae."

And then I'm coming. No warning. Spilling all over my knuckles as I milk myself through it, pumping hotly over and over. Jae's mouth is open partly as he watches, and on pure instinct I flip the camera again and show him the last few spurts of my orgasm. I hear him come a second later and I flip it back, bathing in the glow that is Jaehyun coming. Soft, quick breaths that are delicate and almost feminine, gentle cries that are fucking melodic. He orgasms like he dances, controlled and expertly. But there's a loosening of his body as he comes, an unravelling, like a ribbon in the wind, and it's beautiful to watch.

He laughs softly and I can't help but copy him.

"Well, that was not disappointing," I say and he giggles softly.

"So, you miss my hole?" he ponders and I groan with embarrassment. He laughs harder and I realize that it's somehow become one of my favorite sounds in the whole world. Lee Jaehyun's laugh.

"Never trust anything I say on the brink of orgasm, ever. My brain is entirely in my dick."

"So, then you don't miss it? That is a shame." He pouts, the embers of laughter in the corners of his eyes still.

"I miss every part of you," I say and he sobers immediately.

I do too. Fully taken aback by how utterly sentimental that sounded. How deep it sounded. He looks…scared.

"I just mean, yeah. I miss it. I miss you. I know it doesn't make a whole lot of sense, I know we only spent a few days together, but it felt like it was more than just a few days you know? It felt like a lifetime in some ways. Like a religious experience. I felt like that when I first saw you too. Like I heard angels singing or something."

Fucking hell, what am I saying? Stop talking Rapha. Stop it. When I glance back at Jae he looks amused. Soft and sleepy and not scared. Just amused. Relief hits every cell in my body.

"A religious experience?" He laughs, not derisive, just endearing.

Like he finds me cute or something. "Angels singing? I am starting to think maybe I should not trust what you say *after* an orgasm either. Is your brain still in your dick?"

I laugh at that. "Maybe...you know what, maybe. Or maybe I left it up your ass or something."

He laughs louder and makes a show of looking for it. Between his legs. Up his ass. Then I'm laughing harder, stupid ridiculous laughter with tears in my eyes and I've never felt so fucking...light. Not as a kid or as an adult. Maybe it's just that post orgasm, come-drunk high. But I feel filled with possibility, hope, anticipation.

I'm...happy.

My next thought drags me back to Earth.

Now that I know what this is, surely I need to call Camille. Tell her it's over.

Tell her it's very fucking likely I'm in love (love?) with someone else.

TWENTY-TWO
RAPHAEL

"How was Colarado?" Cleo asks, pulling me into a hug. She's cut her hair, a short pixie-looking style which suits her. "Your mom good?"

"Good. Really good. Your hair looks great." I deflect, scared if she looks too long she'll see something on my face. Like *I fucked a guy is now* printed on my forehead.

She ruffles a hand through it and beams, saying she wishes she'd waited until summer since LA is so cold. We shoot the shit for a bit before Zeke struts in, sporting sunglasses and a full beard. He looks well-rested and eager. Crawf is next, looking like shit. When Mase is nowhere to be seen an hour later we start without him. Jamming mainly, relaxing back into it. My SG sounds like a fucking dream. Clean and pretty, the strings cool under my fingers but the body warm and familiar against mine. It's not as good as Jae feels against me, but it's a close second.

It's another hour before Mason walks in the door. He picks up his guitar without a word and joins in. He too looks like shit, like he's lost weight and has spent the last fortnight hiding from the sun. He doesn't even look at me. Barely looks at any of us actually. I cast a look round at Crawford who just shrugs and plays on.

I play through a couple of the songs I'd come up with, though really they're just words with the barest suggestion of tune behind them, letting the guys fill in the blanks. It's as effortless as ever. First Zeke lays down a beat, Cleo filling in the bass to complement. Crawford then layers his guitar over mine, giving the riff some structure. It's Mase that brings it all together though. With a little modal alchemy, some well-placed grace-notes and a few backing vocals, what sounded like nothing twenty minutes ago now has fucking *wings*. I still get goosebumps from how easily we do this. Sayonara had been a fucking nightmare, but we still pull this stuff together like we were born from it. It just works. Each strand coming together perfectly every single time. Jeff calls through to tell us there's food, but we keep playing, not ready to stop quite yet.

Crawford pulls some insane chord progression out that he says he dreamt about and we're lost to it for another hour. Cleo and I finding some lyrics from nowhere that fit perfectly, Mase adding a section that elevates it further. I just watch him for a bit, envious but proud. He's one of the greatest guitar players on the planet—Guitar World had called him that in 2020 and he just fucking shrugged it off, like it was nothing. Hendrix was in the same fucking list. But it's true. He makes it look so fucking effortless and there's always this moment in the studio when it's like we all remember just how good he is and stop playing just to watch him. His voice is incredible too. Rougher and lower than mine but with a perfect pitch. He's not half bad on the drums either. He was almost our front man and sometimes it's clear why. There are still videos of the guys before I joined with Mase out front, but he'd said he hated it. Said he'd just wanted to play guitar. One night he'd been too wasted to perform and I'd stepped up. Mase said it was the best gig we'd ever done and that he'd never stand out front again. No one had argued.

Watching him now though, I wonder if he ever regrets it. Letting me take this from him. I hadn't meant to, didn't want to, but a front man is just that. The front and center. It's my name people hear first. My face they see first. And sometimes, I wonder if he might hate me for it.

I think of Jae then. Of his band, of how it's always Kai front and center during interviews and press but how when they perform they somehow look like equals on that stage. I think I'll talk to Jae about it at some point. Maybe it's a genre thing, I know bands like his are designed in such a way so that people gravitate towards a favorite. Bands like mine are formed around a front man, and maybe if he's exceptional, a guitarist gets to lead sometimes too. But it's the front men of rock bands in the west that are treated like messiahs.

Finally we stop for food, and after wolfing down two slices of pizza, Mason disappears outside. The others look at me pointedly as he goes. I'd been planning on talking to him anyway, so I finish my slice and follow him.

"Hey," I call out, watching his back tense.

He's sat on the low wall, smoking a joint with his eyes closed and his face turned up to the setting sun. He says nothing as I sit down next to him, only holding the blunt out as an acknowledgement of my presence. I take it and inhale deep before handing it back to him. I try to remember the last time I got high and think it was the night before I went to Jae's apartment. It hits me a little harder than I expect it to for that reason.

"Guess we should talk, properly, huh?"

He looks down at his hands and shrugs. "Yeah, I guess."

I know it's not all my fault that Mase and I are in this weird place right now. It was his attitude about Cleo's brother, and my guess that it's how he would talk about Jae too, maybe even me, that shoved this wedge further between us. But hating him isn't gonna change his attitude, only gonna harden it.

"Look, I appreciate you reaching out in New York," I start. "But that shit about Asher, made me feel really uncomfortable. He's Cleo's brother, and Cleo's a good friend." I look at him. "To both of us. So yeah, it was...not cool, Mase."

He swallows, looking guilty. "Yeah, I know."

I think he's not gonna say anything more but then he sniffs, wiping his hand over his face.

"I was in a dark place that morning, Rapha. But you were right, I was out of line."

We'd just won a Grammy and he was in a dark place? Concern

makes me study him a moment. He looks the worst I've ever seen him look. Eyes, red from the blunt, shadows underneath them, his skin dry and sort of pale. He looks fucking haunted.

"Mase, you doing okay, man?"

I feel him tense slightly. "Yeah, man, you know. Same old shit." He laughs but it's completely hollow. "Hate fighting with you."

I sling an arm around him and pull him closer. "I hate it too." He nods but doesn't relax into my hug, his body still tense. So I let him go, ruffling a hand through his hair instead. "Don't worry about it."

"So, what about you and Cam?" He doesn't look up as he asks this. "You gonna be okay?"

"Yeah, we'll be okay." Not together, not married, but as long as she doesn't hate me then we'll be okay.

He nods, his shoulders dropping slightly. I sit with him while he finishes his joint in contemplative silence. When he's finished he stands and looks down at me. "Let's go back in," he says, as he wanders back toward the building.

"Mason," I call after him.

When he turns he looks so fucking lost, like a kid who can't find his parents at the mall.

"We good?"

He nods, running a hand over his hair. "Course we are. Always, man."

But he looks vacant and rudderless.

When we break again, I send Camille a text asking if we can talk later. I don't want to do this on the phone but I can't avoid it much longer, not now I know. Not now the word love has entered my head in relation to someone who isn't her.

It's twelve hours later when I get a response. She finishes shooting on the 18th and she'll be back in LA on the 19th. Her flight out to Lyon, to her parents place, is the 23rd. *We will talk then*, she says. I don't feel I have the right to push this, so I don't. I respond back with three words. *Ok*. And, *I'm sorry*.

If she didn't already know, I feel like she does now.

It feels over in every way except in words and I'm sorry for it. I really fucking am. But there's a small sliver of relief there too. Because the last two and a half years I've spent inside my head with these weird unnamed feelings for another person has felt like living two lives. Not knowing what it meant, what it was, who *I* was. It's been like having this weight settled on my chest which is gradually getting lighter.

The next few weeks I practically live at the studio. Calling or texting Jaehyun whenever I get a few moments alone. If the band notices, they don't say anything. But I'm certain I've seen a few suspicious looks from Mase whenever I've come back from speaking to him.

It's one night about three weeks out from NY when I get a notification of a message. A picture. I'm high and a little buzzed from tequila when I open it. It's a mirror selfie. Full length. He's naked. Fully fucking naked.

I almost choke on my drink as I swipe out of the picture and glance around me to make sure there's no chance anyone saw it. There's not, but Mase is across the couch from me, slouched low as he strums away at his Telecaster. The others are busy and not looking in my direction. I stand up and wander from the room out into the hallway until I find a corner and then open the picture again.

His fingers are splayed across his abdomen, close to where his piercings are, and his cock is flushed and half hard. Mine is too just looking at it.

He's sent the image with the message: **I am silver.**

That's when I finally notice his hair. With the sunlight hitting it from a window near him it looks bright, polished silver. Glowing. I type back.

Me: You're also naked.

The reply is immediate.

JH: Oh, yes. That too. ,)

I hit the number to dial, knowing that he's likely able to talk if he's sending me nudes. He answers after a couple of rings, his soft laugh floating down the phone.

"I am sorry. I did not mean to distract you from your work," he says without any conviction.

"Well, that's a lie. How was I not supposed to get distracted by that?"

"I thought maybe you would see it later. Before you went to sleep."

"I haven't slept in two days," I say. Which makes it even more miraculous that I'm able to get even half hard right now.

Jae tuts. "Sleep is important, Raphael. I do not want you to be tired when you get to Tokyo. That would be bad…"

"Yeah? How come?" I'm grinning now.

"Because I have lots of plans for us and I need you to be awake for them."

"What sorts of plans?"

"I do not want to distract you from your work by telling you. Plus, some of them are a surprise."

"I do like surprises." I sigh. "And I like your hair."

He laughs. "You do?"

"Yeah, it makes you look…like a fairy."

"I don't understand," he says. "What is…a fairy?"

"You know, the mystical creatures. Little, cute, pretty, with wings. Like Tinkerbell."

"Ah, *Yojeong*?!" He laughs louder. Then, "I am not so little."

"More little than I am."

"This is true…" It sounds seductive. "You are big. Your feet and your hands. And your cock."

The sound of that word coming from his mouth does something to my balls, a deep vibration running up through them. A needy, low thrum.

"Do you like my cock, baby?" I have no clue where it comes from but I blame it on the lack of sleep and the coke and tequila swimming around my blood. I hear him make a small, low, noise.

"Mmm, yes. I do. I like it a lot."

"What do you like about it?" I run a hand over the thing in question, pressing my palm against it.

"How it tastes. How it feels inside… how you fuck me with it."

I bite back a low groan. Fuck, I need to stop this before it's too late. Jae makes a similarly aroused noise and the image of him lying naked on his bed drenched in warm golden sunlight flashes across my mind.

"Are you touching yourself right now?"

"Perhaps." He gasps, whining a little. It gives me the real answer.

"Fuck, I wish I was there right now." I groan.

"*Are you fucking kidding me right now!?*" Comes the voice from behind me. I whip round to see Mase standing there, furious, mouth twisted in disgust.

I swallow, mouth drying up with shock.

Turning back around, I say quietly into the phone: "I'll call you back later, okay?"

"Is everything okay?"

I glance over my shoulder to find Mase's glare fiercer than before. "Yeah, everything's fine, don't worry."

"Text me that you are okay," he says, unconvinced.

"I will."

I hang up the phone and slide it into the back pocket of my jeans as I take a step toward Mase. Something violent flares in his eyes that stops me going any closer.

"You're fucking someone else?" he spits.

"It's not entirely like that, man. It's…complicated."

"*Do you like my cock, baby?*" He mocks. "*Are you touching yourself right now?* You piece of shit. Like fuck it's complicated!"

I try my best to keep my voice calm. To stop this escalating. "You don't know what you're talking about, Mase, so just let it go, okay? Let it go."

He laughs at that, taking a step toward me. "*Let it go?* She fucking worships you! She loves you, Rapha, and you're sticking it somewhere else because you're what, bored? Is that what you were doing in New York? When she was worrying about you? When *I* was worrying about you?"

There's rage in Mase's tone but there's something else too, something desperate and painful. I don't get it.

"I said, let it go. You don't know shit."

I go to move past him but he grabs me, pulling me back to face him. It happens too fast to duck or put my hands up before his fist connects with my face, hot white pain exploding across my jaw.

"You piece of fucking shit. You're not doing this to her!" He goes to hit me again but I manage to block it and then the others are there dragging him back. "You piece of shit!"

"What the fuck?" Zeke is saying as Crawford wraps an arm around Mason and pulls him away from me down the corridor.

"Don't fucking touch me! Get off me, Crawf!" Mase is raging as I touch a hand up to my face to check the damage.

Cleo looks anxiously between us as Mase and Crawford disappear back inside the studio, door slamming closed.

"What was that all about?" she asks me.

"He's been in a weird fucking mood since the Grammy's man," Zeke murmurs.

"He's pissed at me. It's not about you guys." I flex the numbness out of my face.

"He's more than pissed at you, Rapha. What the fuck's going on?"

"Camille and I are over. He blames me for it, I guess." I shrug because I honestly don't get it and I don't know what else to say.

"You and Camille are over?" Cleo asks, shocked, before some weird wide-eyed look passes between her and Zeke. It feels odd, like I'm missing something, but my head fucking hurts and I'm buzzing from the adrenaline so I can't think entirely straight. He actually hit me.

Cleo doesn't look quite as ready to let the thing go as Zeke does, staring at me a long time.

"Let's call it a night," she suggests. "We've all been at this too long. I'll take you home."

She's the only sober one between us and so I wonder if that's why she doesn't seem to be buying the story I just sold them about why Mase punched me. I'm not sure I'm buying it either. She tells me to wait by her car while she grabs my bag and shit from inside the studio. The fresh air feels cool and helps soothe my head a bit as I stand there. When she reappears there's a whole range of emotions on her face as she meets my eye across the roof of her jeep.

"He okay?" I ask.

She gives me another weird look before the door unlocks and she climbs inside.

"Is he?" I ask again when we're both seated.

She sighs. "He will be. He needs to stop doing so much of that shit if he can't act like a fucking adult."

"It wasn't his fault, C. It was mine."

She whips her head round to scowl at me. "You don't see what's right in front of your face, do you?"

I frown. "What's that supposed to mean?"

"Forget it, Rapha." She shakes her head, starts the engine and pulls out of the parking lot.

"I assume you offered to drive me home so you could lecture me about something, so get on with it."

"I offered to drive you home because I don't want you two killing each other." She sighs again. "And with the amount of shit I watched him take tonight, that was a very possible fucking outcome."

I think about that. About how much cocaine I watched Mase do tonight—more than Crawf or I, more than usual. He seemed wasted when he arrived too. I think back to how he was two hours late the first day we arrived too. His mood when we talked. And further back, his mood the day of the meeting when we fought. All of it feels, off.

I was in a dark place.

Something feels…off about it all. The way Zeke and Cleo looked at each other when I told them Camille and I were over and that Mason blamed me for it.

You really don't see what's right in front of your face do you.

I look around at Cleo. She's biting hard on the inside of her lip, hands gripping the wheel as she speeds through Silverlake.

"What the fuck am I missing, Cleo?" I ask her.

My head is loud. So fucking loud. Like an ocean loud. She tenses as she looks round at me, indecision and anxiety warring on her face. But there's something else there too. I don't recognize it straight away. But then I do. Pity. She glances back at the road.

"Rapha, it's not really my place to say this. You and Mason need to talk, work things out."

"Work what out?"

"Look, don't put this on me. This isn't fair, okay." She looks nervous now. "This has been going on so long and you're so fucking clueless sometimes—like a fucking puppy—I've told them that."

Some noise goes off inside my head.

"*Them*? You mean the others?" My head is starting to pound now, narcotics and alcohol being washed away by the building confusion and anxiety. "Cleo, just spit it out. I don't know what the fuck is going on here, but I'd really appreciate it if you'd enlighten me."

She looks at me again, pitiful like. Then closes her eyes and curses something in Spanish.

"Mase and Camille. They were like…together, they fucked I mean. Before you guys got together," she clarifies quickly. "But he's like, fuck Rapha, he's in love with her or something."

Or something.

He's in love with her or something.

"I don't…*what*?" I'm not even sure which part of it I'm not getting. All of it. Any of it. I break each part down: Mase and Camille were together. They fucked. Before we got together. Mason's in love with Camille. With the woman I was going to marry. They fucked. And I didn't know. Didn't even suspect. Mason is in love with Camille.

"I'm sorry Rapha, I know this is weird…it's something we all said you—."

"Pull over," I cut her off.

Cleo glances at me first, concerned, then checks her mirror and pulls over. The street isn't as deserted as I'd like as I throw open the door, stumble out of the Cherokee and empty my guts out onto Hyperion Avenue.

TWENTY-THREE
RAPHAEL

Cleo hands me two white tablets and a glass of water and sits down on the rug in front of me. She crosses her legs and temples her hands under her chin as she studies me, careful, like I'm about to breakdown or something

"I shouldn't have said anything," she says.

I give her a look at that. "Yeah, you should have."

"You were in love with her Rapha, and happy. We didn't want to ruin that."

"You mean you didn't want to ruin this band. Like any of you give a shit about who I am in love with."

She looks hurt as she curls her toes into the carpet. "I wanted to tell you—I told them we should tell you. But then...I stopped. I saw their argument. And like, would you really have wanted to know about this back then? When you saw fucking stars when you looked at her?"

"Yes! I fucking would have! To know you all lied to me, to my face—all this time. How do you think that makes me feel, C?"

She says nothing. Looks down.

"It makes me feel like you care about this band a hell of a lot more than you care about me."

"I care about you, Raphael. I love you. You're one of my best friends." She looks up at me. "But Mase is too. And he was hurting. Watching you together was torture for him."

"Wow, so now I'm to feel *sorry* for him?"

"No, that's not what I'm saying but just like…try and see it from our perspective. It was hard for us to watch. To be torn between you two like that."

"My heart fucking bleeds for you, Cleo, it does. All of you. How fucking sad for you all. Watching me be a clueless fucking idiot all this time must have been real hard for you, yeah, totally. What was it you said, a clueless fucking puppy? That's right."

I stand, storming through to the kitchen to the freezer to fish out the bottle of Grey Goose I keep in there. I don't bother with a glass, twisting the cap off and slugging a large mouthful back. The burn feels nice as it scorches its way down my throat into the bitter heat of my stomach.

Cleo stays where she is on the carpet, watching me with big sad eyes, round with pity.

I hate it.

"When did they fuck?" I ask as I walk back towards her.

"I don't know the details," she says miserably.

"You know the details. Tell me."

"You should talk to them about it, Rapha."

"The two people who've lied to my face every day for years? Yeah, I think I'll pass."

I swig another angry mouthful. I'm a hypocrite, I know that. But it makes no fucking difference right now. It pisses me off that I can't even decide what I'm angry about. *Who* I'm angry with. Camille, maybe. Mase, sure. The others who knew about it and said nothing, who were gonna sit there in that fucking chateau in France and watch me marry someone that fucked my best friend and not say a fucking word about it. A woman that my best friend is in love with. Something hits me then, with all the force of a sledgehammer to the face.

"Does she love him back?"

Am I standing in the way of some great fucking romance? Am I the other person?

Cleo looks confused by this line of questioning. "I...don't think so. I don't know. Honestly, I don't know anything."

"You know more than me."

She gives me another of her sad looks. I take another drink.

We're both quiet for a long time before I say something I hadn't even planned to.

"I've met someone else."

She blinks with shock. So Mase hadn't said anything to the others about my phone call after Crawf had dragged him off. "Does Camille know?"

I nod. "She knows there's someone. She was surprisingly understanding about it," I scoff as I take another drink. Now I'm wondering why.

"Is it...serious?"

"It's a guy."

I'm not sure why it comes out right then. Whether this revelation has shifted a whole lot of others into perspective and so it's easier to say than I imagined it would be. Or if it's just the Grey Goose. But Cleo's mouth falls open and she's getting up off the floor to come sit on the barstool across from me.

"Rapha, that's...wow. You've never been with a guy before, right? Like, this is new?"

I nod, wordlessly.

"Fuck..." she whispers, watching me with something like awe.

"He heard us talking on the phone. Mase. That's why he lost it."

"He knows?"

"He knows there's someone. Not that this someone has a cock."

She covers her mouth and sinks back, sighing loudly. "Holy shit, Rapha. This is fucking huge...how? Like when?"

"I don't know much about this stuff, Cleo but I'm pretty sure it's not something that happens overnight. Like it's always been there, right?"

Cleo's bi. Never not been as long as I've known her. Has had male and female lovers, though more of the former just because of the circles we move in. "So you're like, pan?"

I shrug. "I'm not even sure I know what that is."

"You like guys or just him?"

I think about this though I really don't have to. "I'm pretty certain it's just him."

Her eyes go bug wide again.

"I've known him a while I guess, but nothing happened until New York."

She nods. "So Camille knows it's a guy? Maybe that's why she was sort of okay about it...she knows this is a big deal for you."

I shake my head. "She doesn't know that. Only you and my mom do, so far."

Her mouth shapes into an 'o'. "How do you think she'll take it?"

"Right now? I honestly don't give a shit."

It's a lie. I do care. Of course I do. I'm not sure what my exact feelings about Camille are right now. I need to talk to her. I need to talk to Mason too. But I honestly don't think my brain or body can take it right now. What I *want* is to talk to Jae. Another thirteen days before I leave for Tokyo and it may as well be a fucking year for all the shit I'm going to have deal with before I get on that plane.

I swallow back some more of the Goose. "I don't know how the fuck I fix this, Cleo. How do we all go in there tomorrow and record?"

"I'll speak to the guys and tell them you're done for the holidays, tell them you know everything and you need some time to get your head around shit," she says forcefully. "Talk to Camille and maybe Mason, if you feel up to it. Zeke, Crawf and I can record some more without you. You can lay the vocals down when you get back."

I don't know how I feel about that. I want to play. I'd missed playing. All of us back in one room again made it feel like I still knew who I was. That not a single thing had changed. When everything had. I liked the certainty of that.

"Take your equipment to your mom's and see if you can get anything down?" she suggests, seeing the indecision clear on my face.

The idea of them recording any part of this album without me seems wrong, makes me feel uneasy and a little cut out. But the idea of facing them all tomorrow only hammers home the fact that they already did that. They cut me out when they decided to keep this from me. When they decided to rally round Mason and keep his secret for him.

I manage only to nod as the unease swims over my gut again. Cleo puts a hand on my shoulder and squeezes.

"You need to eat something if you're planning on finishing that." She gestures at the bottle. "I'll make you some grilled cheese."

I don't argue. I could always eat grilled cheese, something she knows only too well. As she busies herself in the kitchen I pull out my phone. There's a message from Jae from over an hour ago.

JH: Let me know you are okay. Sorry about the photo—I did not mean for it to cause problems. :(

When I open the photo in question again, my body physically aches from want. From how much I want to be with him. Feel the angles of his lean body pressed against mine while he sleeps. Kiss the taste of him into my mouth. Hear the soft broken noises he makes when I do. I flick back to the text screen and type out a response.

Me: I'm good. I just really fucking miss you. Call you later?

Then, without giving it another thought, I write:

Me: What are you doing for Christmas?

Mom wouldn't be mad if I missed Christmas in Colorado. Not when I just spent Thanksgiving there. I honestly think if I tell her who I'm spending it with she'd likely squeal with excitement again. He said he's working right up until Christmas Eve but he made no mention of spending it with his family. I wonder if that's because of the stuff he mentioned about his dad. There's a selfish fucking part of me that hopes he isn't spending Christmas with his family, because then he could spend it with me.

I'm waiting for a reply when my phone rings. Not Jae though. Camille.

My body goes completely still as I stare at it. I know then that she's spoken to Mase. Because she does that. She did it when I was in New York too. Clearly it's something they do. Something twists in my gut, bitter and hot, and I take another sip from the bottle as I watch her ring off. The missed call message pops up. Then a text.

Camille: Raphael, please call me. It's not what you think, I promise you.

There's a heart too. A little red one. It swims in front of my eyes as I stare at it trying to decide why *I* feel guilty. I blink it away, but it stays blurry. I'm wasted. There's no response from Jae by the time I'm slouched on the sofa and Cleo comes back with my grilled cheese. The cheese oozes out of the sides and suddenly I'm ravenous.

"You going to be okay? I can stay if you want? Talk this out. Or we can just watch Ghost in The Shell and get wasted?"

She looks worried about me and I sort of understand why. I feel edgy and frayed, a bit unhinged honestly. I've just come out to her, found out my best friend is in love with my (ex?) girlfriend, and almost sank a bottle of quality vodka—all in the space of a couple of hours.

I take a bite of the sandwich and shake my head. "I'm good. Gonna finish this and sleep it off. Thanks." I talk round a mouthful as I hold it up.

She nods, warily. "You call me if you need to okay? I'm here for you, we all are. Even if you don't believe me right now."

"I believe you." I'm not wholly sure if it's the truth, but I also don't think I have the capacity to lie about it right now either. Too much effort.

She leans in and plants a loud kiss on the top of my hair.

"Love you," she says, picking up her keys and heading for the door.

"Cleo," I call after her.

She stops, turning.

"Don't mention it to them. Not yet. I'm not ready to deal with their shit about it yet."

I'm hoping I don't need to clarify which part.

"Of course not. We made all of this shit with you and Camille and Mase about us—which it wasn't at all. And this definitely isn't. This is yours, Rapha. It's no one's business. I've got your back, okay? Always."

I nod. She smiles. Then she's gone. And then I'm alone.

I do turn on Ghost in The Shell. If there's such a thing as a comfort movie, that's mine. I'm not sure when I pass out, but it's after I smoke a joint and sink the rest of the vodka. It's after Camille has called a few more times and sent me another text urging me to call her. It's also before I get a response from Jae. My phone deathly silent from his end. It makes me a little edgy, like maybe I've a form of separation anxiety or something. Makes me think about what he really wants and about what I have left if he doesn't want me as a serious thing in his life.

Happier than I can remember feeling in a long time.

That meant something. This feeling swirling in my gut is paranoia, from all the drugs and alcohol I'd put in my body over the last fortnight. I make him happy. It's real.

When I wake up next morning I feel the worst I can remember feeling in my life.

My mouth is dry as a desert and my head feels like it's being crushed in a vice. Grilled sandwich along with a liter of pure alcohol, fear and panic and anger all sloshing around together in my chest. As I pick up my phone I've a moment of panic that I may have drunk tweeted something publicly, something about Mase and Camille, something about Jae, but I've never been that reckless online. Fuck, did I drunk call Jae? Nah, but I did text him about Christmas.

My phone doesn't light up because it's died sometime in the night. My gut churns some more as I haul my body up from the couch, bone and muscle snapping back into place as I stretch it out. I plug the phone in as I take a scalding hot shower, letting the steam blast away some of my hangover. I stand in there for close to thirty minutes without washing, just staring at the grey tiled wall, wondering how the people I'm closest to in the world could lie to me all this time and have no idea.

Yeah, okay, I know I've kept shit from Cam these past few weeks too, months even, but it doesn't feel the same. *Hypocrite.*

Finally, I scrub the water from my face and wash my hair and body. Then scrub my teeth until they feel sensitive and sore.

My phone is sitting on the desk silent and dark and I'm sort of dreading picking it up. Scared of Camille and the guys, but especially Jae.

What are you doing for Christmas?

What was I thinking? I'm an idiot. A needy, drunken idiot.

With a curse I grab it and press to unlock. There are a few messages from Camille. One from Zeke. One from Cleo. One from mom. I swipe past them all to get to Jae's. There are two.

JH: Good! Glad you are okay!

***JH: Christmas? We have schedule until 24th. But then we are on holiday until 3rd. Why?** ☺

It's embarrassing how much my heart soars from that stupid fucking smiley. How the warmth spreads through my chest, hotter and more healing than the shower I just took. My head clears right up too. It's 6 a.m. there right now, meaning he won't be awake for me to call him, and suddenly I fucking hate this time difference. How the fuck would we even do long distance with this in the way? Would I move to Korea? Right now I'm thinking yes, I would. In a heartbeat.

Me: Call me when you wake up?

My phone rings almost immediately, startling me.

"You're awake?" I move towards the bed but my phone is in the charging point so I turn back, rotating in an aimless circle.

"I haven't been to sleep yet," he says, croakily. Sleep heavy on his voice. "I practiced until late, then I was live for a bit. I thought you might have called back and I didn't want to miss you."

"Fuck, I'm sorry. I passed out." I feel like a dick. He says nothing. "Live?" I ask.

"We-live, for a while."

"Not naked I hope?"

This gets a small laugh. "No, not naked. Why did you ask me about Christmas?"

Whatever bravado I had last night definitely feels dulled by my hangover, but I drag some up from somewhere.

"I was wondering if you'd want to, like, spend it together. With me."

"In LA?" The fact there's no hesitation makes me feel warm.

"Fuck no, not here. Anywhere else."

"Does this mean you cannot come to Tokyo?"

"No, I can. I am, I want to come to Tokyo too. I just…" I clear my throat. "I miss you. I really fucking miss you. And a few days in Japan with other people isn't gonna do it, you know? I want to spend the holidays with you. I was going to go home to see my mom but I think she'd be okay with this. With me coming to see you."

"You…want to spend Christmas with me?"

He doesn't sound horrified, only mildly surprised. At least I hope that's what it is. It occurs to me that I don't know him well enough to tell yet. *I want to spend every fucking minute with you* isn't something I can say right now, not with the paranoia still flickering on the outer edges of my brain.

"Is that too much?" I ask, tone light.

He says nothing for so long I wonder if maybe he's fallen asleep. Then: "Seoul is very pretty in winter," Jae says. "I would like to show it to you."

"You don't have to spend it with your family, or…"

"We don't spend Christmas together," he says, without elaborating.

Nothing else matters then. Not Camille or Mase or the state of our band. Nothing matters except seeing Seoul in winter.

"Then, I'd really fucking like that."

막간
(JAE'S INTERLUDE #2)

I feel anxious and sick. Like I have done something wrong and I'm just waiting to be discovered. This is outside of the rules we've had since our debut.

For eight years, every personal relationship either of us has had or thought about having, has been declared to the company. For the first four of those years, it was forbidden to enter into any. But after that—after Kai and I almost imploded the band—the rules were eased. And as long as we abided by some carefully constructed and mutually agreed protocols, we could see whomever we liked.

No one had ever dated a western, male rock star before. There was no protocol for that.

One of the protocols was to advise the company of any new 'deepening personal (sexual) relationship/s.' So preparations could be made and NDA's drafted. Announcements prepared in case of leaks. There were also defamation lawsuits waiting to be filed if anything false was posted by the media or by our exes about those relationships.

Six months ago, the company had dealt with a fake pregnancy rumor about Boohyin and Saela before it could go public, and there was still the odd rumor in some online circles concerning Kai and me. But since it was mixed in with the usual 'shipping' fans do with bands and their members, it was easy to ignore that.

But the fact remained, no personal relationship had ever been discovered by the press because we followed the protocols.

Until now. Until I'd broken them.

Any serious relationship would make the headlines on Newsen. A relationship with a western artist would make headlines across the world. A relationship with a male western artist? That would destroy us. Certainly here at home. We'd pushed the limits over and over again, of course, but this will not be accepted as easily as the outfits and the lyrics and the music videos. I know that.

My stomach lurches once more and I have to rest a hand against the wall of the elevator to steady myself as my legs lose a little strength.

I should have said no. I should have told Raphael coming to Seoul wasn't possible. But there had been something in his voice that called out to me, saying things that he himself wasn't saying. He said he missed me—*I really fucking miss you, Jae*—but it felt like more than that. It felt as though he *needed* me. I'd never had someone need me before. Not like that. If felt...good.

But this wasn't the same as a few stolen nights in New York. Or a few nights in Tokyo over New Year's. This was him coming here, to Seoul, to my home. Seoul was not New York. We'd not left the apartment together there.

Which is why I have to tell them. All of them. The meeting is our monthly schedule rundown. Where the company tells us where we have to be, when we have to be there, and what is expected of us. It's shorter than usual because we only have a few more things planned before we break for Christmas. So normally we talk about our plans for the holidays, what we need from the company, what they need from us, travel details, emergency contacts and a brief overview of our first appearances of the New Year.

I'm not the last to arrive and the meeting hasn't started yet. Xan and Kai are not here, though no doubt they are above us somewhere in a studio working.

Taejin seems to be in a good mood, laughing with Seungmin about something near the vending machine. Boohyin is looking at something on his phone that has him laughing quietly. Ji-u is eating ramen from a pot next to me, slurping loudly. He slides the pot to me and offers me his chopsticks. I shake my head. I'm going to throw up.

When the door opens and Xan walks in, followed by Kai, the muscles in my back bunch up almost painfully. I can't do this.

I barely hear a word that Seung or Lua say throughout the entire meeting. I'll be sent an email afterwards with all the important details, so it is not critical to listen. We meet in person so we can discuss any issues with the scheduling, any concerns about individual aspects, anything we think might be a problem. It's all very lighthearted and informal though that isn't always the case. Some gifts are exchanged, presents for Lua's children and Seungmin's wife. Then we are talking about the break period and what we are all doing. Who we are spending it with. How much we are looking forward to seeing our friends and families.

"Jaehyun, you are going to Tokyo, right?" Lua asks and it suddenly feels like there is a spotlight on me, a microphone shoved under my mouth, and everyone is staring.

"On the 30th, yes." I nod. "I'll be back in Seoul on the 2nd."

She nods, smiling with genuine warmth. "With Shi-Eun?"

I swallow.

For some reason, I glance at Kai who's been only half involved in this entire meeting, typing on his phone, looking stressed. There's a line between his eyebrows that hasn't shifted since he walked in and he looks very tired.

I'm being a coward, I know this. Why am I so afraid? These people are my friends, my brothers, they care about me, they've always supported me—why would this be any different? I am overthinking it, as always.

I clear my throat and then my mouth is moving and it's too late to second, third, or fourth guess it anymore. I'm not entirely sure what order the words leave my mouth, but they do.

Xan sits up in his chair, Ji-u too, and Kai stops scrolling his phone—the line that had been etched between his eyebrows gone now. I zone in around the end of my little announcement and my voice sounds strange and formal, like I am reading the news. I still haven't mentioned Raphael by name and I'm not sure why. That feels like an additional revelation all on its own.

"...so he will be arriving on 23rd and staying with me at my apartment and then we will go to Tokyo, together. Seungmin-ssi, I will pass the details to you if you can arrange a car from Incheon for his arrival."

There are a few beats of silence in which Seungmin glances

towards Kai, before looking back at me. It makes me think that despite what he promised me, he did tell Seungmin about Raphael. But then Boohyin and Ji-u also glance at Kai and I think perhaps that's not it at all.

"This is a relationship that you are serious about pursuing?" asks Seungmin finally.

"I would not be putting myself through this…" I indicate the room "…if it was not."

The air in the room has changed, and me with it. I feel exposed and peeled raw and for a small fleeting moment, I resent Raphael for it. I think about how foolish I am going to look if this should all fall apart or if he wakes up after a few days with me to realize that he is in fact straight after all.

Seungmin nods.

"There is something else," I say. "Something which makes this more complicated, I suppose."

I glance round the table at everyone and then immediately look down at the grain because everyone staring at me while I talk about Raphael is far too intense. I smooth my finger over the polished wood as I tell them the rest.

"He is…in a group, an American rock group. And well, his sexuality is not announced. Not known. He has only discovered it himself and so—."

"Who is it?" Xan cuts in. His eyes are dark and almost accusatory.

As I try to understand why he's looking at me like that, Kai speaks.

"Raphael Scott," he says.

The room is silent for a beat before it turns very loud.

"You knew about this?"

"You are dating Raphael Scott?"

"Isn't he married?"

"Engaged."

"He's straight?"

"Clearly not."

"This started in New York?"

"This is a disaster."

It is just a babble of noise and questions until Seungmin tells everyone to be quiet.

"This is my business," I tell them firmly, though there is a tremor in my voice.

"Well, that's not technically true is it?" Xan says, who looks furious in a way I don't understand. "Everything we do affects the entire band. Something you are more than aware of, Jaehyun-ah. Have you any idea what this will do to us if the media catches even a hint of it?"

"Of course I'm aware," I snap.

"But you are going to do it anyway." He nods. "No matter how much it affects the rest of us. Because you are as selfish as you have always been."

"That's enough, Sang-kyu," Ji-hoon says, his voice low and authoritative.

The room stills. It's been a long time since I have heard him use that tone with anyone. Since any of us have. But Xan certainly. Xan defers to his elder and says nothing else. But then he stands and storms from the room. Not before throwing another weighted look in my direction.

The meeting wraps up quickly after that, though of course I'm asked to stay behind to run Lua and Seungmin through the scant details of mine and Raphael's holiday plans. It isn't of course, but it also is, very much like I've misbehaved in class and I will explain myself to the teachers.

Before Kai leaves he gives me a look that could be saying any manner of things. Mostly though, it looks like concern.

Seungmin-ssi and Lua want to know the exact nature of Raphael's engagement which is—according to Newsen—very much still on. I can only tell them what he told me—which is that it is over. For some reason, this earns me soft almost pitiful looks from them both and I feel my cheeks heat. It puts a sort of scrutiny on this thing between Raphael and I that I don't like at all. They tell me that while this may be the case, it doesn't ease their concerns about how it will all look if this should get out. To this I say that since it's their job to stop that happening, and since they have always been supremely successful at it, I don't fully understand the concern.

Still, they encourage *me* to encourage *Raphael* to at least formally announce his break-up with his actress girlfriend. Without any mention of us of course. I have absolutely no intention of doing this but of course I nod and tell them I will consider it. Our relationship, or whatever this is, has survived this long only because I've treated it with fragile hands and a tender touch. A butterfly's wings. To which any pressure applied whatsoever will result in a torn and broken body. Mine.

I give Lua Raphael's flight details which he sent last night, so they can arrange a car to pick him up at Incheon and bring him to my place, and then there's a question about sexual health practices which makes me feel like a child. Do I know his status? Have we used protection in each of our instances of intercourse? *The company would prefer to know the sexual status of all partners, but we understand this is not an easy conversation to have so early in the relationship.* I'm reminded that a doctor is available for the partners of all members, and that we can both be tested together if this will make it easier, and then I am done.

Out in the hallway, Ji-u is waiting, jittery with tension as I knew he would be. He lifts his head from his phone and there's a look in his eye like hurt. Betrayal too, perhaps.

"Do you want to get some food?" he asks, despite him finishing his pot ramen less than thirty minutes ago.

I nod though I'm not hungry.

When we're settled in a corner booth of the company restaurant, bowls of steaming Yukaejang in front of us both, he sits back in his seat and stares at me. Brown eyes big and wide, brimming with innocence. He's only two years younger than I am, but some days I feel that gap is far wider.

"You're angry with me," I say.

He thinks about this before shaking his head. "Not angry."

"Disappointed? Confused? Hurt?"

He thinks about this too and then lifts one shoulder in a shrug. "I guess, yes. All of that. There are no men in Korea for you to date?"

I huff out a laugh because he is nothing if not unwaveringly direct. There is no rudeness in him, it is just his manner.

"There are many, I suppose, just not many who want to date me." It is supposed to be a joke but somehow it comes out sounding both joyless and self-important.

"I don't know about that, Hyung. You are…" He waves his spoon in my direction. "You are Jaehyun."

As if this explains everything. Though in some way, I suppose it does. People want to date me because I am Jaehyun, and conversely, the opposite is also true.

"It wasn't planned, Ji," I tell him. "And I didn't keep it from you on purpose. I only wanted to see if it would become something… serious."

"And is it? Are you serious about Raphael Scott, Hyung?"

Fragile hands. Tender touches. A butterfly.

"It is early. I do not know yet," I reply, but it rings with a note of untruth. "But I would like to be."

Ji-u's face softens and he reaches forward to pick up his spoon. Only after he takes a huge slurp and makes a tiny high-pitched noise of pleasure as he swallows, does he answer.

Conversationally almost, he says: "Then it is Ji-hoon-Hyung I'm worried about."

We don't talk any more about Ji-hoon as we eat our soup, but Ji-u's comment does leave some lingering thoughts in his direction after we part.

I take the lift to the studio floor and knock on his door. It's Xan who opens it, pulling it wide to let me inside. I expect some further words of condemnation, but he says nothing. In fact, his eyes are softer than they were downstairs, a note of apology in them now even if it doesn't find its way to his lips.

I glance at Ji-hoon

If they were working before the meeting, they aren't now. Now, they're sharing a bottle of what looks to be his favorite Japanese whisky—the same one I now prefer—as American rap music plays low on the speaker system. Kai is in his high-backed desk chair in front of the computer, Xan's indent on the well-used leather sofa. Xan walks over and picks up his hoodie and pulls it over his head. Then lifts his glass and downs the contents.

"I'll let you talk," he says, with a long look in Kai's direction. As he passes he gives me a look that's definitely a warning.

I roll my eyes.

"See you, Hyung," I say loudly as the heavy door sighs closed behind him.

Ji-hoon reaches across to pour himself another glass. Without asking, he swivels around to lift another glass from the unit behind him and pours me a measure too.

"You spoke with Jong-hyun?" he asks, gently, concerned. "He was waiting outside for you like an expectant father."

I sit on the dented space of the leather sofa and lift the tumbler. "I did. He says he is worried about *you*."

I take a sip, watching Ji-hoon's shoulders tense and then release. His eyes are partly glazed with whisky and exhaustion, his mouth bitten red. The circles beneath his eyes look more pronounced in the low light.

"That is because he knows nothing about your American." His voice and eyes are serious. "It's you he should be worried about. Not me."

"Are you worried about me, Hyung? Is that what this is? That is what you and Xan were talking about? How worried you both are for me." It's a sarcastic, biting comment shaped to draw a reaction. And it does, just not the one I want or expect.

He sighs softly. "I always worry about you, Jaehyun-ah."

"We have spoken about this many times, it is not your place to worry about me."

He wants to argue this point. I see the words form on his tongue.

What he says is: "How can I not? When you do things like this? Telling the company? Inviting him to Seoul? What are you doing?"

"Living my life," I snap.

"He is going to hurt you."

The way you did, is unsaid. Instead, I say, "Then I will be hurt. Again. Then I will recover, again."

That familiar guilty look comes over his face. I don't think he even knows he looks at me like that.

"You deserve better than to be hurt over and over. To have your heart broken over and over."

"We get better the more we practice at something, Ji-hoon. You were the one who taught me that."

"Jae, I..." He stops, hesitates, looks down, back up. "If this is because of me...to prove something to me...to force this thing between us—"

The laughter when it rises up is almost hysterical. "Aishh, not everything is about you, Ji-hoon."

I drink the contents of the glass in three burning gulps while glaring at him. As he glares back at me.

"I suppose you are angry because you shall no longer have a bed to crawl into when you are lonely? Because you cannot bring yourself to let anyone past all of this?" I wave a hand over him, indicating *this*. "I have been a warm bed for you for too long, and it is over."

"You know that is not what you are," he growls, angrily.

He's angry because he cannot face the truth of it. It has always been the same. He has always been the same. An immovable stubborn thing. The qualities that make him strong and dependable are the same that make him bull-headed and unyielding.

"You are more than that, better than that, better than him."

"You do not know him!" I snap. "You know nothing of him but some stupid drunken comment he made once. Almost three years ago. Which he has apologized for. Which he is ashamed of. Hating him purely for this, without giving him a chance to prove what he is not, is not who you are. He is good and kind and when he looks at me...I know how he feels. He doesn't hide from me."

Where I hide from the world, Raphael wears his feelings proudly for all to see. He'd already told his mother about us, about me, like I was important and he was not ashamed.

"And he makes me smile and laugh. He makes me happy, Hyung, and you will not speak about him like you know who he is when you do not." I hadn't been aware that I was crying but I can feel the wetness leak down my face and I scrub at it, frustrated.

"I'm sorry," he says, soft, tormented. "You're right. I do not know him." He lets out a loud breath. "But I...would like to know him. If he's...if you care for him."

"I do. I care for him, Hyung. And I'm scared because...well, you know."

Because I don't want to care for someone again. I don't want to feel that alone again when they don't care for me the way I need them to.

"I will be back in Seoul on 27th," he says reaching out to grip my hand. "Perhaps we could meet, or I could prepare dinner? For all of us?"

I try to imagine that. It sounds awful and ill-advised—for so many reasons—but I can see how desperately he wants to try and it's that which makes me nod. Ji-hoon nods too. I stand.

"I will let you work. Sorry."

"No, I am sorry," he says again. "Let me know what I should make for dinner?"

I nod again and head for the door. "See you on Wednesday."

I'm almost at the door when he calls out. His voice is not loud, but it is firm. Resolute.

"Jaehyun-ah. I am sorry if what happened between us has ever made you feel...unimportant or has caused you to feel..." He looks broken and my chest floods with guilt. "I never ever wanted to hurt you. I love you...I just..."

"I know..." I whisper. It was me who wanted things he could not give me. Things he told me he could not give me.

"You don't see yourself the way I see you, the way the world sees you." His voice has a new weight in it, a heavy solid thing. The next words he says with a slightly resigned tone, but they still take my breath away. "The way your American looks at you too."

The article about Raphael's engagement breaks on the morning of the 22nd. It's forwarded to me by Seungmin. A link to an American news site without any text attached.

My blood turns cold because initially when I see his name in the URL, I think it's something about us. But then the page loads and I see the headline:

Raphael Scott and Camille Le Garde Split.

A source tells ENT, "Raphael and Camille have split up. The source reports that this was a mutual decision. "They both have a lot of love and respect for each other, but it was time for them to move on," the source continued. "Unfortunately they are in different places in their lives." The couple were due to marry in the south of France this summer but decided that ultimately the relationship wasn't working. We have reached out to both Raphael and Camille's spokespeople for comment.

There are pictures of them together in the article. Some candids of them laughing together as they walk down the street holding hands, a couple of them kissing in a coffee shop, and a few of them at public events looking perfect together. Camille Le Garde is beautiful and elegant in a way that is somehow distinctly French. I stare at her smile and try to imagine how she might look tearful and sad, and a sharp stab of guilt pierces my gut. I know it is not possible I am entirely to blame for the end of their relationship, but I played some part, some supporting role in its demise. Raphael looks happy too, by her side. But I suppose he wasn't. People who aren't happy are very good at pretending that they are. I know this.

I switch to Twitter to search for any reaction to the story, scrolling through some of the comments under the articles the news accounts have posted there. It is big news. Most comments appear to be critical of Camille, calling her fake and a bad actress, and accusing her of things I have no clue how they would know, such as cheating on him with a co-star and being critical of his lifestyle.

Then there are the fans of Raphael, flooding the comments about how talented he is, how hot he is, and who they want to see him with now. His bandmate Cleo is mentioned a lot, some even saying that they hope he has left Camille because he is in love with her instead. I click on a few pictures of him and Cleo together and agree that they do look handsome together. They look close on stage and in photoshoots, often smiling at each other and laughing. She's opposite to Camille physically; dark haired and olive-skinned with striking green eyes and a seductive-looking smile.

Amongst a thread of speculation, there is a comment about his father and I remember Raphael speaking about him in New York. It seems incredible to me then that I have not done this yet. Looked up his famous father. I'd realized immediately that the impassive tone in Raphael's voice when he spoke of him wasn't a lack of feeling, but the opposite. It was a sustained and practiced way of hiding pain. I'd recognized it immediately because it's as familiar to me as breathing.

When the page loads in front of me and the wealth of articles written about Raphael's father, Finn Sullivan, pop up, I am even more convinced. How could his father possibly be unimportant to him? He was important to so many people. He was the lead singer of a rock band, just like Raphael is. He was considered a great artist with a far reaching influence who died tragically. A tour bus crash had killed four members of his band, including their manager and driver. Raphael's father's body was incinerated inside the vehicle—there are pictures of the crash too, these I do not click on.

I pull up a YouTube video of a performance of Rapture of Malice. A headline stage at a British music festival and I'm stunned at the sight of Raphael's mirror image screaming into the microphone. Finn Sullivan's hair is a few shades darker than Raphael's, but his angled shoulders and lean limbs move in almost the exact same way, his voice a similar mix of tenor and alto, that youthful whine that can turn so easily to musical screech. *I didn't know him*, Raphael had said. And yet…there is so much of him in his father it's astounding.

Naver takes me to a biographical page about Finn Sullivan and I spend the next two hours reading about Raphael's father. The one who abandoned him and his mother right after he was born. The one who chose fame over family. Who chose stardom over his wife and child.

By some kismet of the universe, my phone rings. It's him. His father's face is gone, replaced by his own as I click on answer. The video screen opens and he's in his car, in the driver's seat. Sunglasses and a ballcap on. Messy blonde hair poking out from under it.

"So we're doing gifts, right?" he asks, like I have dropped into the middle of a conversation we'd already been having.

"Gifts?" I blink.

"Yeah, for Christmas. Like that's a thing you do? In Korea?"

I smile at that, laughing slightly. "Not like Americans do, but yes, we give gifts."

"So I should buy you a gift, then."

"I'd not thought about it. But if you like, yes."

"Is there something you want?"

I laugh again. Mainly at the ridiculous words that want to fall from my mouth at the question. "There are lots of things I want."

Raphael grins. "Are they all sexual? Cause I am down for that. You know that."

"Some of them are sexual. Some are intangible. Some are shiny and expensive."

He blinks. "Okay…I can't get you lingerie, right? Like that would be weird?"

Something hot stirs to life in my belly and lower. Raphael buying me lingerie. That he'd want me to wear. That he'd fuck me wearing. The thought has a lot of images attached to them. I swallow. I've never worn lingerie before, but then I'd never had a reason to. Someone who wanted me to. Raphael wants me to. That makes me feel…hot. Needy. A little desperate.

"Yeah, it's weird. Got it." He runs a hand over his mouth. "Okay, well I'll think on it."

He looks troubled but specifically so, not generally so, given the news that's spreading across the world as we speak. Does he not know it's been leaked? That a source close to him has told the world his engagement is over. I don't want to ask in case he does know and doesn't want to talk about it. My talking about his relationship has never been particularly well received.

"You do not have to buy me a gift. You are coming all the way to visit me in Korea, that is very…romantic."

"It is?" He thinks about it. "Huh. I guess it is."

Then there are a few moments of silence where he just smiles at me. I want to see his eyes. I can't make them out behind the glasses, the reflection of the car cutting shapes across the tinted glass.

"I can't wait to see you."

"You are seeing me now," I say, teasingly.

"I wanna see you closer than this. Hold you. Fuck, I forget what you feel like in my arms." He groans a little in want.

Open. So very open. It makes me bolder.

"Well, I remember what I feel like in your arms," I say.

"Yeah? How's that?"

"Happy. Safe. Very aroused." I add this last to lighten the mood.

Raphael shifts in his seat, chuckling low. "Yeah, we gotta stop that or I'm gonna be even harder than I am right now."

"You are always hard." I point out.

"Only when I'm looking at you." It's not said with a flirtatious tone, but an unexpectedly sweet one. "Oh, I got the testing done you asked about. I'm all good. I'll screenshot and send you my results."

The change of subject, takes me a little by surprise. Unknown to Seungmin and Luan, Raphael and I had already talked about it. I'd told him it was common, likely more common than straight couples, for gay ones to have that conversation early. We were tested monthly at the company, our medical checks done like the servicing of a car. He'd never cheated on Camille, he'd said. But then an odd look had come over his face—as though he had forgotten that's what he has been doing and he'd said he'd go the next day and get it done.

"Oh, you don't have to send it to me. I believe you." Feeling pulsates between my legs at what that means. Raphael inside. Raw and hot. I swallow. "Thank you for doing that."

"Of course. It's no problem, dude."

I can't help the smile that comes from that. *Dude.* "So your mom is really okay with you coming to Seoul for Christmas? She doesn't hate me?"

"Hate you? God, no. She's dying to meet you. I think she'd rather have you there than me to be honest. She's a K:otic. Loud about it too. I've no idea where this has come from, she was into grunge before."

I'm not certain I know what grunge is. "I'd like to meet her," I say.

His eyes go wide and round. "Really?"

"Yes. Really."

"It's my birthday in March. Maybe, if you're free, we can go visit her?" He sounds hopeful.

Comeback starts in April so I'm certain there will be no free time to fly to the US and back, but I can't bear to disappoint him so I say, "Maybe, yes."

"Okay, well, I'm gonna go home, pack my shit. Try and sleep until Thursday night. Don't practice too hard."

I smile at him. "No, I won't. Oh, and the company will send a car for you. To the airport. They have your flight, so they will bring you here."

"Ah, okay cool. Yeah, that's cool. And you'll come later?"

"Yes. But sleep, or take a bath, or there are books." I laugh because suddenly the idea of him being here, in this very room, in less than two days feels very surreal.

"I'll figure it out. Don't worry about me. Maybe I'll go explore your city," Raphael says with an excited grin. "Fuck, I'm gonna see you soon. I can't wait."

"Me too." I nod.

We hang up and my mind starts racing as I try to think about what on earth I'm going to buy him for Christmas. I come by an idea less than a minute later, face heating and cock stirring. I minimize the page on Raphael's father and pull up another website instead.

TWENTY-FOUR
RAPHAEL

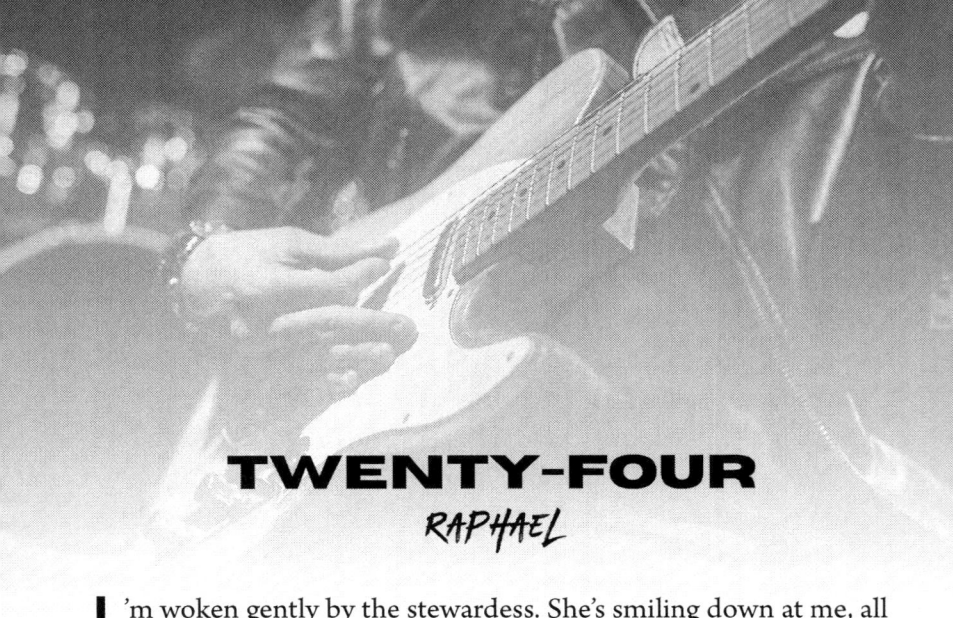

I'm woken gently by the stewardess. She's smiling down at me, all teeth and looking immaculate despite the thirteen hours we've been in the air.

"We're landing in twenty minutes, Mr. Scott," she says.

"Thanks. It's Rapha," I croak, rubbing at my gloopy eyes as I sit up. It's my automatic reaction to whenever anyone calls me that, no matter how out of it I am.

The bed in first class was surprisingly comfortable. Worth the extra $2k. I'd had a couple beers, pulled on my eye mask and earplugs, and was out within an hour of leaving LAX. Which had been a shit show. Phil, the photographer, had been there, a few others too. Asking about Camille, asking if the rumors about me and Cleo were true, asking about my black eye. Had Camille been cheating? Had I cheated on her? Where was I going? Who with? Was I off to Australia to patch things up with my fiancé?

I'd managed to hide my bruising from Jae. Wearing either sunglasses or calling him in the dark with only the light of the TV whenever we'd video called. I was hoping it was gonna be gone by the time I saw him, but Mason's resentment is still flowering around my eye and so I guess I'll have to talk about it.

Jae had told me to wear a facemask when I landed just to be safe, even though no one except them drew crowds to airports in Korea.

And that was because it was planned in advance. My driver is waiting for me just inside the arrival lounge with the name 'Shiro' on his tablet. It's Jae's cat's name. It meant white in Japanese.

I wave at the guy and he bows before reaching a hand out to take my suitcase. I try to protest, but he smiles and bows again and so I let him take it, happy to give him something to do and not wanting to be rude about it since I know manners are a big deal here. I follow him outside to a large, black SUV and he slides open the door for me. I climb in and almost shit myself at the sight sprawled elegantly on the leather seat sat across from me.

His long legs are crossed at the knee and he's wearing smart black tailored pants, a grey sweater with Chanel written in black across the rolled up sleeves, white face mask, and a pair of dangling silver earrings. His eyes are smiling as he looks over at me. The close space of the car means I can smell him. Clean, expensive, floral. He waits until the door is closed behind me until he slips down the mask.

"You are here," he says.

"So are you." I want to lean across the space and kiss him, press my nose to the skin of his neck and breath him in, but I don't know if I can. I feel the tension in my body unfurl at the very sight of him though. A deep contented breath leaving me. "I thought you were working today?"

"I am, but there was some time and I thought about how I'd like to be one of the first faces you saw when you landed in Seoul."

The driver climbs in and says something to Jae in Korean, which elicits a response of a few words and a nod.

"Are we…" I glance at the driver. "Safe here?"

"Inside this car? In Korea?"

"The car."

"We are safe."

It's Jae who moves. Across the distance between the two seats to fucking crawl into my lap. As he burrows his face against my neck and the scent of his cologne floods my nose, I almost groan out loud from how good he smells. He feels almost slight in my arms as they come around him. The planes and sharp edges of his body are hot and hard but yielding and soft as he moves. I nose at his cheek and hair, inhaling deep. My dick is starting to take notice, especially when he presses his lips below my ear and sucks the lobe into his warm mouth.

"I am glad you are here," he whispers, a soft noise falling from his throat.

He places his hands on both sides of my face and brings his head around to press his lips to mine, slipping his tongue into my mouth. My hands press flat against the base of his spine, fingers dipping beneath the seam of the leather belt he's wearing to grab at the top of his ass. Solid muscle, smooth skin. My dick twitches again.

"Are you trying to get us arrested in a foreign country?" I ask against his lips.

"Mmm," he says. "Maybe."

We kiss for what feels like hours, our breathing turning fast and shallow, teeth and lips sliding over each other, hungry and then lazy, fast and then slowing down. I'm fully hard by the time he separates our mouths to lift his head and look down at me. Eyes scanning my face.

"What happened here?" he asks in a roughened tone, lips wet and red from kissing me. The tips of his fingers skim over the bone of my cheek circling towards the bridge of my nose.

"Can we talk about it later?" I turn my head to kiss his fingers and Jae nods, though doesn't look away from the bruise for a long moment. Then he sighs and presses his head into my shoulder, snuggling.

"Fuck, I really missed you."

"My hole?" He smiles against my neck, voice like honey. "Or something else."

"All of you. I missed it all."

I grip him tight to me, an ache deep in my chest that feels like a lot more than just lust, just desire.

I can only stand and stare out at the view in front of me, mouth open and eyes wide.

Jae's apartment in New York was nice. Spacious and stylish. But this is something else altogether. For a start, it's on the 28th floor of what has to be one of the tallest buildings in the city. I'm looking down at other skyscrapers from here. I can see their helipads, for fuck sake. The huge open aspect lounge looks out onto a river, the clustered buildings of the city framed by mountains in the farther distance behind it. Boats move slow down the wide expanse of water that appears to cut through the center of Seoul, restaurants and bars dotted along the riverbank.

As we were driven toward Seoul, he'd sent a link to my phone for an app that he told me to install. Then he'd taken my phone, typed something into the app, scanned his fingerprint, and told me to hold it to the small white box on the door to his apartment. I could only blink and nod, dumbstruck. The car had pulled up in the circular promenade of a group of modern towers made of glass and chrome, the frontage more like a five star hotel than an apartment block.

"I will be home around 7 p.m. Hopefully earlier." Jae looked apologetic.

"No worries, I told you, I can entertain myself." I still had to get him a Christmas gift, so that was first on my list. I had been working on a gift of sorts for a few weeks, but I wanted to give him something I could watch him unwrap. "I'm sure you've a lingerie drawer I can jerk off over or something."

His laugh had been low and embarrassed. When he leaned in to kiss me goodbye I'd felt the outline of something half hard between his legs. It made me grip him a little tighter.

"See you later," he said. "If you have any issues with the door, call me."

I hadn't had any issues. The app had worked for the lift and the door both and now I was standing in his condo, which had to be worth upwards of $10 million easy.

At one side of the lounge is an open wood and chrome kitchen which looks unused, a small library that doubles as a dining area with a solid table that seats ten. Between the window and a wall holding a moderate sized TV, there's a wide sliding door to another room. I'm not sure what I'm expecting to find behind it, but it isn't a large mirrored space the same size as the kitchen and lounge combined that must be his dance studio? Curtains drape from the tall wall of windows, white and sheer, and it hits me—it's the room from the video I must have watched a hundred times or more. I walk to one end and pull up the video in question on my phone and hold it at the right angle, smiling when I see I'm right.

Back out, I wander a few other rooms; a small office, a gaming room, a small-ish bedroom. I open another door, a utility room of sorts, and feel a slight pressure against my ankle. The cat is small and short-haired, pure white with big blue eyes that peer up at me in question. Crouching down, I reach out a hand to let it sniff my fingers, which it does. It's not wearing a collar, but I remember his name.

"Hey buddy. It's Shiro, right? I'm Rapha," I say, letting him bump his nose on my knuckles. He purrs softly so I count it as a win. "Which one of these is your dad's bedroom, huh? Do you sleep with him in there? Lucky lucky, Shiro."

There are two more doors I haven't opened and one is a huge bathroom, half-egg bathtub and dark grey tiles. Double shower on the other side. The last door, at the very end of the long hallway is a paneled sliding door, Japanese style, which glides open so smoothly I wonder if it's on water.

Jackpot.

Jae's bedroom is sunken, a few steps leading down from the door into the large calming space. The sunken floor should give the room a higher ceiling but it looks like it's been artificially lowered; a warm wooden slatted thing that carries through the shelving and bed frame. More books on low shelves that run along the bottom of the bed and above the headboard. There are a lot of plants in here. Dotted around on shelves and above the bed. Some on the floor next to unhung art which leans purposely against white walls.

As I come down the steps into the bedroom, Shiro makes a soft noise behind me. He's sitting on the top step watching, big eyed and curious. To my right is an entrance to what looks like his closet.

A look inside has my mouth falling open again. It looks like a designer store in here. Camille has a closet in our house, but this is insane. It's pristine. Shirts coordinated by color, jeans too, sweaters of the softest-looking material folded in rows. Shoes and boots polished and lined up on shelves. Sneakers below—of which there are considerably few pairs—looking brand new. Jackets and coats, all immaculately pressed.

In the center of the room is a display cabinet with watches and jewelry laid out in shiny twinkling rows. It's frighteningly organized, almost compulsive. But some part of me also finds it incredibly... hot. Like, it tracks. Of course, he has a closet that looks like this. Out there he wears clothes like armor. Never a hair or stray eyelash out of place. Never a crease in sight. Never a step or note missed. It's clinical in here. Like the way he performs is clinical. There's a practiced sort of perfection to everything Jae does.

Something goes off in my brain looking at this closet and it's the understanding that this, *this*, is why watching him come apart under me is so fucking fascinating. Why watching him covered in sweat and come is so insanely hot. I feel myself getting turned on just thinking about it. I shake it off and go to inspect the jewelry stand in the center.

He owns a lot of it. Both silver and gold, both simple and extremely decorative, feminine and masculine. Earrings, rings, necklaces, bracelets, a dozen watches at least, jeweled pins and silk scarves with gems sown into them. There's a dressing table too with make up; brand names Camille used to use, others I haven't heard of. Women's perfume and men's cologne are arranged neatly on a small trolley next to it. At the end of the closet is a door leading into another bathroom. This one is all white marble, no bath, just a shower. More plants and products laid out neatly around the sink.

Since the other bathroom looked a lot less used, I decide to sit my shower bag and toiletries in here. Then I take a shower, wash the flight off, dress in clean sweats and t-shirt before having a look in his fridge for something resembling a snack. I find a cupboard full of all kinds of ramen and some beer in the fridge and I take both to the sofa and bring up Netflix, shoving some anime on until I feel my eyes turn heavy. Shiro comes up at some point, tiptoeing along the back of the sofa to peer at me for a bit before finding a spot close to my feet.

I wake up to the sound of Jae's voice, low and quiet, so that I think at first it's a dream, but when I blink around he's in the kitchen with Shiro in his arms and is kissing him softly on the nose. He's talking in soft Korean to the white cat that stretches his head up to nose at Jae's face. Jae's hair is wet and pushed back—the silver darker than it had been in the car earlier—and he's wearing dark pajama pants and his usual relaxing attire of a long sleeved t-shirt at least three sizes too big. He sets the cat down on the floor in front of a small white box that makes a gentle beeping noise and opens before dropping some kibble into the tray below. As Shiro eats, he goes to the fridge and opens it, stares, then closes it again a moment later.

It's strange watching him move around his house like he would do if I wasn't here. I wonder if he's forgotten that I am.

"What time is it?" I ask and he whips round, gently startled.

"Just after eight. I got home a little early but I thought I would let you rest. The flight is so long from the states." He sounds almost apologetic as he makes his way across the apartment towards me.

"I actually slept all the way over—not sure why I dozed off. I should be fine for sleep until I go home now." I yawn.

He smiles as he flops down next to me and settles a hand on my chest, just resting it there as he gazes softly at me.

"Hello." He smiles.

I reach out and grip his wrist, pulling so that he falls onto my chest. Our lips close.

"Hey."

I lift my head up to kiss him. He strokes my tongue with his own, making a soft noise in the back of his throat. He tastes like toothpaste and something distinctly Jaehyun. That familiar spice and sweetness, like cinnamoned apples or mulled wine. I bring my other hand up to hold his face while I devour his mouth, deeper strokes of his tongue and soft bites of his lips. As I nose his cheek, similar to how Shiro did, he threads his fingers through my hair and turns his head to give me access to whatever I want.

Fuck, I feel starved of him.

Holding his waist, narrow between my hands, I tug him so that he's fully on top of me, thighs nestled on either side of mine.

"I still cannot believe you are in Seoul…" Jae whispers against my mouth.

I push up his shirt so that I can touch him skin to skin. His stomach quivering and warm, nipples already hard little things under my fingers.

"I'm prepared to fly quite a long way when the sex is this good, baby."

It's a lazy, meaningless, joke but I feel him stiffen a little. He sits up and gazes down at me, brow slightly furrowed.

"That was a stupid thing to say, sorry."

Jae shakes his head, says, "It's okay."

Then he's kissing me again, urgent again, moving his body precisely over my hardening cock. I smooth both thumbs over his nipples and he whimpers, arching into it, nibbling and kissing around my mouth as his breathing speeds up. He sits up a little and pulls off his t-shirt and I follow him up, kissing my way up the hot flat skin of his abdomen and chest, across to the sensitive pink rounds. He gasps, holding my head against his chest, needy, thrusting his hips as I play with him with my hands. I kiss my way down his ribcage, across the tattoo that I knew meant *my body, my art*, in Japanese, marveling at how perfect every inch of him is. At how lucky I am that I get to touch him.

I move one hand to his ass, dipping beneath the waistband of his pajamas and sliding my finger down the seam towards his hole. As I circle it, he moans, bucking his hips into me. So I tease it, dry, pressing down on it, smoothing over it, but stopping short of breaching it. I want to breach it, fuck him open with it, stretch and pull and ready it. I want to do it with my finger then my tongue. I lift my head back up, searching for his mouth and thrust my tongue in, fucking it like I want to fuck his hole. Jae trembles.

"Raphael…" He moans into my mouth.

"Mmm, what do you want, baby? Tell me."

He pulls back and looks down at me, panting as he says, "I want to feel you again. Inside me."

"My mouth or my cock?" I tap his hole and he shivers again, his eyes growing heavier. Then I remember what he said on the phone. "You want me to stretch you open on my cock again, Jaehyun?"

His eyes catch fire and he makes a low, completely filthy, sound. Then he nods, biting his lip. I almost come right there.

"Here or in bed?" I ask, my voice barely solid.

"Bed. I want to fuck you in my bed."

I can only smile at that. At how he's phrased it, considering I'll be the one fucking him into the mattress. "You want me to carry you in there?"

He grins sexily, and hops off of me. "I can walk."

"You say that now...we have *days of this.*"

His laugh trails after him as he walks—no, runs—towards the bedroom.

TWENTY-FIVE
RAPHAEL

It seems weird to me now how I assumed I wasn't attracted to men. How such a thing had ever entered my mind. But I hadn't been. I'm not, even. I'm sure, in fact, that my sexuality is defined entirely by him alone.

He redefined me completely that night in Paris.

He moves now, with all the grace of a ballet dancer walking on stage to perform, towards the far side of the bed and presses a button on the wall to draw a light colored blind down over the window. Behind him the lights of Seoul blinker, the boats meandering down the narrow river like slow-moving fireflies.

"Leave it open a little," I say, as I kneel on the bed.

The blind stops moving about halfway and he turns to me. Framed as he is by the view of the city behind him, lean muscular body pale in the low light, he looks like some kind of mystical creature that I've dreamed up halfway to a deep sleep.

I crawl toward him on my knees and reach up to skim my hands over his narrow waist. His chest rising and falling quickly as I lean in to kiss it, then up, mouth skimming over his nipples before they find his collarbone. I kiss here, softly, at odds with what I really want to do, which is bite and pull and suck hard until it turns red and purple. Until I can see my marks on him. I tug gently at the waistband of his pajamas and boxers and pull them down his thighs.

When I look down, I see his cock is half hard and jutting out towards me in invitation. He takes it in his hand and jerks it slowly, other hand drifting lazily through my hair as he looks down into my eyes with some dreamy expression on his face. Soft smile and soft hair.

When I lower my head towards his cock, his movements stall but his hand stays gripped around the base. He doesn't angle it toward my mouth, just waits for me to take it.

Which I do. On my tongue first. I stick it out and let him run his cock against it for a few moments, curling it around the head to lap up the precome here. I keep my eyes fixed on his and he bites down on his lower lip to stifle his moan. Then I close my mouth around it and suck it inside, as far as I can take it until my lips meet his hand, which he then moves to my cheek.

I turn my head so he can feel his cock press against it from the inside. I know he likes it when I tongue the head, and so as I pull back I focus on that, rimming it with the tip of my tongue around my open mouth for a bit before taking it back into my throat. His hand clutches at my hair tighter, fingers digging into my scalp.

When he starts to thrust a little, not forcefully just purposefully, I groan around him. I'm hard. Fully. Because, perhaps startingly, I really fucking love the feeling of his cock in my mouth. The weight of hard, wet skin on my tongue, the sweetly bitter taste of his precome, the smell of his skin where my nose pushes right up against his shaved hair. All of it.

"Raphael..." He groans, pulling himself all the way out of my mouth to trace the head over my lips. "I want to come."

"So come," I say and take him back in.

He works his hand over it as I curl my tongue around the head, flicking it, sucking in the salty sweetness that's leaking out of the slit. When his movements get clumsy and his head falls back, I take over with my hand, gently knocking his own out of the way. Twisting my wrist, I move my head up and down the slick hard skin. His thighs quiver, his grip on my head changing and then he's fucking my mouth. When he stops moving his hips and instead starts pulling my head on and off his cock, I have to grip my dick tight in my fist so I don't come all over myself.

He says my name again, a choking half-sob, and then he's coming, spurting hot and thick into my mouth. His balls draw up under my chin as he falls forward, gripping me to him as he empties his load down my throat. I swallow most of it, warm and almost tasteless, before sitting up on my knees to pull him in for a kiss. What I haven't swallowed I push past my lips into his mouth, scraping his tongue with mine so there's no way he's not tasting himself. It only seems to turn him on more. He climbs on top to straddle me, naked and rutting the aftershocks of his orgasm against my dick.

"I really need to be inside you," I tell him, flipping our positions so that he's beneath me on the bed. "Can you take me right now?"

"Yes." He pants, reaching above him. "Fuck me. I need to feel you inside."

Above the bed is a functional headboard with shelves built into the structure. With a practiced move, he pumps something from a large expensive-looking bottle into his hand before reaching between his legs. I sit up and strip out of my t-shirt and sweats, while he preps himself, though when I'm back between his legs I push his hand out of the way again and slide my own fingers into the hot space instead. He's as tight as I remember, my finger pushing into his body, meeting some resistance.

It hits me suddenly. We're both clean. He saw my status. I saw his. Did that mean...? I glance up at him to find him looking fucked out but turned on at the same time, eyes flitting from where my hand is pushing inside him to my face and back again.

How I haven't blown yet is a fucking mystery, frankly.

"So...did you want to use a condom or...?"

He shakes his head. Bites his lip. "No. But if you want to then we can..."

My voice comes out hoarse and pulled tight. "I really want to feel you without. If you're sure...if you're okay with it."

"I want that too," he says, spreading his legs a little wider for me.

I kiss him hard before pulling back to look down at where my middle finger, palm-up, is disappearing in and out of his body. On the next instroke, I push my index finger inside him too and he gasps and groans, before settling down. His breathing is so fast and his soft spent dick looks so fucking pretty sitting against his inner thigh.

My mind is loud in the quiet of his bedroom, the words *fuck fuck fuck* and *come come come* echoing over and over like some kind of war drum.

"Raphael…" It sounds raw, like purest need. And I want to give him whatever it is he needs but…

"*Fuck,* Jae, you're still so tight."

"I don't care, just fuck me, Raphael."

And then he's grabbing his knees and pulling them up to his chest, presenting himself to me like something from one of my wildest wet dreams. He pulls a pillow from near his head and slides it under his hips and then he's there, glistening wet and desperate and I don't need him to ask me again.

Up on my knees, I settle myself where I need to be, stroking the head of my dick over his still tight hole a few times. The desperately high noise that leaves him as I do this isn't one I've heard him make before and it forces me to do it for a bit longer. When he lets out a groan of impatience, I push in. It's frighteningly tight, the first push, trying to breach this tiny space with the blunt throbbing head of my cock. I can see my hands trembling.

But then it's in and I've never felt anything like it.

His mouth is close to the hot, wet heat I can feel wrapping around my cock, really fucking close, but this is so fucking perfect that I think my head lifts off my shoulders for a second. I feel lucky to be allowed inside it for even heartbeat, it's that good.

His body feels like it's sucking me in, a slow pull inward that gets hotter and hotter the deeper I go. I can feel every bump and ridge of his body over my cock as I push in and each breath comes with some new unexplored sensation. He bites and pants against his lips, gripping hold of my arms in a way that borders on painful. I hope there are marks there when I look tomorrow. I lean in and press my forehead to his as I fight the urge to *fuck*.

"You feel…fucking hell, Jae, holy shit. You're so perfect. So fucking hot in here. I can't…I'm not gonna last."

He kisses me, panting against my mouth, body tense and vibrating beneath me.

"Wait…just wait one moment."

He drops his legs so that they bracket my hips and then he's gripping his cock, jerking himself rough and quick. He's not hard, I don't think, but he pulls on his cock like he is. Then he's moving. Short shallow circles of his hips like he's trying to…like he's *loosening* himself on my dick.

Holy shit I've never felt anything like it. Like he's stroking my cock from the inside out. My body's straining with the effort of holding off my orgasm and so I can only watch and breathe and try not to come as he moves, until the circling of his hips becomes something else, until he's…fucking himself on me.

My brain sort of falls offline, I think, as he lifts his hips up off the bed and falls back on my cock. He's watching me as he does it, calm look in his eye, only the hitch of his breath as he hits something he likes.

"Okay," he says.

I grab his hips and help him do what he's been doing, but it changes the flow of his movements and he's not falling on me now but being pulled and pushed while I thrust up and down. I know when I've found the right rhythm because his whole body reacts like he's been shocked, head falling back and his back arching almost impossibly. Then he lets out something that sounds like a scream.

I *need* him closer. On me. Smothering me. Need to taste his skin and hear his breaths and feel his fucking heart beat inside his chest.

I grab hold of him and pull him up onto me and fuck upwards, clawing and clutching at his back, hands moving over every inch of skin I can touch, mouthing at his throat and collarbone and chest as he rides me upright.

"You're so beautiful, so fucking beautiful, I missed you so much…fuck." I'm babbling, I know that. Sex-crazed words into his neck, against his ear, the sweat of his skin on my tongue as I lick across his pulse point. He tastes sweet and clean and so fucking delicious.

"I love how you feel inside me, Raphael." He moans, before a few words in Korean spill from his mouth. "Don't stop, please don't stop."

I grab his face with both hands as I kiss the words from his mouth, pulling his head to my chest. "I'm going to come…fuck, Jae…I'm…"

I make a move to push him back, to pull out, but he keeps hold of me, legs tightening around me.

"Inside," he whispers.

I'm in no state to refuse him so I push him back down onto the mattress and thrust into him once, twice, and a third before I'm coming inside him. I feel him tense and I wonder if he's coming too, but his hands are nowhere near his cock. He meets every pound of my hips with one of his own, perfect tight strong body arching up into mine.

It's only when I sit up to pull out do I feel it, the sticky wetness between us. He came. Without me touching him, without touching himself. I feel ridiculously proud of that, though I'm sure he did most of the work himself.

He reaches across to his bedside where a small black wooden box sits, and pulls out some tissues which he wipes his chest with, then between his legs. It's intimate and weirdly hot watching him do it. Then he's settling on his side next to me, the front of his body pressed to the side of mine. I feel his hand in my hair, smoothing the damp lengths back off my forehead.

"You are getting better at fucking men," he says, panting.

When I turn to look at him he's not even smiling. Just pondering.

"Have you been practicing?"

"I'm not sure which part of that to be insulted about." I pinch him lightly on the thigh.

He looks fucked out as he smiles and I feel proud of that too. "It was a compliment."

"Well, I haven't been practicing. I mean, unless you count all the times I've fucked you in my head. In that case…yeah, I have. Non-stop."

I grin this dopey grin at him and he smiles back, cheekbones high and eyes almost closed. He traces his fingers lightly over my torso. Over the tattoo of our first album name, badly etched, across my hip bone. It hurt like a fucker, but all I feel is pleasure now as he draws softly over it. I think of the shop front on Venice Beach where I got it done and about where I am now and it makes something light up inside my head.

I want his name somewhere on me. He deserves that. Even if this flickers out and dies, as all things that burn as brightly as this do, he deserves that. He matters more than that first album ever did. And if I don't get to keep him, if he doesn't want this—anything serious—with me, then I need to know that this fucking happened. That I didn't dream it. Because every moment I get to spend with him feels exactly like that.

We're both quiet for a long time before he shifts, propping his head up to look at me. He's on my left and so has a perfect view of it. I should have expected it.

"Will you tell me what happened now?" he says. "With your eye. With your…girlfriend."

I look round at him. "She didn't do this. Though maybe I'd have deserved it…" I give him a meaningful look.

He gives me a grim smile.

I'm still not sure about anything where Mase and Cam are concerned, except that I feel less angry about it all now, now that I'm here. With him. I think I can even understand why Mase did it. Watching me shit all over a relationship he wished he had.

"My best friend did. Mason. He's in our band."

Jae looks very serious, concerned. "He hit you? Why?"

Fuck, where to even start? Jae doesn't want to know this shit—why would he? I don't want to talk about Camille and Mason and the mess I have to go back to. The mess I helped create. I want to pretend that I never have to go back at all. But I know I have to tell him something and so I decide to tell him the fundamental reason why Mase suckered me across the face.

"He heard me on the phone, talking to you. He accused me of cheating on Camille…and I guess he was right."

Jae sits up, looking horrified. "Your best friend hit you because of me?"

"What? No, not *because* of you." I follow him up. "Because of *me*. Because he…well, it's complicated." Jae still looks worried. "He doesn't know about you. No one knows about you, well, except for my mom. Don't worry."

I don't want him to start freaking out about this, about the prospect that anyone would tell anyone about this. I know how strict his company are about this shit. Cleo knows but she doesn't know his name and I know for a fact she won't tell another soul. This is mine and she'll respect that.

"I'm not…" He shakes his head, biting his lip. "I am not worried about that."

I sit forward, closer, so we're facing each other. "Then what are you worried about? Talk to me, Jae."

His hands are knotting the sheets and he's avoiding my eyes; I don't like how it makes me feel. I want to pull him into my arms, kiss him again, but he looks skittish as a scared cat and I'm not sure he wants that.

"You're…this is…" He lets out a little growl of frustration at not being about to find whatever words he needs. He looks at me, at my face, as though he'll find them there. "What are you doing?"

I frown. "What? Nothing?"

"No, I mean, here. With me. This." He motions between us. "Because this is already so difficult for you and you are losing things because of me and I don't know what I can offer you instead of those things, except this sneaking around and hiding and that is not something normal for you. Not like you had with your…with Camille and—"

I surge up so I'm kneeling and pull him into my arms.

"Baby, you gotta stop talking now because you're ruining my post–orgasmic bliss." I kiss his head and then his temple and slowly, so slowly, I feel him soften into me. His body turns pliant and his arms grip hold of my shoulders. "Where'd that come from?"

I pull back to look into his eyes. Milk chocolate with honeycomb pieces. He's still breathing a little hard so I kiss him, licking into his mouth until he starts kissing me back. I separate our mouths gently and nudge his nose with mine.

"Talk to me. Where did that come from?"

He shakes his head, casting his eyes down. "I don't know. I just… everything feels so real now that you are here and I am scared of letting you down, of not being who you need me to be."

I frown at that. "Who do you think I need you to be?"

He casts his eyes about, still avoiding looking at me. I gently tilt his head up.

"Why would you let me down?"

"I…don't think…" He shakes his head. Looking so fucking sad.

I want to kill whatever and whoever made him feel like that, except I'm worried it's me.

"I am not strong like you," he says softly. "I don't think I can give you what you want. I cannot be beside you at events or hold your hand and walk down the street. It would destroy our band. Here in Korea it is…the label…the public…it is not the same as in America."

There are tears in his eyes now and my heart feels like it's being torn apart looking at them. I wrap an arm around him and pull him onto my lap.

"Listen to me, Jae, I don't give a shit about that. About *any of that*." I settle my head on his shoulder and run my hands up and down his back which is still straight and stiff, tension leeching off him. "I want to be with you, whatever that means, whether it's in an apartment in New York, or an apartment in Seoul, or on a boat in fucking Tokyo."

Jae lifts his head to gaze down at me, eyes wary.

"They will try to control everything about us. Even though it will be a secret, they will still try to control it."

"Who?" I frown. The media? The public?

"The label," Jae says, miserably. "They wanted me to ask you to put a statement out about your engagement—before it was in the news. They wanted me to ask you to get a medical. Our lawyers will dig into things about your life, things you don't want them to know—just in case they have to prepare a suit. In case this does not work... so I can come out of it looking well."

Sweat is beading on his forehead and there's a knot of tension in his back that I try to undo gently with my fingers. It's automatic, touching him. I need it like I need to breathe.

I blink up at him. "They asked for the medical? They *know* about us?"

He *told them*?

He shakes his head. "I had to. It is...because you were coming here, and I cannot hide that. But the medical was me. I always ask about it. But perhaps I always ask about it because I know they will. Because my whole life has been like this...living to their rules and protocols. But for them to demand these things, from you, from anyone who is stupid enough to be with me...*Sshi-bal,* it is ridiculous. Why would anyone want this?" He pushes a hand through his hair and looks at me. "Why would *you* want this?"

It's not even a hard question. "Because I want *you*. And if this is what it is, then this is what it is." I stroke my finger under his jaw, over those full pink lips that haunt my dreams. "But is this...what *you* want? With me, I mean. I know we were going to talk in Tokyo about what it was and what was possible. Is all this label stuff what you meant by that?"

He nods, looking small and a little lost and all I wanna do is wrap him up tight and hold him forever, protect him. So I do. Sort of. I tighten my arms around him and lower us down again to lie on the bed, him tucked against my chest, silver hair tickling my nose. I inhale the scent of him.

"I don't care about any of it," I say again. "If they wanna interview me and see if I'm good enough for you then I'll do it. If they want to dig into my life to prepare a lawsuit they're never going to need, then let them—there are no secrets that a dozen music magazines, websites and Reddit threads haven't already talked about, at length. I'm not that interesting, Jae. In fact, you're the most interesting thing I've ever done."

He laughs at that, soft and musical, then turns his head to kiss the base of my throat. He throws a leg over me and hugs me tighter with it, warm cock pressed stickily against my thigh. It makes a contented rumble roll over my whole body.

"But I want to do this with you. Loud or quiet, whatever you want. It doesn't matter to me—not that part anyway."

He's quiet for a long time. Then: "I saw the article. It said that you and Camille have ended things. Mutually. Is it true?"

I'm not expecting the question. I never am. But him saying her name like that, tinged with a breathlessness that could be hope, here, with his naked skin pressed against me—it's overwhelming.

"It is over," I tell him. "But we haven't spoken about it. She's been in Australia and neither of us really wanted to do it over the phone. I'm not sure who leaked that story." A lie because now I think I might know. Mason. I just don't want to go there, right now. "It's not *not* true. It's just not entirely true either."

I feel him nod against me.

"In New York, I told her there was someone else. She wasn't angry. Not really. Just hurt, I guess." Maybe some of it was guilt over what she'd hidden from *me*. "I told her I needed time to think things through and that we'd talk after Thanksgiving. But we haven't yet. I'm certain she knows it's done."

"She does not want it to end," he says quietly.

"I...I don't know what she wants." I admit. "But it doesn't matter. I know what I want." I kiss his head to emphasize what that is.

There's a pause and I know it's because he wants to ask me something. I think I might know what it is too.

"Have you been with her since we have been...doing this? I have no right to ask that, not really, and I don't suppose it matters. We were clear with each other before you came to New York..."

"No. I haven't seen her since the day in New York, and nothing happened."

I feel him soften against me.

"When I get back to LA, I will end it. It's already over, baby, I promise."

"But you haven't ended it already because you were not sure you wanted to?"

I want to flat-out refute that, but there's something in it. Something cowardly that had been holding me back. If I couldn't have Jae then maybe I'd just keep trying with Camille, but that's not how I feel anymore. It hasn't been for a while now. And that was before the shitstorm with Mase.

"I knew that I didn't want to get married. I knew that the way I felt about you, and thought about you, wasn't the way a guy about to get married should feel either. I just didn't quite know what it meant or what to do about it." I debate internally about how much to reveal, but he's already been so vulnerable with me tonight, just minutes ago, that I feel like I want to offer him something too. "I've fantasized more about you the last year than my fiancée—that should have told me something, right?"

He turns his face into my chest and smothers a soft laugh. "You have?"

"You know I have."

He lifts his head and looks up at me, licking his lips. "Tell me about how much you fantasized about me."

"Like a lot. I must have watched that Haven Williams dance video a hundred times," I tell him without shame. "Jerked off after almost every single watch."

He's grinning but I can see the arousal seep into his eyes, his breathing quickens slightly, pretty pink mouth opening a little. "We have a lot to thank Haven for, it seems."

"Fuck, yeah. We do, don't we?" My mind wanders back to the dance video. "You filmed that video here, right? In your practice room?"

He confirms with a nod.

"Looks like we'll be able to turn one of those fantasies into reality then." I raise my eyebrows playfully. "If you're up for it?"

"I am," he says, breathless.

The fantasy of fucking him against one of the mirrored walls blasts itself into my mind, except it's more powerful than any of the others because this time it's filled out with scent and smell and taste and touch. This time I know what he'll sound like when I make him come all over the reflection of himself.

He looks down between us, raising an eyebrow of his own. "You are hard again?"

"I have a very, very good imagination. It's a fucking curse."

He shuffles down the bed and settles himself between my legs, smiling up at me as he presses his mouth to my pelvis and licks across the seam.

"You do not need your imagination here," he breathes, working his mouth across and down and between. When he sucks one of my balls into his soft warm mouth I know he's right. I know that, in fact, my imagination is shit. Because he's much better than I imagined.

He's fucking everything.

TWENTY-SIX
RAPHAEL

Christmas Eve in Seoul is a lot like Christmas Eve in Colorado. Cold and layered with wet snow and crammed with people trying to find last-minute gifts just like I am.

Jae had offered me his driver, or the label's driver I guess, but I'd said no. It wasn't just that after what he'd said last night I now think they might be following my every move, it's that I like exploring new cities. Always have. Plonk me down anywhere and I'll navigate myself around, not quite like a local, but like an experienced tourist at least. Even if everything is in a language I don't know and an alphabet I don't understand.

Cities with great subway systems make it easier. Seoul happens to be one of those. The closest station is literally beneath Jae's building, and everything is colored and coordinated and designed with the tourist in mind. No one gives me a second glance either, which I like. We're not as big in Asia as we are in other parts of the world, but we're still known enough that it's feasible I could be recognized. But it's two days before Christmas in one of the busiest cities in the world and so I'm not particularly worried.

Also, since it's fucking freezing, everyone has their scarves pulled up over their faces including me. It's Jae's scarf. Because I hadn't brought one. He'd pleaded with me in usual Jaehyun style not to catch a cold and ordered me to take his scarf when he checked what

I was going to wear outside. He'd been unimpressed with my leather and duffel combo, relaxing only when I explained about the beanie. I told him again that I'm from Colorado. That I'm not from LA. That I do understand what winter is. But it makes a little curl of warmth settle in my chest that he cares this much about other people catching a fucking cold. It's extremely endearing.

The subway spits me out in the center of the city and it's a wash of scents and noises and giant flashing screens not unlike Times Square. Except that here I can't understand anything they're telling me. It disorients me a second and so I pull up the Chanel store on my phone map again hoping I've taken the right line. I have. It's a cop-out gift, I know that. Lazy. But it's something I know he'll like, and if he doesn't, then at least I have the other gift stored away on my phone as a back-up.

I feel giddy about just being in the shop, looking for a gift for him, like I'm thirteen and he's Daisy Wiseman. Except she didn't like the card I'd stuffed in her locker or the box of cupcakes shaped like daisies I'd left on her stool in science lab. The ones mom had helped me make. Her and her friends had laughed at both before I'd watched her toss them in the trash. Thankfully I hadn't put my name on either. My crush on her had lasted half a year; a quarter the length of the one I'd had on the person I was now going to buy a pair of $4000 earrings for. Five and a quarter billion won. I'm hoping Jae's reaction is better than Daisy's.

The sales guy is fluent in English, dark-eyed and lean; attractive in the way I apparently recognize now. He reminds me of Jae's bandmate a little, the rapper with the tattoo on his neck. Xan. I hadn't learned all of their names yet, but I was trying.

"Your girlfriend is going to love them," he's saying as he hands them off to be gift-wrapped.

I debate whether to say they're for my boyfriend, but there's a part of me that thinks he might know who I am and that he's just professional about not mentioning it.

"How long are you in Seoul for?"

"A few days. Then I'm going to Tokyo for New Year's."

His eyes light up with interest. "Ah, cool. Very Cool. Have you been before? Tokyo is…well, it's not Seoul, but it's a great city for tourists." It's not said in a derogatory way, just well meant.

"Yeah? I'm crazy into anime so I feel like I'm gonna need to try and not turn into some shrieking fanboy the second I step off the plane, you know? I've wanted to go for years."

We'd planned on it for the next tour but I'd get to see the inside of a bar and a venue and then my hotel room, before being flown out the next day. I'd get to see a bit more of it this way.

"I get you, man, I get you." He laughs, genuine. "How about Seoul? Are you liking it so far? It's a bit of a culture shock, right?"

"I mean, I moved to LA for college which was a culture shock, so I guess I'm used to it. But it's great so far. I haven't seen much yet, only got here yesterday, but I'm looking forward to exploring a little."

I like this guy. He'd not normally be the kind of salesperson you get in stores like these and I'm wondering if this is how he normally is, or if it's just me.

"Man, I love LA. I actually grew up in San Francisco, my family are still there. Moved back here about a year ago, felt like it was calling to me or something? But both are home, you know? I miss it."

That's when I know he knows exactly who I am. The finely wrapped box inside the Chanel bag appears in front of him a moment later and then he's handing me the thing, stuffed inside a cellophane bag to protect it from the elements. His voice is quieter when he says.

"Have a great trip, Rapha. Enjoy Seoul, man. Was really great talking to you. And thanks for the commission." He gestures at the bag.

I'm already wondering how this is gonna look when/if he posts about it online. Why am I in Seoul? Buying $4000 earrings when I've just called off my engagement. It's on the tip of my tongue to ask him not to do it, not to post about it. I don't want the risk for Jae—though why the fuck anyone would put us together like that I don't know—but I just nod and offer him my hand.

"You deserve it, man. Merry Christmas. Hey, look me up on IG if you're ever in LA, yeah? If I'm around maybe we can grab a beer?"

It's Machiavellian, but it might work. Is he gonna use this for clout when I've made that sort of offer? I'm hoping not—he seems like a cool guy. "Have a great Christmas."

I bundle out back into the bustling Seoul street. I'm in the central thoroughfare, the giant TV screens flickering brightly in the snow-heavy afternoon.

Glancing up, I freeze.

A thirty-foot Jae is staring down at me. It's a commercial for a sports brand so he's in a t-shirt, trackpants and sneakers—not a look I've ever seen him in before. He's flirting with the camera the way he does, that heavy-lidded stare he's almost famous for, a slow trace of his lips with his tongue.

I can't move for a second as it hits me how huge he is. Not only physically, in front of me now, but here in Korea. There's likely not a single person in this country who doesn't know his name. We're both visible in lots of ways but for him, here, fame is something entirely different. I understand fame and the trappings of it, of course I do, but I've largely been allowed to do whatever the fuck I want with it—sometimes I've been actively encouraged to.

But Jae's brand of fame is something else. It's particular. He's expected to be above scandal. Above anything that might be seen as negative. Like a politician or a priest. He's lived his entire adult life this way. Whilst hiding his sexuality, whilst hiding want he wants and needs; who he is on a base level. The clothes, the jewelry, the precision of his art—it's his armor. And somewhere behind it all there's him. This vulnerable, sometimes sad, beautiful fucking thing that just wants someone to be brave enough to be with him. To choose him for him. To put their fucking name on the box of daisy cupcakes and love him the way he needs and deserves.

His words from last night hit me like a blast of snow-chilled air.
Why would anyone want this? Why would you want this?
I am not strong like you.

Fuck, I think he might be the strongest person I've ever met. How he hasn't collapsed under the weight of expectation and the constant drive for perfection, I don't know. It's suffocating just thinking about it.

I'm still thinking about this as I slide into a metal booth at a little hole–in–the–wall food place advertising "Korean chicken and beer." I'd found it a few blocks off the main shopping area, buried in a slush-filled alley and teeming at the edges with people. I almost walked on to find something else, but an elderly woman with an apron called me back inside, leading me through the cavern-like space and into a table near the back.

The place is loud, Korean voices laughing and shouting good-naturedly. She spoke a little English and seemed to know what I wanted before I even opened my mouth, so I'm eating a basket of fried chicken—a crispy savory orgasm that melts on my tongue—and drinking a Korean brand beer I take a picture of so I can try and pick some up later. Then I wonder if it only tastes this good because of the chicken. But it's the best bottled beer I've ever had outside of Belgium. Mase and I did a beer tasting once when we were on tour there and left the place unable to walk and with $800 worth of beer Sam had to figure out how to import.

Thinking about him, I open the text chat. Stare at it for a bit. The last message I sent him was when he was late for the studio that first day. What the fuck happened that tipped him over the edge? Before finding me in the hall asking Jae if he missed my cock, something had happened. Something that made him not want to face me. Something that had him turn up two hours late on our first day back, wasted.

He'd spoken to Cam when I'd been in New York. Cam had called him? Was that what he'd said? Yeah, he said he called me because *she'd* asked him to. Why would she do that? Why would they even be talking? I turn it over and over in my head and realize Cleo was right, I really don't see what's right in front of my face.

Had he secretly been wanting my relationship to fall apart? So he could sweep in and be the guy Camille deserved.

I try and imagine them together. Not in a physical sex way, just in the usual, couple kind of way and I can't see it. They don't work. Not in my head anyway. Camille deserves better than me, yes, better than someone who had barely been present the last year of our relationship. But is that guy Mason? I don't think it is but clearly there's a lot I don't know about Camille and Mason and what they have.

Startling me out of my spiral, my cell starts ringing in my hand. I blink down at it, half expecting it to be Camille or Mason, but it's not. It's Jae.

"Hey, sorry, it's loud in here," I say as I answer, covering my free ear with my hand.

"Where are you?"

"Some chicken and beer place. I'm almost done—just have to pay." I look about me for one of the wait staff. Of which I'm certain there's only one—the woman who sat me down.

"You are finished with your shopping?"

"Yeah, all done. How about you? You finished work?"

He had a TV show, some 'fan content' to film, and then a magazine interview scheduled for today. I'm not even sure what time it is.

"Almost. Just some photos and then I am done."

He sounds exhausted. Then I feel guilty for keeping him up half the night and waking him early this morning because my jet lag had pulled me awake at five. I'd rolled into him, my dick pressed against his hole and couldn't stop. His alarm had gone off an hour and a half later while I dosed back to sleep, his come drying around me.

"Did you want to do something tonight, for Christmas Eve? There is a company dinner, they have a private room booked at a Hotel in Gangnam—some of the others will be there. And since they know of you now…"

The lady in the apron comes over and takes my card and wanders off with it. I glance down at the check and do the calculation quickly. It's insanely cheap. I reach into my jacket for some cash to leave as a tip.

"Is that what you want? You want me to come meet them?"

We hadn't talked about this and he doesn't sound overly enthusiastic about the prospect, but it could just be tiredness.

I worry that maybe he does want to go, but he'd rather I wasn't there, so I say, "If you want to go I can hang out here in town for a bit, grab a few more beers, and then head back to the apartment. I'll see you there later?"

"No," he says immediately. "I don't want that. It's Christmas Eve and you are in Seoul and I want to be with you."

My chest does little flip flop at that.

"Okay. So tell me where you want me to be and I'll be there."

The woman comes back with my card and a smile, handing me a receipt which has the dollar conversion on it. Twelve fucking dollars. For the best fried chicken and beer I've ever had. I drain the last of the beer and slide the three 50,000 won notes under the empty bottle and head out. Jae is silent all the while. I'm thinking he's fallen asleep when he speaks again. I'm outside now, it's still snowing.

"Would you mind if we ate at home? In our pajamas."

"Mind? I'd fucking love that."

"Really? I promise I will be more fun in Tokyo." He sounds apologetic. "I'm just…tired."

"Baby, I get it. I told you, I just want to be with you. So, when will you be home? Should I head there now or…?"

He sighs softly, all low and sweet. "A couple more hours. You should have some soju and sweet potato. But don't stay out in the snow too long."

I can't help grin at this. I'm sure Jae spends sixty percent of his brain power worrying that people he cares about are going to catch a cold.

"Or, I could send a car for you now? If you want to come here and wait for me. We have a lot of soju here."

I consider it. Seeing Jae do what he does, that fucking aura he has, at work. But then I remember he'll be doing it surrounded by the people who polish his armor and tell him what to do. Who to fuck. How to fuck them. Nah, I'm likely to get drunk and punch someone. Probably Kai.

"I'll wander around for a bit longer—don't worry I'm wrapped up nice and warm. I'll see you back at the apartment."

"Okay, then I will arrange for dinner to be delivered later. Is there anything you want, that will remind you of home? I don't know if they will be able to find it here, but I can try."

Something desperately fond rises up into my throat, sticking there. I have to clear my throat to dislodge it. "Nah, it's fine. I wanna have Christmas in Seoul. Let's do it all your way."

"My way," he whispers.

I can see his smile through the phone. Cheekbones high, dark eyes glittering and teeth poking out behind full lips.

"Okay," he says in a small voice. "I will see you later, at home."

Home. I think my heart actually stops beating for a second.

From somewhere I find my voice. "Hey, wait, should I buy pajamas then? Cause I didn't bring any."

TWENTY-SEVEN
RAPHAEL

"Kai has invited us to dinner on the 27th," Jae says, as he shoves a load of stew into his mouth.

"Really? That sounds great," I lie.

He bites away a small, knowing smile. "Kai is a great cook."

"Yeah, well, it's definitely the food I'm worried about so that's good to know."

I feel loose and warm from the soju. Though maybe it's because Jae is in these incredible short shorts and a thin Gucci t-shirt that's slipping off one shoulder to expose the raised point that I want to trace with my tongue. He looks at me as he sets his chopsticks down, lifting his small shot glass. He's sipping it delicately, not knocking it back as I'd been doing.

"He wants to get to know you," he explains.

"Why?" I raise an eyebrow.

The guy doesn't like me. Hated me on site. Clearly doesn't think I'm good enough for Jaehyun, who he may or may not be in love with. Now he wants to get to know me. It feels like Mase and Camille all over again.

"Because I asked him to."

I frown. "Why?" I'm hoping there's nothing in my voice that sounds like I'm bitter or suspicious or worse, jealous. Though I'm certain I feel all three of these.

"Because I want you to get to know each other. He is important to me, and you are...important to me also."

"You want me to get to know the guy you used to fuck?"

It's out before I can even think about it. Jae doesn't react, just stares openly at me. His eyes are expressionless, inscrutable, so I can't even figure out what tone I used. Whether he's annoyed. I don't think I sounded angry with him, I'm not sure I am. I'm just...confused, I guess. Then I realize what he just said: *you are important to me*.

"He is a lot more than that, Raphael," Jae says in this really deep way that *does* make me angry. That makes something hot and bitter rise up in my chest.

"Yeah? Well, that's real good to know, Jae." I down the last of my drink and drop my fork noisily onto the plate and stand. "I need to piss."

After I empty my bladder I stare at myself in the mirror for a long time, my vision swimming a little from alcohol and disquiet.

When I examine the root cause of that disquiet, who I'm angry with, I realize that it's me. Of course Kai is more than a guy he used to fuck. He's known him years, he's his band leader, he works with him day in and day out. He's a friend and a confidant. He's already told me they don't fuck anymore—that it stopped long before I came along. And Jae has always been open and clear with me from the get go, he's never been underhanded or deceitful about any of this shit—not like Cam or Mase. Or me, I suppose. He said I'm important to him, and that's all I've wanted for as long as I've known him.

If he wants me to get to know the important people in his life then I should be fucking happy about it. We don't speak the same native tongue but this works because we've always been upfront and honest about what we want from each other—there's no room for ambiguity. There's enough different about us already—shitloads that I still need to understand and get my head around—and I'm not willing to create more misunderstandings. Yeah, fuck that.

When I return back to our picnic, he's leaning with his head on the wall of windows, thoughtful as he gazes out at the river scene below. The snow has started up again and it flickers down slow and soft, to and fro, against the wind. When he hears me approach he sits up and watches me closely again, searching my face for something.

"Sorry," I say. "I was being a dick. I want to get to know him too, if he's important to you then I *want* to get to know him."

He smiles hesitantly, searching for something on my face. He's refilled my small glass and I scoop it up and down it again. No misunderstandings. I take a deep breath.

"The night I texted to ask your plans for Christmas, was the same night Mason hit me. I told you that he heard me on the phone talking to you, but that isn't the full story."

Jae sits up straighter, eyes rounding with interest as he prepares to hang on every word.

"They slept together—Camille and Mason—before she was with me. I'm not really sure of the details because I haven't asked. But it turns out he's in love with her or something."

I see the knowledge work itself over his features, and then his head snaps up. Because he gets it. The language we both speak: who we are at our cores.

"You think that it is the same with Ji-hoon and me." It's not a question.

"Is it?"

He gives me a sad kind of look, then he's crawling over and into my lap and wrapping his arms around my neck.

"I did not want to go into this long and sad old thing that is between me and Ji-hoon. But I will if it means you will not worry. If it means you will trust me."

He smooths my hair back off my forehead, digging his fingers gently into the soft part at the back of my head.

"Ji-hoon is not in love with me," Jae says. There's no regret in his voice, it's just softly matter of fact. "And though I thought I was once in love with him, I know now that it was just many other things together that tricked me into thinking that." This time his voice is sad, regretful. "I will tell you everything you want to know about the mess of Ji-hoon and I, if it is what you want, Raphael. I will never lie to you about this."

His eyes are wide and open, so open, and when he presses his lips to mine I nearly forget everything else. I'm certain that's not his intention, but it's always the outcome when he does it. I separate our mouths and look up at him.

"I don't need to know everything." I drop my forehead to his shoulder. "I just needed to know if this…us…is just a stop-gap."

When I pull up he's frowning. "Stop-gap?"

"Like…something you were doing temporarily. Until you and him…worked shit out."

He sits back a little, tilting his head. "Have I ever given you a reason to think that you are temporary? A stopping gap?"

I shake my head and look out through the window. "Not exactly, but neither do you tell me it's permanent either." I look back into his eyes. "You tell me a lot of reasons why it can't work and won't work and so I don't know. Maybe this all started as one thing, for both of us. But now? Now I don't know where I stand or what this is to *you*." I smooth my thumbs over his hips, then squeeze a little. Encouraging.

He blinks at this, slowly, as he does. Carefully considering. Deliberate. Jae smooths his hand over my hair again, fingers curling into the lengths at my nape.

"I told you: you're important to me, Raphael. You make me happy." He holds my eye as his hands come to settle on both cheeks. "*This* is important to me."

The words are warm, like the sun on my face. They're not exactly what I want to hear, not quite what I hoped he'd say, but I'll take them. I nuzzle my face under his jaw, inhaling deeply. That scent I can never get enough of. Cinnamon and spiced apples and something uniquely him. I trail soft kisses up his throat, over his chin to his mouth.

"You're important to me too," I whisper against his lips. "I feel… like…"

My cheeks heat with the intensity of feeling pushing at me from the inside. Need and want and something more than both of those.

"I feel like when I'm with you it's like being lost somewhere. Somewhere new, somewhere that's beautiful and different and smells great." I sniff under his jaw again and he laughs, ticklish. "And I really fucking like it here, Jae."

I lift my head up to look at him. His eyes are glittering and wide and I think for a second he's going to cry but he just...smiles. It's warm and bright and so beautiful that I have to blink my eyes so not to be blinded by it. He buries his face in my neck, clinging to me.

"I really like it here too, Raphael," he whispers.

I'm not sure how long we sit there, him in my lap almost purring against my neck, as my hands trace up and down the warm skin of his back. Contentment buzzes through my whole body, the weight of him steady and so right. When I lift my head, I notice the clock in the kitchen.

"Hey, it's Christmas." I press it as a kiss to his shoulder. "Do you wanna open your gifts? You normally do them before sleeping right?"

"Normally, yes."

"So, do you want to?"

He shakes his head. "I want to go to bed with you. Let's do it in the morning. Like Americans." He moves to get off me and we both stand. He gestures vaguely at the picnic. "We should clear that up…"

"I'll do it. You go ahead. I'll be right behind you."

He stifles a yawn and then nods. "Thank you. Please be quick."

I wrap up some of the leftovers and toss the rest. Then settle the bowls, plates, and glasses in the dishwasher and fold up the throw blanket we'd been sitting on. I'm pushing the sofa cushions back into place when my cell vibrates on the low coffee table. I stiffen when I see Camille's name. Before I can think about it I'm lifting the phone and sitting back on the sofa to hit 'accept'.

I can't fucking run from this anymore.

I hear her make a small gasp of surprise. "Raphael?"

"Yeah. I'm here."

She lets out a sigh. Relief? Frustration? Exasperation? I'm not sure which. "I thought I'd never hear from you again. Where on earth are you?"

"On the other side of the world."

"You hate me that much?"

I sigh. It feels like heartache. "I don't hate you, Cam."

She is quiet for a bit. Then: "What did he tell you?"

"Nothing. He hit me."

"He told me. Are you okay?"

"I can take a punch, Camille. Question is, why did he hit me?"

"Perhaps because you are fucking someone else behind my back."

I don't have much to say to that. So I say nothing and let my thoughts re-order and settle. "Cleo says he's in love with you? Is that true?"

She sighs again. "You will have to ask Mason that, I suppose."

"I'm asking you. I'm asking how everyone around me knew about you and him and I didn't."

"There is no me and him, Rapha."

"No? But there was, right? At one point?"

"Your tone is exceptionally judgmental for someone who is sleeping with someone else right at this moment," she snaps. "Because you are with her now, yes? Where else would you be..."

"This is...different, Cam, he's one of my best friends. And you lied to me about it for the entirety of our fucking relationship! All of you did. Did you all have a good laugh about it whenever I left the room?"

"Of course not! We never said anything because we *love* you!" She sounds devastated that I would even think that. "Mason loves you, I love you. The others, I did not know about. I did not know that they knew... *Putain*, what a mess."

My voice is softer when I ask. "Tell me the truth now. I want to hear it from you."

She's only quiet a moment before she starts. "I met Mason at a party in LA. *Before* you and I were serious. After we met in Paris and flirted a little online. I did not think you were interested in me and so when Mason and I met that night, you did not come up, I did not know who he was at first, did not put the connection together. And when I did, it was not important to say because nothing had ever happened between us. With Mason, it was fun, we got very drunk on free champagne and it was a night I would have probably forgotten if you and I did not meet again in London."

London. London. I try to cast my mind back. We'd met again at a show I'd done in London without the others, she'd called me out on not calling her back after Paris. I'd liked it. I'd liked her. We clicked. She was smart, beautiful, and she made me laugh. The sex was fucking great and I was fucking happy.

"But after that there were a few times when he'd call me, drunk, telling me he had feelings for me. It was sweet, flattering I guess. I like him as a friend, nothing more. The night of the Grammy awards, after you and Crawford left for your party, he told me again that his feelings had not changed. That he even considered leaving the band, because he could not stay and watch us get married."

It feels like a smack across the face. Mason wanted to leave the Poets? Because of Camille? Me? Fuck, they could survive losing me easier than they could him. And he'd had this thought *after* we'd won a fucking Grammy? The next day was when we'd had our fight over Cleo's brother.

"I never cheated on you, Rapha. Never."

It feels shittier than I expect to find I believe her. Given everything I've done. It's guilt and feeling so small that makes me ask the next question. "You never thought I might like to know you'd fucked one of my best friends? That never occurred to you?"

"Oh, Raphael...of course, it did. But when you are falling in love with someone you do not ruin it with things like this. I was afraid I would lose you. I did not want to lose you." *You've lost me anyway,* I want to say.

I lean forward on my knees and let out my own deep sigh. "It's over, Camille."

The words are out and I feel...lighter, there's a lot of space inside me now where they'd been living and it feels good. Good to have said it. For months I'd been terrified that as soon as it was out I'd want to take it right back. But I don't. I want to cement it.

"It was over before Mase hit me, before I found out about you and him. It's not...about that. It's about me."

She says nothing right away and I close my eyes and try and imagine the look on her face. I can see it so clearly; the hurt, the pain, and it makes me feel like shit. How had I gotten myself into this position? How had I managed to do this to the woman I was about to spend the rest of my life with? The woman I loved, the woman who was on paper, my perfect fucking match. Who would have given me everything. It hits me like a truck.

I'm him. I'm fucking Finn.

"You have figured it out then?" She asks, "Are you in love with her?"

My eyes are closed and all I can see is him.

"Yeah, I'm in love with someone else."

Camille is silent again. She's not hung up, I can still hear the sound of people behind her, the soft notes of her breathing.

"I'm so sorry, Cam."

It's a few more beats of silence before she says:

"Merry Christmas, Raphael."

And then she's gone.

I drop my phone and let out a breath. I'm thinking about doing my breathing exercises when I see movement at the side of my eye. I expect Shiro but instead Jae is standing there with his toothbrush in his mouth staring at me. He looks stunned. Dark eyes wide in the low light.

Did he hear me say it? Is that terror on his face? I want to go to him. I want him to say it back. But that's not how it works.

That's not how love works. Love is fucking terrifying. A jump in the dark. Blind fucking faith.

He's still looking at me. That wide-eyed stare coupled with quick breaths. He doesn't look like he's going to say anything, so I bite the bullet.

"That was Camille," I tell him though I'm sure he worked that out on his own. "I figured I'd been avoiding her long enough."

I watch him warily as he keeps staring. He nods once and then turns and scurries off down the hall leaving me sitting there alone.

I push down the anxiety churning in my gut and follow him.

He's finishing up in the bathroom. Smoothing some expensive face cream over his cheeks and forehead, the tip of his nose, his chin. I brush my teeth as I watch him go through his skincare regimen.

He's not looked at me. After the cream, there's a clear liquid, two precise drops onto two fingers and then he's smoothing that on too, mainly around his eyes. Then he washes his hands. When he's done that he finally flicks a brief look at me before dipping back out of the bathroom.

I piss and wash my hands and then wander back into his bedroom where he's lying flat on his back under the striped sheets, staring at the ceiling.

The light is off on his side but not on mine. He tilts his head to watch me walk around the bed and strip out of my sweats before getting in beside him. His skin glows in the dull light and I can smell the faintest trace of the products he's used, orange peel and baby powder.

He stares back at the ceiling as he says, "You told her you are in love with me."

He doesn't sound terrified. Doesn't look it either, not anymore. Maybe he just needed some time to sit with the idea.

"Does that scare you?" I ask.

He turns onto his side so that he's facing me. "That you told her or that you are?" he asks, mouth softening into a semblance of a smile.

"The second one."

"A little, yes," he says in a really small voice.

"Why?" I'm ready for him to say something like; *because I don't feel the same way you do,* or, *what if I can't give you what you want,* or possibly even something like, *you're important Raphael, but I can't ever be with you—not like that.*

But instead, he says; "Because everyone who's ever loved me—who has ever tried to be with me—has always decided that in the end it is too hard. That I am too…difficult." He shakes his head like that's not quite what he meant. "That it is too much hard work to be with me. To love me."

He still looks frustrated. Like he can't quite verbalize what it is he means. It doesn't matter though because I get the gist. And it's pissing me off. Who made him feel like that? His parents? His friends? His bandmates? Ji-hoon?

In any case, loving him isn't hard. It's been easy. Quick and easy. I blinked and it was done. I try for light because I can feel him slipping into someplace dark, somewhere I don't want him to go. Never again if I can help it.

"Then you know a lot of liars because that's not been my experience." I smile, reaching out to smooth my hand around his neck.

He trembles beneath my fingers, eyes slipping closed.

"You have not been doing it very long," he reasons.

"Learning to skateboard was hard. Painful too. I fell off *a lot*. Broke a lot of bones." I count them in my head. "Five; the same one twice. But I never gave up until I could do it. Learning to play the guitar was hard too. I was pretty sure I'd been born with my fingers on the wrong hands because I couldn't get my head around how I was supposed to move them, how to do that quick enough to make it sound good, then do it while strumming too. I practiced until my fingers bled. Until blisters formed over blisters—they never really healed properly."

I lift my fingers to show him the roughened pearly pads. Old callouses that were part of me now. He takes hold of my hand and stares at them, then brings them to his lips to place feather-soft kisses over them.

"Are you going to break my bones, Jaehyun? Make me bleed?"

It's not really a question, but he answers it anyway.

"Never." There's a quiet ferocity in his eyes.

I slide my hand around his neck to pull him closer. "Then how about neither of us hurt ourselves or each other? Not unless it's in a kinky-sex way."

He laughs against my mouth. "A kinky-sex way. You mean like spanking?"

"Maybe. Or biting."

To demonstrate I roll over him and shove my face in the crook of his neck and bite down, not hard enough to mark, but hard enough to make him squeal. He twists his body away, laughing.

"You're so fucking edible, it's a wonder you're still whole honestly." I bite his shoulder next. He squeals.

"Stop! Please, stop!"

He's gasping and giggling as I unlatch my mouth from his skin. Then he's lying under me, hair ruffled and cheeks pink, eyes sparkling with something. He's so fucking gorgeous like this. Loose and open and smiling.

"I love you," I tell him. "I don't need you to say it back, and I don't need you to feel the same. It's soon for you, I get it. But I feel like I've been in this for a long time and now that I've got you like this, I'm all in. I'll take whatever you can give me, Jaehyun. I know all of this is harder for you…that you have to be careful with who you decide to be with or whatever. I get it. But I don't care about any of the stuff that you think I should be worried about, I told you that already." I stroke a section of his silver hair back from his face. "I just want you."

He swallows, mouth falling open a little, breathing still quick from his laughter. When he presses his palm over my heart I think he might be about to say it back and for a minute I wonder if I want him to say it in Korean or not.

But it's not what he says anyway.

"I will give you everything I can, Raphael." It's that small voice again. Soft and gentle and so very sincere. "Please just…wait for me. I want to be with you. I will try hard to give you all that you need, just please wait for me."

He's pleading with his eyes. I lean down to kiss him, deep and rough.

"I'll wait for you, baby." I kiss the words into his mouth as he wraps his arms around my neck. "As long as it takes, I'll wait for you."

막간
(JAE'S INTERLUDE #3)

As the coffee brews, I call my parents' number, hoping as always that it's mom who answers. I consider it my first gift of the day when her soft voice comes down the line.

"Good morning, mama. I wanted to wish you and papa merry Christmas." I take a seat at the dining table.

"Ah, Jaehyun-ah, honey," mama says and my chest tightens. "Merry Christmas. You are at home?"

"Yes, for now. But I have plans later."

She doesn't ask what they are or chide me for not coming home. I try to imagine taking Raphael home to Daejeon to meet them and goosebumps prick at my arms and across my neck. He would be very charming I am sure; but it wouldn't matter. Not to papa at least.

She tells me that he's out, gone to pick up grandma and Min-Seo to bring them to the house. She asks if I am eating well and working hard and makes me promise to try to come home for Lunar New Year. She tells me that she is proud of me, that papa is too, and thanks me for the gifts I had sent to them which they opened last night.

It's not a long phone call but when I hang up I breathe deeply with relief, the imaginary list in my head of things I must do today, a little shorter.

Ji-u is the first to wish everyone merry Christmas in the group chat. Boohyin sends a silly video of a cat dressed as an elf and dancing to an American Christmas song. I send a simple message with some Christmas tree emojis. Ji-hoon wishes me merry Christmas privately first, thanking me for the gift—a piece of art by an artist he likes—and then tells everyone to have a great day in the group chat.

I sip my coffee as I consider what Raphael said last night.

He loves me. It should make me incredibly happy; he is the first man to tell me so in the way I have always wanted. It should fill me with joy and happiness and excitement for the future. And I do feel some of those things. Just not as strong as I feel other things. Fear. Anxiety. Uncertainty. Like the future is rushing towards me at high speed and if I don't jump or move out of the way then I am going to be crushed. Or perhaps it is the past which will crush me. Perhaps Raphael could love me hard enough that it will not matter about all the ways in which I am broken, faulty, imperfect.

I try to consider my own feelings. I do this often very early in the morning or very late at night, because somehow when the world is quiet my mind is always loud. I try to sort through the loudness to the core of how I feel about Raphael. I've not yet accepted it to be love; it is too soon for it, even if love has always come too easy for me. (And not easy enough for those I want to love me back.) Whatever we have feels too new and fragile to be weighed down by such a heavy word as love.

My feelings for Raphael are strong, I know this. Surprisingly strong. He makes me feel cared for and warm and like I am enough. There is happiness in these things. These weeks with him, laughing and learning him, I've been happier than I can remember being for a long time. But some final tether holds me back from falling fully into this with him. Whether it is the fact that I worry I am still a novelty for him, that he will wake up soon and realize that this has all been a fun experiment, I do not know. But he has always been clear with me, and I trust he feels that which he says he does. But I know too that love can be a fickle and changing thing. And almost never unconditional.

He says it's been easy to love me but he doesn't know what it is to love me yet—I worry that he doesn't really know me at all. The life I lead in the quiet, out of the spotlight. He said he'd take whatever I can give him, but he deserves better. He deserves more than to be hidden away and denied, more than to be a lie I tell the world over and over. More than the sad dark nights I can offer him behind a closed door.

Except, is this not what I wanted from Ji-hoon? Something real. Something unhidden.

Raphael is offering me everything I want and it's me, this time, who is unwilling. No, not unwilling—unable.

Shiro mewls at my feet and I scoop him up and kiss him on the nose.

"Merry Christmas, baby. I have some extra special treats for you today. But you have to be good while we are travelling, okay?"

He meows softly, warm little body purring like an small engine as I tuck him under my chin and stand, kissing him again as I move to the kitchen. I set him down near his bowl and start making some eggs and bacon. I'll wake Raphael up when it's ready. We don't have a lot of time this morning before we have to leave for Gyeonggi to spend two days at the forest house before returning to Seoul. The company had arranged for someone to cook dinner for us, but I only had them for a few hours this evening.

When they're done, I spoon the eggs onto the plates and top with bacon, pour two fresh cups of brewed coffee, set the toast in the center of the table and then go to the bedroom.

He's still fast asleep. Lying on his front with his cheek pressed into the pillow. His hair is a blonde tangled mess about his head, long enough that he's been tying it back out of his face when he's writing in his leather notebook or watching TV.

I perch on the bed next to him and gently brush a section of hair back from his cheek. He sleeps deeply, Raphael. As I do. A strand of compatibility I didn't know I cared about. But I like that he sinks into dreams as heavily and completely as I do. My patterns of sleep are strange and often problematic, but when I do sleep it is heavy and deep. I lean in and kiss the side of his neck, the scent of him strong here. Sleep and soap. As I nuzzle my nose against the warm skin, he flutters awake, slow and yawning.

"Merry Christmas, Raphael." I smile as I pull back up.

Eyes still closed, he smiles. "*Keur-iseu-maseu jal bona-eseyo,*" he says groggily, carefully, before his mouth turns up into a shy smile.

I can't hide the small look of surprise on my face.

"Sorry. Did I butcher that? I watched a YouTube video."

I laugh because he looks extremely cute right now. "You did not butcher it."

"I didn't?" His eyes light up, happy.

I shake my head, reaching out to pet his.

"You have no idea how many times I listened to google translate saying that over and over. And there were all these different versions of it, formal and informal, slightly less formal. Us English speaking folk really just said 'fuck it' we're gonna have exactly one way of saying shit, didn't we?" He's laughing now and it makes me laugh too. He slides a hand up under my T-shirt where he flicks a calloused finger over my nipple. "I'm not sure I'm ever gonna be able to speak Korean, baby. I'm sorry."

I shake my head to disagree. "I am sure if you practiced a lot you could. English was very hard for me at first." My cheeks heat as I say, "And you have a very talented mouth."

His eyes glint with mischief as he wraps an arm all the way around me and pulls me fully on top of him. "Yeah? Why don't you tell me more about this talented mouth of mine. Anything in particular you like that it does?"

"There is one song you sing, where your voice sounds very deep, that I like a lot." I sigh with my eyes closed.

He pinches my hip playfully.

"What?" I ask innocently. "You thought I was talking about something else?"

He grins and buries his entire head under my t-shirt, licking and nibbling the warm skin of my stomach. It makes me howl with laughter because I am very ticklish here. My feet too. But he has not found out about this yet. I can feel the familiar stir of want between my legs. I want him as much as I always do. His mouth, his cock, his come, all of it all over me, inside me. When he seals his mouth over my nipple and sucks, I almost abandon all of the plans I made for today.

"Raphael…we…I have…made plans."

He pulls his head out from under my t-shirt and gives me a perplexed look. "Plans?"

I nod. "I have arranged something—I hope you don't mind."

"You have to go see your family or something?" He looks torn. "I can hang out here, it's fine, I don't mind."

"No, not that." He is so desperately sweet. "I mean plans for us. You and I."

"Oh." He looks mildly suspicious now.

I lean in to peck him soft on the nose then slip out of his loosened hold to stand.

"I think you will like it." I give him my sweetest smile. "Now come, eat, and then we will dress and pack."

"Pack?" He blinks. "I haven't even *unpacked*."

"Then it will not take you long. You can comfort Shiro while I pack. He hates travelling."

This makes him sit up, blanket falling to expose his lean, golden body, dabbled with black ink. "We're *travelling*?"

I give him a wide smile. "Come on or your American-style breakfast will be cold."

Shiro *does* hate travelling. But Eun-soo who usually comes to look after him when I am travelling is in Chongju with her family, and so there's no other option but to take him with us. The drive is only a little over an hour, so he will be okay.

I'd told Raphael as little as possible about where we were going. Only that it was in the forest and a popular scenic route. He said he hoped I wasn't doing this for him because he would have been happy to spend the day in bed with me, that he couldn't think of a better way to spend Christmas in fact. I told him that we could do that when we got there if he liked.

I haven't been to the forest house in almost eight months because of our schedule and normally when I am here, it is alone. I prefer it that way. So it will be strange to have another person here. In the rooms that I normally only see myself in.

As I drive, Raphael rests his head back and closes his eyes, strumming some soundless beat on his thigh with his long fingers. He's wearing a white hoodie underneath a Moncler shacket in brushed wool, a bold check pattern of reds, blues, and white which brings out his eyes and the warm Californian tan of his skin. His eyes are ice blue today. Normally they're the blue of the ocean but the stark white of the snow and the bright wool transforms them into something frost bitten. When Shiro lets out a small whine he sits up and turns round in his seat to peer through to the back.

"Hey, we're almost there, buddy," he says in a soft voice. The kind you might use on a small child. It makes a warm sensation move over my chest. "And then your dad is gonna give you so many treats to reward you. I might give you some too."

Through the rear-view I see him poke his fingers through the carry case to wiggle them at Shiro, who only whines louder. It makes me smile. Really the best thing to do when transporting cats is to ignore them completely, talking to them only makes them more vocal.

"Did you have pets as a child?"

"A goldfish once," he says turning back around.

"And how are they as pets?"

"Real quiet."

I can't help but laugh before he tells me they did have a dog once, an old one that his mom found injured by the side of the road and who ended up living with them until he died a few years later. They called him Al, for a song about a long lost friend he then starts to sing. It does not sound familiar but his voice is wonderful.

An easy silence settles as he scrolls through his phone, then there's music playing instead of the low chatter of the radio which he does not understand. I'm not sure what it is, but it is in English. It's pleasant, warm, and faintly seasonal. I feel his gaze turn to me a moment later and then his hand moves across the center console to settle on my leg. His touch is warm through my jeans, large and solid around the top of my thigh.

"I'm really glad I'm here with you today," he says with an easy smile.

"You do not know where I am taking you yet." I laugh and he grins adorably.

"You, know…I don't actually care." He sighs. "If you and the little guy are there, then I'm good."

I want it so much then it almost hurts. This. Raphael. Out and unhidden. I want to take drives with him and wake up with him. I want to exchange gifts on celebration days. I want it almost as much as I wanted the life and the career that now means I cannot have it.

"It has a heated pool?" Raphael exclaims excitedly as we drop our bags by the bed.

Outside the bedroom, the wood deck area leads to the large heated pool where steam lifts off amidst the chilly afternoon air. It's partially covered, a wooden construction which wraps around and over it and sections off the deck in zones. The hot tub and sauna to the left of the pool, the outdoor dining area and kitchen to the right and then a large sunken seated area.

The house when we opened the door smelled of roasting meat and a homely mix of Christmas spice, and Raphael's eyes had lit up at the roaring fire and Christmas tree I'd had the company arrange when they did the cleaning—the presents I'd sent ahead wrapped and arranged beneath.

The two men in the kitchen had given us polite hello's before quickly getting back to work. Everything, they said, would be ready in around an hour. The table was already set and they'd serve up the food and carve the turkey and ham before leaving us alone. I could already tell there was going to be far too much food. Raphael had a big appetite, as did I, but it was a dauntingly large amount for just the two of us. Still, we would try.

Raphael spins round suddenly and pulls me into his arms.

"I'm sure I said let's do Christmas the Korean way. Now here I am in a house in the snow covered forest, turkey with all the trimmings, a crackling fire, and a Christmas tree."

He pretends to look cross but it just looks cute. He loosens his hold and dips his head to kiss me. It's a lick of his tongue first, one that has me parting my lips, and then he moves in deeper, tasting me fully as he makes a soft noise in his throat.

"I can't believe you did all this for me," he whispers.

My cheeks feel hot. My ears too.

"I thought we could meet halfway. Have an American–style Christmas in Korea."

"You're amazing, do you know that?"

I push at him gently. "Stop it. It is nothing."

"You gave me Christmas as a Christmas gift. It's…insane."

I frown, moving away to lift my suitcase onto the bed. "Oh, this is not your gift. Those we will open after dinner."

"Are you fucking serious?" His mouth drops open. Then he groans. "Shit, my gifts are fucking terrible. I feel bad."

Now it is my turn to frown. "I do not believe that. Gifts are a gesture, you coming here to spend the holidays with me is a huge one. There is nothing I need."

He comes toward me and slides his hand around my waist, his eyes turning mischievous.

"Nothing?" He raises an eyebrow. "Like nothing at all." His hands begin to fumble with the button on my jeans and then he's dropping to his knees, head upturned as he licks his lips showily. "Hmm, what about this…? Like, as a thank you?"

"Raphael there are two men next door. You cannot be serious…"

"Baby, they could barely look at your extremely famous face, you seriously think they're gonna come into your bedroom?"

I begin to protest again but then his mouth is over the fabric of my underwear and he's…sucking. Hot, wet loud kisses along the length to the tip that feel *so* good. I gasp, sliding my hands into the lengths of his hair.

"Okay…then you will have to be very quick." I am panting a little as I bite down on my lip.

He smirks. "And *you* will have to be very fucking quiet…" And then he's pulling down the white material and swallowing me down almost entirely. I cover my mouth to stifle my cry of pleasure.

TWENTY-EIGHT
RAPHAEL

"I think I'm going to explode," I tell him, sitting back in the chair with a pained groan.

I've eaten my body weight. I think my stomach is about ready to rip open and there's still a mountain of food on the table.

He's still eating. Which is a wonder really given his frame. He's been eating turkey and mashed potato and creamed corn with chopsticks and I've been struggling to think of anything as fascinating or as fucking adorable.

"It's fine. We can eat it later. Or tomorrow," he says around a mouthful of gravy covered mashed potato.

I nod and lift my wine, watching him over the rim. He's wearing this oversized cardigan thing, his face bare and scrubbed clean from the shower we took earlier, and his hair fluffy and soft-looking. I'm pretty sure this is my favorite version of him. When he's like this. Unwound and soft.

Although…the sight of him coming down my throat is a close second. And the sight of him on his knees with his eyes closed in bliss as he mouths at my cock, like he had in the shower, a very close third.

I'm smiling about this as he looks up and catches my eye and smirks, like he knows where my mind is. He lifts his wine and sips at the red slowly, letting it darken and wet his lips.

"So what do you normally do after eating?" he asks.

"At home, we'd normally lie on the couch in a food coma and watch some TV. My mom will normally find a British period film to watch—they're her favorite."

The fact that I haven't heard from my mom yet is weird, but she runs about crazy on Christmas day ferrying people around and cooking so she'll call me later.

"British period film?"

"Yeah, you know. Those ones where women just sit about in rooms drinking tea and talking. '*Oh, they only have six thousand a year, Miss Havisham! He's such a scoundrel, Elinor!*'"

My attempt at an English accent isn't that bad, but he's bent over and laughing at it anyway. His hand covering his mouth as his shoulders shake with soft giggles.

"Is that what you want to do now?" he asks, when he's stopped laughing.

"I wanna open our gifts."

His eyes light up and then he's nodding, before jumping up from the dining table and rushing out of the room while I can only blink after him.

"Should I follow you? " I call out after him. "Is my gift in the bedroom?"

I hear him laugh. "No, there is one in my suitcase that I did not send with the others."

I'm hoping his are also shit because I really don't feel good about some overpriced earrings and an unfinished song right about now. Not after everything else he's done today. Maybe I can make it up to him with my mouth or my dick, fuck maybe even my ass if it goes *that* badly.

While he's in the bedroom, I fill our wine glasses and carry them to the living room. I'd put his under the tree earlier, and my phone is charged and the backing track ready to play. I can only hope my mom doesn't call while I play it for him.

I take a small second to consider how fucking cheesy it is. Writing him a song. I've never done it in my life, not for Camille, not for any girl. And there's a reason why. It makes me want to throw myself off a bridge from embarrassment. But I wrote it for him, about him, and there are more where that came from too, so I suppose I need to know how it will make him feel before I do it again.

In the livingroom, he's setting a small parcel on top of two larger ones by the tree. One of the parcels is big, a large rectangular shape that's not much smaller than him, another about quarter that size, and then a small thin one on top of that. All are wrapped in silver paper that glints in the low light.

My cheeks heat as I reach down for the Chanel bag I'd hidden near the back, turning to him. He looks at me, then looks at the parcel in my hand, and then beams wide.

"You bought me Chanel."

I hold it out to him sheepishly. "This is where you tell me you're actually a brand ambassador and that you already have everything in their collection."

He steps closer and takes it from me with a small shake of his head. "I am a brand ambassador for Valentino, but Chanel is my favorite," he whispers. "Please do not tell anyone."

I pretend to think about it. "Maybe if you're good I'll keep your filthy secret to myself." I bend my head to kiss him on the underside of his jaw. "Merry Christmas, beautiful. Next time I'll do better. I have one more gift but first…" I turn around to pick up his wine glass and hold it out to him. "I have to get you good and drunk."

His eyes turn a little darker. "Oh? I do not have to be drunk to do something naughty with you, Mr. Rockstar. Don't you know that by now?" He reaches up to ghost a kiss over my ear and whispers, "You only have to ask, Raphael. I will do it."

I turn my head to catch his mouth, my dick twitching to life when he pushes a wine-sweet kiss onto my lips.

"Good to know," I whisper against his mouth, before kissing him again, harder.

He melts, our breaths turning quick and hot against each other for a few moments. But then he pushes me away gently before flouncing back down on the sofa with his giftbag and his wine.

"Open the smallest first," he says, waving a hand in the direction of my gifts without looking up from his own.

I sit cross-legged by the tree and do as I'm told, picking up the smallest one first and gently pulling the paper away from one corner. It's expertly wrapped, the paper a thick embossed parchment that feels almost like canvas. I hear Jae gasp loudly from beside me and I turn my head. He is looking at me with this almost frightened look on his face.

"Raphael...these are...so expensive," he says, gazing down at them.

"Do you like them? I mean, will you wear them?"

He nods emphatically. "I will. But rarely. I will be afraid to lose them. I normally wear things like these for a few hours only." He's reaching into the white velvet box and lifting one out to hold it up to the light. "They are so beautiful. I saw them on the...brochure... but I do not...I never buy myself these kinds of things. It feels so... isn't it too much?"

I think about the glass cabinet back in his apartment that is laden with jewels and gold and designer watches and frown, confused.

"You don't buy yourself jewelry? But you have loads."

He unfixes the earring from its box. "Gifts. They are all gifts."

I try not to think about who the fuck else is buying him four thousand dollar earrings but I fail. Kai? Other guys he's been with? Some hot twist of jealousy flares up inside me which is fucking ridiculous. Of course, he's been with other people. Of course, they've given him gifts. The fuck is wrong with me?

But then, like he can sense the direction of my thoughts he says, quickly, "Brands. Brands send us a lot of things. And once Ji-u spent a ridiculous amount of money on a necklace for my birthday, but I am so afraid of losing it or damaging it that I have worn it only once."

He's taking off his subtle silver hoop earrings now and I watch, transfixed, as he puts the new ones on. They glint and gleam under the low light, sitting gorgeously against the elegant line of his neck. Smooth skin against the pearl and silver of the earring. He does the same with the other and tilts his head this way and that to show me them.

"How do they look?"

I blink a few times and shake my head to clear it. "Amazing."

He grins and then stretches himself out toward me, feline and elegant, so he's on his hands and knees in front of me.

"Thank you," he says, kissing me slow. "I love them very much."

I close my eyes and chase the soft cherry of his mouth, licking my tongue across soft lips.

"I really liked buying you them," I murmur. "I want to buy you presents all the time. Spoil you."

I can feel his mouth curve against mine. "Mmm, I would not complain about that. Now hurry, open yours."

He sits up and back, expression turning serious as he gestures with his head to the half opened parcel in my lap. I drag my gaze away from him and look down, then continue to tear the paper off what is a small, slim hardback book. **Learn Korean, fast!**

I laugh as he giggles at what he says is a joke present.

"You know, this is actually perfect since I really hate those Duolingo characters." I flick through the pages.

He's not sure what Duolingo is and so I pull out my phone to show him which results in him proclaiming that the characters are in fact very *cute-ah*. I lean in to place a kiss on his cheek.

"Not as cute as you."

At this he rolls his eyes and points at the largest parcel before immediately sitting back, folding his arms across his chest. He looks nervous for some reason.

I wait for him to say something, something to explain, pre-emptively, what is in the huge box and why it has him so nervous, but he doesn't say a word.

It's immaculately wrapped again, and the box underneath the paper is solid. Heavy too. So I don't try and lift it up, I just peel the paper back carefully to reveal a polished wooden box, black lacquer with what appears to be Korean lettering across its surface in delicate gold script. I wonder if what's in it is what's written here, or if it's just the maker's mark. I glance briefly at Jae who's expression hasn't changed at all.

Carefully, I pull the paper out and away from the gorgeously crafted box, smoothing my hand over its edges and curves, around to the front where a gold lock and key sit stylishly against the black wood. It sort of reminds me of those boxes that have very expensive bottles of whisky inside, though I'm certain that's not what this is.

"Should I open it?" I ask and he nods once, offering me the faintest of smiles.

Turning the lock gently, I hear a soft snick, before I push up the lid to get a look at the contents.

Sitting in an intricate woodcut frame, is a guitar. Acoustic, the body carved of the same black lacquer as the box itself. The neck is stained red and the strings and pegs are that same gorgeous burnished gold of the lettering on the box. And in the lower corner of the body is that same Korean script most certainly denoting a maker. I'm clearly a philistine because I don't know a single Korean guitar manufacturer. But what I do know is it's the most beautiful guitar I've ever seen.

"It is handmade. One of the producers at the company told me that these are very rare," Jae explains. "There are only fifty in the world. Because he makes only six per year and has refused to let them be made by machine. I think he is perhaps a little strange."

He laughs a soft nervous laugh.

I want to tell him I don't deserve it. That my hands aren't even close to worthy of playing this, that it's the most special gift I've ever been given by anyone. But I can't get any words to come out.

"I'm sorry if it is not your style. I know you play electric guitar, but I thought it was very pretty, and I suppose I liked the idea of you playing a Korean guitar. Maybe you would think of me when you played. I believe there is only one other in Northern America, though Beomgyu says it is in a museum…in the place where the country music is made."

He's still nervous, scared that I hate it, because he's talking quickly and breathlessly and before I even realize what's happening

I'm fucking crying. I turn to look at him and his words peter out. His expression transforms to shock.

"Jaehyun, this is fucking incredible. It's the most beautiful gift anyone's ever given me," I look back at the guitar with awe. "I don't know what to say. I don't even want to touch it…it's…seriously beautiful."

I shake my head as I reach out and draw my fingers over the gold strings. It reminds me of him. Sleek, immaculately crafted, and jaw-droppingly beautiful.

"I do not know much about instruments but I am certain they only work when you touch them."

I laugh, wiping my tears away with the back of my hand. When I look at him again, he's watching me closely. When he reaches across to take my hand, kissing the fingers softly, he doesn't look nervous anymore.

"Will you play something for me on it?"

I take a deep steadying breath and nod. The guitar glides out of its box, far lighter than I was expecting. I stand, taking a seat on the footstool instead as I rest it on my thigh—it fits against me perfectly, just like he does—and start to tune it. Though I barely have to. It sings clean and sharp on each chord, the strings humming warmly beneath my fingers.

"I was gonna play this for you from my phone," I tell him.

"Play what?"

"Your second gift." I give him an embarrassed smile as I lean over to take a deep gulp of my wine. "I might have sort of wrote you a song."

His eyes light up brighter than the Christmas tree as he settles himself back on the sofa and sips his own wine. "Oh, this will be very good. Please tell me you will sing about my asshole."

I splutter out a laugh as I sit my glass back down. "That's actually the title."

"Of course." He nods, proudly. Then his face melts into this gorgeous smile and my heart trips over itself. I love him. I seriously fucking love this guy. Person. Human.

"You should know I'm really embarrassed about this," I say, as I play through the first few notes of the first song I ever learnt. It's one of Finn's. A B-side from his first EP.

"I am certain it's not that bad." Jae smiles, stretching out on his side with his knee bent up, head resting on his upturned hand. His t-shirt rises up over the flat warm skin of his abdomen making my mouth water.

"Writing a love song and playing it to the person you wrote it about is the most embarrassing thing a musician can do."

"Is that so?" He reaches his foot out to toe me into action. "Then I think I like you embarrassed. You look very pretty when your cheeks are pink."

"I don't think you'll find it so pretty when I shit myself."

He laughs. "Sing for me, *Mr. Rockstar.*"

I give him one last stupid smile and then I switch the tempo, slowing it down so that the chords shorten and my fingers have to pluck rather than strum. Then I sing for him. I thought I wouldn't be able to look at him while I did it. While I sang about being lost and found in a foreign place. How needing is so very different from wanting. How green tea reminds me of him.

But I find out quickly that I can't look *away* from him. My eyes trace over every inch of his face; dark eyes warmed by the wine and the fire, pink full mouth licked wet, the stretch of his pale throat disappearing under his top, nipples faintly visible. His hip dips inward before rounding out around a perfect thigh, teasing smooth supple flesh. His soft smile mirrors my own for the opening verse, and the bridge, but then his expression changes. And because I'm watching him so closely, I see his throat move as he swallows. The sweet kiss of a smile melting away into something darker and heavier, seeping into his eyes like a rain cloud across the sky. He stands up and then he's gone from the room in a flash.

I stop playing immediately. I still had another verse to go.

A door closes down the hall and I sit and contemplate the lyrics I've just sung, combing through it for anything he might have taken offence to. Anything insulting. There's nothing. So I conclude that it's the fact I wrote him a song at all. Maybe he thought it would be fun and then when it turned out to be sickeningly sincere he just couldn't handle it. I don't blame him. I reach across to sit the guitar back in its case and take up my red wine, gulping the last of it back down as I try to figure out what to do.

He's been gone about ten minutes when I decide I can't wait this out. My insides are gnawing me to the bone. I wander down the hall in the direction he went. There's a faucet running in the main bathroom, light spilling out from under the thick wooden door. I rap it softly with my knuckles.

"You okay?" I ask through it. "I'm not sure what happened there. Sorry if I embarrassed you."

He says nothing.

"I'd love to say it won't happen again but I can't make that promise. I'm embarrassing as fuck when I'm this into a person."

Still nothing. I press my ear against it.

"Jae? Can you unlock the door?"

"It is unlocked," he says after a moment.

He's sitting on the floor between the tub and the sink, back pressed against the wall and his knees pulled up to his chest. His hair is pushed back from his face, and though he isn't looking in my direction I can see his cheeks are red and splotchy. Tear stained.

"I'm sorry," I say again.

Jae turns to glare at me. Then he waves a hand in the direction of the living room.

"You cannot…do things like that," he says, voice quiet and angry.

"Things like…?" I need to know so I can expressly prevent myself doing them ever again.

"That. You just cannot…"

He wipes the back of his hand across his face and even this is done angrily. But when he looks at me again, I see it. He's not angry, not really. The anger is hiding something else, something bigger. Fear. He's shit fucking scared.

I go towards him immediately and lower myself to the floor across from him.

"Talk to me, baby. Tell me what you're scared of."

He squeezes his eyes closed and takes a huge breath, but he doesn't talk.

"Or did you just really hate the song? It's cool if you did—not everyone likes my song writing."

It's said lightly, with a small suggestion of playfulness. It earns me another glare, incendiary in its intensity. It's distracting because he looks fucking gorgeous with his pink cheeks and glittering eyes. His mouth is shaped into an angry pink pout and it takes all of my strength not to lean in and kiss it.

"I thought it was going to be…funny." He sniffles, giving me a wide-eyed serious sort of look. "You really wrote that *for me*? About me?"

I nod and he launches himself at me, climbing into my lap.

"I hate you," he says quietly against my neck.

"I don't think you do." I press a kiss against his cheek.

He's trembling when he pulls back to look at me.

"I am scared, Raphael," he says in a small voice.

"What of? Tell me. I bet it's not that scary."

"Of everything," he says. "Of having you and losing you, of having you and losing everything else." He buries his head in my neck and breathes deep, like the very scent of me is comforting to him.

"You know, before that night in New York…I think I was more terrified than I've ever been in my life."

He pulls back, studying me. "Really?"

"Yeah, really. I threw up before I came to your place." I wasn't ever going to tell him this, but it feels important right now that I do. It feels like something he might understand. Might get comfort from.

"And you still came?"

"Twice as I remember it? Or was it three times?" I smile and he hits me playfully on the shoulder. "I was terrified, Jae, but I'd never been more certain of what I wanted than I was sitting on the bathroom floor of that hotel room with the taste of vomit in my mouth. I was scared of losing everything too. But when I thought about what

I might gain from it…" I squeeze him tighter then, meaningfully. "It was so fucking worth it."

"I wasn't scared then," he admits. "But I am now."

"I can't control everything else, but I can promise you that I won't hurt you, Jaehyun."

It's the one thing, the only thing, I know for certain. I'd never ever hurt him. And if he wants it, I'll give him everything. He can have every single part of me: the talent, the lack of it, the daddy issues, the successes, the failures.

"If you want this, with me, then we're doing it together. And I'll be right fucking here beside you as long as you want me to be, however you want me to be."

He stares back at me a long time without saying anything, then says: "And if I tell you that I want you as a friend, that I cannot offer you any more than that?"

The ground falls away and my breath catches in my throat. Jae as a friend. One I can look at but never touch. One I can talk to and listen to, but not have. Would I seriously be okay with that?

"Is that what you want?" I ask.

Those ten seconds he takes to think about it are the longest of my life. But in them I decide that yes, I'll take that. I said I would and I meant it. I'll take whatever he's willing to give me.

"No, it is not," he replies. "I want more, Raphael. I want to love you."

I almost sag with relief as he reaches for the button of my jeans, undoing them to pull me out. I do the same, then maneuver him closer so that our cocks are lined up, hot smooth skin against hot smooth skin. It's dry but it still feels like fireworks going off under my skin. Sparks of pure white pleasure across my thighs and balls.

I kiss him hot and hard, my hips fucking up into his fist as I try to jerk him off at the same time. I come quick and without warning, my orgasm rushing out of my body like a fucking geyser. He spreads it over the head of his own cock and arches his body backwards, resting on one hand, to fuck up into his own fist now. When he's about to come, I lean in and catch the spill of him on my tongue, chin and cheek. Hot streaks of white that taste of him.

When he's done, he buries himself against me again, wrapping his arms tight around my neck. His breaths are soft and hot and quick from his orgasm. Moments later, long after they've slowed, he speaks, "Thank you for the song. It was very beautiful."

I press my lips to his hair and whisper, "You're welcome."

TWENTY-NINE
RAPHAEL

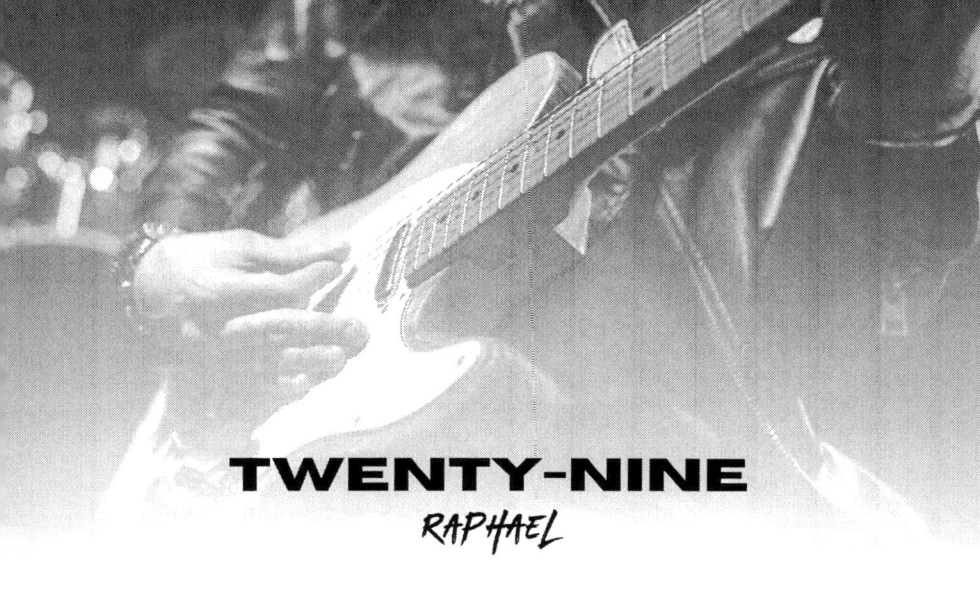

We arrive back in Seoul in the afternoon of the 27th. I'd have been happy to stay in the mountains—avoid the fuck out of this dinner tonight—but these are his friends (and his ex) and I've already decided that what's important to him is important to me. So I'll go. I'll be fucking charming too. Not give this guy any reason not to like me.

Jae had won my mom over. She'd called late on Christmas day and asked—demanded—I put him on the phone.

This was after he'd given me his last gift, which I can't think too much about or my head will explode. Because it was lingerie. *Fucking lingerie.* After he'd made me open the last gift, he'd disappeared into the bedroom to change into them. Lace white panties and thigh-highs which he'd let me bend him over the couch and fuck him in, after we'd showered and changed into pajamas.

With mom he'd been overly polite and nervous, smiling his high-cheeked smile (still pink from the shower) and nodding at everything she said. Even when she invited him to her birthday dinner in February. I'd told him later he didn't have to make it, but he said that he didn't have his schedule yet but that he would do everything he could to make it there. If that's what I wanted.

Tonight for Kai's dinner, I'm wearing the Gucci shirt Jae bought me in New York and a pair of black jeans, my favorite pair of well-worn black boots and half my hair pulled back into a knot. He'd looped some silver around my neck from his jewelry collection; a long necklace with a cross on it and two shorter ones which sat higher up. He appraises me with a warm look which I think might be about the shirt but which I hope is about more than that.

"Very sexy," he says, fixing one of the earrings I gave him for Christmas to his right ear.

He's wearing the tightest pair of jeans I've ever seen—so tight I'm seriously concerned for his cock and balls—and another of his Chanel sweaters, both black. The glint of the earring against his styled silver hair makes him look sleek and expensive.

"I knew that shirt would look good on you."

"I knew those earrings would look good on you."

He smiles as he finishes putting on the other one. I'd watched him put make-up on earlier. A dab of something under his eye, a flick of mascara over his lashes and a tint of pink cream on his cheeks and lips. He smells incredible too. The cologne I'd always thought reminded me of chocolate and Christmas I see comes in a small golden orb-shaped bottle with a Korean name. He'd looked shocked when I told him I didn't really wear cologne. Then offered me something 'manly' from his collection.

We're at the door when he pulls on a leather jacket from the closet there. This time I'm the one who questions the jacket's ability to keep *him* warm.

He only smiles and says, "We do not have to go far."

He's carrying a small gift bag and a bottle of wine as we head out and take the lift down to the tenth floor. The apartment complex is connected to the other blocks by covered glass walkways on intersecting floors. We cross the neon lit bridge to another building and then take the lift back up, this time to the 20th floor.

"Do you all live in the same building?" I ask him, as I watch the city grow smaller below us.

"No," Jae says typing something on his phone. "Only Ji-hoon and I are here. Ji-u, and Taejin are still together in the dorm and Xan and Boohyin are in Itaewon."

I try not to think too hard about the fact that he lives in the same building as his ex and the guy I suspect broke his heart. Then we're exiting the lift and coming up to a walnut door which Jae knocks on with three sharp knocks. It faces the opposite side of the building to Jae's apartment and so when it's pulled open I see a different view of Seoul spill out behind Kai.

This one has high-rises spread out across an indigo sky, lights of all colors picking out the shapes of buildings. Kai throws an arm around Jae first, a hug where his nose brushes his hair as he says something in Korean. He gives me a long look—not unfriendly but not entirely friendly either—before stretching out a hand.

"Welcome," he says.

"Thanks for having me, man." I shake his hand and Kai nods, stepping back to let me inside.

Following Jae's lead, I slip out of my boots at the door and shove my feet into a pair of the Korean house slippers I'm definitely going to order a batch of when I get back home. They're just more comfortable than walking around hardwood floors in your socks. I feel a little like a dick in them but since everyone is wearing them, I don't feel too self-conscious.

The apartment is a similar design to Jae's except it's flipped, the hallway open to the lounge and kitchen, already filled with a group of people, wine glasses in hand and foreign voices animated in conversation. There's music floating gently out from above us—sounds like modern jazz—and the scent of food causes my mouth to water.

When the group spots Jae there are loud exclamations and then he's being pulled into a chatter of excited Korean leaving me hovering on the periphery of the kitchen.

"Drink?" Kai asks from my right.

"Yeah, thanks. That'd be great."

"You drink whisky, yeah?"

There's a drinks cabinet pressed against the wall between the kitchen and lounge, bottles arranged on top and on a glass shelf above.

"Whisky is good, whatever you have is fine."

I cast a look over my shoulder. Jae's head is thrown back as he laughs at what the guy next to him says. The two women are laughing too. The other guy is checking his phone.

"You guys have a good Christmas?" Kai asks as he hands me the tumbler.

It's about three fingers full with one large ice cube in it almost the same circumference as the tumbler itself. He hadn't asked how I drink it. Which is normally neat. I lift it to my mouth anyway.

"Jae took you to the house in Gyeonggi?"

I nod as the whiskey slides sweet and cool down my throat. "Yeah, it was beautiful. Really peaceful up there, isn't it?"

Kai nods, watching me carefully. "How do you like Seoul?"

"It's a cool city, though I haven't seen much of it. I'd definitely like to explore a bit more before I fly back."

"Which is when?" It's asked so nonchalantly that I almost miss the flicker of hostility in his eyes.

I give him my most charming smile. "I have a flight out on the night of the second, but who knows what'll happen." I look over Jae. He's pouring himself a glass of wine from the open bottle on the counter, listening and nodding intently to what one of the women is telling him. "Maybe I'll just stay here."

"Our schedule is insane the next few months," Kai says. "I think it'd be better for him if you weren't around to distract him."

I stiffen at that. "Yeah, well, we already know that what you think doesn't really matter, does it?" I give him another smile and cut across the room towards Jae.

He introduces me to the rest of Kai's friends by my name and nothing else which makes a pit open up in my stomach, but a moment later he slides a hand around my waist and pulls me in to kiss me on the lips. The move gets a squeal from the women and low murmur of approval from one of the guys, the other just watching impassively. Almost coldly. It's only when he moves away to talk with Kai who's behind the stove that I recognize him by the neck tattoo. He's cut his hair and dyed it a shocking orange color, but it's the rapper from his band. The one who looks constantly angry. Xan. Except I'm certain that's not how Jae introduced him. Though I'm still repeating their names over in my head so as not to come off as the ignorant fucking American.

Jae's explaining how the two girls are in another band, one who are about to tour the US and who's name I may have heard (I haven't) and how the other guy, Su-jin, is a producer at YJK, who has worked on every single K:OS album. He speaks English fluently, as does one of the girls—Ada—and they all seem to have heard of The DPs which makes me feel less of an outsider. I'm normally more than fine in these kinds of situations, but being the only person here who doesn't speak Korean, and having two of Jae's bandmates glaring daggers into my back, sets me kind of on edge.

Where Jae has that mirrored space he uses to dance in, Kai has a dining room. A huge, round dark-wood table set for the seven of us at the center of it, there are black and white art prints hanging on the walls and another with vinyls, books, and modern-looking knick-knacks. It's curated. Stylish in a different way from how Jae's is. There's a turntable on the vinyl wall—this is where the quiet foreign jazz is coming from—that is wired into speakers in the four corners of the room.

Jae goes around pouring everyone's wine, pouring ours last, before taking his seat next to me on my left. Ada to my right. Kai and Xan bring the dishes through, setting them on the center of the table which has its own spinning mechanism. Then there are glasses of soju in front of us and we're toasting to the coming new year. The seating arrangement puts Xan directly across from me and he alternates between glaring and ignoring me for the first half hour. His cold, impassive gaze landing on Jaehyun a few times too.

The dinner is in staggered English, with Jae explaining anything he thinks I might have missed in between. The food is, begrudgingly, the best I've had since I got here. Including the American Christmas Dinner Jae paid a private chef to cook for us, and I don't mind telling Kai that. He looks genuinely pleased by the compliment.

Jae is helping clear the plates and Ada is asking me about our next tour and when we might be in Korea when my phone vibrates in my pocket. I slip it out to check. It's Camille. I stare at it a moment, a weird slither of unease moving over me, before shoving it back in my pocket.

Ada is chatting to Su-jin now and so I take the opportunity to go for a piss. Xan and Jae are side by side in the kitchen, loading the dishes into a dishwasher. Jae's body language is defensive and tight, his head turned away from Xan. While Xan's empty coolness I've been staring at for hours, is gone. He's gesturing quietly, passionately even, at the side of Jae's head. I want to go over, insert myself between them, but then Jae turns his head and says something—too low for me to hear from here over the music—and Xan stiffens. His face softens and a new look comes over it. Chastened. He looks at Jae a long time before turning his head back to the task at hand. I don't quite understand the dynamic, but Jae doesn't look threatened by his bandmate.

I watch them a moment more just to make sure before slipping out of the living area and down the hall. Since the apartment is the mirror of Jae's, I know which door is the bathroom. I piss quickly and wash my hands. When I pull open the bathroom door, Kai is standing in the hallway, hands in his pockets as he gazes at a large wood-framed canvas on the wall opposite. He turns his attention on me leisurely. It's not that I find him attractive, but he is, objectively good-looking: model appearance coupled with a sharp, detached edge that borders on dangerous. A quiet dominant air that adds to the aura.

I hold his stare and wait for him to say something. When he doesn't, I move out of the doorway and back toward the others.

Then I hear him say, "If you hurt him, I will make you regret it."

I turn back slowly. "Excuse me?"

"You heard me."

I smile a little. "I'd have pitched jealousy a few levels beneath you, man."

He does a weird thing with his face. "It is not jealousy, he's my brother."

"A brother you used to fuck."

He hides his surprise well. Meaning he thought I didn't know. Meaning he thought Jae wouldn't have told me. We're not speaking loudly, but I still don't want any of this to travel, and so I take two steps towards him.

"Yeah, he told me," I say. "Does that bother you? That he trusts me that much?"

I see his jaw clench so hard it changes the shape of his face.

"You think you know me, don't you? A lot of people do." I keep my voice easy, light even. "That's why you're standing out here threatening me—because you think you know how I'll respond. You want me to what, hit you? Embarrass him? Listen, I get it. If I was in your position I'd be pissed too, man."

"My position?"

"You had him and you lost him and maybe you can't fucking deal with it."

I see a glimmer of real violence in his eyes then. It doesn't give me anything like the kind of satisfaction I hoped for.

"You do not have the faintest idea of what my *position* is," he says. "You do not know me."

I hold my hands up. "That's true, I don't. But he wants me to; that's why I'm here. So what do you say we just pretend we get along for his sake. Sound good?"

He opens his mouth to speak but his eyes flick over my shoulder. The way his body reacts tells me exactly who's standing behind me.

Jae is watching us, both worry and suspicion on face. "We have decided to go to Dal's. Ada is meeting some friends there." He looks at me for agreement. "It is a club."

I give him a bright smile, one I turn on Kai next. "Yeah, okay. Whatever you want, I'm in."

Kai forces a smile onto his face too; it changes his whole demeanor.

"Yes, of course. Let's go to Dal's."

THIRTY
RAPHAEL

Jae doesn't do drugs. In any form. But neither was he disapproving as Su-jin offered me a line of perfectly cut white powder on a wooden board that Kai brought through from his kitchen. I'd looked at him before accepting—he'd given me a soft shrug of his shoulders with a half nod and upturned hand that said 'your decision'—and so I bent my head to partake. With the soju and wine already sloshing around in my veins, it settles nicely into a sparkly warm buzz under my skin. Neither Kai, Ada, Jae or Li take anything, which makes me wonder if it's something about drug testing at their company, but then Xan does a line and I think it's probably just personal taste.

Two Ubers arrive a short time after and we bundle in and are whisked through the wintry Seoul night. Ada, Jae, and I had taken the first one and so we arrive a few minutes before the others at a narrow street in what Jae tells me is Gangnam-gu. We wait around in the cold for a few minutes but I don't feel it, blood warm from the alcohol and narcotics, but mainly from how beautiful Jae looks right now. He's wearing a face mask and a thick woolen hat and so I risk it and pull him into me, nuzzling my face into his neck. His eyes are warm and fond, sparkling as he slips his hands about my waist and gazes up at me. Starbursts go off in my chest as his cheeks curve up into a smile.

"Fuck, I love you," I tell him.

His cheeks curve up even further. "You are high."

"You are beautiful."

He laughs and hides his face in my chest. The others arrive a few moments later and Su-jin leads the way into a very small–looking bar with the word 'Dal' in warm lighting above the door. It's misleading though because the thing stretches out ahead of us through an inner courtyard with small tables and heaters all around and filled with people and trees wrapped in fairy lights.

At the end of the courtyard, there's another door and through this is the club. It's warm inside, a blast of hot air hitting us the moment we step inside. Su-jin waves ahead of us at someone and then we are being ushered into a corner table next to the DJ booth. It's a low ceilinged space with a bar at one corner and a wall of paned windows looking out into the courtyard we just passed through. The vibes are good. Warm and funky with the faint scent of incense hanging in the air. Ada is hugging the DJ friend I assume is Dal, and then Kai and Xan do the same.

Beside me Jae is shirking out of his jacket and stuffing it on the back of the booth that runs the length of the wall. I take mine off and do the same. There are speakers above us so Jae has to lean in and speak close to my ear.

"I am going to say hello to Dal-hyung," he says.

I nod. "I'll go to the bar. You're drinking soju?"

He shakes his head. "Drinks are coming," he says and then moves off to where Kai and Xan and Ada are talking with the DJ.

Ada is first to come back, sliding into the booth and scooting next to me. She leans in.

"He seems happy." She has a warm smile on her face.

I glance at Jae to see he's laughing again, head thrown back and hand covering his mouth. Kai and Xan are gone.

"You have it very bad, my friend," she says which drag my eyes back to her. Mischief lights up her contact-colored eyes.

My tongue wants to say a million things in response to that— partly because of the coke, partly because it's true—but I shake my head and shrug. This makes her laugh. It's only then that I notice Li isn't here. That she never got out of the Uber with them.

"Is Li okay?" I ask her. "She didn't fancy it?"

She shakes her head. "She has an early photoshoot. And her and Dal used to be together. It did not work out." She makes a face that tells me it was a little more than that.

"Ah, got it."

The music is a bass-heavy city beat, funky in a way that feels distinctly Korean. It fits the vibe of this place, which is all umber wood and pale orange walls. The people are mixed; stylishly-dressed students, mixing with guys in business suits, mixing with K-pop idols.

Jae slides back in beside me just as the drinks arrive via an exceptionally pretty server. Colored tattoos stretch up both their arms to the sides of their long graceful neck. Pale purple hair matches their lipstick and nails. There's something distinctly feminine in the way they move but something masculine in the features. It takes me a full minute to look away and it's only because I feel Jae's hand on my thigh under the table, distracting me.

Two ice buckets filled with little bottles of soju have been set down, along with a bottle of Scottish malt whisky and seven glasses. A jug of ice water next to that. Jae thanks them in Korean and the server bows and moves off. He pours himself some water first, then fills the same glass with an inch of whisky, before asking me which I want. I point at the soju. He takes a long sip of his drink and settles in next to me.

"Now you will tell me what Kai said to you," he says, settling comfortably.

Next to us, Su-jin has slid in next to Ada and the two of them are talking in Korean. They're not listening in any case.

"Nothing really," I shrug.

"Nothing, really?" He looks entirely unconvinced. "I will not stand for him being rude or mean to you. We have already talked about it."

I smile at his cute, fierce, little angry face. "You think I can't stand up for myself?"

"In America, perhaps. But not here."

This makes me laugh. I reach out to touch his face, smoothing my thumb across his cheek. He leans into it.

"Listen, he's very protective of you, I get it. I would be too. But you don't have to worry about me, I can handle it." I tuck his hair behind his ear as he slides a little closer. Beneath the table his hand moves higher up my thigh.

"Okay, but if he is mean to you again you will tell me."

"Is this your feisty side?" I settle my hand on the back of his neck and pull his head close. He thinks about this a moment—the word, I think—and then he nods. "Well, I like it."

I press our mouths together and Jae swipes his tongue past my lips to touch it against mine. Then bites my lip softly.

As if on cue, Kai and Xan reappear from the crowd. Kai sits on the opposite side of Su-jin, and Xan stays standing. They give Jae a look and he moves back, putting a little space between us. But then he leans forward on his elbows, resting his head on his hands which he then tilts in my direction. He gives me a slow, loaded smile. It hits my balls first. Then my dick. A low, warm thrum of desire that makes me want to drag him into the bathroom and fuck him senseless.

Another image then. One that makes me choke slightly on my drink. Something I want so fucking badly I can barely breathe. I want him to fuck me. I want it. That door that was unlocked when he stuck his finger in my ass had been forcefully kicked the fuck open.

I swallow around the breath stuck in my throat, and ask, "So how do you guys know Dal?" I need to focus on something else to stop the rampant thoughts careening through my head.

Jae glances at where the young DJ is bent over talking to Xan and Kai.

"He was in our group," Jae says. "When we first began."

I look at Dal anew. He's about Kai's age I'd guess, good-looking and wearing a pair of thick–rimmed glasses. Tattoos stretch up the length of both his arms.

"But after three years as a trainee, he simply left. Said it was not the life he wanted. He opened this bar and now he DJ's and is happy."

There's a look on Jae's face as he stares at Dal that might be envy.

"What would you be doing if this wasn't your life?" I honestly can't imagine Jae doing a normal job. Sat behind a desk, clocking in for a pay check. He's too…extraordinary. Stands out too much. Feels like he was born to be idolized. "What did you wanna be when you were a kid?"

"That is the funny thing," he says with a sad smile. "I always wanted this. I dreamed of it."

It hurts, watching the lost, sad look in his face. He holds it a second, then shakes it out with a gentle toss of his head.

"And now you don't want it? Your dream?"

He laughs, softly. "Dreams are safer when they are unachievable. Anyway, it does not matter what I want. Now this is bigger than my dreams, or Kai's, or Xan's. It is bigger than all of us."

"Yeah, I get that." Under the table I settle a hand over his thigh and give it a light squeeze. For comfort only. "So all you can do is try to be happy outside of it."

I hope he gets what I'm saying. That I want to be that for him. That I'm going to be that for him for as long as he wants me to be.

"Life is a struggle, man. We grow and we learn and we evolve, and all we can do is try to find some fucking happiness along the way." I lean my head on my hands, a mirror pose to his own. "Let me be that for you?"

He holds my stare a moment and then without breaking it, lifts his drink and downs the last of it.

"And what about when you decide this is not what you want anymore?" he asks. "What shall I do then?"

"Nice try, but I already told you: I'm not going. Not unless you tell me to. And even then…"

My smile is playful but I'm deadly serious. I feel his hand settle over mine beneath the table and he squeezes my fingers inside his own. He gives me a single look of resolve and then he's kissing me. His free hand tangles into my hair and his body slides forward and everything falls away around us. Everything is his mouth and the soft warm press of his body and the expensive smell of his skin. It's me that pulls back from his mouth, licking the taste of him from my lips.

"Fuck, I really want to get out of here..." It comes out as a groan as I stare at his mouth.

The side of his mouth lifts up, seductive as sin. "We can get out of here."

It starts in the alley outside and continues in the Uber. I can't keep my fucking hands off him. The thing I've been trying to keep contained the entire night, in front of his friends, I let loose now. The warm angles of his body vibrate under my hands, the soft low noises as my fingers tease his cock and nipples over his clothes wrap themselves around me.

It's almost feral, the need building in me. By the time we reach his apartment building my dick is hard as stone and his cheeks and mouth are painted red from my kisses. I'm not gonna last long. Which is fine, I suppose. Sometimes it's like this, quick and rough and filthy.

We just stare at each other in the elevator. But then he casually brushes a hand across the front of his jeans and licks his lips and the head of my cock pulses out something warm and wet. The instant the door of his apartment is open, I'm pushing him inside and against the wall, back to me. He unbuttons his jeans by himself, making it easier for me to yank them down, and then I'm kneeling behind him with my face buried in his ass. I spread him open and lick a stripe across the tender warm hole, groaning when he lets out a strangled noise from above.

He twitches around my tongue, the opening clenching at the attention. I tilt my head and flick the point of my tongue against the rim teasing and licking at it, but it's not enough. I need to be inside it.

"Spread yourself open for me," I tell him. "Let me see it."

I feel completely out of it and entirely fucking focused at the same time. My voice is a low dark hiss in the half-light of his hallway. He groans as he does what he's told and it's so hot I think about letting go and coming right there.

"Raphael, please..." He whines. He's got his head pressed sideways against the wall, eyes squeezed closed. I stare back at his hole. All pink and desperate and clenching. He's fucking his hips into the wall as he can't use his hands, because they're holding his ass open for me.

"You're so fucking hot, Jaehyun. So beautiful, I wish you could see yourself like this." I jerk my cock a few times, brave. Stupid. "Tell me what you want, baby. Tell me...I'll give you anything you want."

He lets out a tormented sound. "Your tongue...please...put it back...I want to feel it inside."

The last part is whispered against the wall but he doesn't need to ask again. I want it too. I nose upward from the back of his balls past the hole, inhaling him. It's intense here. Sex and skin and heat. My mouth waters and I collect the wetness on my tongue and lick it over his hole, past the ring of muscle into the soft heat inside. Its resistant, slow to open, but as I flick and press I feel it begin to soften, yielding to me. I lose myself to it. Hours maybe. Flicking and sucking and kissing it. Worshiping it with my tongue and then my fingers, so that when I stand and slide my cock into it, I think it's never felt as loose.

His back arches and his head drops backwards onto my shoulder making it easy for me to grip hold of his hair, hard. It's rough. Rougher than it's ever been between us. Desperate raw fucking half dressed in a dark hallway. It only turns me on more. He uses the wall for leverage to lower himself and fuck backwards onto me, then he gives up, goes loose and begs for it. I'm certain I bite his throat. I know I pull on his nipples, and when I feel him reach for his dick, I bat it out of the way and take hold of it instead.

Even after I feel him come all over my hand I keep jerking him off. He's loose-limbed and begging for me to come but I can't. I can't really think past the feel of him wrapped, clenching, and gasping around my cock. Skin hot and slicked with sweat. Just when I'm certain the ability to come has been wiped out by the drugs and soju, it rushes up at me in a wave. I suck in a deep breath and let it drown me.

Pulse after pulse after fizzing pulse. It sparks and pops through my entire body. I'm not even sure how I'm still standing not to mention how I'm managing to hold Jae upright. I stay inside him until my breathing evens out, which takes longer than normal.

"You're so perfect…" I tell him through kisses I press against his hair and his cheek. "Fucking hell, that was incredible."

"It was." He laughs, breathless. "Let's go to bed and do it again."

I groan because I think I need to sleep for a week before I can do that again. But then I'm slipping out of him and he's moving away from me down the hallway with my come dripping out of his ass, and I think that just maybe I might be able to rally.

THIRTY-ONE
RAPHAEL

I'm not asleep long, I know that much. My eyes popping open only a few hours later. Coke does that, I find. My phone tells me it's just after five and that Camille has tried calling again. There's a text too.

Call me, Rapha. It is urgent.

My chest does a weird flipping thing. I worry that maybe she's found out about Jae but I don't know how that would be possible. I've a horrible thought and I flip open Twitter and search through my name but there's nothing new and nothing about Jae, so I relax a little.

Next to me he's dead to the world asleep. Naked as sin and his lips pouting and pink.

I'm on edge now though. Camille's text prodding at any chance I have of going back to sleep. What can she have to tell me that's urgent?

I slip out of bed quietly so not to wake him and move through the apartment to the kitchen without putting on the lights. Shiro appears from the shadows, languid and yawning in the pre-dawn light. I feed him a couple of his treats, though it's likely too early, then I gulp down a glass of water. I pour another and carry it to the sectional and take a seat in the dark. I stare into space for a bit before dialing her number.

She answers on the third ring. "Rapha…"

"Yeah, it's me. Is everything okay?"

She laughs a little, empty and sad. "Not really. I am pregnant."

Everything stops. My breath, my heart, the world around. Everything just stops. Then it all rushes back in, bigger and louder than before.

"Since when?" I manage to get out. "I mean, how? I don't understand how..." She's on birth control.

"I don't know how. It just happened."

Do these things just happen? I didn't think they did. I feel sick. I'm silent for a long time until she prompts me.

"Say something, Raphael."

"Did you know when we spoke on Christmas Eve? Did you know then?"

"Yes."

"Why didn't you tell me?"

She says nothing and it gives me the answer I'm looking for.

"You were going to..." She was going to get rid of it. "Without telling me?" My voice is harsh in the darkness of Jae's living room.

She sniffs. "I thought about it, yes. But I cannot do that—I am not that person. But I thought that if you do not love me anymore and I did not want to be a single mom..."

I close my eyes and lean forward, pinching the bridge of my nose.

"I never said I didn't love you anymore, Cam. That's not..."

Our relationship as it was, is over. Love was something else altogether.

"You are in love with someone else, Raphael," she says as though speaking to a child. "This is not...what you want."

This hurts. The pain in her voice *hurts*.

"This changes things, Camille. You know it does."

"It changes some things, yes, but not others. You do not want to be with me and I am not going to force you into something you don't want."

"You're not... *forcing* anything." I sigh. "This happened to us both and we're gonna work through it, together. Decide, together. Do it, together." Something Finn never offered my mother. "How...I mean, do you know how far along you are?"

"Perhaps eleven weeks or so, I am not certain."

Eleven weeks. Pre-Grammy's. Pre-New York. Pre-Jae.

"You're still in France?"

"Yes."

"When are you coming back to LA?"

"I have an appointment with my doctor in LA on Friday. So I will be home on Thursday. I wanted to talk to you before saying anything to Giselle or the studio."

I nod. "I can come home too. If that's what you need me to do. What you want me to do?"

I can't hide from this in Jae's arms, as much as I want to do just that.

She hesitates a moment. "Yes. Okay."

"I'll look at flights now and send you the details."

She sniffles again, some choked sad sound bubbling up from her throat.

"Look, it's gonna be okay. Don't worry about anything, Cam, we're gonna figure this out. Together, okay?"

"Okay."

"Okay. I'll see you at home."

It's hours later before Jae comes stumbling, sleepily, though to the living room.

The sky is a different color to how it was when Camille told me she was carrying my baby, now a grey thing heavy with impending snow.

I still feel as lost as I did four hours ago. I'd managed to book a flight out to LAX at 5 p.m. tonight getting me there tomorrow morning. There'd been an earlier flight, but I'm not ready to say goodbye to him yet. If that's what this is going to be. I'm terrified at how he's going to react. My heart aches at the thought of how he might view this, my leaving. Going to Camille. I feel guilty and weighed down with mistakes I've not made yet.

"You did not come back to bed." He yawns, wandering barefoot towards me.

He's pulled on a long-sleeved sweater which falls past his wrists and uses the cuff to rub at his sleep-clogged eyes. He flops down next to me and drops his head on my shoulder with another yawn.

"Have you eaten already?"

The normality in his voice and in his line of questioning is heart-breaking. I settle my hand on his thigh, squeezing it gently. He turns his head into my neck and inhales.

"Wasn't hungry." I place a kiss on his sleep-ruffled hair. It's now deeply familiar scent makes my chest constrict tightly.

Please let me have this again. Please don't let this be the last time.

He lifts his head up to look at me then, something in my voice tickling his instinct. Then he takes in the fact that I'm dressed. His eyes look deep into mine for a few long moments, slowly coming more awake.

"What is wrong?" he asks.

I'd thought about it for hours. The words I'd use. How I'd use them. But nothing felt right, nothing made any of it easier, less devastating.

"Camille is pregnant."

Nothing happens right away. Like he's still asleep and I've said it to his prone unconscious body. Which, god fucking forgive me, I'd also considered. Packing quietly as he slept and slipping out just so I didn't have to do *this*.

He edges back from me ever so slightly until we're no longer touching anywhere. It hurts more than I thought it would.

"You are leaving," he says. Not a question. He's still looking into my eyes like all the information about what is about to happen to us is in there. "You are going back to her."

I turn my body fully to face him. "Right now, I have to. I need to talk to her and work this out. I've run from this, from her, long enough. She needs me."

He blinks, some heart-breaking look coming into his eyes. Then he turns them away from me and nods. "I understand. You should go to her." His voice is frighteningly calm. "This has been fun, Raphael."

He stands and goes to move away but my hand shoots out, grabbing hold of that too–long sleeve.

"Jae, *please,* this doesn't have to be the end of this…us."

He turns big glittering brown eyes on me. "What do you want from me, Raphael?"

"I don't know," I say and immediately regret it.

He gives me a look of disdain, which I deserve, and pulls his sleeve out of my grip and wanders back in the direction of his bedroom.

"*Fuck,*" I hiss when I'm alone again. I do know. I know what I want from him.

I fly out of the sofa and toward his bedroom, throwing open the door. He's sitting in the center of the bed with his knees pulled up to his chest, his head resting back against the headboard.

"I do know, I want you. That hasn't changed, Jaehyun."

He looks at me, unmoved. "We all want things we cannot have. Now, go home to your girlfriend and be a father to your child. I wish you both happiness."

He may as well have slapped me in the face. The pain makes my temper flare. My voice is sharp when I stalk closer to the bed and say: "And what about you? What do you want? All that honesty and clarity you offered me at the start, how about you give me some of it now? What do *you want*?"

I see him swallow, pale throat drawing my eyes like a moth to a flame. "What does it matter? I cannot have the things I want."

"It matters to me. And I'm fucking asking you, what do you want, Jaehyun?"

"It changes nothing. You will go home to your girlfriend and raise your child and I will be alone."

"Being this kind of pathetic doesn't look good on you, Jae," I snap.

His eyes go wide with shock.

"Tell me what you fucking want. You act like everything is

inevitable, like no matter what happens the outcome is gonna be the same regardless. I've told you what I want over and over again, I've promised I won't hurt you, but here you are, *still* so fucking scared to put everything out there. To take what you want. Camille being pregnant has nothing to do with us. It changes things, yes, but it doesn't have to be the end of it. But you need to be honest with me again, now, what do you want? From this, from me. I need you to say it. *Clearly."*

He looks fucking tormented, his face pale as snow and his eyes shimmering and huge. I can't see his hands under the sleeves but I know they're fists. There's a war on his face. A whole battlefield of *what-ifs* and *maybes* and *I can't give you this* and *what does it matter* and I want to go to him and shake him the fuck out of it. I'm not breathing as I stand there, between life and death, waiting on him to fucking say something. Call ceasefire on this. Put me out of my misery. When he does speak, his voice is calm like those moments after some earth shattering event.

It tells me the war is already over. Lost.

"This has been enjoyable for us both. Let's not make it into anything more than that." He gives me some practiced kind of smile and shuffles his body gracefully off the bed. "I am going to take a long bath, so I will be out of your way while you pack."

Like it's a kindness.

And then he's gone.

He closes the door to his ensuite gently behind him.

Rage and loss threatens to incinerate me. It's bullshit. All of it. I know he feels something and I know he's scared, but I don't know if this now is him deciding it's just not worth it. Has Camille being pregnant just made that decision all the easier for him to make. Or is it something else? Does he want me to fight for him harder? I want to? But what's the point in fighting something that isn't fighting back?

All manner of disturbing notions play through my mind. Like going in there and grabbing him, fucking him senseless over the bathroom counter, falling to my knees at his feet and begging him to tell me not to go, to say that he loves me back, pleading with him to just say the fucking words. That I'll do anything if he just…told me it's what he wanted. That I'm what he wants. But I do none of that.

I pack, instead.

I pack while my brain vibrates inside my skull, a headache pounding at my temples. I didn't bring much, I realize. I'd snuck out of LA like a fucking criminal and now I'd do the same in Korea. In the lounge, I eye the black lacquer case of the guitar he bought me. I could take it to the airport and pay whatever they want to fly it out of here but it feels wrong to take it now, under this storm cloud. If he wants me to have it after this then maybe I can have Halcyon arrange the transfer. It's a heartache I can deal with another day. My heart feels too battered and bruised to deal with it now. A limping, war-ravaged thing.

An hour later he's still not appeared from the bathroom. Maybe he has no intention of coming out until I've gone. I grab a beer from his fridge and sit by the wall of windows and look out at a snow covered Seoul. A notification from the airline tells me my flight is in three hours. Thirteen hours in the air to debate my entire fucking future.

Maybe I could ask Sam to arrange a last minute tour so I could lose myself in it and not need to think about anything else except getting from one stage to the next. Was that what Finn had done when my mom said she was pregnant? Run?

So no. I'm not running. Because I'm not fucking him.

"You are still here," he says from behind me. Close. I hadn't even heard him moving into the room, lost miles and years away. Twenty five years away. I'm on my third beer, the peeled labels littering his dining table. He slides into the seat beside me, fragrant and scrubbed raw, face wiped of any emotion I can name. My heart physically *aches* from how much I want to reach out and touch him. Pull him into my lap and bury my head in his neck. Breathe him into my body. Beg him not to tell me goodbye.

"Did you hope I'd be gone?"

He doesn't have to say it. The guilty look is enough. *Yes.*

"I can call the company and have them arrange a car to take you to the airport," he says.

"I've booked an Uber already. It'll be here in a half hour."

"You are going home to LA?"

"Yeah."

He nods then moves to sweep up the peeled labels into one hand, lifts the two empty beer bottles in the other and goes to the kitchen. I hear him discard the trash and potter about in there for a few minutes before he's back, cup of green tea steaming from a cup in front of him. I almost smile. *Green tea reminds me of you.*

He feels so distant, so formal, it reminds me of the night back in Frida's where he'd sat across the booth from me. I could barely draw breath that night. At least he'd looked at me then. Something he isn't doing now.

"I don't want this to be over, Jae," I tell him honestly.

What's the point in leaving here with shit unsaid? I want to tell him I love him again but it feels like it would be unwelcome here, now.

"I know," he says with a sad smile. "But this was never going to have the ending you hoped for, Raphael. I thought maybe I could have…" He looks down and shakes his head. "But this was never just about me. Having you would affect not just me but our whole group. Everything. A public relationship with a woman is not permitted." He looks up at me, imploring me to understand this. "With a man? It is…it cannot be done."

In that moment it's not about me, or us, or about what he can and can't give me. I'm angry for a whole other reason.

"So you just hide who you are? Forever."

"No." But he looks like he's seriously considering it. "It is not forever. Only until we are no longer important." He lifts a shoulder as he looks down at his tea.

I want to fucking hit something. Like there would be a time when he wouldn't be important.

"So, I'll wait. I can wait. I don't need a public anything, we can do this however you want to do it. Quiet. We don't need to tell anyone."

I sound fucking desperate because I am. He looks up at me, eyes wide. He looks tired and so fucking young—like a kid. One who's been worked too hard for someone else's profit—and a flare of protectiveness so strong rises in my chest it burns all the way up to my throat.

"We can work through this, Jaehyun. I can wait and we can work through this. We'll find a way of making it work. Look, I know this is harder for you, I get it okay. I just wanted…you to try."

For you to think I was worth it. For you not to walk away. For you to fucking **choose me**.

"And what about this?" he asks gently.

I don't know what *this* is right then, I'm so focused and ready to bat away any new obstacle he tosses in our way.

"You are going to be a father, Raphael. Your child will need you. That is where your focus should be now—not on this, us." He waves a small pale hand, like it's inconsequential. Like he's nothing. Like *we're* nothing. "It has been…fun being with you. But now we should both move on. I think that maybe it is better this has happened now. Now you do not have to choose."

He sounds fucking genuine when he says it too. Like he's seriously talking about me being the one who has any kind of choice to make. When I'd already chosen. I'd chosen him.

It hits me like a fucking truck. He's already chosen too. This *is* him choosing. And he's not choosing me.

Just like Finn didn't choose me.

I stare at him a long time before it gets too painful to look at him. I want him so much it's like a solid thing in my chest, my throat, choking me. I stand, my legs weak from the impact of that truck he just hit me with. My bag is by the door next to my boots and I go pull them on. Coat next. Bag shucked over my shoulder.

"I told you I would have taken whatever you wanted to give me. Whatever that looked like."

It takes all of my control not to shout it at him, to rein in the hurt and pain burning a path through my insides, familial and familiar. I've no right to blame him. He warned me over and over and over again about all the reasons this couldn't work. He never said he loved me either. Never said he was ready to do this with me. He never really promised me anything. Still, I would have taken the scraps. Pathetic as that is. Likely Finn's fault again because he'd left a hole so big it made me that desperate for Jae's love now. A desperation that really I shouldn't be afflicted with because my mom had always loved me enough.

He turns in his chair to look at me, a smile so beautiful and sad on his face it almost brings tears to my eyes. "Love cannot bloom hidden away in the shadows, Raphael. Eventually it will wither and die. It would not be fair to offer you a love like that, one that is half in the dark and dying from the start. You deserve something better than what I can give you."

"And what about what you deserve? You deserve to be fucking loved too. And I would do that, I would love you enough for fucking both of us, okay? Just…let me…" *Keep doing it.* I can't force the rest of the words past the thickness in my throat.

"This is the life I chose, Raphael, the love I chose. I am happy—you do not have to worry about me."

The love he chose. The *life* he chose. Neither of which involve me.

From the corner of the living room Shiro is watching us with sharp blue eyes, watching it all with impassivity. I envy him. Envy this fucking cat. Envy the love Jae has for him, envy the life he gets to live here, envy that Jae gets to be the center of his fucking universe so completely, so easily.

I scrub a hand over my face and nod as Jae stands and comes toward me. We look at each other for a few moments before he says, without a trace of fucking irony, "I hope that everything goes well for you in the New Year, and that you are healthy and happy."

I open my mouth, close it again, then nod again. "Yeah. You too."

He hesitates a moment, hands fidgeting by his sides, before he moves forward and wraps his arms around me tightly. I practically sag into him, one arm wrapping around his waist and one cradling his head as I bury my face in his hair. I nose down behind his ear, kissing him in the space where he smells so fucking good.

It's him who turns his head to kiss me, slow and careful at first before it catches fire. Our tongues and lips falling quickly into those desperate, urgent pulls on the other until we can't breathe, until we're both half hard and rutting against each other like fucking dogs in heat.

Of course it's him who finds the strength to end it, pulling back like he's been burned even though his eyes are dark with arousal. I'm breathing hard and licking the taste of him from my mouth when my phone alerts me that my Uber is downstairs.

There's not a set of words in my vocabulary that would fit inside this moment, so I don't even attempt it. I give him another nod and heft my bag back onto my shoulder and say all I'm capable of saying which is:

"Goodbye, Jae."

He smiles again. So beautifully sad again. "Goodbye, Raphael."

I don't look back once. I let his apartment door close behind me and walk to the elevator, pathetically hoping to hear his footsteps running after me or the sound of his voice shouting my name. I don't.

It's the loudest silence I've ever heard.

I stare at my phone all the way to the airport. Gripping it tight in my fist as I check in and go through security, as I huddle myself into a corner to wait by Gate 32 with my hood pulled low over my eyes. There's a text from Cam to say that she won't be back in LA until the day after tomorrow and I reply that I'm at the airport, before going back to simply staring at the screen. I think about what I'd do if he called me now and asked me to come back. If he asked me to choose him over the child growing inside Camille and I almost throw up from the realization.

I guess I am a lot like Finn after all.

막간
(JAE'S INTERLUDE #4)

The second the door closes behind him, I go back to bed. I text Mae Li to say that something has come up and I cannot make it to Tokyo for New Year's and that we can catch up when she is back in Seoul. Then I turn off my phone.

I try not let my mind return to the thoughts I'd had while sitting in the scalding, then tepid, then cold bath. Of what *might* have been. Of what I could have had. Had I been braver or a different person or chosen another life.

I had not lied to Raphael; this was the life I chose. I wanted it. I worked eighteen hours a day for eight years to have exactly this and it is greed and ingratitude that sits low in my stomach now. Heavy as stone. I cannot have both. I cannot have both my dream and him. Not now and not here. No one can have everything. Least of all me.

This is better. This way I can let him go without guilt. Now he gets to go back to his life before me, to a woman who can love him loudly and boldly and without shame or fear. Now he will have a child who will love him unconditionally. My heart warms at that. At the kind of father Raphael will be. A love as beautiful and strong and immovable as the sun. As fierce and certain as the moon. A love he had offered me.

I'd love you enough for both of us.

I curl onto my side and clutch at my stomach as the sobs grow louder and more intense, the words I'd been swallowing down for days making it hard to breathe.

I told you I would have taken whatever you wanted to give me. Whatever that looked like. I love you.

"I love you too," I whisper to no one. "In another life I would have chosen you."

It feels like hours before exhaustion makes the tears dry up. Lying there in the fading light with Shiro curled around my feet and Raphael curled, immovable, around my heart.

He would be in the air now.

I wake up sometime through the night with my bladder full and my stomach tight and sore from crying. I drink some water, refill Shiro's bowl, and go back to bed, falling asleep again almost instantly.

A horrendous banging wakes me. Startling me awake, panicked and afraid. The apartment is draped in low afternoon light and I know I've slept well into the day. I pat around the bed and under the pillow for my phone to check the time but I hadn't switched it on again. As I power it up, the banging goes on, louder and more urgent. It's from the front door, I realize. Then Ji-hoon's voice bellows down the hallway toward my room. He has the lock code so I'm not sure why he is not using it.

"Jaehyun-ah! It's me! Open the door!"

Groaning, I haul myself out of bed, exhaustion still clinging to my bones despite the days' worth of sleep I've managed since Raphael left. My eyes are crusted and dry from crying and I know how I must look, but it doesn't prepare me for the expression on Ji-hoon's face when I pull open the door. He blinks at me in shock, drawing his gaze down my body and back up.

With a sigh, I back away from the door.

"You have the combination, why did you have to knock so loud?" I rub at my eyes as the light stabs at them.

"I didn't know if you'd be alone. Naked. Whatever." He looks around the apartment as he closes the door behind him. "Where is Raphael?"

"Gone," I say and the tone must be revealing because Ji-hoon's face does a whole manner of things. Finally settling on curiosity. "Coffee?" I ask him from the kitchen.

"Have you been online?"

"I've been asleep, Hyung."

Another curious look. This one melts into something else, pity I think. But there's more to it. It makes me pause refilling the coffee machine. I think about pictures of a reunion between Raphael and Camille, the announcement of their baby, a marriage, and I have to set my hands on the counter and take a deep breath in.

But I haven't been asleep that long. And it can't be that because he thought Raphael was here.

Ji-hoon is pulling his phone out of his jeans and coming towards me. He punches something in, flicks through, and then he's sliding it across the kitchen counter towards me.

It's a video. Grainy but still clear. It's Xan and Kai behind the DJ booth at Dal's but then the camera pans to the left and it's Raphael and I. Our heads are close, whisper close, the angle is such that you can see all of my face and only part of his but it is disputedly him. The tattoos confirm it.

He whispers something into my ear and I grin and nod like a stupid careless idiot in love and then he is kissing me. It's soft and gentle and the memory of it makes my mouth open in readiness as I watch. Ji-hoon takes his phone back and taps something, then there is another, of us leaving the bar hand in hand.

"They are all over. The company are trying to get them taken down here but it's not just Korea, Jaehyun-ah." He sounds...sorry for me.

I back away from him and run to the bedroom to swipe my phone off the bed, opening Naver to search my name. It is article after article asking if I am in a relationship with Raphael Scott. Links to screen grabs of the video and the video itself, hundreds of them, thousands, multiplied and zoomed in and cropped and in each one of them we are very clearly in love with each other. I look happy. I was happy. And now...

Some posts call it fake and edited, proof on why this is the case are listed in the tweets below. From those who don't think it is fake there is mainly shock and disbelief. On the trending page on Twitter it is my name, and when I click on it there are thousands of posts reacting to the video. Humorous reaction gifs and lots of emoji's and people using a lot of capital letters.

There are negative comments too but they are noticeably…rare. And many of these seem to be because if I am with Raphael then it means I am not in a relationship with Ji-hoon.

Some have pictures of Raphael on stage, topless, soaked with sweat, and screaming into the microphone and appear to be congratulating me. Some compare Camille and I by saying that Raphael has good taste. Some are even saying Raphael is more attractive now that he also likes men. I know the reactions will not be the same on his side of the internet, they cannot possibly be. He is—was—the straight, lead singer of a rock band. He was engaged to be married to a beautiful French actress.

I think of the names they will call him. I think of the words he and his bandmates used when they thought I could not understand them. Fury and guilt grip me. He was always so nonchalant, always acting as though this thing between us could not damage him in any way.

I wonder how he feels now.

As I examine my own feelings, I realize that absent is the horror I expected to feel should such a thing as this ever happen. Absent is the fear and the shame I had prepared for my whole life, should who I was be discovered.

For so long I feared such a thing as this; my private life, my sexuality, the core of who I am being exposed for the world to see. For my father to see. But now, all I can focus on is how happy I look in this stolen moment. How completely seen I always felt when Raphael looked at me. And I simply let him…walk out of my life. So easily. Without a word of protest.

Dumbstruck, I look up to find Ji-hoon standing in the doorway. I search his face for anger at me for what I've done, for what I've allowed to happen, but I don't see it.

"We have a meeting." He glances at his watch. "You should shower and dress. The car will be here soon."

Shaking my head, I whisper. "What have I done?"

He is next to me a moment later, strong and warm, as he wraps me in his arms. My body sags into him, clutching at his strength, at the solid reliable weight he has always been for me.

"It is going to be okay," he says against my hair. "I promise you it is going to be okay. You will see."

He thinks I mean this; the group, the company.

But I don't.

The members are all looking at me how Ji-hoon did. Sad and filled with pity. Even Xan. Xan who has always seemed to see my faults and weaknesses more clearly than the others; almost as clearly as I see them myself. He has always called me selfish and careless and he was right. With Raphael, I was careless and selfish and this is what has happened. I expect Xan to say it now, but he doesn't. He looks concerned and sad and there's a grim kind of determination on his face that I don't quite understand. I don't have enough energy within me to figure it out either.

Ironic since in *this* moment, now, I want to be selfish. I want only one thing. And I'm shocked to find that it is not K:OS.

"I will go on hiatus," I say and as the words leave my mouth I realize how much I want it. What it might mean. That perhaps I could have Raphael for a while longer.

If he still wants you.

"If you wish me to return after a period of time, then I will. If not, then I understand this too. The last thing I want is to cause any shame. It has never been what I wanted. Maybe I can bring forward my enlistment?" I look at Lua in question. "Then it will be only Ji-u left to complete his."

This is my back-up, my last resort. If Raphael doesn't want me.

This is apparently the most controversial thing I could have said because the entire room erupts. There are incredulous shouts and angry refusals and hearty disagreements. After a few heated minutes of raised voices, Seungmin manages to calm the noise. And then he's looking at me and asking a question I hadn't heard the first time he said it.

"What do you want, Jaehyun?" he says again.

"What do you mean?"

"I mean, what do *you* want? Do you wish to go on a break? Do you need some time by yourself to come to terms with this? The schedule in January is quiet. We can put out any statement you want." He glances down at the tablet in front of him, scanning it. "It will not be hard to remove you from things for some time. If that is what you want."

It is three times now he has asked the question. *What do I want.* What I want has never felt possible so it has never been something I've thought much about. It was why I found it so hard to answer Raphael when he asked.

Seungmin shifts in his chair, fixing me with his most sincere look. "What is it that you want the company to say about this? Before Christmas you told us this was a relationship you were serious about pursuing. Is this still the case?"

"You speak like I have that option now, as though I have ever *truly* had that option. What are you proposing, Seungmin-ssi? That you put out a statement declaring that Raphael and I are in love? That we are together and that the company gives our relationship its full support?"

My voice is pitched high and hysterical but the room is silent and very serious.

"Why not? It would be the truth." It is Ji-hoon who speaks.

I turn to him, tears threatening at the corners of my eyes.

"You are in love with him."

I swallow around the lump in my throat, very aware of the ten pairs of eyes on me. I could not say it to Raphael in those moments before he left. Not because I did not want to, but because I did not want it to be the reason he stayed.

"Yes." In the end they are simple and easy enough to say. "But it does not matter." I lift a shoulder. "We cannot be together. I cannot be in a public relationship with a man."

As I glance around the room, at Ji-u and Taejin, at Xan and Lua—Boohyin is in Jeju with his family—I don't see the same looks of pity they had in their eyes when I arrived. Taejin is smiling at me, a small strange smile filled with mischief. Jonghyun looks fragile, like he might cry at any moment. Xan is studying me very carefully.

"It is true it has never been done in our industry," Lua says finally. "There is no precedent for an out, gay idol. But we would not be who we are if we did not push those precedents forward—if you all did not redefine what it means to be idols. That is why you are so successful. Why you have the reach that you do." She looks straight at me, sitting up straighter in her chair. "If this is what you want, Jaehyun-ah, then we will support it. Song Nim will too."

"*Support it?*" I ask, unable to believe my ears.

I must have misunderstood something. I frown and look to Ji-hoon for clarification, as I always do when I'm told something or asked something I don't understand. His smile is small and close-lipped. It says something like *I promised you it would be okay.*

"I don't understand. I thought this would be...that I would have to..."

I cannot breathe. Cannot think around the words I'm trying to say. I did not think I would be able to have it all.

My body collapses under the weight of relief, and I'm crying again. Pushing the chair back from the table and turning to fold my body onto my knees. I don't hear Seungmin's gentle suggestion that the others leave the room, I don't hear Ji-hoon say he will stay behind, but then he's in front of me, crouched low and rubbing soft circles into my back.

"It is okay, shh, it's okay, Jaehyun-ah."

And I believe him. It is going to be okay. If Raphael wants me. *Still.* Then it is going to be okay. If he doesn't, then it will be heartache the likes of which I've never known, but at least I won't have to hide this part of me anymore. At least there is hope on the other side. Hope that someone else will love me the way that Raphael was ready to.

God, no. I don't want someone else. I want him. I want Raphael Scott to love me.

My tears dry up immediately as I'm gripped with a breath-taking urgency. I sit up straight and look at Ji-hoon.

"I need to go to Los Angeles."

I'm standing up and charging toward the door of the large conference room. I can hear Ji-hoon's confusion as he blinks after me. Pulling open the door, I find Lua and Seungmin outside, standing in the center of the squared-off seating area in deep discussion.

"I need you to book me a flight and hotel in Los Angeles. A driver too. I want to leave today."

Lua smiles and nods.

I don't want him to tell me it's too late or not to come, or that this video has ruined his life. I want to look him in the eye and tell him everything I should have said before. Then he can decide if he still wants to love me. If it is still easy to love me.

What do you fucking want, Jaehyun?

"You." I whisper to no one. "I want you, Raphael."

THIRTY-TWO
RAPHAEL

Sam calls first, pulling me awake from a sleep that's half emotional exhaustion, half jet-lag. It was so deep that I awaken like I've been underwater, sucking in breaths like I'm drowning.

I feel around for my phone on the bedside.

"Yeah," I croak into it.

"Where are you?" Sam is outside but talking quietly, so it's a fight to hear him over the noise of the traffic while my brain is still offline.

"At home, why?"

"I thought you were out of the country? When'd you get back?" He says 'out of the country' weird. Like the way he might say 'you're vegan?'

"Can you call me back when I'm awake, Sam? I got in at four, I've only been asleep for…" I crane my neck to check the clock by the side of the bed. "Five hours. I'm not even sure what country I'm in right now."

"I'm coming over. You need to check the internet."

And then he's gone.

I have to fight hard not to fall back under the weight of sleep because my head feels like a whole planet on my neck. The feeling of loss creeps in as I come more fully awake, consciousness ushering it in like an unwelcome visitor.

It's over. He's gone.

Scrubbing a hand over my face, I sigh and flick open the stupid fucking bird app.

Another story about Camille and me, I presume. The baby then. I wonder how the fuck the baby news is out and wonder if this is somehow down to Mason too. Does he know? His feelings about it are suddenly way too important.

When I pull up the search bar to search my name, my eye is drawn down to the trending topics. Because at the top is 'JAEHYUN'. Beneath it, 'KOSJAEHYUN'. This isn't unusual. He or his bandmates are trending on here every other day. He wears a short-sleeved top, shows an ankle, goes to an airport and the internet has a breakdown.

But this time, beneath his name, there's mine.

And below that, 'JaehyunxRaphael'.

I'm all the way awake in a fucking nanosecond. Sitting up and pulling off the sheet I click on both our names. For the second time in as many days, my entire fucking world stops.

While I'd been asleep my entire life had changed. *Unraveled*.

It was a video of Jae and I kissing in Dal's. The tattoo across my hand as I hold his face make it impossible that it's anyone else. The look on my face makes it impossible that I'm not very much in love with him. The look on his…fuck… had he really looked at me like that? Like he loved me back?

Fuck, Jae.

I don't look at anything else, I don't care about anything else. I flick out of Twitter and pull up his number, closing my eyes as it rings off to voicemail immediately. I debate over whether to leave a message. Does he even want to hear my voice? Especially right now. But I can imagine the fear and the shame and the devastation he'd be feeling right now and decide that maybe he'll want to hear a supportive voice right now. From someone who loves him no matter what the world now thinks.

"Hey, it's me. I just woke up. I saw the video and I wanted to… fuck, I don't know, see how you were doing, I guess? Are you okay? Baby, I'm sorry. I need to know you're okay though, so can you call me? Also, tell me what you want me to say? I'll say whatever you want. Or nothing at all. Just…yeah, call me. Let me hear your voice. I'm sorry…I… I love you."

It's moments after I've hung up, staring out at the broken brown and green landscape of the valley, before I feel the presence of someone behind me. I hadn't heard her come in, come upstairs, come into the room.

But Camille is standing just inside the bedroom door, weekender bag on her shoulder and small suitcase by her feet. She's holding her cellphone tight in her hand, her eyes red-rimmed with exhaustion and wide with something sad.

"Cam, I'm…sorry. I'm so fucking sorry…I didn't…"

She storms toward me, dropping her bag on the bed and then she…wraps her fucking arms around me. A tight, warm, fragrant hug I didn't know I needed.

"It's okay. Shhhh, it's going to be okay," she says softly as I rest my head on her shoulder. "I promise it's okay. You're okay."

Camille has her arms folded as she stares Sam down, the power of her glare pressing him into the opposite side of the couch.

"He has already told you he will say nothing and post nothing until he hears from Jaehyun."

Hearing her say his name is surreal, like hearing Carl Sagan tell me the moon is, in fact, made of cheese.

"Now is that all? Honestly I do not know why you're even here, Sam. If you came over here every time a story appeared online about Rapha then you may as well live in the pool house."

She tuts, frenchly, and stands. Code for telling him it's past time that he left.

He sighs, standing. "This isn't just any story."

"No, I suppose not. It involves him with another man. Apparently Halcyon choose to be extremely interested when the story has a non-hetero theme." She gives him a terrifying, pointed glare.

"That's not what this is."

"No, I am sure you are just concerned about the welfare of your artist, hmmmm?" She looks at me, then back at Sam. "You know who else is concerned about the welfare of their artists, Samuel? Sony. Interscope. Geffen. And if Halcyon do not remember who they work for, then Raphael's solo release will find a new home. That part of his contract is under conditions, yes?" She gives him her red-carpet smile.

"Fuck, Camille. Do you want a job?" Sam says, with a shake of his head.

"With Halcyon?" She snorts. "No, thank you. Now if you don't mind, we have a lot to discuss and you are here uninvited."

Sam nods, beaten, then looks at me. Just wait until he finds out she's pregnant. "If you could just give me a heads up before…"

"Before I say anything, post anything, do anything." I nod. "Yeah, I got it, Sam. Just call me if you hear from YJK, yeah?"

I'd asked him to contact Jae's people to see what he wanted me to say about this. As yet, there'd been nothing. As yet, Jae still hadn't returned my call.

Camille shows Sam out and returns to sit by me on the sofa. After we'd hugged for a bit she'd sent me to shower while she made coffee—she'd had tea because, yeah, she's pregnant—and then Sam had turned up. He'd known nothing, had been hit with it the same as I had the second he opened his eyes this morning.

Jae's company hadn't put out any kind of statement yet despite being ahead of it by almost eight hours, and I didn't know if that was bad or not.

The worst thing about watching that video isn't the invasion of our privacy. It isn't the questions I am about to be asked, or the explanations I'm now going to have to give to the people around me. It's the ache of loss it evokes over my entire body, inside and out. It's watching us together and knowing I'll never get to touch him like that again. Never get to be that close to him again. Never get to breathe in the scent of his skin after sleep, see his eyes up close when he smiles, or hear the noise he makes when he puts that first bite of food into his mouth.

In that video he looked like mine, happy and warm and mine, and the notion that he isn't any more is the worst pain I can ever remember feeling. I'd watched it over and over and over before dialing Jae's number a second time. Then a third. Each time going to voicemail.

I can't begin to imagine how he's dealing with this. What this means for him and his band. Maybe he blames me so much he can't bear to hear my voice. I can imagine his panic and his fear and I feel responsible for it. I'd been the one who was high, I'd been the one licking at his fucking mouth like a cat at a milk bowl, I'd been the one who'd pushed and pushed and fucking pushed. If not for me...

"Why didn't you tell me in New York?" Camille asks, pulling me out of my head. "I would have understood if you'd just talked to me."

I nod. "I know *you* would have, Cam, But *I* didn't. I didn't know what it was for so long until suddenly...I did." I give her an apologetic look. "I guess since I'd convinced myself I didn't know what it was, it was like I wasn't cheating around on you."

I look down, guiltily, its bullshit. I know it is. She deserved better. Better than what I gave her.

"And when you knew, was the day you told me it was over?"

I shake my head. "I knew before...but I didn't want to tell you over the phone."

She makes a small soft sound and reaches across to take my hand, curling her fingers around mine tight. "You are not your father, Raphael."

My head lifts at that as I frown at her detour. "What?"

"It is why you are here, no? Because you are so afraid of being him? You are willing to risk your own happiness to show that you are nothing like him. Rushing to my side has left him alone to deal with this. Of course, you did not know it would happen, but you came here to be with me now because you wanted to prove that you are not like Finn."

It feels like another slap in the face. A truth as loud and obvious as any I've ever heard. I try shaking my head to disagree but of course I can't.

"I thought about it a lot on the plane," she goes on, pulls one leg up under the other to get comfortable. "I thought about a lot of things—it is amazing how much thinking a jet engine will force you to do."

My phone rings then and I jump towards it, desperate to see Jae's name on there. But it's Crawford's. I let it ring off and sit back, focusing on Camille again.

"I know that when I have this baby you will be there for our child in all the ways he was not."

I hate talking about him. I won't talk about him. Instead, I say, "You're keeping the baby?"

She nods. "Yes. I am going to have this child. But, that is not to say you have to be any sort of father, Raphael."

I frown at that. "You're saying how I'm not him, but then you're saying *that*?"

Cam smiles at me. "I wasn't finished. What I was saying…was that you do not *have* to be any sort of father, but I know that you will be an incredible one. Our child will not be short of love, will not have to wonder if their father loves them. Because I know you will be there to tell them. But I do want you to not feel constrained by this—it is my choice and I do not want you to think for a moment that it means you are tied to me forever. I understand that what we had before is over, Rapha. I know that you are in love with someone else—the whole world knows that, in fact. But I will also say this now; if you choose to be in our child's life then it is permanent. You do not get to pick them up and place them down when it is convenient. So you must think about it, carefully."

"I don't have to think about it, Camille."

"Non, I did not think you would. Then we are going to be parents together, are you afraid?" She pats my knee, beaming at me. It all feels fucking surreal honestly. How is she this cool about all of this?

"Yes. I'm terrified, actually. Can you seriously imagine me as a dad?"

She studies me carefully, and then, a little giddy, she says: "Yes, I can—you will be great. And me? I will make a good maman, no?"

"The best. But seriously, what the fuck happened, *you* sounded terrified on the phone?"

She waves that off. "I told you, the jet engine made me think. On the phone, I was tired and emotional and in my parents' house. I always feel worse when I am there, you know. Also, now I know that you did not leave me for another woman."

"Are you serious right now?"

"Of course, always. And you, you will tell me what happened with you and Jaehyun, yes? I deserve to know that, at least."

An ache burns its way across my chest, so bright and painful that I have to rub at it to soothe it. Will it ever stop aching? I want to watch the video again.

"Yeah, you do. But I just…" I don't want to talk about it right now because it hurts too fucking much. "It's over, I think. I mean, he never wanted any of this." I wave in the direction of my cell phone. "And I don't know what he's thinking or how he's feeling. Fuck, he must be so scared. He must hate me right now."

I honestly can't stand thinking about him over there alone, without any support. With the glaring disapproving eyes of Kai and Xan and his company. Kai cares about him. That much was evident in his warning to me, so surely he'll have his back now? Surely he's not gonna hang Jaehyun out to dry with this?

I reach out for my phone again, just as it starts ringing. It's Cleo now and so I reject the call and pull up his number instead, trying it again. It's still switched off.

Desperate, I pull up Jae's account on Instagram and navigate until I find Kai's tag in one of his photos then I click to send a message. I debate no more than a few seconds on the words:

Please ask him to call me. I need to know he's ok.

I close it without even glancing at the notifications and thousands of DMs I can see are sitting there. My stomach sinks at what might be in there. I see my follower count is up but I don't really register what that means. Ghouls probably. Fuck them. All of them.

Camille is watching me quietly, stare heavy. When I look round at her she gives me a small smile.

"He will not hate you." She reaches out to brush my hair back, whisper soft. "You are a very hard man to hate, Raphael. And a very easy one to love." She stands. "I am going to shower and nap. I will see you in a few hours."

Her hand drops off my hair and I feel adrift and alone again.

"Cam," I call after her. "I love you, you know."

She stops and turns back. "I know, puppy."

"I don't think…I don't deserve you." My voice feels fragile, paper thin. Like I might cry.

"I am very fabulous, but I believe everyone should have a me in their life so…" She shrugs. Her playful look fades and she's serious again. "It is going to be okay, you'll see. Now do not sit and mope. Perhaps think about baby names, yes? Perhaps we do as your mother has done and name them after our favorite artist? Salvador? Pablo? Frida for a girl?"

"Go and nap, Camille, you're not thinking straight."

She laughs and disappears toward the bathroom.

My chaotic thoughts rush back in the moment I'm alone again.

It's going to be okay, you'll see. I don't know if I believe her. All I want is for that phone to ring and for Jae's name to be on it and for him to tell me *he's* okay.

I manage to avoid Crawford, Zeke, and Cleo's calls the rest of the day. Rather than reply to them separately, I send a text to the group chat telling them I'll call them tomorrow and tell them everything. The band don't appear to be questioning the validity of the video, just my entire existence. I half expect them to turn up at my door but it doesn't happen. I'm pretty sure my French bulldog would chase them away if they did. Mason hasn't been in touch at all. Not a single fucking word. If my mind wasn't already full to bursting, I'd wonder what that means, but as it is, I don't care.

I'd switch my phone off, but delusional or not, I'm still waiting for Jae to call back. Kai saw my message two hours ago but hasn't responded, which I'm taking as a positive because he could have told me to fuck all the way off and blocked me, which he hasn't. Yet. Jae hasn't been online for hours either which is scaring the shit out of me and it's this that forces my hand in the end.

I send a second message to Kai close to 1 a.m.—when the video has been out there almost eighteen hours and Camille has gone back to bed.

At least tell me he is okay.

This time, he replies only a few minutes later:

He will be.

What the fuck is that supposed to mean? I stare at it until my head hurts and the letters blur, wanting desperately to ask Kai to explain. *He will be?* He will be as soon as he forgets about me? He will be as soon as he wakes up from his fucking coma? He will be when?

I get my answer an hour later. It drops into my phone with a small, upbeat, chime against my skull. I'd fallen asleep on the sofa with Ghost in The Shell playing low on the TV and all the lights off. A picture message from Jae. I wonder for a second if I'm still asleep and dreaming but as I sit up and swallow back the stale taste of Cheetos and the thumping inside my skull, I know I'm not.

"Holy shit," I whisper, standing up.

For the third time in as many days hours my entire world stops.

It's a picture of Manhattan Beach pier, of the very same spot that I'd stood waiting for him all those weeks ago.

The second message comes through a second later.

I'll wait for you.

THIRTY-THREE
RAPHAEL

Manhattan Beach Pier is just the same as it always is, but it feels like a temple as I walk towards it. The wooden planks the nave of some holy place I've come to be baptized and Jae's my fucking priest.

I saw him the second I got out of the car, small neat frame leaning against the railing gazing out to sea. I'd tracked every breath he'd taken as I'd made my way down towards him, counted and curated each one.

He's wearing a long trench coat in cargo green, black slacks and a black beanie pulled low. A large scarf wrapped around his neck and the lower half of his face. I see and feel him stiffen as I come to stand next to him, my arm brushing his as I mirror his pose.

The ache of loss inside me goes deathly silent a moment, calmed by having him near me again, but then it roars up louder than before. I want to touch him. Kiss him. Bury my face in his neck and nose a path across that sweetly scented throat. I can see shadows under his eyes, put there by me, by a thirteen hour flight, by a video that no one had the right to record and release out into the world. I'd been thinking on the drive here what I would say first, do first, but in the end it comes out without thought.

"Jae, I am so sorry. I never meant for that, I know you never wanted that…" I stumble over the words. "I'm just so sorry."

He turns his head, then says with a frown: "You are not wearing a jacket."

I blink, looking down. I'm wearing a hoodie and a pair of jeans I'd pulled on dirty from the wash. Thankfully I'd brushed my teeth and pulled my unwashed hair back into a ponytail. "No, I just…ran out."

"You'll catch a cold. We should go somewhere warmer."

I don't want to talk about this. I want to kiss him. "I'm not cold, baby. It's LA."

"*Baby…*" He smiles, blinking up at me slowly. "I did not think I would hear you call me that again."

Clearly I'm feeling better because I make a joke. "I'll call you whenever and whatever you want."

He smiles and I'm glad I risked it. Then he's serious again. "The world knows about us."

"I know."

He's searching my face for something. "Your girlfriend knows?" he asks.

When I nod he appears to wince.

"And your band?"

"Yeah, they know."

He nods, worrying his top teeth over his plump bottom lip.

"What about you? Everyone in Korea must know by now. Well, South Korea at least. The north have a lot of other shit going on, I guess…" It's another attempt at a joke, except this one falls flat.

"A lot of people in Korea know," he confirms, eyes on his feet.

I look down to see my boots are unlaced and I've no socks on through the openings.

"The company. The members. A lot of the fans do not believe it but a lot do and yes…they know."

The urge to touch him is fucking overwhelming. So I give into it. Reaching out to skim his chin with my finger, raising it gently to his cheek. It's so warm and soft.

"What do you want to do? I'll say whatever you want. Deny everything if you want. Tell me and I'll do it. I just want…"

I just want you to be warm and happy again.

He doesn't like this. His eyes round with hurt that god forgive me, makes hope swell in my chest.

"Is that what you want? To deny everything? To go back?" His voice is so small, so soft.

"You know what I want, Jaehyun. I told you in Seoul. Nothing's changed for me. I never cared about any of this. People can say whatever the fuck they want. They already do. They always have." I hold the back of his head. "I want to be with you. I want *this,* with you."

His eyes begin to shimmer. "But what about your baby, about your girlfriend?"

"Camille stopped being my girlfriend when I fell in love with you," I tell him. "Camille and I are good. We talked, and we're gonna be parents—I'm going to be a dad—but that doesn't change anything about how I feel about you. I told you, Jae, I'll give you anything you want. I'll take anything you want to give me. I just want to be with you."

I'm pretty sure it's clear, but for some reason he looks confused.

"How can that be when *everything* has changed?" He shakes his head. "I do not know how to do this. Be with someone like this. I have never been with anyone, not like this, I…"

He stops, takes a breath and tries to find his words again. "I used to think that the world finding out who I was would be the worst thing that ever happened to me. That it would be the end of everything I had worked for, that it would mean that I could not do what I loved anymore, and that I would never be happy again. But then you left me in Seoul and it hurt so much. It felt like *that* was the worst thing that could ever happen to me."

He brings a small pale hand up to wipe at his wet cheek. I want to pull him into me, kiss his hair, hold him tight. But I also want to hear him speak.

"So when Kai showed me that video, when he told me that everyone knew about us, about *me,* I did not care. I was…relieved." He whispers the word like he's afraid of it. "It did not hurt a fraction as much as you leaving had hurt."

He turns fully to me, eyes pleading with me to understand. "When I let you leave, I thought I was doing what was best for you; for both of us. I thought that if I let you go, you would see in the end that it was the right thing to do and that you would thank me for it. But I did not want to let you go, Raphael. I do not want to be without you. I want…"

He takes hold of my hands and squeezes them tight in his smaller ones. "I want to be with you. I love you and I want to be with you and I am not afraid anymore of what the world thinks of it. I want to love who I want to love and do what I love to do. I want it all even if it makes me selfish. If you give me another chance I promise I will give you everything I could not before. I promise not to be scared, I promise to try to be everything you want me to be…I promise I will love you loudly and not in the shadows, I promise…"

I kiss the next words out of his mouth, swallowing his small, delicious gasp of surprise. We kiss like that for what feels like a long time, my hand in his hair—his beanie clutched tight in my free one—his hands in the back pockets of my jeans, our breaths hot against each other's lips.

When I pull back, he looks dizzy. His mouth is kissed red and his cheeks pink and he's never looked more beautiful. So I tell him that. And when he smiles that shy smile at me, I decide that I'll tell him that every fucking day.

"You don't need to promise me all of that, baby." I pull him against me to kiss his hair. "You don't need to do anything except let me make you happy. Just…let me love you and make you happy. That's enough. You're enough." I press a kiss to his forehead, then the tip of his cold nose and he sinks against me. "This is gonna be great, you know."

He lifts his head to smile at me. "It is?"

I nod. "I'm gonna write so many love songs about you. You're going to be tired of hearing them. Every Christmas, birthday, Chuseok, Seollal."

He laughs, happy tears shining in his eyes. "You have been reading your *Learn Korean, Fast!* book."

I nod, proudly and he buries his head into my chest and giggles. My arms wrapped around him he turns his head to look out at the Pacific.

"We are really going to do this," he says, soberly.

"We already are." I kiss his hair again.

"I do not want to hide anymore, Raphael. I am tired of hiding."

"You don't have to hide. But neither do we have to do anything different to how we've been doing it. We do this however you want to do it, baby."

I get to be with him. That's my prize. Without lifting his head from my chest, he reaches into the pocket of his coat to pull out his phone, lifting it at an angle that puts us both in the picture. His head half buried in my chest and my face half buried in his hair, the lights of downtown LA behind us.

He takes three and asks me to choose my favorite.

"Are you sure?" he asks, his finger hovering over the Instagram post button.

I don't have to think about it long. Any reservations I have aren't about him or about us, it's about what the world might do to this perfect thing we have. This thing that's existed between just us for so long.

But then I think about how it became stronger when I told my mom, how I became more sure of it when I told Cam, how badly I wanted it back when the stranger with the camera showed me what I'd lost.

"Yeah, baby, I'm sure."

I press a kiss to his cheek as he presses 'post' on the picture he's taken of us and tagged me in.

@ljh: ♥

HIDDEN TRACK (EPILOGUE)
RAPHAEL

Two and a half years later

Lottie reaches across to switch off the recording on her phone and lets out a huge sigh. I'm hoping she's not been holding her breath the entire interview. Not that it felt like an interview. More like a therapy session.

I certainly feel as light and clear-headed as I do after a session. Though in there we don't really talk about Jae as a subject matter. He's more of a constant point of reference before Jae, after Jae.

"Thanks for being so candid, Raphael. I really appreciate it."

I shrug. "I'm an open book. I'm fucking exhausted now though."

She smiles, nodding in understanding. "Cathartic?"

"Yeah, I guess so."

"You're still happy to talk about your dad on Friday? It's no trouble if you've changed your mind." She sounds genuine, but I know it's important to her to square the circle with Finn, since she already did the podcast on him.

"I'll be fine."

Then we're standing and I'm walking her out. The light is fading a little, though the traffic noise outside is louder. A glance at the clock tells me it's just after 5 p.m. He lands in two hours. The thought of it is enough to melt away a little more of the knot of anxiety in the pit of my stomach.

"Where are you staying?" I ask, to make some conversation.

"I'm in Sorbonne, just near the Latin Quarter."

"Just over the river, cool. It's a good vibe there."

"It is. I love Paris. I've often thought about moving here for a couple of years too."

I'd told her that we were moving to New York in a year or so, when Lili starts pre-k there. But that we'd planned to live for a bit in every city we loved eventually. She'd looked inspired.

"I would recommend it. I love it here too. Be sad to leave it."

"New York is wonderful as well though, right?"

"Yeah, it is."

We shoot the shit for a little longer while she switches out the house slippers with her boots and then she's gone. To be back on Friday to do the part about Finn.

About my father.

I don't have the same issue I used to have in calling him that. Yeah, I still have *some* issues, but they're different ones. They're more about loss and grief than anything else. Because once I'd dealt with the resentment and the hatred and the bitterness, I'd uncovered a whole lot of other shit under there.

I'm working on those too. I'm getting there. I'd even visited his grave. It was a whole process. One I'd never have imagined for myself ten years ago. But there were a lot of things I didn't imagine for myself ten years ago.

I grab a quick dinner of leftover chicken and salad, and then take a shower. I think about jerking off because I haven't seen him in person in eight days and I don't want to blow my load as soon as he walks through the door. But I decide against it. He'll be here in a matter of hours. I can wait that long for fuck's sake.

There's a text on my phone when I get out telling me he's landed and is in the car.

Camille calls to check the plans for Sunday, which we'd already gone over multiple times. She doesn't get stressed often, Camille, but when she does it's normally related to Lili. I tell her it'll be fine and that since she's three and won't even remember it, it doesn't matter if it all goes wrong. Surprisingly, *that doesn't fucking help, Rapha.* She hangs up straight after, warning me not to be late with the cake.

I hadn't meant to dose off, but I'm woken by the feel of my journal being extracted from my hands, the distinct presence above where I'm lying on the couch. When I open my eyes, he's staring down at me with a soft mouth and softer eyes.

"Bonjour, mon amour," he says.

I reach out and take his hand, pulling him on top of me. He buries his face in my neck and sighs, before leaning up to kiss me, deep and slow.

"How was your flight?" I ask, as I place kiss under his jaw, under his ear.

"Long. I did not sleep."

"No? But you had your own bed, *your own room?*"

The fashion label had sent him and Ada a fucking jet to fly them from Seoul to Paris for the show tomorrow, even though he'd have been coming here anyway. The currency of brands and their brand ambassadors during Paris Fashion Week was private jets and pretty clothes.

"Yes, but I lay awake wishing you were there so we could join the airplane club and so I couldn't sleep."

I smile. He's fucking adorable. "It's the mile high club, baby. But yeah, I can see how that would have been distracting."

Jae settles comfortably on top of my chest, tucking his head under my chin. He smells good even with thirteen hours of flight on him. His hair is his natural brown black these days—had been for a while now—and it was my new preference. It matched his eyes and made his skin look like sculpted marble. After five years, he's still the most beautiful thing I've ever seen.

"You saw Lili today?" he asks, sleepily.

"Not today. I had the interview with Descript, remember."

"Ah, yes, sorry. It went well?"

"I think so. We talked a lot about your asshole."

"My religious, soul-shifting asshole?" He laughs but it sounds heavy with exhaustion.

"Did you eat on the plane at least?"

"A little." He lifts his head and looks up at me. "But I think I would like some pizza. With mushrooms. Some pizza and wine and we can eat it in bed. Then I will suck your cock."

I raise an eyebrow at him. "I think you'd fall asleep with it in your mouth if you tried to suck my cock tonight, baby."

He looks mildly offended for a minute, then concedes. It's with a great effort he peels himself off me and stands up.

"You will order pizza while I shower?"

I nod and he wanders away from me towards where his case is just inside the living room door and wheels it out into the hall.

"With mushrooms!" He shouts.

"I got it. Don't fall asleep in there."

I sit on the couch staring into space a few moments.

I do this sometimes. Checking in with various parts of my body to make sure they're tangible and physical and that I'm real, because sometimes it feels like I might be dreaming. That I get to have this life. With him. With my daughter. With my mom. With my music. With all the things that make me feel like the luckiest person on earth. People shouldn't be this lucky. But I am. And I try to make sure everyone around me, everyone who helps make me feel it, knows just how grateful I am

After calling in the pizza order, I open a bottle of red and pour us both a glass and carry it into the bedroom. He's out of the shower, white towel wrapped around his waist while he rummages in his suitcase. His lean body drips water onto the wooden floor where he's crouched low. I eat up the sight I'd been starved of for eight days, mouth desperate to suck those droplets right off his skin. The thought is headier than the wine in my hand. He finds what he's looking for—a small Gucci toiletries bag—and stands, only now seeing me standing there.

His own gaze dips over me appreciatively, eyes stalling at my crotch where I'm half-hard from just watching him.

"You're so beautiful."

He still blushes every fucking time. "So are you."

"Lie on the bed," I say softly.

He swallows, visibly, sets the shower bag on the bedside and does as he's told.

"Lose the towel."

He smirks before peeling it slowly away from his hips—too fucking slowly—and flattening it on the bed. His perfect cock is stiffening under my look, filling out nicely against his muscled thigh.

My mouth waters.

I take a deep sip of wine and let it sit on my tongue as I cross toward the bed. Setting the glasses down on the nightstand, I climb on and settle my head between his legs, pushing his thighs apart a little further to fit me. He's perfectly still as I just stare at him here. When I lean in to lick the very tip of his cock, he squirms a little. Glancing up, I find him watching me intently.

"I love you," I tell him.

"I love you too," he whispers.

"You're perfect."

At this, he smiles. Mouth parting with want.

"Perfect and so fucking beautiful." I breathe hotly over his cock, then kiss it.

"Raphael…" It's a protest and a whine and a prayer all at once.

"Ask me to do it and I will. I'll do anything for you, you know that. Give you anything you want; you just need to ask baby."

I lick the tip again. He squirms again.

"Suck my cock," he begs. "Please suck my cock."

"On one condition."

He half groans half laughs, bringing his hand to jerk his own dick, impatient. I bat it away.

"Fine," he snaps but there's no heat in it. "What is your condition?"

"Marry me."

His entire body goes rigid with shock. Eyes widening.

"What?"

"You heard me."

"I want you to say it again."

"Marry me."

He blinks at me a few long moments, then sits up. I can't help but notice his dick is still very fucking hard.

"You want...me to marry you?"

"I really do."

"But...I can't...it's not..."

"Not legal in Korea, I know. But it is here. It is in lots of places actually."

"But..." he says again.

I'm aware then that my mouth this close to his cock is actually pretty distracting for us both. So, I sit up. "But what?"

He flounders. "I don't know. It's not something I ever thought I would be able to do. So, I have never really thought about it." He looks a little...embarrassed by this? That he had never thought of it.

"Okay, well, are you thinking about it now?"

Jae nods, carefully.

"And so how do you feel about it?" I reach out and take his hand, stroking my fingers over his smaller ones.

He looks at our hands, then up at my face, then down at our hands again.

"Why do you want to marry me?" he asks.

"Is this you fishing for compliments again? Cause I'll take the bait, happily." It's a joke but he doesn't laugh. He just looks up at me all wide-eyed and uncertain.

"You did not want to get married before. To Camille."

I can't hide my flinch of surprise. "Yeah, well, because I didn't want to marry Camille."

"But you must have thought you did. You asked her. Why would you ask her if you did not want to marry her?"

I feel my dick shrinking at that. It's a valid fucking question, it's just not where I expected this conversation to go. I'd expected I'd have his dick in my mouth and him nodding an emphatic yes at this point. I scrub a hand over my face and let out a sigh.

"I guess, at one point, I thought I wanted to marry Camille."

"But then you changed your mind."

I know where this is going. He doesn't even have to say it.

"I'm not going to change my mind about you, Jae."

"You sound certain now, but how can I know you will be certain in two more years? Five?"

"Isn't that the same with any marriage proposal? Any marriage? Why does anyone get married in that case? There's always a possibility that minds and feelings will change."

He nods. "That is a good point, yes. So then why do you want to get married? To me. If that is a possibility?"

"I don't think it is. Not with you."

He gives me a look. *Be clear, Raphael. Clarity, always.*

"Because I love you. Because every single day I feel lucky that you *let me* love you. That you chose me, that we get to have this." I motion between us and around the room.

"Getting married would not change that, Raphael." He squeezes my hand and gives me the fondest smile. "I love you too. So much."

"So you don't want to marry me?"

He thinks about this again, hard, biting his bottom lip as he does. "I do not think it would be fair."

I frown. "Fair to who?"

"Everyone else." My frown deepens. I see him reform his words, take a deep breath, start again. "Because of who I am, I am allowed to have my career and have this. With you. But to get to marry you also? It does not feel fair. To get married when so many men, and women, in my country cannot. When our society still views it as wrong. When they would not recognize it for what it is." He shakes his head. "I am sorry. I love you, Raphael, I do. But I cannot marry you."

"Shit…" I let out a breath. "I never thought about it. Not like that."

I'd thought him lucky, lucky that he could get married even though his country didn't allow it. But he's right. It would be a privilege so many others don't get to have. And it shouldn't have to be a privilege—it should be a fucking right. I squeeze his hands tighter, loving him even more, though I hadn't thought it possible. "It's okay, baby. I get it. I…I'm sorry."

He reaches up to smooth a hand over my cheek. "Do not be sorry. I am not saying never, because one day it *will* be legal in Korea; support is growing. I am hopeful it will happen soon. On that day we will get married, okay?" He gives me one of his heart-stopping smiles.

"Deal."

"Deal."

He waits a few beats before he asks, in an innocent, impossible-to-resist voice.

"Will you still suck my cock?"

The cameras are going absolutely nuts and there are far too many people around us. Too close to us. Pushing and shoving towards the small circle Jae's bodyguards have created for us out of sheer strength and determination.

I don't like it.

Screams and rabid sounding shouts of our names make me grip hold of his hand harder. It's not the first appearance we've done together, we've done plenty now, but it's the most intense I can remember. Apart from the time we'd landed in Korea after the story about us broke. But that was planned. We knew it was going to happen.

This feels uncontrolled and fucking feral.

I chance a look over at Jae. His expression is almost serene as we are herded through the crowd. There's a tightness around his mouth though, that's the only sign of how he really feels. That and the way he's white-knuckling my hand between our bodies. I let go of his hand and pull him closer, angling him in front of my body with my arms around him as I feel a shove at my back.

I practically growl over my shoulder at the bodyguard behind me but he's shouting over his at the crowd of fans and photographers to give us room.

I hate this. I fucking hate it.

This is mainly Jae's fame; something on a level he is used to but that I can't get my head around no matter how hard I try. Add me to the mix and it's become a potent cocktail of hysteria that makes my anxiety spike through the roof.

The screams die out as we're ushered through the glass doors into the museum. I turn on the bodyguard closest to me, practically growling.

"What the fuck was that? There isn't a back fucking door we could go through if you knew it was gonna be that insane?"

Jae's hand lands on my arm, gently comforting. "It was arranged, mon cheri, it is okay."

I blink at him. "You agreed to *that*?"

"The brand wanted a loud arrival, and yes we agreed." He smiles hesitantly.

We? There wasn't a *we*. There was *his fucking label*.

"I am sorry I did not tell you. You were not supposed to be here."

"Well, I'm glad I fucking was."

He leans up to kiss me, soft and quick. "I am fine."

I wrap my arm around him and pull him against me, pressing my mouth to his hair. My body is still vibrating, panic speeding wildly through my blood.

"I hate it."

"I know," he whispers and pulls me toward the junket.

Then it's insane again. This time with cameras and press, but at least this time they're behind a barrier. The brand's name is emblazoned behind us, in the press and cut of the clothes we're both wearing, on the lanyards everyone in headsets is wearing. They shout both our names like we're dogs they own, commanding us to turn and look and smile, this way and that way, lower, higher, to the right, left. I do my best, but I know I'm gonna look like a moody fucker in the photos.

But since Jae isn't smiling either—he perfected the smoldering fashion pose years ago—it won't look too out of place. I'm not exactly new to press photos, but it's always far more intense with him by my side.

I move away from him and let the photographers get him alone, he's the ambassador after all. I'm only still news because I'm here with him, as his partner. Maybe when Hamartia is out in the world people will care about me for me again, but I don't particularly give a shit either way.

When he's done, he retakes my hand as we're led through an atrium filled with people, into the place they've converted for the show. It's a huge gallery-room, long and bright with frescos on the ceiling and a domed skylight in its center. Marble statues are set in recesses along the length of the space, six rows of seats on each side set up in front of the catwalk. The place is almost full as we're shown to our seats, a prime spot in the front row on the left-hand side. We pass Ada as we go and Jae and I say our hello's, quickly, before being urged on again.

I almost laugh when I see who've they've seated us beside.

Haven squeals loudly and jumps up, rushing toward us.

"If it's not the hottest couple on planet earth! Maybe the solar system." She moves to hug us both at once. "God, look at you both." She practically drools over Jae's outfit; a dove-grey tailored suit cut to perfection. "Stunning, you look so good. You too," she adds, turning to me.

"Did you ask to be seated here? Seriously, Haven you need to stop this or we're gonna have to get a restraining order."

"Listen, I take all the credit for this." She laughs, waving a hand over us both. "I'm practically the reason you're together."

"Yeah, we hear that a lot, don't we, baby?" I look at Jae and wink. "We'll remember to invite you to the wedding."

As Haven demands *we damn well better*, Jae gives me a loving look and lets Haven pull him down to sit next to her, looping her arm under his. With his free hand, he reaches across to take mine settling them both on his thigh. Haven's talking animatedly to him about fashion trends she's hoping to see, and he listens, but every now and then his eyes stray to mine, warm and happy and filled with love.

"Saranghae," I mouth.

He beams. "I love you," he mouths back.

I debate pretending to Camille I forgot the cake but the crazed, intense look in her eye tells me she wouldn't appreciate the joke.

"It's in the pantry, yeah."

"How did it look?" She kisses me on both cheeks in greeting.

"I didn't open the box." Then add, "But the box looked great."

She looks at me as though I'm entirely useless and turns to Jae, pulling him into a hug.

"I opened the box," he tells her. "It is perfect."

She smiles gratefully at him and offers us both a drink from the tray of pink champagne she's pointing at.

Jae lifts one while I decline, since I drove here.

"Where is she?"

"In her room with Mathèo, she wanted to show him the doll's house."

Mathèo was Julien's son. Julien was Camille's husband, who is currently carrying a serving tray of pink champagne to the other parents floating around the large Livingroom of their apartment. There are rainbow balloons everywhere and banners saying 'Joyeux Anniversaire' on more than one wall.

Julien turns his head and nods at me, hands far too busy to wave, and smiles brightly. I like him, and he's an amazing second (or is it third) dad to Coralie. He's ten years older than Cam, widowed, and with a seven-year-old son who Lili adores. He directs plays and ballets and is as perfectly French as Camille's dad always wanted her husband to be. The only person who Jérémie would have hated more than me as Camille's husband would have been Mason—Mason who sobered up, got over Camille, and married a sweet Australian girl in the space of six months. He now has five-month-old twins and lives on a ranch in Albuquerque. We talk every other day.

"You need me to do anything?" I ask, dutifully.

Camille shakes her head and hurries off to do something else. While Julien stops to say hello to Jae, I sneak out of the room and down the hallway toward Lili's room. As I get closer, I can hear the sound of her sing-song voice babbling animatedly in French.

The door is open and so I stand there for a bit, watching as she directs Mathèo to place this there and that there. She's wearing a white summer dress with purple cats on it and a set of white cat ears—the K:OS branded ones Jae had gifted her for Christmas. Of course she's a K:Otic.

Since I don't speak French, not on any proper level at least, I can only watch her expressions as she chats to Mathèo, and his for clues to what she's telling him. It appears to be some kind of lesson in interior design.

When she stands up to walk around to the back of the doll's house, she sees me.

"Papaaaaaaaaaah!" she cries excitedly.

The way her face always lights up when she sees me makes my heart full to bursting point every fucking time. It makes me think of myself as a little kid too, how desperately I wanted my dad to walk back through that door. I don't feel bitter about this anymore, just sad. Sad for little Raphael.

Lili places the little toy chair down carefully first before barrelling toward me, blonde curls streaming out behind her.

"Joyeux anniversaire, ma jolie chérie." I plant a kiss on her reddened cheek as I lift her up.

"Merci, Papa," and then she starts babbling in French.

"English words, princess, remember?"

"I'm sorry, papa. I try to learn engish with maman every day. Julien too."

"I know baby, you're so smart, and papa isn't."

She giggles at this and starts talking to me in broken 'engish' about her dolls house, but then she lets out another excited cry and squirms for me to let her down.

"*Jae-un!! Papa, it's Jae-un!!*"

I let her down and she runs down the hall toward him, arms wide and laughing happily. Jae doesn't lift her, instead crouching down to her height so she can wrap her little arms around him and give him two pecks on the cheek. Then she turns her cheek so he can do the same. Then he wishes her happy birthday in French.

"Bonjour, Raphael," comes the little voice from beside me. Mathèo looks up at me with big doe-like eyes. I settle a hand around his tiny shoulders.

"Hey buddy, how's things? You good?"

"Yes, I am well, thank you. And you?"

I smile at how practiced it is. "Really good, Matty. Really good. How's your guitar playing coming along."

"Good! Will you listen to my song later? I learned it for Lili's birthday." He whispers this second part.

"Oh, she's going to love that. Of course, I'll listen to it, I'd love to. Your dad says you're getting really good."

Mathèo smiles wide at this, little chest puffing out.

"I want to be as good as you one day," he says making some intense rush of emotion hit me squarely in the chest.

"Yeah? I bet you'll be better than me soon." I ruffle his hair a little as we walk toward Lili and Jae who are deep in conversation like two old friends, Lili's eyes filled with hero worship and love. Like father like daughter in that sense, I guess.

So fucking lucky, I think again. *So fucking lucky.*

ACKNOWLEDGEMENTS

I have so many people to thank that led me to writing Jae and Raphael's story but let me keep it super short.

Kseniia, Clotilde, Rachel, Sian, Laura, and Lindsey. You ladies were instrumental in helping me get this story out of my head and onto the page, thank you so much for being there for this.

Thank you to all the fanfic writers out there who write gorgeously inspiring stories and don't get nearly enough credit for them. You are amazing.

Thanks to those incredibly talented people out there writing soul-shifting, life-changing queer love stories. You've changed my life!

Thank you lastly to all the wonderfully funny, beautifully kind, marginally obsessed K-pop fans out there. My beautiful baby Jaehyun was inspired by so many awe-inspiring idols—I hope you found a little of your bias in there somewhere. Saranghae. ♡

If you enjoyed this book I would urge you to leave a review on Amazon and Goodreads—it really does help us indie authors and I would be so grateful for that!

Alternatively, if you would just like to come say hello and ask me what I'm up to next, then you can find me on the socials below.

Twitter: @scarlettedrake
Instagram: @scarlettedrake
Goodreads: www.goodreads.com/book/show/91122393

Printed in Great Britain
by Amazon